## Praise for the novels of Robyn Carr

"The Virgin River books are so compelling—
I connected instantly with the characters
and just wanted more and more and more."
—#1 *New York Times* bestselling author Debbie Macomber

"*Virgin River* is sexy, tense, emotional and satisfying.
I can't wait for more!"
—*New York Times* bestselling author Carla Neggers

"A thrilling debut of a series
that promises much to come."
—*New York Times* bestselling author Clive Cussler

"Jennifer is a beautifully drawn character
whose interior journey is wonderful to behold."
—*RT Book Reviews* on *Runaway Mistress*

"This is one author who proves a Carr can fly."
—*Book Reviewer* on *Blue Skies*

"Robyn Carr provides readers [with] a powerful,
thought-provoking work of contemporary fiction."
—*Midwest Book Review* on *Deep in the Valley*

"A remarkable storyteller..."
—*Library Journal*

"A warm, wonderful book about women's friendships,
love and family. I adored it!"
—Susan Elizabeth Phillips on *The House on Olive Street*

"A delightfully funny novel."
—*Midwest Book Review* on *The Wedding Party*

# ROBYN CARR
# SHELTER
# MOUNTAIN

MIRA®

ISBN-13: 978-0-7783-2974-9

Recycling programs
for this product may
not exist in your area.

SHELTER MOUNTAIN

Copyright © 2007 by Robyn Carr.

All rights reserved. Except for use in any review, the reproduction or
utilization of this work in whole or in part in any form by any electronic,
mechanical or other means, now known or hereafter invented, including
xerography, photocopying and recording, or in any information storage or
retrieval system, is forbidden without the written permission of the publisher,
MIRA Books, 225 Duncan Mill Road, Don Mills, Ontario, Canada M3B 3K9.

This is a work of fiction. Names, characters, places and incidents are
either the product of the author's imagination or are used fictitiously, and
any resemblance to actual persons, living or dead, business establishments,
events or locales is entirely coincidental.

MIRA and the Star Colophon are trademarks used under license and registered
in Australia, New Zealand, Philippines, United States Patent and Trademark
Office and in other countries.

For questions and comments about the quality of this book please contact us at
Customer_eCare@Harlequin.ca.

www.MIRABooks.com

Printed in U.S.A.

Karen Garris, another precious daughter, with love.

# ACKNOWLEDGMENTS

Thanks to Pamela SF Glenn, CNM, MS—without whose expertise in midwifery this story would not have been possible. My deepest gratitude to you for poring over manuscript after manuscript with sharp eyes and a ruthless pen, keeping me straight. And to Sharon Lampert, RN, WHNP, for sharing your expertise as a women's health nurse practitioner, but mostly for picking up your cell phone no matter where you were and answering delicate questions about female anatomy and function with directness and honesty. I'm sure there are people out there still talking about what they overheard in the grocery store, beauty parlor and Department of Motor Vehicles. The passion and devotion with which you two professionals serve your women patients is inspiring, and was an enormous help in shaping the character of a dedicated nurse practitioner and certified nurse midwife.

Thanks to Paul Wojcik for sharing your experiences in the United States Marine Corps, and to Richard Gustavson, RN with twenty-three years in the Navy Reserves. I thank each of you for reading the manuscripts and for offering your invaluable technical input.

Kris Kitna, Chief of Police, Fortuna, California, thanks for valuable information on local law enforcement, not to mention help with details about hunting, fishing and firearms.

Kate Bandy, the best assistant a writer can possibly have, my dear friend of many years, thanks not only for reading copy and offering suggestions, but especially for accompanying me on an exciting research trip to Humboldt County. Without you there I would have floundered...or slipped off a mountain.

Denise and Jeff Nicholl—thanks for reading first drafts, taking exhaustive notes and answering a million questions. Your friendship and support during the whole process mean the world to me. Many thanks to Nellie Valdez-Hathorn for her help with my Spanish.

Other early readers whose input was critical included Jamie Carr, Laurie Fait, Karen Garris, Martha Gould, Pat Hagee, Goldiene Jones and Lori Stoveken—I'm deeply in debt to you for your comments and suggestions.

Huge thanks to Clive Cussler, Debbie Macomber and Carla Neggers for reading and commenting on Virgin River. For you to take the time, with your busy schedules, is a monumental compliment.

Huge thanks to Valerie Gray, my editor, and Liza Dawson, my agent, for your commitment to helping me craft the best series possible. Your hard work and dedication made all the difference—I'm so grateful.

To Trudy Casey, Tom Fay, Michelle Mazzanti, Kristy Price and the entire staff of Henderson Public Libraries, thank you for the monumental support and encouragement. I've never known a more hardworking and motivated group of public servants.

And finally, thanks to Jim Carr for your loving support. And my God, thank you for cooking! I wish I'd known years ago that you could!

# One

A fierce and unseasonably cold September wind blew chilly rain against the windows. Preacher wiped down the bar, and while it was only seven-thirty, it was already dark. No one in Virgin River would be out on a night like this. After the dinner hour was past, people tended to stay in on cold, wet nights. The campers and fishermen in the area would be locked down tight against the storm. It was bear-and-deer hunting season, but it was unlikely any hunters would pass en route to or from lodges and blinds at this hour in such weather. Jack, his partner and the owner of the bar and grill, knowing there would be little if any business, was tucked away with his new wife at their cabin in the woods. Preacher had also sent home their seventeen-year-old helper, Rick. As soon as the fire burned down a little more, Preacher planned to switch off the Open sign and lock the door.

He poured himself a shot of whiskey and took it over to the table nearest the fire, then turned a chair toward the hearth and propped up his feet. Quiet nights like this were to his liking. He was a solitary kind of guy.

But the peace was not to be. Someone pulled on the door, causing him to frown. It opened a little bit. The wind

caught the door and it flew open with a bang, bringing
him instantly to his feet. Entering and then struggling to
close the door was a young woman holding a child. The
woman wore a ball cap and had a heavy quilted bag slung
over her shoulder. Preacher went to get the door. She
turned, looked up at him and they both jumped back in
surprise. She was likely startled because Preacher looked
intimidating—he was six foot four, bald with bushy black
eyebrows, a diamond stud earring and shoulders about as
broad as an ax handle was long.

Under the bill of the baseball cap, Preacher saw a
pretty young woman's face bearing a bruise on her cheek
and a split lower lip.

"I'm… I'm sorry. I saw the sign…."

"Yeah, come on in. I wasn't expecting anyone to be
out tonight."

"Are you closing?" she asked, hoisting up her burden,
a little boy, not more than three or four years old. He was
asleep on her shoulder, his long legs dangling limply.
"Because I… Are you closing?"

"Come on," he said, stepping back for her to pass. "It's
okay. I don't have anyplace better to go." He extended an
arm toward a table. "Sit by the fire there. Warm up. Dry off."

"Thanks," she said meekly. She went to the table by
the fire, and when she saw the drink, said, "Is this where
you're sitting?"

"Go ahead. Take it," he said. "I was having a shot
before calling it a night. But there's no hurry. We don't
usually close this early, anyway, but with the rain…"

"Did you want to get home?" she asked him.

He smiled at her. "I live here. Makes me real flexible
on the hours."

"If you're sure…"

"I'm sure," he said. "If the weather's decent, we
usually stay open till at least nine."

She took the chair facing the fire, the boy's gangly legs straddling her lap. She let her quilted shoulder bag drop to the floor and pulled the child closer, hugging him tight, stroking his back.

Preacher disappeared into the back, leaving her to warm herself for a minute. He came back with a couple of pillows from his bed and the throw from his couch. He put the pillows on the table next to her and said, "Here. Lay the kid down. He's probably heavy."

She looked up at him with eyes that seemed to want to cry. Oh, he hoped she wouldn't do that. He hated when women cried. He had no idea what to do. Jack could handle it. He was chivalrous; he knew exactly what to do with a woman under any circumstance. Preacher was uncomfortable around women until he got to know them. When you got down to it, he was inexperienced. Although it wasn't intentional, he tended to scare women and children simply because of how he looked. But they didn't know that underneath his sometimes grim countenance he was shy.

"Thanks," she said again. She transferred the child to the pillows on the table. He immediately curled into a ball and put a thumb in his mouth. Preacher stood there, lamely holding the throw. She didn't take it from him so he put it over the boy and tucked it around him. He noticed the boy's cheeks were rosy and his lips bright pink.

When she reclaimed her chair, she looked around. She saw the stag's head over the front door and flinched. She turned full circle, noting the bear skin on the wall, the sturgeon over the bar. "Is this some kind of hunting place?" she asked.

"Not really, but a lot of hunters and fishermen pass this way," he said. "My partner shot the bear in self-defense, but he caught the fish on purpose. One of the biggest sturgeons in the river. I got the buck, but I'd rather fish than hunt. I like the quiet." He shrugged. "I'm the cook here. If I kill it, we eat it."

"You can eat deer," she said.

"And we did. We had a great winter of venison. Maybe you should have a drink," he said, trying to keep his voice soft and nonthreatening.

"I have to find a place to stay. Where am I, anyway?"

"Virgin River. Kind of out of the way. How'd you find us?"

"I…" She shook her head and a small laugh escaped. "I got off the highway, looking for a town with a hotel…."

"You got off the highway a while ago."

"There aren't many places wide enough to turn around," she said. "Then I saw this place, your sign. My son…I think he has a fever. We shouldn't drive anymore."

Preacher knew there wasn't anyplace to get a room nearby. This was a woman in trouble; it didn't take a genius to figure that out. "I'll fix you up with something," he said. "But first—you want something to drink? Eat? I've got a good soup tonight. Bean and ham. And bread. I made the bread today. I like to do that when it's cold and rainy. How about a brandy to warm you up first?"

"Brandy?"

"Or whatever you feel like…"

"That would be good. Soup would be good, too. I haven't eaten in hours. Thanks."

"Sit tight."

He went to the bar and poured a Remy into a snifter— fancy stuff for this place. He hardly ever used the snifters on the usual crowd—but he wanted to do something special for the girl. For sure she was down on her luck. He took her the brandy and then went back to the kitchen.

The soup was put away for the night, but he took it out of the refrigerator, ladled out a scoop and put it in the microwave. While it warmed, he took her a napkin and some utensils. By the time he got back to the kitchen, the soup was ready and he got out the bread—some of his best: soft, sweet and hearty—and nuked it for a few seconds. He put that and some butter on a plate. When he came out of the kitchen he saw her struggling out of her jacket, like maybe she was stiff or sore. The sight of it stopped him briefly and made him frown. She threw a look over her shoulder, as if she was caught doing something bad.

Preacher put the food in front of her, his mind spinning. She was maybe five foot five and slight. She wore jeans and her curly brown hair was tucked through the back of the ball cap like a ponytail. She looked like a girl, but he guessed she was at least in her twenties. Maybe she'd been in a car accident, but it was more likely someone had smacked her around. The thought alone got him a little hot inside.

"That looks great," she said, accepting the soup.

He went back behind the bar while she ate. She shoveled the soup in, smeared the bread with butter and ate it ravenously. Halfway through with her meal she gave him a sheepish, almost apologetic smile. It tore through him, that bruised face, split lip. Her hunger.

When she'd sopped up the last of her soup with the last of her bread, he returned to her table. "I'll get you some more."

"No. No, it's okay. I think I'll have some of this brandy now. I sure appreciate it. I'll be on my way in a—"

"Relax," he said, and hoped he didn't sound harsh. It took a while for people to warm up to him. He transferred her dishes to the bar, clearing her place. "There isn't anywhere around here to get a room," he said when he returned to the table. He sat down across from her, leaned toward her. "The roads aren't so good out this way, especially in the rain. Really, you don't want to head back out there. You're kinda stuck."

"Oh, no! Listen, if you'll just tell me the closest place… I have to find something…."

"Take it easy," he said. "I got an extra room. No problem. It's a bad night." Predictably, her eyes widened. "It's okay. It's got a lock."

"I didn't mean…"

"It's okay. I'm kind of scary-looking. I know it."

"No. It's just—"

"Don't worry about it. I know how I look. Works great on guys. They back right off." He gave her a small smile, not showing any teeth.

"You don't have to do this," she said. "I have a car…."

"Jesus, I couldn't stand to think of you sleeping in a car!" he said. "Sorry. Sometimes I sound as bad as I look. But no kidding—if the kid's not feeling so good…"

"I can't," she said. "I don't know you…."

"Yeah, I know. Probably makes you wonder, huh? But I'm way safer than I look. You'd be okay here. Better here than at some hotel on the freeway, guaranteed. A whole lot more okay than out in that storm, trying to deal with those mountain roads."

She looked at him hard for a minute. Then she said, "No. I'm just going to press on. If you'll tell me how much—"

"Pretty rough-looking bruise you have there," Preacher said. "Can I get you anything for that lip? I have a first aid kit in the kitchen."

"I'm fine," she said, shaking her head. "How about if we settle up and—"

"I don't have anything for a kid's fever. Except a room. With a lock on the door so you feel safe. You don't want to pass up an offer like that in this weather, with a kid who might be coming down with something. I look big and mean, but I'm about as safe as you get. Unless you're wildlife." He grinned at her.

"You don't look mean," she said timidly.

"It can make women and little kids real nervous—and I hate that part. You on the run?" he asked her.

She lowered her eyes.

"What d'you think? I'm gonna call the cops? Who did that to you?"

She immediately started to cry.

"Aw. Hey. Don't."

She put her head down on folded arms on the tabletop and sobbed.

"Aw. Come on. Don't do that. I never know what to do." Hesitatingly, squeamishly, he touched her back and she jumped. He touched one of her hands, very lightly. "Come on, don't cry. Maybe I can help."

"No. You can't."

"Never know," he said, lightly patting her hand.

She lifted her head. "Sorry," she said, wiping her eyes. "I'm exhausted, I guess. It was an accident. It was really stupid, but I was struggling with Chris—" She stopped suddenly and looked around nervously, as though worried about being overheard. She licked her lower lip. "I was trying to get Christopher in the car, hanging on to stuff, and I opened the door right into my face. Hard. You shouldn't be in a hurry, you know? It was just a little accident. It's fine." She lifted the napkin to her nose.

"Right," Preacher said. "Sure. Too bad about that. Looks sore."

"It'll be fine."

"Sure it will. So—what's your name?" When she didn't answer for a long moment, he said, "It's okay. I'm not going to repeat it. If anyone came looking for you, I'd never mention seeing you." Her eyes grew round and her mouth stood open slightly. "Oh, damn, that was the wrong thing to say, wasn't it?" he said. "All I mean is, if you're hiding or running, it's okay. You can hide or run here. I won't give you up. What's your name?"

She reached out and ran her fingers gently through the boy's hair. Silent.

Preacher got up and flipped off the Open sign and threw the latch on the door. "There," he said, sitting down with her again, the little boy taking up much of the table beside them. "Try to take it easy," he said softly. "No one here's gonna hurt you. I can be a friend. I'm sure not scared of the weak dick who'd do that to a woman. Sorry."

She looked down to avoid eye contact. "It was the car door…."

"Not afraid of any mean old car door, either," he said.

She gave a little huff of laughter, but had trouble looking him in the eye. She picked up her brandy with a slightly trembling hand and lifted it to her mouth.

"Yeah, there you go," Preacher said. "If you think the boy needs a doctor tonight, there's one right across the street. I could go get him. Or take you over."

"I think he's just coming down with a cold. I'm keeping a close eye on him."

"If he needs medicine or something…"

"I think he's okay…."

"My buddy, the guy who owns this place, his wife is a nurse. A special nurse—she can give medicine, see patients…. She takes real good care of the women around here. She'd come in ten minutes. If a woman makes a difference, under the circumstances."

"Circumstances?" she asked, a panicked look floating across her features.

"Car door, and all that…"

"No. Really. It's just been a long day. You know."

"Yeah, must've been. And the last hour or so off the freeway, that must've been pretty awful. If you're not used to those roads."

"A little scary," she admitted softly. "And not having any idea where I am…"

"You're in Virgin River now, that's what matters. It's just a little crimp in the road, but the people are good. Help out where they can. You know?"

She gave him a small, shy smile, but her eyes were downcast again.

"What's your name?" he asked again. She pursed her lips tight, shaking her head. Her eyes welled up again. "It's okay," he said softly. "Really."

"Paige," she whispered, a tear running down her cheek. "Paige," she repeated in a small voice.

"Yeah, that's good. That's a pretty name. You can say your name around here without being afraid."

"Your name?"

"John," he said, then wondered why he had done that. Something about her, he guessed. "John Middleton. No one calls me John, though. I'm known as Preacher."

"You're a preacher?"

"No," he said with a short laugh. "Way far from it. The only one ever to call me John was my mother."

"What did your father call you?" she asked him.

"Kid," he said, and smiled. "Hey, kid," he emphasized.

"Why do they call you Preacher?"

"Aw," he said, ducking shyly. "I don't know. I got the nickname way back, when I was just a kid in the Marine Corps. The boys said I was kinda straitlaced and uptight."

"Really? Are you?"

"Nah, not really," he said. "I never used to curse at all. I used to go to mass, when there was a mass. I grew up around priests and nuns—my mother was real devout. None of the boys ever went to mass, that I remember. And I kind of hung back when they went out to get drunk and look for women. I don't know…I never felt like doing that. I'm not good with women." He smiled suddenly. "That should be obvious right away, huh? And getting drunk never really appealed to me."

"But you have a bar?" she asked.

"It's Jack's bar. He watches over people real good. We don't let anybody out of here if they're not safe, you know? I like a shot at the end of the day, but no reason to get a headache over it, right?" He grinned at her.

"Should I call you John?" she asked him. "Or Preacher?"

"Whatever you want."

"John," she said. "Okay?"

"If you want. Yeah," he said. "Yeah, I like that. Been a while since anyone called me that."

She lowered her eyes for a moment, then raised them again. "I really appreciate this, John. You staying open and everything."

"It's not a big deal. Most nights we're open later than this." Preacher inclined his head toward the boy. "He going to wake up hungry?"

"Maybe," she said. "I had some peanut butter and jelly in the car, and he went through that pretty fast."

"Okay, there's an extra room upstairs, right above the kitchen. You help yourself in the kitchen—I'll leave a light on for you. Anything you want. There's milk in the refrigerator. And orange juice. Cereal, bread, peanut butter, more of that soup in the fridge and a microwave. Okay?"

"That's very nice of you, but—"

"Paige, you look like you could use some rest, and if the boy's coming down with something, you don't want to take him out in that cold, wet mess."

She thought about it for a second and then said, "How much?"

He laughed in spite of himself, then sobered quickly. "Sorry, I didn't mean to laugh. It's just that—it's my old room. It's not a hotel room or anything. I lived up there for two years, but then Jack and Mel got married and I got his apartment out back. That room over the kitchen—smells a little like bacon and coffee in the morning, but it's a good size, with a big bathroom. It would do for a night." He shrugged. "Just being a good neighbor. Okay?"

"That's generous," she said.

"I'm not putting myself out any—it's an empty room. Glad to help out." He cleared his throat. "Got a suitcase I can get for you or anything?"

"Only one, on the backseat."

"I'll get it for you. You get your brandy there," he said. "Give yourself another shot if you need it. If I were you, I'd need it, after driving through these hills in the rain." He stood up. "Bring it with you and I'll show you the room. Upstairs. Um—you want me to carry the kid up for you?"

She stood, as well. "Thanks." She stretched her shoulders—as if stiff from a long drive. "If you don't mind."

"Not a problem," he said. "Listen, so you don't worry, your room and my apartment aren't even connected— we're separated by the kitchen and stairs. You just lock your door and rest easy." He gently and clumsily lifted the little boy into his arms. His head went onto Preacher's shoulder and it felt odd. Preacher didn't have a lot of experience with carrying around children, but he liked the way it felt. He gave the boy's back a few long, slow strokes. "This way."

He led the way through the kitchen and up the back staircase. He opened the door and said, "Sorry. It's kind of a mess. I left some things up here, like my weights. But the sheets are clean."

"It looks fine," she said. "I'll get out first thing in the morning."

"Don't worry about it. If you need a couple of days, we can work it out. Like I said, it's not exactly for rent or anything. Just sits empty. I mean, if the kid's got a little bug or something…"

He laid the boy gently on the bed, strangely reluctant to put him down. The warmth of the child against his chest was comforting. He couldn't resist touching his floppy blond hair. Beautiful little kid. "How about some car keys? Might as well go get that suitcase…."

She dug around in her quilted bag, which looked kind of like a diaper bag, although the boy was too big for diapers. She passed him the keys.

"Just be a minute," he said.

Preacher went to her car, a little Honda, and got in. He had to put the seat all the way back and his knees still rubbed against the steering wheel. He pulled it around to the back of the building and parked it beside his truck where it couldn't be seen from the main street in case someone was looking for her. He wasn't sure how he'd explain that—he wouldn't want her to be afraid.

He plucked the suitcase out of the back; it was way too small for someone who was taking a trip. It was the right size for someone getting out with the clothes on her back.

When he was back in the upstairs room, she was sitting tensely on the edge of the bed, her son behind her. He put down the suitcase, placed the keys on the bureau right inside the door and shuffled a little in the doorway. She stood up and faced him. "Look. Ah. I moved your car—put it right out back by my truck. Off the street. It's out of sight from the road now. So if you get up or look out, you're not confused about that—it's right out back. I recommend you sit tight, wait out this rain, travel in dry daylight. But if you get—you know—nervous, the bar only locks on the inside and here are your keys. It's no big deal if you… Like if you can't relax and have to leave, it's no big deal if the bar door's left unlocked—this is a real quiet, safe place. Sometimes we forget to lock up, anyway. I'll get it locked for sure tonight, you and the kid being here. Um…Paige…you don't have to be worried or anything. I'm a pretty reliable guy. Or else Jack wouldn't leave me with the bar. Okay? Just get some rest."

"Thank you," she said, and it was barely a sound.

He pulled the door closed. He heard her move the dead bolt, protecting herself. For the first time since coming to this little town, he wondered why that dead bolt had ever been installed.

He stood there a minute. It had taken him about five seconds to conclude someone—ninety-eight-percent chance a boyfriend or husband—had belted her in the face and she was on the run with her kid. It wasn't like he didn't know that stuff happened. It happened all the time. He just never understood what satisfaction a man could get out of hitting a woman. It made no sense to him. If you have a pretty young woman like that, you treat her right. Hold her safe against you and protect her.

He went to the bar, turned off the lights, checked the kitchen, leaving a light on in case she came downstairs, then went to his apartment behind the kitchen. He was only there a few minutes when it occurred to him that there were no longer clean towels up there—he'd emptied the bathroom and moved all his downstairs. He went to the bathroom, gathered up a stack of clean white towels and went back upstairs.

The door was open a crack, like maybe she'd already been down to the kitchen. He could see a glass of orange juice sitting on the bureau inside the door and it pleased him that she'd helped herself. Through that space of an inch, he saw her reflection in the bureau mirror. Her back faced the mirror and she had pulled her bulky sweatshirt up over her head and shoulders, trying to get a glimpse of her back and upper arms in the mirror. She was *covered* with bruises. Lots of big bruises on her back, one on her shoulder and upper arms.

Preacher was mesmerized. For a moment his eyes were locked on those purple splotches. "Aw, Jesus," he whispered in a breath.

He quickly backed away from the slit in the door and got up against the wall outside, out of sight. It took him a moment to collect himself; he was stricken. Horrified. All he could think was, what kind of animal does something like that? His mouth hung open because he couldn't imagine this. He was a warrior, a trained fighter, and he was pretty sure he hadn't done that much damage to a man equal to him in size, in a fair fight.

Some instinct kicked in that told him he shouldn't let on that he'd seen. She was already afraid of everything, including him. But there was also the reality that this wasn't a woman who'd been smacked. She'd been pummeled. He didn't even know the girl, yet all he wanted was to kill the son of a bitch who'd done that to her. After five or eleven months of beatings, then death for the sorry bastard.

She shouldn't know he was feeling that; it would scare her to death. He took a few deep breaths, composed himself. Then he tapped lightly on the door.

"Huh?" he heard her say, sounding startled.

"Just some towels," he said.

"One second, okay?"

"Take your time."

Momentarily she opened the door a tiny bit farther, her sweatshirt back in place.

"I forgot, I took all the bathroom stuff out," he said. "You'll need some towels. I'll leave you alone now. Won't bother you again."

"Thank you. John."

"No problem. Paige. Get some good rest."


Paige pulled the bureau carefully, as quietly as possible, in front of the door. She really hoped John hadn't heard that, but as close as she could figure out, the kitchen was right beneath this room. And—if the man meant her or Christopher any harm, he could have already delivered it, not to mention that a locked door and empty bedroom dresser couldn't possibly keep him out.

As much as she'd have liked a hot soak in a tub, she felt too vulnerable to get naked. She couldn't talk herself into the shower, either—she might not hear the doorknob rattle or Christopher call out to her—so she washed up in the sink and put on clean clothes. Then, leaving the bathroom light on, she lay carefully on the bed, on top of the covers. She knew she wouldn't sleep, but after a little while she calmed down. She stared at the ceiling, the wood slats forming a perfect V over her head. What came to mind was that this was the third time in her life she'd lain in bed looking at such a ceiling.

The first time was in the house she grew up in—the beams were bare, pink insulation puffing out between them. The house was small, only two bedrooms, and already old when her parents moved in, but the neighborhood had been clean and quiet then, twenty years ago. Her mother moved her into the attic when she was nine; she shared her space with boxes of stored household goods pushed back against one wall. But it was her space, and she escaped to it whenever she could. From her bed she could hear her mother and father arguing. After her father's death when she was eleven, she could hear her older brother, Bud, argue with their mother.

From what she had learned about domestic battery in the last few years, she should have expected to end up with an abuser, even though her father never hit her or her mother, and the worst she ever got from Bud was a shove or slug in the arm. But man, could the men in her family yell. So loud, so mad, she wondered why the windows didn't crack. Demand, belittle, insult, accuse, sulk, punish with the meanest words. It was just a matter of degrees; abuse is abuse.

The next time she had found herself staring at a ceiling like this one was after she left home. She'd gone to beauty school after high school and stayed home with her mother, paying rent, until she was twenty-one. Then she and two girlfriends—also beauticians—rented half an old house. Paige had happily taken the attic bedroom, though it wasn't even as large as her childhood room and most of the time she had to crouch to keep from hitting her head on the slanted walls.

Tears came to her eyes because she remembered those two years with Pat and Jeannie as the happiest in her life. Sometimes she missed them so much it made her ache. Three hairdressers, mostly broke after rent, food and clothes—it had seemed like heaven. When they couldn't afford to go out, they'd buy popcorn and cheap wine and make a party of it at home, gossiping about women whose hair they cut and frosted, about boyfriends and sex, laughing till they couldn't sit up straight.

Then Wes came into her life, a successful business-man, six years older. It was shocking to realize he'd been the age she was now—twenty-nine. Yet he'd seemed so worldly, mature. She'd been styling his hair for only a couple of months when he asked her out and took her to a restaurant so fine the hostesses were better dressed than she was. He drove a brand-new Grand Prix with cushy leather seats, darkly tinted windows. And he drove too fast, which at twenty-three didn't seem dangerous. It was thrilling. Even though he yelled at and flipped off other drivers, it seemed his right—he was powerful. By her standards, rich.

He had a house already, which he didn't even have to share with roommates. His career was trading stocks and commodities; an exhausting job that required brilliance and high energy. He wanted to go out every night, bought her things, pulled his wallet out of his pocket and said,

"I don't know what you really want, what little thing would just make you cry it's so perfect, so I want you to shop for yourself. Because you being happy is the only thing that matters to me in the world." He'd peeled off a couple of bills and handed her two hundred dollars, a veritable fortune.

Pat and Jeannie didn't like him, but there was hardly a mystery in that. He wasn't all that nice to them. He treated them like wallpaper, furniture. Answered their questions with one word when he could. In fact, she couldn't remember what they said about him when they tried to warn her off.

Then came the insanity of her life spiraling out of control that to this day seemed impossible: he'd hit her before they married, and she'd married him anyway. They'd been in his fancy car, parked, having an argument about where she was living—he thought she'd be better off at home with her mother rather than that old half a house in a questionable neighborhood with a couple of dykes. It got pretty nasty; she'd said her share of ugly things to him. He said something like, "I want you with your mother, not in some little whorehouse in the ghetto."

*Just who the fuck do you think you are, calling where I live a whorehouse?*

*How do you use that language with me?*

*You called my best friends dykes and whores and it's my language you criticize?*

*I'm just thinking about your safety. You said you wanted to marry me someday, and I'd like you to still be around when that happens!*

*Well up yours, because I love living there and you can't tell me what to do! And I'm not marrying anyone who can talk about my best friends like that!*

There was more. More. She vaguely remembered calling him a bad name, like prick or asshole. He called

her a bitch, a difficult bitch. In any case, they both contributed, she was sure of that.

He'd slapped her, open palm. Then he immediately
broke down, collapsed, cried like a baby, said he wasn't
sure what had happened to him, but maybe it was because
he'd never been in love like this before. It was wrong, he
knew it was wrong to overreact that way, he was crazy, he
was ashamed. But…he wanted to hold her in his arms
every night, take care of her for the rest of her life, never
lose her. He apologized for what he'd said about the roommates—maybe he was jealous of how loyal she was to
them. In his mind he couldn't see past her; there was no
one in his life he valued like he valued her. He loved her
so much it made him nuts, he said. She was the first person
he'd ever felt that way about. Without her, he was *nothing!*

She believed him. But she never used profanity
around him again.

She hadn't told Pat and Jeannie because even though
she was stupid about what was happening, she knew
better than to risk their further disapproval. It only took
her a couple of days to get over that slap. It wasn't much
of a slap. It didn't take more than a month for her to
almost forget it happened and trust him again; she thought
him handsome, exciting, sexy. He was edgy and confident. Smart. Passive men couldn't get the kind of success
he had. She wasn't attracted to passive men.

Then he said, "Paige, I don't want to wait. I want us
to get married as soon as you're ready. A nice wedding—
screw the cost, I can afford whatever you want. Ask Pat
and Jeannie to stand up for us. And you can quit your
job—you don't have to work anymore."

Her legs hurt; she was getting bunions. Fixing hair six
days a week was no easy job, even though she had liked
it. She'd often thought how much more she'd like it if she
only had to do it about six hours a day, four days a week,

but that seemed an impossible dream. She could barely make ends meet as it was, and her mother had been working two jobs since her father died. In her mother, she saw her future—alone, weak and worked to death. A picture of her surly roommates wearing pretty satin at her wedding, smiling, envious of her good fortune and the cushy life she'd have. And she'd said yes.

He hit her again on the honeymoon.

Over the next six years she'd tried everything—counseling, police, running away. He got out of jail right away, if they even bothered to take him in; he found her in hiding, and it just got worse. Even her pregnancy and Christopher's arrival hadn't stopped the abuse. She discovered by accident that there might be a little more to this equation—a certain chemistry that gave him such energy to work those long hours and wear himself out keeping track of her, the fits of euphoria, the skull-splitting temper—some white powder in a small vial. Cocaine? And he took something his personal trainer gave him, though he swore it wasn't steroids. A lot of traders used amphetamines to keep up with the demands of the job. Cocaine users tended to be reed-thin, but Wes was proud of his body, his build, and worked hard on his muscles. A coke and steroid regimen, she realized, could make his temper hair-trigger short. She had no idea how much, how long. But she knew he was crazy.

This was her last chance. Through a shelter she'd met a woman who said she could help her get away, change her identity and flee. There was an underground for battered women and children in hopeless situations. If she and Christopher could just get to the first contact, they would be passed along from place to place, collecting new ID, names, histories and lives along the way. The upside was—it worked a lot. It was nearly foolproof when the woman followed instructions and the children were young enough. The downside was, it was illegal, and for *life*. Life like this, covered in bruises, afraid she'd be killed every day—or a life of being someone else, someone who isn't hit?

She started squirreling away money from her grocery allowance and packed a bag that she hid with a contact from a shelter. She managed almost five hundred dollars and fully intended to get herself and Christopher out before another bad episode occurred. With the last beating, she knew she was nearly too late.

And here she was, looking at her third V-shaped ceiling. She knew she wouldn't sleep; she'd hardly slept in six years. No worries about the drive—with so much adrenaline going on, she'd make it.

But then she woke up to sunlight and a regular *thwacking* noise outside. Someone was chopping wood. She sat up cautiously and smelled coffee. She had slept after all. And so had Christopher.

The dresser was still pushed against the door.

# Two

Preacher barely slept. He spent half the night on the computer. It was like this little machine was invented for him, because he liked to look things up. He had been trying to get Jack to put the inventory and receipts on the computer, but Jack had a clipboard that was like an extension of his arm and wanted nothing to do with Preacher's technology. It was slow, there being no cable hookup out here, but he was patient. And it got the job done.

The rest of the night was spent trying to catch some sleep, which eluded him completely. He got out of bed several times and looked out the back window to see if the little Honda was still there. He finally got up for the day at five, when it was still black as pitch outside. He went into the kitchen, started the coffee, laid a fresh fire. There was no sound from upstairs.

The rain had stopped, but it was overcast and chilly. He'd have liked to go ahead and split logs, work off some aggression, but Jack liked doing that, so he let it go. At six-thirty, Jack came into the bar, all smiles. This was the happiest man in Virgin River since he got married. It was as if he couldn't stop grinning.

Preacher stood behind the bar with his coffee mug and

lifted his chin in greeting to his best friend. "Hey," Jack said. "Good rain."

"Jack," he said. "Listen. I did something…"

Jack shrugged out of his jacket and hung it on the peg inside the door. "Pee in the soup again, Preacher?"

"I got a woman upstairs…."

Pure shock settled over Jack's face. Preacher didn't have women around. He didn't prowl, didn't flirt, didn't do any of that. Of course, Jack didn't really know how he lived like that, but this was Preacher. When the guys, the Marines they had served with, were all out looking for women to pass the night with, Preacher stayed behind. They jokingly called him the Big Eunuch. "Oh, yeah?" he asked.

Preacher took down a mug and filled it for Jack. "She came in last night, during the storm," he said. "She's got a kid with her—little," he said, measuring with his huge hands. "Kid might be coming down with something. He's got a fever, she said. I gave her my old room because there's no place to stay around here…."

"Well," Jack said, picking up his coffee. "That was nice of you. I guess. She steal the silver or anything?"

Preacher made a face. They didn't have silver; the only thing worth stealing was the cash, locked up tight. Or liquor—way too much trouble for a woman with a kid. Not that any of that ever crossed his mind. "She's probably in some trouble," Preacher said. "She's got… Looks like maybe she's been in some trouble. Maybe she's running or something."

Again, Jack was shocked. "Huh?"

Preacher stared hard into Jack's eyes. "I think she needs some help," he said, when in fact he *knew* she needed help. "She's got a bruise on her face."

"Oh, boy," Jack said.

"Mel coming in to Doc's?" he asked.

"Of course."

"She needs to have a look at the kid—make sure he's not sick. You know. And the woman—Paige—she says she's all right, but maybe… Maybe Mel can—I don't know—be sure."

"Yeah," Jack said, taking a sip from his mug. "Then what?"

Preacher shrugged. "She's gonna want to get out of here, I think. She's all skittish. She seems scared. I want her to at least see Mel."

"Probably a good idea."

"Yeah. That's what we'll do. Ask her to let Mel have a look. But I can't make her, you know. I think you should do it. Talk to her, suggest it to her…."

"Nah, Preach, you can handle this. It's your deal—I haven't seen her or anything. You just talk to her. Quiet and soft. Try not to scare her."

"She's already scared, which is how I figure she's in some trouble. The kid hasn't seen me yet, though—he was asleep. He'll probably run screaming."

At seven-thirty Preacher fixed up a tray with some cereal in bowls, toast, coffee, orange juice and milk. He went up the back stairs and gently tapped on the door. It opened immediately. Paige had showered and dressed. She wore the same jeans and a long-sleeved chambray shirt. A little black-and-blue spot peeked out from the opened collar and Preacher immediately felt steamed up, but he tried to keep it from showing on his face. Instead, he focused on her eyes, which were a deep emerald-green, and her damp hair, which fell in curly tendrils to her shoulders. "Morning," he said, trying to keep his voice quiet and soft, like Jack would.

"Hey," she said. "You're up early."

"I've been up forever," he said.

"Mom?" came a voice from behind her. He looked past her and saw the little kid, Christopher, sitting cross-legged in the middle of the bed.

*Robyn Carr*

She opened the door for Preacher and he came in, putting the tray on the bureau just inside the door. He stayed by the door and gave the kid a nod. He tried to relax his features into softness, but wasn't sure how to do that. "Hey, little buddy. You want some breakfast?"

The kid shrugged, but his round eyes were wide and focused on Preacher.

"He's not so good with men," Paige whispered softly. "Shy."

"Yeah?" Preacher asked. "Me, too. Don't worry—I'll stay back."

He looked at the child and tried out a smile. Then the kid pointed at Preacher's head and said, "You hafta shabe that?"

It made Preacher laugh. "Yeah. Wanna feel?" he asked. He approached the bed slowly, carefully, bending his bald head toward the kid. He felt a small hand rub over his dome and it made him laugh again. He raised his head and said, "Cool, huh?" And the kid nodded.

Preacher went back to Paige. "My buddy's wife, Melinda, she's coming to Doc's this morning and I wanna take you over there. Let her have a look at the kid, make sure he's okay, and if he needs medicine or anything, she'll fix you right up."

"She's a nurse, you say?"

"Yeah. A special nurse. A midwife. She delivers babies and that."

"Oh," Paige said, a little more interested. "That's probably a good idea. But I don't have much money—"

He laughed. "We don't worry about things like that around here, if someone could use a little help. It'll be fine."

"If you're sure…"

"It's all good. Come on downstairs when you're ready. Mel will be over there about eight, but take your time. Not too many people get sick around here and they're not usually busy."

"Okay. Then we'll press on…."

"Um, if you need to, you can stay a couple of days. I mean, if he's not feeling so well. Or, if you're tired from driving."

"I'll probably just get back on the road."

"Where you headed?" he asked. "You never mentioned."

"Just a little farther. I have a friend… We're going to visit a friend."

"Ah," he said, but if it had been just a little farther, she'd have kept going. "Well, you think about it. Open offer."

While Christopher sat cross-legged on the bed to eat cereal, Paige leaned toward the mirror, dabbing makeup on her purple cheek, covering it as best she could. It had at least lightened somewhat. But there was nothing she could do about the split lip, which was scabbing over. Christopher would touch it and say, "Mommy's owie."

Her mind wandered back to that last beating. The part that still shook her was not being able to remember what had really started it. Something about Christopher's toys being strewn all over the family room, and then Wes's suit not back from the dry cleaners. He wasn't happy about what she'd made for dinner. Or was it what she had said about the toys? "Jesus, Wes, he has toys—he plays with them. Just give me a minute…" Had he slapped her then? No, right after that, when she muttered, under her breath, "Don't get excited, don't get mean, just let me do it…."

How could she not know that he'd react like that? Because she never knew how he would react. They'd had months of no violence. But she had seen it in his eyes when he came home from the office. It was already there—eyes that said, I'm going to hit you and hit you and hit you some more and neither of us will know exactly why. As usual, by the time she zoned in on that dangerous gleam, it was too late.

She had started spotting then, in danger of losing the baby—the new baby that she'd recently told him about. Big surprise—since he had kicked her. So she dragged herself out of the bed and went to pick up Christopher at day care. The girl behind the desk, Debbie, had gasped when she saw Paige's face. Then she stammered, "M-Mr. Lassiter asked us to call him if you came for Christopher."

"Look at me, Debbie. Maybe you could forget to call him. Just this once. Maybe for a while."

"I don't know…"

"He's not going to hit *you*," she had said boldly.

"Mrs. Lassiter, maybe you should call the police or something?"

And Paige had laughed hollowly. Right. "I guess you think I haven't."

At least she'd gotten out of town. With her one suitcase, almost five hundred dollars and an address in Spokane.

And here she was, waking up under another V-shaped ceiling. Still scared to death, but at least in the moment, apparently safe.

While Christopher ate, she poked around a little, not touching anything. It wasn't a real big room, but there was enough space for Preacher's bench and weights. She looked at a couple of barbells on the floor—sixty pounds each. On the press he had stacked four hundred pounds; Wes had bragged incessantly about his two-fifty.

There was a medium-size bookcase against the wall, full, books stacked on the floor beside it and on top. She held her hands behind her back; force of habit—Wes didn't like her touching his things, except his dirty laundry. Weird titles—the biography of Napoléon, World War Two warplanes, medieval armies. *Hitler's Occupation*—that sent a chill through her. Most of them were pretty worn, old. Some new. She couldn't spot a fiction title—all nonfiction, all military or political subjects.

Maybe they had belonged to his father or an uncle. He didn't exactly look like a big reader, though he sure looked like a weight-lifter.

When Chris was done with his breakfast, she put on his jacket, then her own, picking up the quilted bag to hang over her shoulder. She left the suitcase, packed, on the bed and carried the breakfast tray down the back stairs. John was in the kitchen wearing an apron, flipping sausage patties, an omelet pan steaming over a high flame. "Go ahead and set that down right on the counter and give me one minute," he said. "I'll walk you over."

"I could wash these up," she said meekly.

"Nah, I got it." Paige watched as he pressed the patties with his big spatula and sprinkled cheese on the omelet, then deftly folded and flipped it. Toast popped up, was buttered and everything put on a large oval plate. He took off his apron and hung it on a hook. He was wearing jeans and a black T-shirt that was stretched so tight across the broad expanse of his chest it looked like it should split. The biceps on the man were like melons. If he'd been wearing a white T-shirt, he'd look like Mr. Clean.

He plucked a denim jacket off the peg and shrugged into it. He picked up the plate and said, "Come on," and walked into the bar. He put the plate down in front of a man who sat at the bar, quickly refilled the man's coffee and said, "I'll be back in a few minutes. Here's the pot. Jack's out back if you need anything."

Paige stole a look out the back door window where she saw a man in jeans and a plaid flannel shirt hefting an ax over his head and bringing it down to split a log. That had been what woke her. She took note of the muscular shoulders and broad back—not as pronounced as John's, but still impressive.

Wes was not nearly as big as either of these men; he was about six feet and in good shape, but as for muscles, nothing by comparison, even with his chemical assistance. If John raised a fist to a woman the way Wes had done, she wouldn't live to tell about it. She shuddered involuntarily.

"Look, Mommy," Chris said, pointing to the mounted stag's head over the door.

"I see. Wow." The place did look like a hunting lodge.

John stuck his head out the back door and yelled, "Jack! I'm walking over to Doc's. Be right back."

Then he turned toward her and gave a nod. He opened the door for her to follow him outside. "How's he feeling this morning?" he asked.

"He ate breakfast. That's good."

"That's good," John agreed. "The fever?" he whispered.

"I don't have a thermometer with me, so I'm not sure. He feels a little warm."

"Good to let Mel check, then," he said, walking alongside her but careful not to get too close. She held her son's hand, but Preacher put his in his pockets. He glanced at the boy; the boy glanced around his mother at him. They eyed each other warily. "It'll be okay," he said to her. "Mel's the best. You'll see."

Paige looked up at him, smiled sweetly, and it made him feel all soupy inside. Her eyes were so sad, so scared. She couldn't help it, he understood that. If it weren't for the fear, he might actually take her hand to give her courage—but she wasn't just afraid of whoever did that to her. She was afraid of everything, including him. "Don't be nervous," he said to her. "Mel's very kind."

"I'm not nervous," she said.

"After I introduce you, I'll go back over there. Unless you want me to stay? In case you need me for anything?"

"I'll be fine. Thanks."

Melinda sat on Doc's front steps with her morning coffee, listening to the loud crack of Jack's ax as he split logs. He had called her when he got to the bar and said, "Put a wiggle in it, babe. Preacher's got a patient for you."

"Oh, yeah?" she asked.

"Some woman stumbled into the bar last night during the storm and he put her up for the night. Says she's got a kid who might be feverish. And he also said he thinks she might be in trouble…."

"Oh? What kind of trouble?" Mel asked.

"No idea," he said. "I haven't even seen her yet. He gave her his old room, upstairs."

"Okay, I'll be along shortly." Out of instinct, she put her digital camera in her bag. Now, watching the front of the bar, she saw something she had never expected to see. Preacher held the door for a woman and a child and walked them across the street. He seemed to be talking to her in soft tones, leaning close, a concerned look on his face. Amazing. Preacher was a man of so few words. Mel thought she remembered being in town for a month before he said ten words in a row to her. For him to take in a stranger like this was both very like him, yet so unprecedented.

As they neared, Mel stood up. The woman appeared to be in her twenties with a dark stain on her cheek that she'd tried to cover with makeup. She couldn't cover the split lip, however. There's the trouble Preacher had seen. It made Mel wince. But she smiled and said, "Hi. Mel Sheridan."

She faltered. "Paige," she finally said, then looked over her shoulder nervously.

"It's okay, Paige," Preacher said. "You're safe with Mel. Everything with her is top secret. She's ridiculous about it."

Mel laughed as if amused. "No, I'm not ridiculous. This is a doctor's office, a medical clinic. We're confidential, that's all. It's very simple. Standard." She reached out to shake Paige's hand. "Nice to meet you, Paige."

Paige took the offered hand and looked over her shoulder at Preacher. "Thank you, John."

"John?" Mel asked. She laughed lightly. "I don't think I've ever heard anyone call you John." She tilted her head a bit. "Kind of nice. John." Then she said, "Come with me, Paige." And she led the way.

Inside the house they passed by Doc, who sat at the reception desk behind a computer. He looked up briefly, gave a nod, then went back to his work. "That's Doc Mullins," Mel said. "This way." She opened an exam room door and let Paige precede her into the room. She closed the door and said, "I'm a nurse practitioner and midwife, Paige. I can have a look at your son if you'd like. Now, I understand you suspect a fever?"

"He's kind of warm. Not too much energy…."

"Let's have a look," Mel said, briskly taking charge. She bent down and asked the little boy if he'd been to the doctor before. She hefted him up on the exam table, showed him the digital thermometer and asked him if he knew what to do with that. He pointed to his ear and Mel laughed happily. "You're an expert at this," she said. She picked up the stethoscope and asked, "Mind if I listen to your heart?" He shook his head. "I'll try not to tickle, but it's hard for me, because tickling is kind of fun—I just love hearing the giggles." On cue, he laughed, though softly. Mel let him listen to his own heart, then hers. She palpated his lymph nodes while he listened to his chest, his leg, his hand. She looked in his ears and throat, and by the time she'd gotten that far he was already getting comfortable with her.

"I think he might have a little virus—doesn't seem to be too serious. His temp is only a hundred. Have you given him anything?"

"Children's Tylenol, last night."

"Ah, then he's in pretty good shape. His throat looks a little red. Keep up the Tylenol, lots of fluids. I don't think you have to worry. If he gets worse, of course…"

"Then it's safe to just keep driving…?"

Mel shrugged. "I don't know, Paige. Want to talk about you? I'm here to help, if I can."

Her gaze instantly dropped and that was really all it took. Mel knew where this was going. She'd spent years in a big-city emergency room, and had seen more than her share of battery victims. The bruise on the young woman's face, the split lip, the fact that she wanted to keep driving…away…

Paige lifted her gaze. "I'm a little pregnant. And spotting."

"And a couple of bruises?" Mel asked.

Paige averted her gaze and nodded.

"Okay. Would you like me to have a look?"

Paige looked down. "Please," she said softly. "But what about Chris?"

"Oh, not to worry. I've got that covered." She bent at the waist and smiled into Christopher's handsome brown eyes. "You like to color, buddy? Because I have a ton of coloring books and crayons." He nodded shyly. "Good. Come with me." She helped the little guy down off the exam table and with the other hand, pulled a gown out of the cabinet and handed it to Paige. "Why don't you put on this gown. I'll give you a few minutes. And try not to be afraid. I'll go slow, be gentle."

"Um… Are you leaving him alone?" Paige asked.

"More or less." Mel laughed. "I'm leaving him with Doc."

"He seems a little…shy…around men."

"It'll be fine. Doc's good with kids, especially the shy ones. He'll just make sure this guy doesn't do surgery or run away. Beyond that, it's just coloring. At the kitchen table."

"If you're sure…"

"We do it all the time, Paige. It'll be okay. Try not to worry."

Mel took Christopher to the kitchen, and after setting him up with coloring books and crayons, she refilled her coffee. Decaf. She wasn't enjoying coffee nearly as much these days. Then she went to the office and got out a new patient form. Given the situation she believed she faced, she would examine the patient first before frightening her with paperwork. Clipboard in hand, she asked Doc to keep an eye on the child in the kitchen while she performed a pelvic.

Being a few months pregnant herself, Mel had a sick feeling at the thought of anyone hitting a pregnant woman. It never ceased to amaze her that a man could live with himself after doing something like that. Forms on her clipboard, her small digital camera in her shirt pocket, stethoscope around her neck, coffee in hand, she tapped on the door and heard Paige softly say, "Come in."

She put the clipboard and her coffee on the counter and said, "Okay, then… Let's get your blood pressure first." She picked up the blood pressure cuff and went to apply it to Paige's arm and was frozen. There was a huge hematoma that covered much of her upper arm.

Mel put the cuff aside and gently pulled the gown away from Paige's back; she had to concentrate not to gasp. She pulled the gown over Paige's shoulder, down her arm, exposing the bruises on her back, arm, chest. She carefully lifted the gown at the bottom, exposing her thighs. More bruises. She looked at the girl's face. Tears glistened on her cheeks. "Paige," Mel said in a whisper. "My God…"

Paige put her hands over her face. Shame at having let it happen.

"Have you been raped?" Mel asked gently.

She shook her head, tears flowing. "No."

"Who did this to you?" she asked. Paige just closed her eyes and shook her head. "It's okay. You're safe right now."

"My husband," she answered in a whisper.

"And you're running away from him?"

She nodded.

"Here, let me help you lie down, slowly. Carefully… Are you all right?" Paige nodded, not making eye contact, and reclined on the exam table. Mel gently moved the gown around. Her chest, breasts, arms, legs—all covered in bruises. Mel palpated her abdomen and Paige winced. "Does it hurt here? Here?" When Paige nodded or shook her head, Mel moved on. "Here? Here?" Mel gently rolled her from one side to the other—her buttocks were bruised, as were her lower back and upper thighs. "Any blood in your urine?" she asked, and Paige shrugged. She didn't know. "The only way I can get a clean urine specimen if you're spotting is with a catheter, Paige. Would you like me to do that? Just to be sure?"

"Oh, God… Do you have to?"

"It's okay. Let's check what we can, first. Any chance you've had an ultrasound with this pregnancy?"

"I haven't even been to the doctor yet," she said.

Another symptom, Mel thought. Battered women didn't take care of themselves, or their pregnancies, out of fear.

Paige sucked on her sore bottom lip, staring at the ceiling through glassy eyes while Mel examined her. "Okay, let me help you sit up. Easy does it." Mel listened to Paige's heart, looked in her ears, checked her head for lumps and lacerations. "Well, Paige, you don't appear to have broken bones. At least none that I can detect. I wouldn't mind getting an X ray of your ribs, just to be sure, since you have some tenderness there, but with you being pregnant and all… Frankly, if it were up to me, I'd admit you to the hospital."

"No. No hospitals. I can't have any records of any kind…."

"I understand, but realize, this looks very scary. How heavy is the bleeding?"

"Not too bad. Less than, say, a period."

"Okay, lie back and slide down. I'll be as gentle as possible."

When she was in the position, Mel pulled on her gloves and took her stool. She touched the inside of Paige's thigh before touching her external genitalia. "I'm not going to use a speculum for this exam, Paige. Just a pelvic to estimate the size of the uterus. If you have any discomfort at all, please tell me." She inserted two fingers, gently pressing down on her lower abdomen with the other hand. "Do you know how far along you are?"

"Just over eight weeks."

"Okay. When we're done here I'll have you take a pregnancy test. If the fetus was still viable—alive—as of a day or so ago, it should come out positive, but it won't tell us much about the past twenty-four hours, I'm afraid. I don't have an ultrasound, but there's one a couple of towns over that we use when necessary. But… One thing at a time. Uterus is normal for an eight-week pregnancy." Mel made a derisive sound. "Paige, you've been through such a lot." She removed her gloves and offered her hand. "Can you sit up for me, please?"

Paige sat up and Mel took her stool, looking up into her eyes. "You're how old?"

"Twenty-nine."

"I understand how hard it is in situations like yours to get help, but I'm wondering if you tried to call the police."

"I've done that," she said very softly. "I've done everything. Police, restraining orders, shelters, moving out, counseling…" Then she laughed. *"Counseling,"* she said. "He had the counselor in love with him in five minutes." She took a breath. "It didn't go too well after that."

"I understand completely."

"He's going to kill me one of these days. One of these days soon."

"Has he threatened to kill you?"

"Oh, yes." She looked down. "Oh, yes," she said again, softly.

"How'd you find Virgin River?" Mel asked.

"I think…I got lost. I got off the highway looking for a place to stay, to eat. And I got lost. I was going to turn around when I saw the town, the bar."

Mel took a breath. Time for a reality check. Not only was it hard for the battery victim to make charges stick if the police weren't called to the scene right away, half the time the victim bailed the abuser out of jail in fear for her life. And it wasn't an idle threat—abusers did kill their victims. All the time. "Paige, I worked in emergency medicine in Los Angeles before coming up here and, unfortunately, I have some experience with situations like yours. We have to get you some help."

"I was trying to get away," she said with a sniff of emotion she was trying desperately to contain. "Then I got lost, Chris wasn't feeling good, I'm so sore I could hardly drive another minute…"

"Where are you headed?" Mel asked.

Paige hung her head, shaking it, and said, "To a friend he doesn't know about."

"Stay here a few days. Let's see how you're doing before—"

Her eyes shot to Mel's. "I can't! I'm in a hurry now! I'm already behind schedule! I have to—" She stopped suddenly. She seemed to gather herself up and try to speak with composure. "I have to get where I'm going before he can report me missing. Before my car is being—"

"No, you're okay," Mel said calmly. "It's okay, Paige. Leave your car behind the bar, out of sight. When it's time to go, take a butter knife out of the kitchen, to loosen the screws on the license plate holders. Switch plates with someone. If you don't speed, drive erratically or get in an accident, no reason for a highway patrolman to run your plates." She shrugged. "No one around here will notice switched plates for weeks. Months. I'd never even look."

While Mel spoke, Paige stared into her eyes and her mouth dropped open slightly in surprise. "Did you just suggest I steal someone's…?"

Mel smiled. "Oh! Did I use my outside voice? I should watch that…."

"You act like you know…"

"Let's not talk about what you're doing," Mel said. "I did a little community service in a shelter once. It killed me," she said. "It tore me up. But I learned a couple of things. Just let me say this—it's worse if you rush. If you hurry. You might drive too fast, drive too sore or tired. Take a few days, heal a little, let the boy's fever go down. Then do it smart. Wherever you're going—it'll be there in a few days or a couple of weeks. You're hurt."

"What if he finds me here…?"

"Oh, my Lord, if he finds you here, I seriously don't like his chances."

"He has a gun, too. Though he's always kept it locked up."

"Handgun?" Mel asked, and Paige nodded. Mel actually heard herself let out a breath of relief. Mel, who had been so afraid of guns before coming to Virgin River. There weren't many handguns here, but there were a lot of guns that could kill a bear with one shot. Or blow a man in half. "There is so much you don't know about our men. Okay, with your permission, I'd like to take some pictures."

"No!"

Mel touched her forearm. "Just as a record, Paige. I promise you, what happens to them will be entirely up to you, but we should have a record for your use, in case you decide you need it. I'm not going to ask your last name or where you came from, all right? I'll make up a chart without a last name but I'll date it. I'll take some pictures with a digital camera. And if you can be convinced to stay put for a day or two, I'd like to take you to Grace Valley for an ultrasound—see how that baby's doing. Just stay long enough to be sure your injuries aren't any more serious than I can tell from this exam. By now you know— while you're under Preacher's care, no one can hurt you."

"He said… John said I could stay a couple of days. But he's…"

"He's what?" Mel asked, frowning.

"He's a little scary."

Mel chuckled. "No, he's a lot scary. Looking. First time I saw him, I was afraid to move. But he's been my husband's best friend for something like fifteen years now, his partner in that bar for more than two. He's gentle as a lamb. He takes a little getting used to…. But he's so good," she added softly. "His heart… It's so big. As big as he is."

"I don't know…"

"You could come out to our place," Mel offered. "We could find another bed. Or stay here in the clinic. We have two hospital beds upstairs for patients. But Preacher can protect you better than Doc or I can, I guarantee that. Whatever you decide—just so you're comfortable. Now, I'm going to slip the gown off your shoulder a little bit," Mel said, pulling the camera out of her shirt pocket. "We'll make this as painless as possible." She pulled the gown off her shoulder slightly. "There we go," she said softly, snapping. She put the gown back up. Then she went to the other shoulder, slowly, gently, quickly getting the picture. One body part at a time; her back, her thighs, her arms, her chest above her breasts. Last, her face, and in that picture, Paige's eyes were closed.

After the pictures were taken, Mel asked for a complete medical history. "But with no last name. It's only for medical purposes, so you can be treated if it becomes necessary. After we're done, you should lie down. Where would you like to go?"

"What about Christopher?"

"Maybe he'll nap a little bit. Or we can keep an eye on him. Between us—my husband, me, Preacher, Doc— we can keep him occupied. Girl," she said, "you have no idea what a piece of luck it was that you stumbled into Virgin River. This place doesn't have so much by way of technology or shopping, but you won't find a town with more heart." She smiled. "Or better food."

"I don't want to burden my problems on this little town," she said miserably.

"Well," Mel said, gently touching her hand, "you would hardly be the first."

# *Three*

Jack was behind the bar having coffee while one of his breakfast regulars was eating when Paige and Christopher came in. Paige stopped inside the door, looking across the room tentatively. Jack gave a small smile and a nod. "Preacher's in the kitchen," he said.

She looked down as she walked past him into the kitchen. Jack gave her a few minutes, refilled Harv's cup, then went to the kitchen. Preacher was alone; he'd just lifted a rack of glasses out of the dishwasher. "If you say it's okay, she's going to stay a couple of days. Till the kid feels better," Preacher said.

"Is that all it is?" Jack asked. "She in some trouble?"

Preacher shrugged and put the rack on the counter.

"You don't know her, Preacher. Don't know who did that to her face."

"I'm not worried about *who*," he said. "Jesus. I'd love to see *who*."

"If you want her to stay, she stays. I'm just saying…"

"This is your place," Preacher said.

"Do I make you feel like that? That it's my place? Because—"

"Nah," Preacher said. "You're good that way, even if

it really is your place. I just don't want you to make her…them…feel bad about it."

"I won't do that. Don't screw with me. You know I consider us partners. This is your place, too. That's your room."

"Okay, then." Preacher took the rack of glasses out to the bar.

Jack followed. "If you're okay here, I'm going to step out."

"Sure."

"I'll be right back," Jack said.

Jack walked across the street to Doc's. There were no patients, but Doc and Mel were inside the front door where, behind the reception counter, Doc was sitting at the desk, eyes focused on the computer.

Mel stood behind Doc, her hand on his shoulder. She looked up when Jack entered and inclined her head slightly, indicating he should come behind the counter. Her eyes were so troubled and angry, he went toward them. Mel glanced back at the computer screen.

Jack had never done anything like this before; Mel had never pulled him into her medical business, even though confidentiality was as safe with Jack as with either of them. She didn't confide medical issues with her husband because that was an ethic she was firm about.

There on the screen were the pictures from the digital. Paige's battered body was on display in many different angles. The bruises were astonishingly bad. If he saw bruises like that on Mel, it would be impossible for him to keep from killing someone.

"Good God," he said in a breath. He wondered if Preacher knew there was a lot more to his houseguest than a little bruise on her cheek.

Mel looked up at her husband and saw the grim set of

his jaw, the pulsing of a vein in his temple. His narrow eyes. "This goes no further," she said.

"Of course not."

"Do you understand why you're standing here, looking at this with us?"

"I think so. She's at the bar. Preacher wants her to stay."

"Well, you should know, I told her she could stay with us if she wanted to. I think she feels okay at your bar, especially since I vouched for Preacher. We have to get her some help or this beast will kill her."

"Of course. You think Preach knows how bad this is?"

"I have no idea. I'm not sharing this with him, but you need to know what's going on if she's under your roof."

"Our roof," he said. Mel and the baby—they were his life. He couldn't imagine laying anything but a loving hand on her. "You know anything about her? Because I don't want Preacher getting used. Or hurt."

Mel shrugged. "I don't even know where she came from. But I don't think Preacher's the one you have to worry about at the moment."

"He's already caught up in this. Taking it on."

"Well, good for him. She needs someone to take this on. And Preacher can take care of himself."

"Yeah, we just went over that."

Mel leaned against Jack and he put his arm around her. "I've never seen anything like it, and I've seen a lot," she said in a breath. "This is one dangerous son of a bitch."

"I don't want you in over your head, either," he said.

"Save it. I have a job to do."

"This is really bad, Mel," he said.

"Even more reason why I'd better do my job."

Preacher was surprised that Paige came back from Mel deciding to stay a couple of days. She seemed so hell-bent to take off. She took Christopher upstairs in the morning and there hadn't been a sound from up there. They missed lunch altogether. But, he reasoned, if the kid didn't feel good, maybe he'd sleep extra long, which would give his banged-up mother a needed rest.

During the quiet of the afternoon was when he usually got dinner ready, but today he got out one of his older cookbooks. He had great admiration for Martha Stewart, even though most of her recipes were too fussy for a bar. But he liked the real old-fashioned ones—old Betty Crocker, Julia Child—before everyone started eating light and watching their cholesterol.

He looked up *cookies.*

Preacher didn't know a lot about kids, and there wasn't much call for cookies in a bar, but he had tender memories of his mother making cookies. She had been a little tiny thing. Tiny, high-principled, soft-spoken but stern, and real shy—he'd inherited the shy part, probably. His dad had died when he was young, but he hadn't been a big guy, either—just average. And here came Preacher. More than nine pounds at birth, almost six feet by the seventh grade.

He didn't have cookie stuff on hand. But he had flour, sugar, butter and peanut butter—a good thing. Those ingredients would make the soft, sweet kind of cookies, anyway. While he was mixing the dough and rolling little brown balls he found himself thinking about the sight of his mother and him sitting together in mass—her narrow shoulders, high-buttoned dress, graying hair pulled into a proper bun at the nape of her neck. And he, beside her, taking two spaces in the pew by the time he was fifteen. While he was gently pressing the little balls flat with a fork, he chuckled to himself, remembering when she taught him to drive. It was one of the only times he heard her raise her voice, get all flustered and upset. His feet were so big and his legs so long, he was rugged on the accelerator, the brakes. *Jesus, Mary and Joseph, John!*

*You have to be gentler! Slower, more graceful! I should have sent you to ballet lessons instead of football!* It was a surprise she didn't die of a heart attack, riding with him.

She did die of a heart attack a little while later, the summer before Preacher's senior year in high school. She didn't look like the kind of woman with a weak heart, but how would anyone know? She never went to the doctor.

Preacher was working on his second tray when he glanced up and saw that little blond head, peeking at him from the bottom of the stairs. "Hi," Preacher said. "You sleep?" Christopher nodded. "Good," he said. "Feel better?" Chris nodded again.

Watching the boy's face, Preacher slowly pushed a fresh-baked cookie across the counter with one finger until it was at the edge. It was a good minute before Chris took one step toward the cookie. Almost another full minute before his little hand touched it, but he didn't take it. Just touched it, looking up at Preacher. "Go ahead. Tell me if it's any good."

Chris slowly pulled the cookie off the counter and to his mouth, taking a very small, careful bite.

"Good?" Preacher asked. And he nodded.

So Preacher set him up a glass of milk right where the cookie had been. The boy nibbled that cookie in tiny bites; it took him so long to finish it that Preacher was pulling out the second cookie sheet and taking off the cookies before he was done. There was a stool on the other side of the counter near the milk and eventually Chris started trying to get up. But he had some stuffed toy in his grip and couldn't make the climb, so Preacher went around and lifted him up. Then he went back to his side of the counter and pushed another cookie toward him. "Don't pick it up yet," Preacher said. "It's kind of hot. Try the milk."

Preacher started rolling peanut butter dough into balls,

placing them on the cookie sheet. "Who you got there?" he asked, nodding toward the stuffed toy.

"Bear," Christopher said. He reached his hand toward the cookie.

Preacher said, "Make sure it's not too hot for your mouth. So—his name's just Bear?" Christopher nodded. "Seems like maybe he's missing a leg, there."

Again the boy nodded. "Doesn't hurt him, though."

"That's a break. He ought to have one, anyway. I mean, it wouldn't be the same as his own, but it would help him get by. When he has to go for a long walk."

The kid laughed. "He don't walk. I walk."

"He doesn't, huh? He should have one for looks, then." He lifted one of his bushy black brows. "Think so?"

Christopher lifted the small, worn brown bear. "Hmm," he replied thoughtfully. He bit the cookie and immediately opened his mouth wide and let the sloppy mouthful fall onto the counter. For a second his look was stricken. Maybe terrified.

"Hot, huh?" Preacher asked, not reacting. He reached behind him, ripped off a paper towel and whisked away the spit-out. "Might want to give it about one more minute. Have a drink of milk there. Cool down the mouth."

They communed in silence for a while—Preacher, Chris, the three-legged bear. When Preacher had all his little balls rolled, he began mashing them with his fork, perfect lines left, then right.

"What's that yer doing?" Christopher asked him.

"Making cookies. First you mix the dough, then you roll the balls, then you smash them with the fork, nice and easy. Then they go in the oven." He peered at Chris from underneath the heavy brows. "I bet you could do this part. If you were careful and went nice and slow."

"I could."

"You'd have to come around here, let me lift you up."

"'Kay," he said, putting his bear on the counter, getting off his stool and coming to Preacher.

Preacher lifted him up to sit on the edge of the counter. He helped him hold the fork and showed him how to press down. His first solo attempt was a little messy, so Preacher helped him again. Then he did it pretty well. Preacher let him finish the tray, then put it in the oven.

"John?" the boy asked. "How many of them we gotta do?"

Preacher smiled. "Tell you what, pardner. We'll do as many as you want," he said.

Christopher smiled. "'Kay," he said.

Paige came slowly awake, her first realization being that she'd slept so hard, she'd drooled on the pillow. She sleepily wiped her mouth and turned her head to look at Christopher, only to find his side of the bed empty. She sat up with a sudden start that jolted her bruised and sore body. She got up and looked around the bedroom quickly, but he wasn't there. She went down the stairs in her stocking feet. When she got to the bottom, she stopped suddenly.

Chris was sitting up on the counter, John standing beside him. They were both rolling brown dough into small balls. She crossed her arms over her chest and watched. John had heard her come down and smiled at her. He gave Chris a nudge and inclined his head toward Paige, so Chris turned.

"Mom," he said. "We're makin' cookies."

"I see that," she said.

"John said Bear needs a leg—"

"He's been getting along fine—"

"For looks," Christopher said.

Paige thought that Bear had been looking pretty awful for a long time now. But for the first time in too long, Christopher looked okay.

\* \* \*

When Rick came to work after school, it was just Preacher in the kitchen, working on dinner. Rick, now seventeen, had been Jack's shadow since Jack first came to town. Preacher came not long after and it was a three-some. Rick lived with his widowed grandmother, his parents long dead, and the guys took him on, let him help in the bar, taught him to hunt and fish, helped him buy his first rifle. Sometimes he was a pain—talked too much. But he'd only been a kid in puberty then—zits trying to beat out freckles—and a little hyper. He'd grown taller in the years since, filled out, quieted down. After about a year of building, the bar opened and they put him to work there.

"Rick. You need a briefing," Preacher told him.

"Yeah? What's up?"

"There's a woman and kid upstairs in my old room. I'm looking out for them. Kid doesn't feel so hot right now—he might be coming down with something. They're staying awhile. Looks like maybe… Well," Preacher said, struggling with the words. "She's got a bruised face, a cut lip. I think she ran into some trouble and she's on the move. So… We're not going to say their names around, just in case someone's looking for her. Her name's Paige, the kid's name is Christopher—but we're not going to say names for a while. And they're going to stay until they feel better. You know?"

"Holy God, Preach," Rick said. "What're you doing?"

"I told you. I'm looking out for them."

Preacher had no experience with children and wasn't planning on having his own. He was thirty-two and hadn't had a single serious relationship with a woman. He figured he and Jack would fish, run the bar, hunt a little, have regular reunions with the squad, but he couldn't see life changing much. That Jack fell in love and got married hadn't upset Preacher's expectations because he thought Mel was the best. It just hadn't changed his own life. One of the reasons he liked Virgin River—it was less obvious he'd always be alone.

Then his life began to change in days. Really, in hours.

Christopher would run down the stairs in his pajamas before his mother could grab him, stop him. He liked to eat his breakfast at the kitchen counter and watch while Preacher diced vegetables, shredded cheese and whipped eggs for omelets. Then there was sweeping to do, and Chris liked having his own broom. There was that bear skin and mounted buck's head—which he needed to be lifted up to touch. They got some coloring books and crayons from Mel's clinic so Chris had something to do while Preacher worked on lunch or dinner. And there were more cookies to bake than there were to eat—cookies were not exactly bar food. Then, amazingly, Paige helped with the washup in the kitchen—probably to be near Chris, who wanted to be with Preacher, and maybe a little to earn her keep. He found this not only helpful, but awful pleasant.

Paige needed to rest, though at first she was reluctant to leave her child in John's care. She seemed to get beyond that nervousness, probably because she was usually near and Chris seemed to be relaxed. And on the fourth day of her stay, at Mel's convincing, she actually left Chris with Preacher while she went somewhere with Mel. Preacher made no speculation of where they were going—he was just flattered that she had come to trust him enough to babysit without supervision.

But still, he used the time to his advantage.

Preacher had been on the Internet, learning about domestic abuse and California law regarding the same. He had done this late at night because there were things he needed to understand about her situation, her terrible bruises, her flight. First of all, it didn't matter if it were a husband or boyfriend, either were equally dangerous. Then there was lots of stuff about how she could be cited with parental kidnapping if she'd taken a man's child away, even after what had been done to her, and how whoever beat her up could be let off with misdemeanors the first couple of times, but the third time was a felony, which carried a prison sentence.

He also read about the psychology of this syndrome, how you could be sucked in, manipulated, terrified—and suddenly find yourself in a life-threatening situation. Battered women who were threatened with death if they told, if they fled, if they fought back—were often killed. It chilled Preacher to the bones.

So, while Chris was napping and Paige was off somewhere with Mel, Preacher called one of his best friends from the Corps, one of the guys who came up to Virgin River regularly when they gathered for fishing, hunting and poker. Mike Valenzuela was LAPD—a sergeant in the gangs division. Too bad he couldn't be in the domestic violence division. Preacher called him, told him about Paige.

"She doesn't know I happened to see," Preacher said. "It was just a little crack in the door and I saw her in the mirror, and Jesus… She was so beat up, it's amazing she's not dead. She's running for her life, man. She ran to get her three-year-old kid out of there. So how is it he can file kidnapping charges against her and get her back?"

"Parental kidnapping. But here's the thing—if there's evidence that he's battered her in the past, if he has a record, she might have to return and face her kidnapping charges, but they'd probably be pleaded down or dismissed, given the situation. And she could probably gain at least temporary custody at that time, a divorce, a restraining order, what she needs to stay safe."

"But she'd have to go *back,*" he said, a note of desperation in his voice.

"Preacher. She wouldn't necessarily have to go back alone. Hey, how into this woman are you?"

"It's not like that, man. I'm just trying to help out. That little kid—he's a good little kid. If I could help with this, even a little, it would make me feel like I'd done something that mattered. For once."

"Preach." Mike laughed. "I was with you in Iraq! You mattered damn near every day, for God's sake! Hey—where did you learn all this stuff about battery DV? Huh?"

"I got a computer," Preacher answered. "Doesn't everyone but Jack have a computer?"

"I guess." Mike laughed.

"One thing I can't get online—I wanna know who she is, how guilty he is, and what's the best way to go here. All I know is her license plate.... California plate..."

"Aw, Preach. I'm not supposed to do that."

"Couldn't you be curious?" Preacher asked. "Because there could actually be a crime in here somewhere. All you have to do is look, Mike."

"Hey, Preacher," Mike said. "What if it's not good news?"

"Would it be the truth?" Preacher asked. "Because I think that might be important here."

"Yeah," Mike said. "Might be."

Preacher swallowed hard and hoped it would be okay. "Thanks," he said. "Go ahead and hurry, huh?"

Paige had gone with Mel to Grace Valley where Dr. John Stone examined her and performed an ultrasound, showing her a small, beating heart in a little mass that didn't look anything like a baby. But it gave her hope. She had gotten out in time. Barely in time.

The pregnancy was an accident, of course. Wes didn't want children. He hadn't wanted Christopher—it interfered with his focus, which was his job and his possessions, Paige being chief among them. Perhaps this new baby precipitated the beating; she'd only told him a couple of days before. In fact, she'd been terrified to tell him. But then, if he didn't want it, why put her through so much? Why not just suggest termination?

The larger question was how could Paige be so relieved to learn the baby had survived when Wes's merest touch repelled her? She was, that's all. But then, she'd come to think of her son as the one good thing that could come out of the biggest mistake of her life. *Have you been raped?* Mel had asked. Oh, no—not rape. She wouldn't dare tell Wes no…

When she got back to Virgin River, she found Chris making bread with John, kneading and punching the dough, laughing.

Such an uncomplicated scene, she thought. So many times when Wes was stressing out and getting himself all worked up about his job, the financial pressures of their lifestyle, she had told him that simplifying things would actually appeal to her. No, she didn't want to be dirt poor and worked to death, but she could be so content in a smaller house with a happier husband. Not long before Chris had been born, Wes bought the big house in an exclusive, guarded, gated L.A. community—more house than they could ever need, and hanging on to it was killing him. Killing her.

So, here she was. The baby had made it. She had to get going, to that address in Spokane, to the first step in her underground escape. The dresser had not been pulled against the door since the first night and she thought she'd give herself another twenty-four hours to rest, then leave in the quiet of night. If there was no rain, the roads wouldn't be so difficult and it would be easier to travel at night while Chris slept.

There was a soft tapping at the door. It was her instinct

to ask who was there, but there was only one possibility. She pulled the door open and there stood John, looking nervous. Looking, in spite of his height and girth, like a teenager. He might've had a flush on his cheeks.

"I closed up the bar. I was thinking about a short drink before calling it a night. How about you? Wanna come down for a little while?"

"For a drink?"

He shrugged. "Whatever you want." He peered past her. "He asleep?"

"Out like a light, despite an overdose of cookies."

"Yeah, I probably gave him too many. Sorry."

"Don't worry—he loves making them. If he makes them, he has to eat them. It's fun—sometimes that's more important than nutrition."

"I'll do whatever you say," Preacher said. "I could cut him back. He likes 'em though. He especially likes burning his mouth on them. He doesn't wait so good."

"I know," she said, smiling. "You have anything like…tea?"

"Sure. Aside from sportsmen, I serve mostly little old ladies." He took on a shocked look. "I didn't mean…"

"A cup of tea would be nice. Good."

"Great," he said, turning and preceding her down the stairs, looking almost grateful to get away.

He got busy brewing tea in the kitchen, so Paige went into the bar and sat at the table where she saw his drink by the fire. When he finally brought her that cup of tea, he said, "You have a good time with Mel today?"

"Yes. Was Christopher a lot of trouble?"

He shook his head with a chuckle. "Nah, he's a kick. He wants to know everything. Every detail. 'Why is it a quarter teaspoon of that?' 'What does the Crisco on the tray do?' And man, yeast blows him away. I think he has a little scientist in him."

Paige thought, he couldn't ask his father questions. Wes didn't have the patience to answer them. "John, do you have family?"

"Not anymore. I was an only child. And my folks were older, anyway—they didn't think they were going to have kids. Then I surprised 'em. Boy, did I surprise 'em. My dad died when I was about six—a construction accident. And then my mom when I was seventeen, right before my senior year."

"I'm so sorry."

"Yeah, thanks. It's okay. I've had a good life."

"What did you do when you lost your mother? Go live with aunts or something?"

"No aunts," he said, shaking his head. "My football coach took me in. It was good—he had a nice wife, good bunch of little kids. Might as well have lived with him. He acted like he owned me during football, anyway," he said with a laugh. "Nah, kidding aside, that was a good thing he did. Good guy. We used to write— now we e-mail."

"What happened to your mom?"

"Heart attack." After a moment of respectful silence, looking into his lap, he laughed softly. "You won't believe this—she died at confession. That really tore me up at first. I thought maybe she had some deep, dark secret that threw her into a heart attack—but I was tight with the priest—I was his altar boy. And it was hard for him, but finally he leveled with me. See, my mom was the parish secretary and real…how should I say this? Kind of a church lady. Father Damien finally told me, my mom's confessions were so boring, he used to nod off. He thought they'd both just fallen asleep, but she was dead." He lifted his eyebrows. "My mom, good woman, not a lot of excitement going on there. She lived for that job, loved the clergy, loved the church. She'd have made a great nun. But you know what? She was happy. I don't think she had any idea she was boring and straitlaced."

"You must miss her so much," Paige said, sipping her tea in front of the fire, trying to remember when she last had a conversation like this. Unhurried, nonthreatening, warm in front of a friendly fire.

"I do. This is going to sound stupid, especially since I'm no kid—sometimes I pretend she's back there, in that little house we lived in, and that I'm just getting my stuff together to go see her."

"That doesn't sound stupid...."

"There anybody you really miss?" he asked her.

The question caused her to suddenly go still, her cup frozen in midair. Not her dad, so scrappy and short-tempered. Not her mom who, without knowing or meaning to, had trained her to be a battered wife. Not Bud, her brother, a mean little bastard who had failed to help her in her darkest hour. "I had a couple of really close girlfriends. Roommates. We lost touch. I miss them sometimes."

"You know where they are?" he asked her.

She shook her head. "Both got married and moved," she said. "I wrote a couple of times.... Then my letters came back." They didn't want to be in touch with her; they knew things were bad. They hated Wes; Wes hated them. They had tried to help, briefly, but he ran them off and she rejected their help out of pure shame. What were they supposed to do? "How'd you get so close to Jack?" she asked him.

"Marines," he said with a shrug.

"Did you go into the military together?"

"Nah." He laughed. "Jack's older than me—by about eight years. I've always looked older than I was—even when I was twelve. And Jack—I bet he's always looked younger. He was my first sergeant in combat, back in Desert Storm." And for a split second he was back there.

Changing a tire on a truck when the tire exploded and the rim knocked him back six feet and he couldn't get up. He remembered it like it was yesterday—he had always been so huge, so rock hard, so strong, and he couldn't move. He might've been unconscious for a little while because he saw his mother leaning over him, looking right into his eyes and saying, "John, get up. Get up, John." Right there in that paisley, high-collared dress, graying hair pulled back.

But he couldn't move, so he started to cry. And cry. *Mom!* he'd cried out.

*Yeah, you have a lot of pain, buddy?* Jack asked, leaning over him.

And Preacher said, *It's my mom. I want my mom. I miss my mom.*

*We're gonna get you back to her, pal. Take a few deep breaths.*

*She's dead,* Preacher said. *She died.*

*She's been dead a couple years at least,* one of his squad members told Jack.

*I'm sorry, Sarge, I couldn't help it. I've never done this before. Cried like this. We're not supposed to cry…. I never did before, I swear.* But he cried helplessly even as he said that.

*We cry over people we lose, buddy. It's okay.*

*Father Damien said, remember she's with God and she's happy and don't soil her memory with crying about it.*

*Priests are usually smarter than that,* Jack had said with a disapproving snort. *You don't cry over something like that and the tears turn into snakes that eat you from the inside out. The crying part—it's required.*

*I'm sorry….*

*You get it out, buddy, or you'll be worse off. Call her, call out to your mom, get her attention, cry for her. It's damn past time!*

And he had. Sobbed like a baby, Jack's arms under his shoulders, holding him up a little. Jack rocked him and said, *Yeah, there you go. There you go....*

Jack sat with him for a while, talking to him about his mother, and Preacher told him that he made it through that last year of school, tough and silent. Then, with no idea where to go or what to do, he joined up. So he could have brothers, which he had now, but it wasn't enough to take away the need for his mother. And that goddamn tire rim almost cut him in half and it was like the pain of losing her came pouring out. It was humiliating, to be six four and two-fifty, sobbing for your five-foot, three-inch mommy. Jack said, *Nah, it's just what you need. Get it out.*

After a little while, Jack pulled him up, hoisted him over his shoulder and carried him about a mile down the road to meet their convoy. And Jack had said, *Let it out, buddy. After you get it all out, you stick to me like duct tape—I'm your mother now.*

"It's no good to lose touch with people who mean a lot," Preacher said to Paige. "Ever think of trying to find those girlfriends again?"

"I haven't thought about that in a while," she told him.

"If you ever want to try, I could maybe help."

"How could you do that?"

"On the computer. I like to look things up. It's kind of slow, but it works. Think about it."

She said she would. Then she said she was awful tired and had to get some sleep, so they said good-night. She went up the stairs and he went to his apartment out back.

That's when she decided she'd better get moving. She couldn't afford to get comfortable here. No more cozy little chats, no more late-night questions. Attachments were completely out of the question.

# *Four*

Paige got the suitcase ready. She pulled the covers back from her sleeping son to search for Bear, but he wasn't there. She nearly stripped the bed around him, looking. Then down on her knees to look under the bed, in the bathroom, in every empty drawer of the bureau—nowhere. She'd check in the kitchen before leaving, but if Bear was lost, he would have to be left behind.

She pulled two hundred dollars out of her billfold and put it on the bureau, then sat, still as stone, on the edge of the bed next to Christopher. Palms together, hands pressed between her knees, she waited. At midnight, she put on her jacket and crept quietly down the stairs. The cabin was so solid, not even a board squeaked.

He'd left a light on in the kitchen for her. This was the only time she'd come down after bedtime since that first night, but she suspected John left that light on for her every night. She tiptoed stealthily toward the door to his apartment and listened. No sound, no light under the door.

She'd located a flashlight in the kitchen when she'd been helping John clean up, a stroke of luck. Up to that point, the best idea she could come up with was a book of matches to light the night while she dealt with the license plates. Once the plates were switched, she'd fetch the suitcase, then Chris. She took a butter knife from the drawer and slipped quietly out the back kitchen door.

Once behind the bar, she was relieved to see no lights on in John's little apartment. She crouched to the task of removing her plates, easily done even though her hands were shaking. Then she got to work on John's, taking the license plate off his truck and replacing it with hers. Then back to the Honda, bending down to fix the new plate in place.

"Getting back on the road again, Paige?" Preacher asked.

She jumped, dropped the plate, flashlight and knife, straightening, her breath cut off and her heart hammering. The flashlight lit a path along the ground that illuminated his feet. Then he took a couple of steps toward her and came into complete view.

"That isn't going to do the trick," he said, nodding toward her car. "They're truck plates, Paige. Anyone, like the sheriff or CHP sees your little car with truck plates—they're gonna know right off."

She felt her eyes well up with tears. Something like that would never have occurred to her. She shivered in the cold night, her hands shaking worse. Inside, her stomach was gripped in a tight, hard knot.

"Don't panic," he said. "I don't think you need different plates, not yet, but we can get it done. Connie's got a little car right across the street. She'd never miss 'em."

A tear rolled down her cheek and she stooped to pick up the flashlight. "I… Ah… I left some money. Upstairs. For the room. The food. Not much, but…"

"Aw, Paige. You do something like that, it makes me look so bad. You gotta know I never thought about money."

She hiccuped tears back and said, "What *did* you think about?"

"Come on," he said, reaching a hand out toward her.

"It's cold out here. Come back inside, I'll make you some coffee so you don't fall asleep on the road, then I'll switch the plates for you. If that'll make you feel safer on the drive, even if you don't really need 'em."

She stayed out of his reach, but walked alongside. "Why do you say that? That I don't need them?"

"No one's looking for you," he said. "At least not officially. You're still okay."

"How do you *know* that?" she asked, ready to fall apart and sink into helpless sobs.

"I'll explain," he said. "I'll throw a log on the fire, get you warmed up and we'll talk. Then I'll switch the plates for you if you want. But after we talk about it, you'll probably want to go back upstairs and sleep till morning, drive in daylight. Besides," he said, holding open the back kitchen door for her, "I got the bear. I'll get it for you—you can't leave without the bear."

She started to cry as she walked into the kitchen, pressing her fingers against her lips. She felt like a caught felon. It made her feel even worse that he was being so nice to her. "I looked everywhere for that damn bear," she said softly with a whimper.

Preacher turned toward her. Hand pressed against her mouth, eyes overflowing, she seemed to jerk with the effort not to add sound to her crying. Then slowly and carefully, he pulled her by her shoulders toward him, against his big chest, gently circling her with his arms. And she collapsed from inside, sobbing against him. No holding back the sound now, she was racked with tears. "Aw, you been holding that in too long, haven't you? I been there, all right. It's okay, Paige. I know you're scared and worried, but it's going to be okay."

She doubted it, but she was helpless in the moment. All she could do was cry and shake her head. She tried to remember when someone had pulled her sweetly into strong arms and tried to make her feel safe. Long ago. So long ago, she couldn't remember the last time. Not even Wes in the early days, at his most manipulative. No, *he* would cry. He'd hit her, beat her, then *he* would cry and she'd comfort *him*.

Preacher rocked her back and forth in the dimly lit kitchen for a long time until she quieted down, then with a hand on her back, pushed her through the kitchen into the bar. He directed her to that same chair near the fire, stirred up the flame and threw on a new log, and went behind the bar to fix her a brandy. When he put it in front of her, she said, "I have to be ready to drive."

"You won't be any good to drive unless you calm down. Just a sip, then if you want coffee, we'll make some." He sat down in the chair next to hers and, with elbows on his knees, leaned toward her. "When you came in here, I had no idea what happened to you, but I knew it wasn't good and I knew it wasn't a car door. You have California plates. So, I called a good friend of mine— someone I knew I could trust. He checked out the plates, registered to your husband. He's been booked for battery domestic before." Preacher shrugged. "I didn't need to know much more than that, did I?"

Paige's eyes closed, then slowly opened again, focused on his face. She lifted the brandy to her lips and took a tiny sip, not confirming or denying anything.

Preacher went on, "He hasn't reported you missing, so no law enforcement's looking for you. I don't know what your plan is, Paige, but if you take Christopher out of state, you'd be breaking the law—that could go hard on you trying to keep him. I figure you must be thinking that way, 'cause you came all the way from L.A. and you're almost out of state now. If you're thinking of running off on your own and disappearing, whew, I don't think that's a good idea. You just don't know what you're doing—

you'll get tripped up. You don't know the difference between truck and car plates. There isn't much devious going on in that head of yours."

A huff of rueful laughter escaped her. Maybe that had been her problem; she wasn't sneaky enough.

"Maybe you have someplace to go where they'll keep you hidden and safe—that's a better idea. I just hope wherever that is, there's a bunch of big, mean, angry guys like me and Jack around, ready, on the off chance the son of a bitch hunts you down and finds you."

"I don't have a lot of choices," she whispered. "I have to get away."

"'Course you do," he said. "Do you know there's one more way to go? You wouldn't have any trouble getting custody of Chris, at least temporary custody, given the father's record, even if they weren't felony charges. You don't need his okay to get a divorce. Not in this state. It's no fault." She was shaking her head, closing her eyes again, another tear spilling down her cheek. But Preacher went on. "There's restraining orders, and even if he ignores 'em, it keeps the law on your side. You ever think of these things, Paige?"

"How do you know all this? Did your friend tell you?"

"I wanna find out something, I look it up," he said.

"Then do you know while I'm trying to do that, he's going to kill me? He's mean, and he's crazy. He's going to kill me."

"Not if you stay here," Preacher said.

She was stunned silent for a moment. Then she said, "I can't stay here, John. I'm pregnant."

Then it was Preacher's turn to show shock. Silent and dark. It settled into his eyes and over his expression slowly as he sat back in the chair, then stood. He went behind the bar and poured himself a shot, throwing it back. When he returned to the chair by the fire, he asked,

"Did he know? When he beat you, did he know you were pregnant?"

She nodded and looked away from him, pursing her lips tight. Intellectually, she knew none of this was her fault, but there was an emotional misfire in her brain that said, you married him, had a child with him, didn't get out in time, let it happen, screwed up, got pregnant again, never ran in time, never saw it coming and it was plain as day.

"You ever been to a shelter?" he asked her. She nodded.

"Here are your choices," Preacher said calmly. "You can stay here and try to get your ducks in a row so when you do leave, you're not breaking the law or hiding for the rest of your life. It's okay if you stay here—there are medical people across the street if you need them, you can help out in the kitchen if you want to, so you don't feel like you're taking advantage, and if you happen to run into that son of a bitch around here, we're ready for him. You think of it as a shelter, like any other shelter—sometimes people just want to help out. Or you can go if you want—continue on with your plan. Whatever it is. You don't have to run in the night, anyway. Safer in daylight. Huh?" He stood up. "You sit a minute, think, have a little brandy there—it won't hurt that baby, a tiny sip of brandy, and I think maybe you need it. I'm going to take care of those plates for you, then I'm going to get you the bear. Whatever you decide to do, you can't leave without the bear, you know that."

He left her, going through his apartment. She could hear him go out his back door. He must have found the bear in the kitchen and put it in a safe place. A log in the fireplace dropped and she pulled her jacket tighter around her, taking another tiny sip of brandy that burned its way down her throat and did, miraculously, settle her stomach and her nerves, if slightly. Or maybe it was the news that

Wes didn't have the police after her that calmed her a little. A while later, John came back from his apartment, still wearing the jacket he'd obviously fetched, and holding the bear.

"Connie'll never know the difference on those plates," he said, holding the bear out to her. "Besides, if she knew what was going on here, she'd tell you to take 'em."

She frowned as she looked at the bear, changed. He had a new leg, sewn out of blue-and-gray plaid. It wasn't exactly the same shape as the surviving leg; it was just a stuffed flannel tube stuck on the bear, but he was symmetrical now. "What did you do?" she asked, taking the bear.

Preacher shrugged. "I told him I'd give it a try. Looks pretty silly, I guess, but it was a good idea at the time." He put his hands in his pockets. "Think you can get a little rest tonight? You still feel like you have to go right now? I could brew you up some coffee if you wanna just get out of here. I think I even have a thermos I could—"

She stood up, leaving the brandy on the table, holding Bear close against her. "I'm going back to bed," she said. "I'll leave in the morning, after Chris has a little breakfast."

"If that's what you want," he said.

Paige awakened to the dim light of morning streaking through the dormer window and the sound of an ax striking wood. She rolled onto her side to see Christopher still sleeping peacefully, gripping the bear with the blue-and-gray flannel leg and she knew she should think about this for a while. It scared her to take a chance like this. But it didn't scare her any more than driving on to some address in Spokane and a commitment to a life she knew nothing about, and might not be devious enough to pull off.

She'd like to think she had learned one or two things from her experiences. If anything, in any way, made her feel threatened, caused her radar to go up, she'd be gone in a flash. She wouldn't bother with license plates or goodbyes.

Then there was that guilt—she didn't want to put these people in Wes's path, in danger. But her reality was that wherever she went, whether to family, a shelter, into hiding—the people who helped her were at risk. Sometimes it was unbearable to think about.

She dressed quietly, without waking Chris, and crept down the stairs to the kitchen. Preacher was standing at the counter, slicing and dicing for his morning omelets. When he saw her at the bottom of the stairs, his hand on the knife froze and he waited.

"I'm going to need to borrow your washer and dryer," she said. "We didn't bring too much."

"Sure."

"I guess it makes more sense to stay here. A little while. I'll be glad to help out. If you're sure."

He began to dice again, slowly. "We can do that easy. How about minimum wage plus the room and meals. Keep track of your own hours. Jack'll pay you when you want him to—doesn't matter. Daily, weekly, monthly. Doesn't matter."

"That's too much, John. I should help for just the room and meals."

"We open by six, stay open past nine, there are two of us plus Rick after school. Two days and you're going to be complaining it's slave labor."

She smiled and shook her head. "I'm not ready for the rest—the restraining order, the custody thing... Court documents like that have to reveal where I am, and I'm not up to that."

"Understandable," he said.

"Eventually, he's going to come after me. File charges, have police looking, maybe hire a detective. But he's going to try to find me. He won't let me walk away."

"One thing at a time, Paige," Preacher said.

"Just so you know…"

"I'm not worried about that. We'll be ready."

She took a deep breath. "Okay. Where's that washer?" she asked.

"In my apartment. The door's never locked." He stopped chopping again and, looking at her, asked, "What made you decide?"

"Bear's new leg. That old blue plaid flannel…"

"Old?" Preacher asked, smiling slightly. "That was a perfectly good shirt."

Preacher took breakfast to Ron and Harv in the bar, and on his way back to the kitchen, glanced out the window to see Jack at the stump with the ax. He heard the sound of the washing machine start up in his apartment.

He poured two cups of coffee and walked out back. When Jack saw him coming, he left the ax stuck in the stump. Preacher passed him a cup.

"Delivery service," Jack said. "Guess you have something on your mind." He took a sip, watching Preacher over the rim of the cup.

"I was just thinking, we could probably use a little help around the bar."

"That so?"

"Paige mentioned she's looking for something. The kid's no trouble."

"Hmm."

"Seems like a good idea to me," Preacher said. "Don't have any use for that bedroom over the kitchen, anyway. You can pay her out of my check."

"The bar makes money, Preach. It can take on an

employee. She doesn't want fifty grand and a 401(k) or anything, does she?"

Preacher made a face. Jack thought he was funny. "It'll probably be temporary."

"My responsibilities are changing," Jack said. "Growing," he added with a proud smile. "Be nice to have a little help in there, in case I have other things to do."

"Good, then. I'll let her know." He turned as if to leave.

"Ah, Preacher," Jack said, and the man turned back. Jack held out his cup for Preacher to take back into the kitchen. "You already let her know, didn't you?"

"Might've let slip I thought we could use her."

"Yeah. One question. She cover her tracks on her way into town?"

"No one knows she's here, Jack. Not that it's any of our business…"

"I'm not nosy, Preacher. I'm prepared."

"Good," Preacher said. "That's good, I like that. Anything changes on that, I'll let you know."

There were things about being in Virgin River that gave Paige peace of mind. Small things, like her car sitting behind the bar between two big, extended-cab trucks, a car she had no reason to take out for a drive. The sound of log-splitting in the early dawn hours that coincided almost exactly with the smell of coffee. And the work—she liked the work. It started with bussing tables and doing dishes, but before even a couple of days had passed, John was showing her how he made his soup, bread, pies.

"The real challenge here is making use of what we have," he told her. "One of the reasons this bar does well and we can get by like we do—we cook what we kill or catch, we make use of Doc and Mel's patient fees that come in produce and meat and we concentrate on making sure our people are taken care of. Jack says, if we think first about making sure the town is taken care of, we'll do just fine. And we do."

"How do you take care of a town?" she asked, confused.

"Aw, it's real easy," he said. "We put out three good meals a day, on their budget, and the sharp folks know about the leftovers. When we shop, since we go all the way to the coastal towns and big stores and have our trucks, we check with people who don't drive so far—old folks, infirm, maybe new mothers—see if we can get them anything. They appreciate that—take a meal or two at the bar. For special occasions we just open up the place, the women bring in the casseroles and the only thing we sell are mixed drinks. We put out a donation jar for the space, sodas, beer—and we make out better than you'd think. We lay in good liquors for the hunters and maybe fly fishermen out this way for contests, but we charge the same prices and they duke us up, real nice." To her perplexed expression he said, "Tip us, Paige. They know what Johnny Walker Black costs. They like how we try to have what they're gonna want—they have money. They leave it on the tables and bar." He grinned.

"Brilliant," she said.

"Nah. Jack and me—we've been hunters, we fish. It's good to take care of the people that put up with us. Maybe the most important thing is remembering them when they come in—makes 'em feel welcome. Jack's good at that. But then there's the food. We're small and not very experienced, but the food's getting a good reputation," he said, sticking out his chest.

"Yeah," she said. "Fattening, but good."

Paige felt that staying in this dinky country bar was like a cocoon, sheltering her from the outside world. Rick and Jack were good about having her there, both of them giving her things to do. It didn't seem that her minor contributions were so much, but they went on about her as if they didn't know how they'd gotten by before. Then there were the customers who came in almost daily, sometimes twice a day. It took no time at all for them to regard Paige as someone who'd been there a long time.

"We're sure getting lots more cookies around here these days," Connie said. "It took a woman in the kitchen to get it right."

Paige didn't bother to explain that it was all John's doing, for Christopher. It was not for the folks in the bar who'd come to like cookies with their coffee.

"What'd he cook tonight, Paige?" Doc asked.

"Bouillabaisse," she said. "It's wonderful."

"Ach, I hate that crap." Doc leaned close. "He hide any of yesterday's stuffed trout back there?"

"I'll look," she said, grinning, already feeling a part of something.

Mel was in the bar at least twice a day, sometimes more often. When the place was quiet and she didn't have patients, she'd sit and talk awhile. Mel knew more about Paige's special circumstances than anyone, and it was Mel who asked about her recovery. "Better," Paige said. "Everything's better. No more spotting."

"Looks like this was a good idea of yours," Mel said, looking around and indicating the bar.

"It wasn't my idea," Paige said. "John said I could stay, help out around here a little. If I wanted to."

"It looks like you might be enjoying it," Mel said. "You're smiling a lot."

With a shock of surprise, Paige answered, "I am. Who would've guessed? This has been a good…" She paused. "Break," she finally said. "I guess I can make this work for a while, at least. Until I start to…" Again she paused. "Show," she said, looking down at her middle.

"Does John know?" Mel asked.

She nodded. "It was the only decent thing to do—to tell him, when he made the offer."

"Well, even though hardly anyone knows the circumstances that brought you here, I think it's fair to say everyone around here understands you must have had another life. Before Virgin River. I mean, you do have a son."

"There's that," Paige agreed.

"Besides," Mel said, sitting back, running two hands over her small tummy. "Lotsa people are starting to 'show.' Did you know I'm four months now?"

"That looks about right," Paige said, smiling.

"Uh-huh. And I've been in this town seven months. Married to Jack less than one. I was married before Jack. I was widowed, and according to the experts, completely incapable of conceiving a child." Paige's eyes grew round, her mouth forming an *O*. Mel laughed. "Obviously, I need better experts. Oh, you think you're the only one who came to this place by way of a wrong turn."

"There's more to this story," Paige said, lifting one brow.

"Just the details, sister. We have plenty of time." And then Mel laughed brightly.

Paige had been in the little room over the kitchen for ten days, the first four of which she'd been planning her departure. Preacher told her he thought it was working out pretty well. They had a nice little routine. Right after Chris had his breakfast and Paige was showered and primped, she plunged into kitchen work, cleaning up after breakfast. While Chris was with John, either coloring, playing War with a deck of cards, sweeping or doing other chores, Paige would take care of her room and their things. Because she didn't have much with her, there was frequent laundry in John's laundry room—so while the washer and dryer hummed along, Paige did a few things she hoped would help him out—cleaning his bathroom, dusting, making up his bed, running the sweeper around his room. "Can I throw in a load of clothes for you?" she asked.

"I'll take care of that. Listen, you don't have to clean up after me."

She laughed at him. "John, I spend all day in the kitchen, collecting your pots, pans and dishes. It's becoming a habit." She laughed at his shocked expression. "You look after my child all day long—you're pretty much helpless, since he won't leave you alone. The least I can do is help out."

"I'm not looking after him," John said. "We're buddies."

"Yeah," she said. And thought, yeah—buddies.

Lunch was usually busy, and Paige served and bussed. Dinner, from five to eight, was also busy, especially this time of year—fall, hunting season with fishing getting good. After eight there were occasionally lingerers, hanging out over beer or drinks, but the cooking was over for the night. That's when Paige would take Chris upstairs for his bath and bed, and after that she'd only check in to see if anything needed to be done before she called it a night. Occasionally, she'd have a cup of tea with John.

Preacher liked that time of night, when there was no more dinner to be served, when the kitchen was cleaned, when he could hear Paige running water upstairs. Sometimes he could hear her singing play songs with Chris. Before pouring that last shot for the day, he'd look at his cookbooks, planning dinner for the next day or maybe the next week, making supply lists. The process made him feel he had everything managed efficiently. Preacher was very well organized.

It was about eight-thirty and there were a few hunters in the bar. Jack was handling the front. Buck Anderson had brought Mel a couple of nice-size lamb shanks, which came straight to Preacher. He was reading about lamb shanks hestia with cucumber raita when he heard a small shuffle. He looked over the counter to see Christopher standing at the bottom of the stairs, stark naked, book under one arm, Bear under the other.

Preacher lifted one bushy brow. "Forget something there, pardner?" he asked.

Chris picked at his left butt cheek while hanging on to the bear. "You read to me now?"

"Um… Have you had your bath?" Preacher asked. The boy shook his head. "You look like you're ready for your bath." He listened upward to the running water.

Chris nodded, then said again, "You read it?"

"C'mere," Preacher said.

Chris ran around the counter, happy, raising his arms to be lifted up.

"Wait a second," Preacher said. "I don't want little boy butt on my clean counter. Just a sec." He pulled a clean dish towel out of the drawer, spread it on the counter, then lifted him up, sitting him on it. He looked down at the little boy, frowned slightly, then pulled another dish towel out of the drawer. He shook it out and draped it across Chris's naked lap. "There. Better. Now, what you got here?"

"Horton," he said, presenting the book.

"There's a good chance your mother isn't going to go for this idea," he said. But he opened the book and began to read. They hadn't gotten far when he heard the water stop, heard heavy footfalls racing around the upstairs bedroom, heard Paige yell, "Christopher!"

"We better get our story straight," Preacher said to him.

"Our story," Chris said, pointing at the page in front of him.

Momentarily there were feet coming down the stairs, fast. When she got to the bottom, she stopped suddenly. "He got away from me while I was running the tub," she said.

"Yeah. In fact, he's dressed like he barely escaped."

"I'm sorry, John. Christopher, get over here. We'll read after your bath."

He started to whine and wiggle. "I want John!"

Paige came impatiently around the counter and plucked him, squirming, into her arms.

"I want John," he complained.

"John's busy, Chris. Now, you behave."

"Uh—Paige? I'm not all that busy. If you'll tell Jack I'm not in the kitchen for a bit, I could do the bath. Tell Jack, so he knows to lock up if everyone leaves."

She turned around at the foot of the stairs. "You know how to give a child a bath?" she asked.

"Well, no. But is it hard? Harder than scrubbing up a broiler?"

She chuckled in spite of herself. She put Chris down on his feet. "You might want to go a little easier than that. No Brillo pads, no scraping. No soap in the eyes, if you can help it."

"I can do that," Preacher said, coming around the counter. "How many times you dunk him?" She gasped and Preacher showed her a smile. "Kidding. I know you only dunk him twice."

She smirked. "I'll see if Jack needs anything, and then I'll be up to supervise."

Paige was peeling and slicing apples, Preacher rolling out pie dough, when Jack came into the kitchen. "Mel's out front," he told them. "She's going over to the Eureka mall, Paige—she can't get into her pants anymore. She said you can ride along, if you need anything."

Paige looked at John, lifting her brows.

"Go on, Paige," he said. "Chris won't be up for another hour and I got the kitchen. You probably need all kinds of things."

"Sure, thanks," she said, putting her apple and knife in the bowl, taking off her apron.

"Listen," Preacher said, wiping his hands on a dish towel. "I don't even know if you have credit cards, but you have to be real careful about that. You should shop with cash—huh?" He pulled out his wallet, took some bills out and began to unfold them, peeling off one, then another, then...

Paige went completely pale, her eyes round and clearly frightened. She started shaking her head and backing away. "Tell... Tell Mel I have to do...some things... Okay?"

Jack tilted his head, frowning. "Paige?" he asked.

Paige backed up until she was against the wall, her hands behind her back, her face as white as alabaster. Then a tear rolled down her cheek.

Preacher put his wallet on the counter and said, "Give us a minute, Jack." Then he took off his own apron and walked toward her. As he neared, she slid down the wall to the floor and put her hands over her face.

Preacher got on his knees in front of her and gently tugged at her hands, pulling them away from her face and holding them. "Paige," he said softly. "Paige, look at me. What just happened there?"

Her expression was panicked. Tears ran down her cheeks, but her voice was a whisper. "He did that," she said. "Got his money out of his pocket and said, 'Go buy yourself some nice things.' He did that so much. Later, he'd throw the money at me and say he couldn't afford to have a wife that looked like a vagrant."

Preacher sat on the floor right next to her. "Did you hear what I said? I didn't say anything like that, did I? I said, you have to be careful, don't use your charge card."

"I heard you," she said in a whisper. "Did I tell you I married him because my legs hurt?"

"You haven't said anything about him," Preacher said.

"Nothing at all. That's okay—you don't have to say anything unless you want to."

"I was a beautician. Hair, I did hair. Sometimes twelve-hour days because the pay was so low. We really worked hard. I never had enough for the rent and my roommates and I lived in a real dump. I loved it, but I was tired, broke. Sore. My legs hurt," she said again. "I knew he was bad for me, my friends hated him, and I married him because he said I didn't have to work anymore." She started to laugh and cry together. "Because I didn't have anything. Because I had nothing…"

"Guys like that know just what to use for bait," he said. "They have a sense for it."

"How do you know that?"

He shrugged. "I read about it." He wiped a tear from her cheek. "It wasn't your fault. None of it was your fault. You got tricked."

"I have nothing again," she said. "A little suitcase, a car with stolen license plates on it, a child and one on the way…"

"You have *everything*," he said. "A car with stolen license plates, a son, a baby on the way, friends…"

"I had friends before," she whispered. "They were scared of him. He ran them off and I lost them forever."

"Do I look like the kind of friend he can scare? Run off?" He pulled her gently onto his lap and she rested her head against his chest.

"I don't know why I stay so crazy," she said softly. "He's not anywhere near. He'll never guess this place. But I'm still scared."

"Yeah, that happens."

"You're never scared," she said.

He chuckled softly, stroked her back. He was scared of a bunch of things, number one being the day she got these problems managed and left with Christopher.

"That's what you think," he said. "In the Marines, they used to say everyone's afraid, so you have to learn to use fear to your advantage. Man, if you ever figure out how you do that, let me know. Okay?"

"What did you do when you were scared?" she asked.

"One of two things," he said. "I'd either pee myself, or I'd get mad."

She lifted her head off his chest, looked at him and laughed a little.

"That's a girl," he said, wiping off her cheeks. "I think you need to get out of Virgin River a little bit. But you're probably in no shape to go shopping today."

She shook her head. "I'm sorry. I made a scene."

"It's a little country bar, Paige. We live for those." He grinned. Then he sobered. "They also used to say, stare it in the face—fake brave. They taught us to look mean."

She shuddered.

"Never mind all that. Tomorrow I'll go for supplies instead of Jack. He can get lunch for once. I'll take you and Chris, get you out of town for a break. You can pick up a few things, if you want to. I'm not buying you anything, though. I'll use the bar charge card so we can get our annual perks, you save your receipts and catch me up later, after a payday or two." He touched her nose. "Chris is running around naked. Suggests a wardrobe problem."

Jack had backed out of the kitchen slowly when Preacher asked for a moment. As slowly as he could, because something major was happening and he was curious. When he got back to the bar, Mel was waiting, up on a stool. "What's up?" she asked.

Jack put a finger to his lips, shushing her. "Something's going on," he whispered.

"Yeah?" she asked, none the wiser.

Jack stuck his head back close to the door. Eavesdropping.

"Jack!" she scolded in a furious whisper.

He put a finger to his lips again. Then with a frown on his face, he went behind the bar and glared down at his pretty young wife. "Paige is having a breakdown in there…."

"Oh? Does Preacher need help?"

Jack shook his head. "He asked me to step out. I heard a couple of things, purely by accident."

"I saw…"

"She has a car with stolen license plates?"

Mel sat suddenly straight, eyes wide. "No kidding?" she asked. "I guess I better check mine, see if they're still mine." Then she smiled cutely.

"And there's a baby coming?"

"Really?" she asked.

"You're not fooling me," he said. "You know things."

Mel made a face at him, as if to say, *Duh. Of course I know things. Patient things.* She might have shared Paige's bruises with him, so he could be prepared for anything and help protect her, but she wasn't a bigmouth. She got off the bar stool and went to the swinging door to the kitchen. She peeked; Preacher was sitting on the floor, gently rocking Paige on his lap. Ah, that was probably exactly what she needed at the moment. Better than a sedative.

Mel walked behind the bar and got up on her toes to kiss Jack. "I don't think she wants to go shopping. Tell her I went ahead—I have to cover up the baby."

"You do that."

"Um, Jack? I don't quite know how to explain this to you. You and I have such different life experiences with things like this…."

"Starting with, I would *never* hit a woman."

"That's lovely, Jack. That's not what I mean. Hmm,"

she said, looking skyward. "It might be easiest for you if you thought of Paige as a POW."

"A POW?" he asked, looking startled and confused at once.

"That's the closest thing I can think of that you can relate to. I'll be back as soon as I have a bagful of elastic waistbands, okay?"

"Sure. Okay."

A couple of hours later, with still plenty of time before the dinner hour, Jack was sitting on the porch, tying off flies for fishing. Paige came onto the porch holding a slice of fresh apple pie on a plate. He took it and said, "Oohh, still warm…"

"I'm sorry about before, Jack. I'm a little embarrassed."

He looked up at her, saw a sweet, docile face—the face of a devoted young mother, a pregnant woman running to protect her unborn baby. And, as he had been instructed by Mel, he imagined an enforced barricade, deprivation, regular beatings, fear of death—for *years*. It was not only hard to imagine a young woman like Paige, so helpful and tender, going through something like that, it was *impossible* to imagine the kind of man who might subject her to it. "Don't worry about that, okay? We all have our moments."

"No, we don't. Only I—"

He cut her off, laughing. "Oh, don't go there. Don't go the 'only I have this baggage' route. Ask Mel—not long before I married her, I had a fantastic meltdown. Come to think of it, so did she!" Then he frowned slightly. "On second thought—could you take my word for it?"

Paige tilted her head. "She wouldn't want to be asked about that?"

"Nah, I don't think she'd mind. It just pisses me off—the way she never tells me anything, and I just lay it all out there. I don't know how she does it."

"That's okay, Jack." She laughed. "I won't ask. I apologize, however."

"No need, Paige. I just hope you feel better."

John took the supply list, Chris and Paige to Eureka. They went to Target first so the groceries wouldn't go bad in the truck while they shopped. She bought a few things—underwear, jeans, shirts. John held Chris's hand outside the dressing room while she tried things on. They stopped at the bookstore. John spent some time in the history section, picking up a couple of books—the same type she'd seen on his bookshelf. Then when he came to the children's section to see if they were ready to go, Paige put up the books they'd been looking at and said, "Okay."

"Maybe we should get a new book or two," he said.

"We have his favorites," she said.

"We could use two new ones," he said. "Okay if I do this?" he asked.

"Sure," she said.

Maybe the best part of the outing was the drive. She'd come into Virgin River at night, in the rain, and except for her quick trip to Grace Valley along the back mountain roads, hadn't seen much of the countryside. John took them for a little drive along the high cliffs of the Pacific Coast—so different up here in the north than in L.A. He passed through a redwood grove, then up into the mountains toward Virgin River.

She looked over at him as he drove; he was grinning. "Why are you smiling?" she asked him.

He turned to look at her. "I've never been shopping with a woman before," he said. "I didn't hate it."

# *Five*

During her stay in Virgin River, Paige started out in the bedroom above the kitchen, reluctant to step outside. Next the kitchen, then the bar, then late evenings with John in front of the fire, talking. And then she'd begun working, getting to know the locals. Gradually her circle widened until she'd been to the corner store a few times, then she'd gone to the little library, open on Tuesdays, to get picture books for Chris and novels for herself.

In only three weeks, she no longer felt like a guest. A newcomer, certainly, but for the first time in years, at ease with her surroundings. The days were long, the work wasn't light. Her legs hurt again, and this time she was grateful for the opportunity to spend this kind of physical energy rather than being locked up and emotionally drained from the constant tension and uncertainty of her life. She fixed her own breakfast and lunch, ate dinner in the kitchen with Rick and John between hustling meals and doing dishes, and it felt *good*.

After Chris was asleep, she read for a couple of hours, and actually fell into the story, something she hadn't been able to do in years. She left her sleeping boy to go downstairs to get herself a glass of milk, smiling as she descended the stairs—there was always a night-light on in the kitchen, welcoming her. She noticed a glow from the bar and peeked in. John sat in the darkened bar at the table in front of the fire, his feet up on the open hearth. She walked into the room.

"Isn't this awful late for you?" she asked.

He jumped in surprise, put his feet on the floor and sat up straight. "Paige! I didn't hear you come down."

"Just prowling around, getting a glass of milk. What's the matter? Can't sleep?"

"Having a little trouble, yeah. I'll go in a minute."

"Want some company?" He had a strange look on his face. "Oh, I guess you want a little time to yourself."

"That's okay…" he said.

"No, I understand. You've been here alone all this time and now you have people underfoot. I'll just see you in the—"

"Sit down, Paige," he said, somber. Unhappy.

"Is everything all right?" she asked, pulling out a chair.

He shook his head. "It's not so good. I didn't want to do this tonight. I wanted to save this for morning."

"Did I do something?" she asked, frowning. "Is there something I need to—"

"You're perfect," he said. "It's not you—you're perfect. I got some bad news a little while ago. Wes did it—what you expected. He finally did it. Reported you and Chris missing. Almost two weeks ago."

She was stunned speechless for a moment. She sank weakly into the chair. While she was settling in, growing more comfortable with her surroundings, her new friends, he had crossed her mind often. She'd look over her shoulder; she couldn't help it. A shudder would pass through her now and then and often her heart would start to beat a little wildly and she'd have to focus her energy on breathing evenly, reminding herself he was nowhere near, and it would pass.

She closed her eyes briefly. "I'll go up and pack," she said softly. "I'd better get going. Get back to the plan…"

"Don't pack yet, Paige," he said. "Let's talk about it."

She shook her head. "There's nothing to talk about, John. He's after me—I have to get us away. I can't afford to take a chance."

"If you run, you're taking a bigger chance. If they pick you up, they're going to take Chris to him and arrest you. You have to do it, Paige. Face him down," Preacher said. "I'll help. I'll find a way to get you through this."

"There's only one way through this—I have to get out of here. You said it yourself, he'll outsmart me."

"I never said that," he argued. "I said you're not devious. But I think you can beat him. I know a couple of people— my buddy the cop, for one. There's a judge in Grace Valley I've been fishing with—I know he'll help if he can. Jack's little sister, Brie, is a lawyer—a hotshot lawyer in the state capital—and she knows everyone. Brie—she's so smart, it's scary. We have to ask some of these people how you can get out of this mess and have a real life. I'll see it through with you, till you're free and safe."

She sat forward in her chair. "Listen, why are you doing this? What do you think you'll get out of it?"

"Me? Sleep, that's what. When this is over, I'll sleep at night knowing you're not getting beat up, knowing Chris isn't growing up mean, learning how to beat on women. Paige, I saw. That first night, when I brought you clean towels, the door was open a little and you had your shirt pulled…" He stopped and hung his head. Then he raised it and looked her dead in the eye and said, "That was no little slap. No little argument."

She looked down into her lap. It was unbearable to think he'd seen that awful mess.

"Listen," he said, lifting her chin with a finger. "I was okay with my life until you walked in the door that night, with your kid and your bruises. It was all right with me to fish and cook and clean up—I never minded being alone. I'm never going to get married, have kids of my own—I know that. But I can do something about this—"

"*This* isn't your business!"

"It is now! Even if you're not counting on me, that kid is! He counts on me every day, from the time he comes running down here in his jammies until he's finally sound asleep! When you and Chris leave here, I'm going to know we did everything we could to keep you safe from that bastard!" He took a breath. "Sorry," he said. "I can sound as scary as I look."

"You don't look scary," she said so softly he barely heard. "And if this doesn't work?"

He straightened. "Then I'll help you get to someplace safe. I'll do whatever it takes. Jesus Christ, Paige, if I don't do this, what am I gonna do with my life? When something like this hits me square in the face and I ignore it, what am I worth then, huh?"

She gazed at his pleading expression and shook her head almost sadly. "How do you know you'll never get married and have kids?" she asked him.

"C'mon," he said, frustrated.

"Really."

"To start with, there's not a single unmarried woman over eighteen and under sixty in this town—that might be one clue."

"There're lots of towns…"

"Jesus, do we have to make this about me? Your kid, he's the only kid ever came near me. Christ, they hide behind their mothers when they see me."

She smiled at him. "You're swearing like mad. I bet your mother's turning in her grave…."

"Spinning," he agreed. Then, pleadingly, "I know you're scared. Are you too scared to try to stare the bastard in the eye and face him down if I swear I have your back? If you have lots of help?" He took a breath. "Did you know, when you come face-to-face with a bear, you never run? You straighten up tall as you can. Puff up and try to make yourself big. Make a lot of noise. Act tough, even if you're not tough." He shook his head. "You'd have trouble doing that, little as you are. But you should think about the theory. If you act like you're not scared and you have help, good and strong and smart help—you might get this behind you. We'll help. The judge, Mel, Jack, Brie. Mike."

"Mike?" she asked.

"My buddy the cop. Mike." He swallowed. "He says what you really have to do right now is turn yourself in— maybe not to the police. But to someone in the law, someone who will listen to your story. I'm thinking a lawyer, or the judge."

"Okay," she said.

"Okay?" he repeated, surprised.

"Okay. I'm terrified, but okay." She shuddered. "It's your way or running, hiding. Either way, the danger is pretty much the same. Him." Then, quietly, "Thank you. For offering. To help."

"It feels good to help," he said. "Just do it for Chris. Let's get him outta this mess."

"Yeah, I'll try that," she said, but her voice was shaky.

Preacher didn't look like the kind of guy who could use looking after, watching over, but this is what Jack did. It was partly out of habit—he'd had the big man's back since they were in the Marines together; Preacher had served under him twice, the first and second Iraq conflicts.

There was another reason Jack was watching closely right now, and that was because Preacher was changing. Jack recognized it at once because it hadn't been so long since he went through similar changes—although Jack had known exactly what was happening to him, and he suspected that Preacher did not.

After twenty years in the Marine Corps and three in Virgin River, Jack had never formed a strong attachment with a woman. It never occurred to him to settle down, commit to one woman. The closest he'd ever come was one woman at a time. And then Mel came to town to work alongside old Doc Mullins and before she'd been here a week, Jack was cooked. It was the right time, the right woman, the right circumstances. And while it shook him, startled him to feel what he was feeling, it never confused him. It was unmistakable. He'd fallen in love with such a horrendous crash it surprised him that the redwoods hadn't trembled, as though an earthquake shook them.

It had happened almost as quickly to Preacher. Paige appeared that rainy night just three weeks ago with her child and her bruises and Jack could sense a fire in Preacher right away. At first it appeared to be an intense need to right a wrong, to protect—typical of Preacher. He was that kind of man—tough on the outside and soft on the inside. Justice and loyalty—those values were everything to him. But in the days since what he saw had evolved. Preacher watched over Paige with an intensity that spoke of something more than the goodness of his heart. He would glance at her and his eyes would grow dark. Glow. He'd shake himself, look away, and his brow would furrow as though he were trying to make sense of feelings he hadn't had before.

Jack and Preacher had such different histories with the opposite sex. Jack had never done well with abstinence—he had always had a woman somewhere. He was driven by those needs. But Preacher was solitary. And while a very private person, he wasn't secretive. In fact, he was candid. Transparent. Jack was sure that if he'd had women around, Jack would know about it. No, he was fairly sure—this was a first for Preacher. He was powerfully attracted to a woman and didn't have any idea what to do about it.

Jack watched Paige, as well, because he cared deeply about his friend. This was a kindhearted and vulnerable woman, and she was tender toward Preacher—but it was entirely possible it was no more than gratitude. If she were ever able to put the threats she faced behind her, she would probably go away. Back to a family somewhere, perhaps. Or even some new place.

For now, they were inseparable. The three of them. Preacher kept Paige and Christopher under his protective wing, as though danger loomed nearby and might strike at any moment. When there were no patrons in the bar, Preacher and Paige sat at one of the tables and talked or played cribbage; if Christopher wasn't napping, he was on Preacher's knee. When the place was busy, fishermen dropping in for drinks or dinner after a long day on the Virgin, Paige and her son would be in the kitchen with Preacher, helping out or just keeping him company. She worked in the bar, apparently content with her duties and constantly checking with Preacher to ask what he'd like her to do.

It was obvious what Preacher was beginning to feel. Not so obvious what Paige was feeling. And no time presented itself in which Jack could talk to Preacher privately. Of course, he wasn't sure what he'd say, anyway. But there was one thing Jack had heard—these domestic situations were probably more dangerous than war. Volatile, unpredictable, lethal. Cops often said they'd rather walk into an armed robbery than a domestic. Jack didn't want anything bad to happen to this woman—he liked her. But he also didn't want anything bad to happen to Preacher.

With this on his mind, he wanted to talk to his wife about it. "I'm going to step out for a while," Jack said to Preacher. "You got the bar?"

"Got it," he said.

Jack walked across the street to Doc's where he found Mel and Doc playing gin at the kitchen table. Mel had a nice little stack of pennies sitting by her hand. When she saw him standing there, her blue eyes sparkled and she smiled at him. "When you're done with the game, can you go for a ride with me?" he asked.

"Where?"

He shrugged. "Just for a ride. Me and you. The sun's out for a change."

"You can be done right now," Doc said. "I haven't had gin once." He threw his cards down and stood up.

"You need to work on your sportsmanship," she told him.

"I need to work on my cheating," Doc returned, heading out of the kitchen.

Mel got her coat and walked outside with Jack. "Where are we going?" she asked again.

"Just for a ride. Tell me about your morning."

They held hands as they walked out to Jack's truck and he opened the door for her. When he was in beside her and driving, she said, "We haven't had anything very interesting. This nasty weather we've been having seems to be bringing out the viruses—lots of runny noses, coughs, fevers. We're running through the decongestant. I think I feel a cold coming on."

"Are you sick?"

"No, but my head is stuffy and one ear is plugged. And I can't take the decongestant because of you-know-who."

"Maybe you shouldn't be working in a doctor's office right now. All those germs," he said.

"Oh, stop." She laughed. She smoothed her hands over

her little pooch of a tummy. "You're going to be a little on the overprotective side."

They drove out of town to the west for about ten minutes and Jack turned off the road, then he stopped. "It's bumpy. The road sucks. That okay?"

"As long as I don't hit my head on the ceiling, we're okay. What is this?"

"Something I came across and wanted to show you. Hang on and I'll go slow. We're going up." And up and up, along a winding dirt road wide enough for only one vehicle, through the trees. Then momentarily they broke out in a big, grassy clearing from which you could see for miles. "I thought you'd love this view."

"Oh. My," she said, taken with it. She looked across fenced pastures, ranches, farms, orchards, a vineyard. Behind them the pine-covered hills rose and in front of them, the hill sloped down to the valley.

"Come on," he said, opening his door.

They got out and stood on this grassy knoll, looking out across the foothills and valley below. Off in the far distance what appeared to be clouds rolled in from the Pacific Coast. Jack put an arm around her shoulders and she leaned against him. "Jack, this is beautiful. I didn't even know this place was here."

"Me, neither. Mel, what if this spot, right where we're standing—what if this spot was your front porch?"

She snapped her head up to look at him, her mouth open slightly, her eyes wide. She said his name in a breath. "Jack!"

"I think I can get it. It's the Bristols' land—too craggy for planting, too far from their pastures and too much forest for grazing. And we don't need much—just a couple of acres, maybe."

Tears filled her eyes. "Oh, Jack," she said again. "You've been looking for land."

He laughed. "I've been sneaking around the back acreage of neighbors' properties, looking for a good piece someone might be talked out of. A view, a good yard, somewhere where the deer might wander right up to the house, destroy your vegetable garden…"

"I've never had a vegetable garden."

"You like it?"

"I love it," she said. "I love you."

He moved behind her and slipped his arms around her. His hands went under her jacket, under her sweater to where the jeans she could no longer close were gaping open. He put his large hands over her tummy and she put her hands over his, leaning back against him. They stood and looked out across the beautiful land, and then there was a little movement within her. These tiny flutters had just begun. "I'm sorry you can't feel that yet," she whispered. "The baby just fluttered."

He bent to kiss her neck. "She likes it."

"How can you not? Oh, Jack, you shouldn't have shown it to me. Now if you can't get Fish and Carrie Bristol to part with it, my heart will break." She pressed down on his hands.

"Think positive," he said. He gently massaged her tummy. "I thought men were supposed to get all freaked out when their wives were pregnant. Not want to touch them. Not want to have sex."

"Not all men," she said.

"God, I want you more than ever," he said, kissing her neck again.

"That—" she laughed "—is simply impossible."

"Want to christen the new home site?"

She laughed at him. "I'm not going back to Doc's with grass stains on my butt. Control yourself."

"I'm going to build you a house here," he said. "First thing I'm going to do is get the road graded and widened, then have the land excavated. I can't do that myself. While that's happening, we're going to have some plans drawn up. I'll need help with the foundation, but after that—"

"Jack, stop. You have to buy the land first."

He turned her around. "I'm going to build you a house here, Mel."

"Okay," she said. "You just do that."

Eventually, they went back to the truck, but they sat there a long while, silent, looking out over the valley. Mel was remembering last March when she arrived, a recent widow looking for a fresh start, and the first thing she thought was that she'd made a terrible mistake in coming to this washed-out little town. She wasn't made to live in the woods—she was a city girl. Now she looked out at the most glorious landscape in America and knew she would never leave it.

Next March, their baby would arrive, a baby John Stone, her OB, said would be a girl. How far she had traveled, emotionally and physically. From a woman who thought she'd never love again, to a woman in the most intense romantic relationship she could imagine. From a woman who thought she'd never have a child to mother.

"You're very quiet," she said to her husband.

"Yeah. I think too much," he said. "Mel. Talk to me about something. Help me with something."

"Oh, you didn't bring me out here to show me the view. No—you would have surprised me with this later, when you were sure you had it locked up. You wanted some privacy," she said. "What's bothering you?"

"I've been watching Preacher," he said.

"Ah. Lots of people have."

"What's up with that?"

"Well, it seems pretty apparent. He's growing very attached to his houseguests."

"Yeah. That's what I think, too. I have a feeling he doesn't know what hit him."

She reached for Jack's hand. "He'll work it out."

"Mel, I'm not sure the looks Paige gives him mean anything but thank you. I mean, Preacher—he's the kind of guy you want around when someone's about to take you out."

"Turns out feeling safe for once is a big item," Mel said. "That was one of the things you gave me that meant the most."

"But she's been hurt bad, Mel. Real bad. When the damage heals and she isn't afraid anymore—"

"Jack, stop. I was damaged. You never let it discourage you for a second."

"Maybe this is different...."

"You're worried that he's going to get hurt," she said.

"Yeah, I might be."

She laughed, but she squeezed his hand. "You're a mother hen," she said. "He's a big boy. Let him be. Let her be."

"I saw the way that woman was beat up. You know the guy who did that to her is obsessed. Mean as the devil himself. She's going to have some crazy bastard after her and I'd hate to have Preacher caught in the crossfire."

"Jack, you'd better listen to me—this isn't up to you."

"I've been watching out for that guy for years now," he said. "This just surprises the hell out of me. Preacher never had much traffic with women. I'm not sure he knows the score."

"He doesn't have to know the score, but I bet you're wrong about that, too," she said, laughing. "He just has to know how he feels and what he wants. This isn't your bone, Jack—don't chew on it. And if you try to warn him off, he's going to break your jaw."

"Yeah," he said sullenly. "Yeah."

He started the truck and drove them back to town. When he let Mel off and went back to the bar, he found

Preacher behind the bar and Paige sitting up on a stool in front of him. The boy must have been napping; it was only the two of them. And Preacher was holding her hand.

"Good, you're back. We need a minute with you."

"Sure," Jack said.

"I need a day, if you can spare me."

"When?"

"Tomorrow or the next day. Soon."

"Tomorrow's okay."

"I want you to know what we're doing. We're going down to Grace Valley to see Judge Forrest. I hope you don't mind, but I called Brie. I asked her about getting a lawyer for Paige in L.A. in case she needs one. But what she's after from Judge Forrest is a restraining order, custody—at least temporary. From her husband, who beat her up. A lot."

Jack looked from Paige to Preacher. "Is that what you want to do?"

"Yeah, Jack. I'm backing Paige up so she can get out of this mess and keep her kid and her baby safe." Paige looked down as if ashamed. Preacher saw that and nudged her, then with a finger, lifted her chin and said to her, "You didn't do anything wrong, Paige." Then to Jack he said, "I told Paige we'd all back her up. Not let anything bad happen."

"Bad happen?" Jack repeated.

"Paige is pregnant. She needs our help."

"Sure," Jack said.

"Thing is—here's something about that restraining order. The husband—he can find out where she is."

"Whoa," Jack said. He hadn't known that. "You sure that's the best way to go? I mean, what are the odds someone's going to find her here, if you just stay quiet?"

"Can't really get around it," Preacher said with a shrug. "The husband—he's reported her missing. And Chris, missing. If anyone does sniff her out here, even worse things are going to happen. We're just going to have to face it."

"Just remember, if you do this, these domestic things can be dicey. Real dangerous."

Preacher glowered at Jack. "Looks like it already was. That shit's gotta stop. And Paige needs us to help put a stop to it."

"Okay, yeah. I'm there. Anyone comes around and makes trouble, you know we can handle that. But—you sure you want to dive into this? It might not come out the way you want," Jack said. "Have you looked at alternatives?"

"He's right, John," Paige said. "It could be a mistake. You could get hurt."

"I'm not getting hurt. No one's getting hurt. Except, best-case scenario, him."

"At least think about it, Preacher," Jack said.

Preacher's expression darkened and his eyes narrowed. "We're doing this, Jack," he said.

Jack took a breath. "Okay, Preach. Okay, whatever you want."

Preacher sensed that Paige had a bad case of nerves, and he didn't blame her. He blamed Jack. It was wrong of him to raise questions, put Paige on the defensive as he had. The very night of that discussion with Jack, right after Christopher was put to bed, while there were still a couple of guys at the bar, Paige quietly said, "I think we should reconsider this plan."

"There's no need to be afraid, Paige. There's only one real danger—losing Christopher in the court. And I may be just a big dope, but I can't see that happening. Not after what's been done to you. He has a record, Paige. It's not like it's your word against his. They'd be putting Chris in danger. I can't believe any judge would let that happen."

"Jack's right—you shouldn't be getting yourself into this mess. We can still get away, me and Christopher. I can get to that address in Washington, get things in order.

Get into that underground that gives women and children new identities…"

"Don't be afraid," he said again. "It's going to be okay. I talked to Judge Forrest and he's optimistic about working this out."

"There are alternatives to taking this kind of chance, is all I'm saying…."

"Paige, if it comes to that, I'll take you away myself. Stay with you until you get into some safe place."

"You don't have to—"

"I made a promise, Paige."

"I'm not going to hold you to that."

"I made a promise to *myself.*"

When Preacher proved intractable, Paige just said good-night and went up the back stairs. But, worried about her, after he closed the bar and locked the door, he crept up those stairs and tapped lightly at the door. When she opened it, he could see she'd been crying. Her eyes were red and her face pink from the tears.

The little suitcase was open on the bureau, clothes neatly folded inside.

"Aw, Paige," he said, pulling on her hand, drawing her out of the room so that Christopher wouldn't be awakened.

She leaned against him and wept onto his chest. He put his arms around her and held her for a little while, gently stroking her back. Finally he said, "Come on. Come with me."

He took her downstairs, his arm around her shoulders, and led her into his room, leaving the door open so they could hear Christopher if he woke. Taking her hand, he directed her to the sofa in the living area, now crowded with the weight set he'd taken out of his old bedroom. He sat in the big leather chair at a right angle to her. He scooted forward and reached for her hands. Holding them, looking into her eyes, he asked, "Are you so scared you were going to run?"

She nodded, and he ran a finger along the line of her jaw. "Let's try to get through this," he said.

"Even if it works, there's no way I can ever repay you," Paige said.

He just shook his head. "I don't want anything from you, Paige. Except that no one ever hits you again. Ever."

Paige just had to touch his face. She put her small palm against his cheek and whispered, "You are such an angel."

"Naw. I'm just an average guy." He laughed a little. "A below-average guy."

She shook her head and a tear escaped and rolled down her cheek. Preacher carefully wiped it away. "It doesn't make any sense to me," he said. "If a man has a family like this—you and Christopher and a new baby coming—why? It seems like he'd do anything in the world to keep you safe, not hurt you. I wish…" He shook his head sadly.

"What do you wish, John?"

"You deserve to have a man who loves you and never lets you forget it. Someone who wants to raise Christopher into a solid and strong man, a good man who respects women." He put his hand against her hair, grabbing a silky fistful. "If I had a woman like you, I'd be so careful," he said in a whisper.

She looked into his tender eyes and smiled, but it was tinged with fear and sadness.

"Come here, let me hold you," he said, pulling her to him. She slipped onto his lap, pulled up her legs and curled against him, her head on his shoulder, his arm around her back. She nestled like a little kitten against his broad chest.

Preacher leaned back in the chair and closed his eyes, his arms around her, holding her against him. All I have to offer is this, he thought. Help. Safety. We'll get this bastard out of her life, she'll grow strong and confident again. And then she'll go. Somewhere down the line there will be a man—one who treats her right. But until then, sometimes she might need someone to hold her for a little while. And if it gets to be me, those few times, I'll make the most of it.

He sat like that until the small clock on the wall said that it was midnight. Paige had not moved in hours; she slept in his arms. He could stay there until dawn, just feeling her small body against his. With a deep sigh, he kissed the top of her head. Then he stood, carefully lifting her in his arms. She roused briefly, looking up at his face. "Shh," he said. "Let's get you to bed. We have a big day tomorrow."

He carried her up the back stairs and into his old room. Preacher lowered her to the bed, next to her son, and brushed the hair away from her brow. "Thank you, John," she whispered.

"You don't have to thank me," he said. "I'm doing what I want to do."

Jack was splitting logs at 7:00 a.m. when Preacher came out of the back door of his living quarters and walked toward him. Jack leaned the ax against the tree stump and turned toward his friend. Then, noting the menacing look on Preacher's face, tipped his head slightly and frowned, wondering what was wrong.

Before he could wonder for long, Preacher landed a shattering blow to Jack's face, knocking him backward about three feet and flat on his ass. It felt like a bomb going off in his head. "Jesus—"

"What the hell are you thinking, making her feel like she's doing something wrong?" Preacher demanded. "You oughta have more brains in your head than that!"

"Whoa" was all Jack could say. He stayed where he was, a hand pressed to his jaw. He didn't dare get back on his feet until he was ready to fight the man. And when Preacher was this pissed, that seemed a stupid idea.

"The girl's already scared to death and doesn't think she deserves any help, and I got *you* questioning *me*. What the hell's the matter with you?"

"Uh, Preacher…"

"I would've expected more out of you, Jack. It's not like you haven't been there. Mel came up here with some shit on her back—not the same shit, but shit just the same. And if I'd told you, right in front of her, that you shouldn't be getting involved, you would have taken me out on the spot!"

"Yeah," he said slowly. He moved his jaw back and forth with his hand. Not broken. He said, "Yeah. Okay." He touched his cheek right below his eye. Now, that might be broken.

"I thought I could count on you to step up. You could always count on me!"

"Okay, so the girl's gotten real important to you…" he said carefully.

"That's not what this is about! I'm just trying to help out—I don't expect anything. But I sure didn't expect you to try to back end me out of helping her."

"You're right," he said. "I'm sorry."

"I never do anything I don't want to do!"

"I know. Boy, do I get that." He started to get up and Preacher put out his hand. Jack took the assist only to find himself shoved back onto the ground.

"If you can't help, then at least shut the fuck up!"

And with that Preacher turned and stomped back into his quarters.

Jack stayed down another minute. He drew up his knees and circled them with his arms. He tried shaking the cobwebs out of his head. Whoa, he thought. Damn.

He got slowly to his feet and decided the log-splitting could wait. He was seeing a few stars. He mean-dered over to Doc's and walked in. Mel was not yet in town but Doc was in the kitchen making coffee. He turned as Jack came in and squinted at him. "How's the other guy look?" Doc asked.

"I think I might've stepped on Preacher's little toes," he said. "Have an ice pack?"

A half hour later the front door opened and Mel came in. She left her medical bag in the reception area and went to the kitchen for coffee, where she found Jack sitting at the table, an ice pack held to his eye. Something about this seemed not to surprise her terribly. She leisurely poured herself a mug and sat down at the table. "Let me guess," she said, wearing a very superior expression. "You felt the need to give advice."

"Why don't I listen to you?" he asked, lowering the ice pack to reveal a bruised cheek and black eye that was threatening to swell shut. She shook her head in disgust.

"As it turns out, Preacher does know what hit him," Jack said.

"Toldja," she said, leaning her chin into her hand, elbow on the tabletop.

"He took some exception to my advice that he might want to give serious thought to getting involved in this mess."

She tsked so that he would know she found him stupid without coming right out and saying so.

"Okay, I said I was sorry. That he was right and I'm sorry."

"After he cleaned your clock, I assume…."

"Well, yeah. After."

"Men."

"We're usually on the same team," he pointed out.

"When there's not a woman between you."

"I'm getting that."

"You know, there's this little rule about opinions. They're only good when someone actually asks you for them."

"He did say something about how I could just shut the fuck up."

"There you go. Who'd figure Preacher for sage advice?"

He made a face at her and put the ice back against his face. He winced.

"Hurts, huh?"

"Damn, that boy's got an arm."

"You're welcome to sit over here and hide out for as long as you want, but sooner or later you're going to have to kiss and make up. Aren't you at the bar today so he can go over to see the judge?"

"Yeah. But I was going to give him time to cool down a little. I'm going to need at least one eye to see out of."

"Oh, I think if Preacher had more in mind for you, he'd have already delivered it."

A little while later Jack walked into the kitchen at the bar and saw Preacher scowl his greeting. Bravely, Jack walked up to the counter. "Hey, man," he said. "You were right, I was wrong, and I'd like us to get back on the same team."

"You sure this team of mine isn't too much trouble for little you?" Preacher asked.

"Okay, you about done? Because this really hurts and I'm trying not to deck you right now. We could've just *talked* about it."

"I wanted to make sure I was clear," Preacher said.

"I get it, Preach. Now, come on. I'm only going to ask once."

Preacher seemed to think about it a second, then slowly put out his hand. Jack shook it and said, "Don't do that again."

"Don't make me want to."

It wasn't long before Paige came downstairs with Christopher. "Oh, my God," she said, looking at Jack's face.

"It's much worse than it looks," he told her.

"What in the world happened?"

"I got too close to the rear end of a mule." He pulled a disc out of his back pocket. "Mel told me to give you this—some pictures she took. In case you need it. But she said it should come with a warning—they're very scary pictures, whatever that means," he said, pretending he hadn't already seen them. "She still has copies, so you can leave this, if someone asks for it—like the judge."

# Six

Judge Forrest served in the Superior Court and made his home in Grace Valley. In his seventies, he was spry and had a serious, perhaps grim countenance. But for Preacher he had a ready smile and handshake. They met not in the courtroom, but in the judge's office. Preacher and Paige sat in chairs facing his desk, Christopher in the outside office with the judge's secretary. Judge Forrest asked Paige some questions about her life in Los Angeles.

Paige explained that she had been married to Wes Lassiter for six years, that Christopher was her three-year-old son and she was a little over two months pregnant. The abuse began right away—he'd actually hit her once before they were married. It became increasingly worse and horribly violent in the past couple of years. "But I should have seen it coming from the beginning," she said. "He was very controlling even before we were married. And he had a temper, rarely at me, but just about things in general. You know, like driving. Or anger about something at work. He's a trader. Stocks and commodities—very high stress."

"And the most recent abuse…?" the judge asked.

With a trembling hand, she slid a disc across his desk. "When I got to Virgin River, the nurse practitioner in the doctor's office examined me because I was threatening to miscarry. She took pictures."

"Jack's wife," Preacher explained, for the judge had been fishing with Jack. "Mel."

"This was the last time," Paige said. "The one that sent me running. Once again."

Judge Forrest took the disc and slid it into the portal on his computer. He clicked the mouse a few times, then turned his eyes toward her. "Why didn't you notify the police?" he asked her.

"I was afraid."

"Have you ever notified the police?" he asked.

"Twice. And I had a restraining order once, which he violated. I couldn't even stay with my mother—he threatened her, as well."

"Mel Sheridan dated these pictures," the judge said.

"I know. She said she'd take a medical history, no last name, date it and have it handy in case I needed it for treatment, or whatever...."

"You needed it. Your injuries are dated September 5. He reported you and your son missing on the twelfth." Judge leaned toward her. "Young woman, this is a dangerous man. If you don't press charges, there is no hope of stopping him. You certainly can't stop him on your own."

"To tell you the truth, I'm surprised he didn't file charges against me sooner."

"I'm not," Judge said. "He wouldn't want you recovered and returned to L.A. while you looked like this." He popped the disc out and handed it back to her. "I'm granting you a TRO and temporary custody based on these pictures and what I can safely assume will be the testimony of your practitioner, and others. He beat you up, then waited until you had time to get away, possibly out of state, before reporting you missing—which presupposes you told him you were leaving. As far as I know, with his permission." Paige opened her mouth, and Judge held up his hand to silence her. "Don't say any more without a lawyer, young lady. That week that he waited before missing his wife and son speaks volumes. But you're going to need some legal help. With any luck, you can obtain a divorce and permanent custody in absentia, but don't be too surprised if you're required to go back to L.A. If that happens, don't stay with family. Your location should be undisclosed. And don't go alone."

"I'm seeing this through," Preacher said.

Judge gave a nod of approval. "Your paperwork should be ready in about an hour. Maybe two. Go have some lunch and come back." He stood up. "I wish you good luck."

Later in the afternoon, as they drove back to Virgin River, Paige said, "Now comes the scary part."

Rick was whistling as he arrived at work. He came from the back, through the deserted kitchen, into the bar. Jack was going through some receipts at the bar as Rick came in. "Hey, Jack," Rick said. And Jack looked up. "Holy God!" Rick said, jumping back. "Man!"

"Yeah. Kind of ugly, huh?"

"Who hit you?"

"I ran into a door," he said.

"Nah," Rick said, shaking his head. "That door has a name. And there's only one guy I can think of who could get one like that off on you. What did you do to piss him off?"

Jack shook his head and chuckled. "Too smart for your own damn good, aren't you? I had an opinion I should've kept to myself."

"Uh-oh. You told him not to get mixed up with Paige, didn't you?"

Jack straightened indignantly. "Now, why the hell would you say something like that?" he demanded.

"Well, it's pretty obvious how Preach feels about her, and her kid. Where is the big man?" Rick asked, looking around.

"He took Paige over to the county courthouse to see a judge. He should be back any time now."

Rick's face split in a huge grin. Then he started to laugh. He plunged his hands in his pockets, rocked back on his heels, shaking his head. Laughing.

"What?" Jack demanded.

"Aw, Jack," he said. "Did you tell him not to do that?"

"No!" Jack insisted. Then he let out a huge sigh. "I'd be dead now if I'd told him not to." He pointed at his face. "I got this for telling him he might want to think about it."

"Oh, my Jesus," Rick said. "Preacher-man is all in. Got a woman."

"Yeah, well, I'm not sure he gets that yet, so watch your step."

Rick stepped close and gave Jack a shot to the arm with his fist. "Come on. I'm not dumb enough to get between him and a woman."

"Yeah?" Jack said. And he thought, am I the only one around here without a brain?

Jack left the bar a little early because he was tired of people asking him what happened to his face. He was having a quiet evening in the cabin with Mel when the phone rang. When Jack heard the voice of his youngest sister, he beamed. "Brie! How you doing?"

"Hi, Jack. How are you?"

"Great. Listen, Preacher told me he asked you for some advice about this young woman he's helping out. That was good of you, Brie. It's a bad situation."

"Yeah, I'm calling with some names for you to write down. Got a pen?"

"You sound a little rushed."

"Yeah, a little. Ready to copy?"

"Sure," he said, picking up a pen. "Go."

She rattled off a few names of lawyers, a couple in L.A., a couple in northern California, spelling for him when he asked her to. "Tell the woman to contact one of these local lawyers immediately, before she makes a move, before the husband can make another move. Immediately."

"Sure. Why do you sound so pissed off?" he asked her. "Bad day in court?"

"Big case," she said shortly. "Not my best day."

"So, what's Brad up to? He around?"

Without missing a beat she said, "Put Mel on."

"Sure," Jack said. "You okay?"

"Great. Can I talk to Mel, please?"

Jack held the phone toward Mel, who, with a perplexed look on her face, got off the couch and went to him. She took the phone in confusion; she said hello.

"Listen," came Brie's stressed voice. "I need you to tell him for me, because I can't talk to him about this yet. Tell Jack—Brad left me. Left me for another woman. He hasn't even taken his clothes, which tells me he might already be moved in."

"Brie?" Mel said in question. "What…?"

"My best friend," she said, rage dripping from every word. "Christine, my best friend. I never knew. Never even suspected."

"Brie, when did this happen?" Mel asked, and that question spoken into the phone brought Jack back to the kitchen, hovering.

"It's been almost a week since he told me he's been fucking her for a year! We were talking about babies—he said he wanted a baby. We've been having sex like mad, and he's been having it like mad down the street." She laughed bitterly. "You suppose she wanted a baby, too?"

"Ah, Brie…" Mel tried.

"He wants to come back for his things. I'm thinking of burning everything on the front lawn."

"Brie…"

"He's seen a lawyer already. He knows better than to face me without a really good lawyer. He wants a divorce—fast." She laughed. "Maybe she's pregnant or something. Wouldn't that be rich?" And then her voice broke for a moment.

Mel had only known Brie a short time. For that matter, she hadn't known Jack all that long. But of Jack's four sisters, she felt closest to Brie; they were around the same age and Brie was Jack's pet. The baby of the family.

Jack and Mel had just been to Sacramento—it was where they were married. Unless she was completely blind and distracted, it had looked to her as if Brad and Brie were the most loving, the most openly affectionate couple out of his four married sisters. This didn't seem possible, a few short weeks later.

"Tell Jack for me, okay? He thinks all the brothers-in-law are true brothers. This'll go down hard. You tell him—"

"Brie, stop!" Mel insisted. "Come to us. Take a week off and come up."

"I can't," she said, sounding suddenly deflated. "I have a big case building. Brad knows all about my case," she said. "He broke it to me now, when my defenses are down, when I have nothing in me to fight with." She laughed bitterly. "Do you fight for a man who's been sleeping with your best friend for a year?"

"I don't know," Mel answered, her heart sinking.

"Mel, tell Jack I'll call him in a while. Tell him I don't want to talk to him about this yet. Please…"

"Sure, honey. Whatever you want. You have someone to lean on? Your sisters? Dad?"

"Yeah, I'm leaning like crazy. But I have to be strong

through this—strong and mad. If I talk to Jack, he's going to make me cry. I can't afford to fall apart yet."

And then abruptly, Brie hung up, leaving Mel holding a dead phone with a completely shocked expression on her face.

"What is it?" Jack asked.

"She asked me to tell you Brad moved out. Asked her for a divorce."

"No," Jack said. "He couldn't have."

Mel nodded. "And she said, please, she doesn't want to talk to you about it right now. Later. She'll call later."

"Bull*shit,*" he said, grabbing for the phone.

"Shouldn't you respect her wishes?" Mel asked, even as Jack punched in numbers.

He stood with the phone at his ear for a long time as it rang. Then, apparently Brie let the machine come on, because he said, "Pick up, Brie. Come on—I have to hear your voice. Goddammit, pick up! I can't do this—waiting around like this. Brie—"

Mel was close enough to hear Brie say, "You absolutely never do as you're told, do you?" And Jack sighed heavily. Mel left the kitchen.

The cabin was very small, so going as far as the living room didn't really afford Jack much privacy as he stood by the kitchen sink, but he turned his back and talked in soft tones for a long time. There was plenty of quiet to indicate he also listened, something Jack was pretty good at, for a man.

Mel looked at her watch a couple of times. It was more than thirty minutes before he put the phone down and sat beside her on the couch. "You make her cry?" she asked him.

He nodded. "'Course I didn't mean to—I just had to know about this, that's all. I want to talk to *him.* She threatened to kill me if I call him."

She ran a finger under the bruise on his cheek. "I had no idea, when I married you, how much you're in everyone's business."

Jack stood and left the room. He went to the empty bedroom where he stored boxes of things he'd brought from his quarters behind the bar. He had a dusty, framed black-and-white photo in his hand and rubbed the sleeve of his shirt over it, cleaning it off. It was Jack, age sixteen, holding Brie, age five. Jack held her on his hip, her arms around his neck. He was looking off, pointing at something; she was laughing, her golden curls lifted by the wind. "She was always like my shadow," he said. "I couldn't shake her. When I went into the Marines she was only six. All the girls got sloppy about me leaving, but Brie was heartbroken." He took a breath. "I know she's a big-shot prosecutor. I hear she's one of the scariest prosecutors they have—a real killer. But it's hard for me to think of her as anything but my baby sister, little Brie. I wanna do something…."

"You should let her tell you what she needs," Mel advised. "Don't get her all mixed up in your agenda."

"My agenda…" he said absently.

"You've suffered a loss, too, Jack. It's a real tight family you have—I saw that. This is going to shake up everyone. Just try not to make your loss taxing on Brie's emotions. She has enough hurt. Okay?"

"Yeah," he agreed. "Yeah." He sat back on the couch, the picture resting on his lap. The expression on his face darkened. "I thought of him as a brother," he said. "I trusted him with the care of my sister. I don't think I'll ever understand how he could defect like this." He grabbed his wife's hand. "You know, in the middle of all that, while Brie's trying not to cry, she says to give Paige her phone numbers. To tell Paige she's prosecuted batterers and knows all their tricks.

Mel, I usually understand the things that men do. Right now men don't make any sense to me."

Paige called Brie and one of the recommended lawyers. Brie advised her to be prepared for contact from her husband—it was probable he'd get in touch. Argue, maybe threaten, try to use their child as leverage. "I know," Paige said. And peaceful sleep through the night was impossible, even though John assured her they were locked up tight and he wouldn't miss a sound.

She was jittery and distracted; the smile patrons had grown accustomed to as she served and cleaned up was missing. She looked outside a lot, scanning the area. Every time the phone rang, she tensed. "John, if he called here, you would tell me, wouldn't you?" she asked.

"Of course. But he has your lawyer's name—he should really call him."

"But he won't," Paige said.

Mel tried to cheer her up, lure her out. "Have you been outside in the past three days?" she asked Paige.

Paige leaned close. "I'm fighting the urge to load Chris in the car and run for cover."

"Yeah, I'm sure," Mel said. "With any luck, the lawyers will battle this out quickly and settle."

"That would be a miracle."

"I'm going to walk across the street and watch the afternoon soap with Connie and Joy. Come with me—laugh a little."

"I don't know…"

"Paige, you haven't seen the sky in three days. Come on. It's just across the street. We'll look both ways."

Preacher, overprotective, walked out onto the porch at the bar and watched them cross, noting nothing out of the ordinary on the quiet main street. But when the soap was over and the women were returning, Paige's worst fear was waiting for her, right in broad daylight, right on the street. Parked alongside of the bar was an SUV, and leaning against it was a man. Mel didn't even notice. She was chattering about the older women's running commentary on the soap opera when Paige stopped walking.

"Oh, God," she said in a breath. She tugged at Mel's sleeve, stopping her in the middle of the street.

He was positioned between them and the bar, one leg lazily crossed in front of the other, hands in his pockets as he watched them, a satisfied smile shaping his lips.

"No," Paige whispered.

"Is it him?" Mel asked.

"It is," she said, drawing a fearful breath.

He pushed himself off the car and walked toward them, slowly and leisurely. Mel instantly put herself between Paige and the man. "You can't be here," Mel said. "There's a restraining order."

He pulled a large, folded document out of his back pocket, kept coming and said, "There's also a court order for Paige to return my son to Los Angeles for a custody hearing. I'm here to pick him up. Paige," he said, "who do you think you're screwing with, huh? Come on, we're going home!"

"Jack!" Mel yelled, shielding Paige from his approach. "Jesus. *Jack!*"

"No—" Paige said in a near cry.

As Paige continued to back slowly away, moving in the direction of the store, Mel held her ground. While the man approached, although he had a sinister twist to his mouth, he was clearly no match for the men waiting just inside the bar, waiting to protect Paige. This preppy man in his pleated pants and Florsheim Chester loafers was not like the big Virgin River men. How could he inflict so much power, so much damage? He was smaller than Jack; *so* much smaller than Preacher. Goodness, he was about Rick's size! Not quite six feet with short, moussed, spiky brown hair. A pretty boy from the city. He was going to be very surprised.

Mel caught a glimpse of Jack coming onto the bar porch just as Paige turned and broke into a run. Wes Lassiter shoved Mel roughly out of his way to give chase. Mel stumbled backward and fell. Her fleeting thought was, Oh, Jack will have seen that. She could hear Jack's heavy tread into the street before she could refocus and watch his running approach. She glanced over her shoulder to see that he wasn't fast enough to save Paige. Lassiter caught up with Paige, grabbed her by the hair on the back of her head and threw her to the ground. In a blur of unreality, Mel watched as he drew back his foot and kicked her, shouting, "What the *fuck* do you think you're gonna do, huh? *Leave* me?"

Jack glanced down at Mel and she glanced up at him briefly as he ran on to Paige's rescue.

Just as Lassiter drew his foot back to deliver another kick to Paige's stomach, Jack hooked an arm around his neck, lifted him clear off the ground and away from Paige. He whirled him and threw him from his victim; he landed a few feet away.

Preacher, who had no doubt been in the kitchen when Mel screamed, was the next one out of the bar, Rick on his heels. A glance at Paige found her struggling to sit up, a hand covering her face, her nose bleeding from her head-first plunge onto the ground. Mel crawled the short distance toward Paige as Jack was trying to help her sit up, when Preacher came running into the street.

Preacher saw that Mel and Jack were with Paige and he went directly to Lassiter, who was still down. Preacher bent at the waist, grabbed the man under his arms and lifted him straight up, clear off the ground. They were face-to-face, Lassiter's feet swinging in the air. For a moment, a look of sheer terror showed on Lassiter's face as he stared into Preacher's enraged eyes.

"I could hit you *one time,* jag-off, and you'd never get up," Preacher snarled into the man's face.

"John!" Paige cried. "John!"

Preacher felt Jack's hand on one of his arms. "Preach, go get Paige."

He looked over his shoulder at her, sitting up, crying, her hand pressed over her nose and blood running down her chin. He held Lassiter off the ground effortlessly; he wanted to pummel him till he cried. He looked back at Lassiter's shocked face, staring into his frightened eyes for a second, and thought, *I can't do violence in front of her. She might think I'm like him. I'm not like him.* Preacher dropped the man to the ground. He bent his face close to Lassiter's and said, "Do *not* get up." Then he straightened, whirled and went to Paige a few feet away.

"God," Preacher said. He got down on one knee and lifted her off the ground, into his arms. He stood with her against him.

"I'm okay," she wept against his chest. "I'll be okay."

He pulled her hand away from her face, saw the blood coming from her nose.

"Aw, Paige, that should never have happened to you," he said. He started to carry her to Doc's.

Jack helped Mel to her feet. She brushed herself off and stood for him. "I'm not hurt," she said. "I just got off balance…."

"You sure?" Jack asked.

She nodded and Jack turned toward Lassiter, still crumpled on the ground. His look of fear was gone and replaced with a narrow-eyed sneer that made Jack furious.

Rick bravely put himself between Jack and Lassiter. When Jack turned from Mel, Rick took one look at the storm gathering on Jack's face, the way he clenched his fists open and closed, and stepped out of his way.

Jack walked over to Lassiter and stuck out a hand to assist him in standing. "Good thing you stopped him," Lassiter said, putting out his hand for assistance. "I'd have had his ass."

Jack pulled him to his feet with a snarl, and once he was upright, threw a punch into his face that blew him across the street four feet. He walked the few feet and stood over Lassiter, looking down at him. "Now you gonna have mine?" he asked.

Lassiter looked up at him, blood immediately spurting from his nose. "What the hell…?" He got clumsily to his feet and faced off with Jack, his fists up as a boxer would do. He shuffled his feet a little, dancing, ready to land a blow with a closed fist.

Jack actually laughed, completely loose, relaxed. "You're kidding me, right?" he said. He wiggled his fingers. "Come on."

Lassiter came at him, then retreated suddenly, whirled in a crouch and came up with a high kick aimed at Jack's head. But Jack stopped the assault of Lassiter's foot with a fast hand that grabbed his ankle. Jack yanked hard and Lassiter landed on his back, his ankle still in Jack's grip. "What you going to do, buddy? *Kick* me?"

"Let go!"

Jack dropped the leg and reached down to pull him to his feet by the front of his expensive shirt. He threw a punch into his gut, doubling Lassiter over. Then another one to his face, reeling him backward onto the ground.

At Doc's porch steps, Preacher turned around and looked over his shoulder at what Jack was doing, then continued on.

"You've had it now," Lassiter said with a strained, breathless voice.

"I haven't had it quite yet," Jack said, pulling him up again. He delivered one more blow to the man's face, sending him airborne a few feet before he landed in the dirt, rolling around, semiconscious. Jack brushed his hands together to remove the stain. "Now, I've had it," he said. "Rick, tie his hands behind his back. I'm going to call the sheriff."

"Sure, Jack," Rick said, sprinting off to the bar in search of rope.

Mel shook her head. "Shame on you," she said to Jack.

"I'm sorry, Melinda. But someone had to knock the shit out of this asshole at least once, and if Preacher had done that, this idiot would never walk again."

"Well, if you get into trouble, don't come crying to me," she said, and turned to follow Paige and Preacher into Doc's.

Paige lay on the examining table in Doc's clinic and Preacher held her hand in both of his. "I let you down," he was saying, so softly Mel barely heard.

"No," she whispered. "No."

"Paige, were you afraid I was going to hurt him?" Her eyes shifted away from his face and he brushed a soft hand against the hair at her temples. "Paige, I could've hit him—but I don't lose control. Paige," he said, putting a finger and thumb on her chin, turning her eyes back to his face. "Paige, I don't lose control. Okay?"

She nodded weakly. Mel put an ice pack on Paige's face and told her to hold it there, then noticed that a dark stain was spreading in the crotch of her jeans. "Preacher, please step out of the room and call Doc so we can examine Paige."

"I'm sorry," he said to Paige. "I let you down."

Paige put a hand on his face. Preacher put a light kiss on her forehead and left, hanging his head. Mel knew the only way this could have turned out differently was if Preacher had been strapped to Paige's side twenty-four hours a day. Lassiter was quick and mean. Obviously crazy.

And Paige was bleeding, perhaps miscarrying.

Mel shook out a sheet to cover Paige. She leaned over her and said, "Help me pull off your jeans, Paige. We have a problem. You might be miscarrying."

Although she cried softly, she was able to lift her hips enough for the pants to be removed. Blood immediately began to pool beneath her and Mel decided not to examine her; she didn't want to aggravate a hemorrhage. Rather, she fixed her up with a Peripad, covered her with the sheet, and told her she'd be right back.

She met Doc in the hall before he came into the examining room. "We need to transport her, at least to Grace Valley—and maybe on to Valley Hospital. Will you call John Stone and have Preacher bring the gurney?"

"Spontaneous AB?" he asked.

"At least. I just hope it's not a uterine hemorrhage. The girl is only twenty-nine. I'm not going to examine her. I'm going to leave that to John. Will you please tell him there was severe abdominal trauma? Bastard kicked her."

Doc grimaced, but then he nodded and went to talk to Preacher.

Back in the exam room, Mel bent over Paige. "I'm taking you to the OB in Grace Valley, Paige. We need a specialist. Possibly a surgeon."

"Am I losing the baby?" she asked weakly.

"I'll be honest with you—it doesn't look good. I've asked that Preacher bring the gurney back. Would you like him to go with you?"

"No. I have to talk to him, though."

When Preacher rolled the gurney to the exam room, Mel told him to take a moment with Paige, quickly, then she would need his help to load her. He stepped into the room and took her hand, the one that wasn't holding the ice pack to her face. "John," she said, "please make sure Christopher is all right. That he doesn't see his father. That he knows Mama is okay. Please."

"Mel and Jack can—"

"No, John. Please. Take care of Chris. I'll be all right, but I don't want him scared and I don't want him to see his father. Please?"

"Anything you want," he said. "Paige…"

"No, no more apologies," she said. "Take care of Chris."

Preacher assisted Mel in sliding Paige from the exam table to the gurney, and the bright red puddle of blood left behind as she was moved caused his own blood to roar in his ears. As he pushed the gurney out of Doc's office, Rick ran to help him lift it down the porch stairs to the waiting Hummer. His vision blurred as his eyes clouded with unshed tears. "Everything will be all right, Paige," he said. "I'll take care of Chris."

Wes Lassiter had achieved a kneeling position in the street, his hands bound behind his back, his face bloody and swelling. He'd begun to draw a crowd. Several men were leaning on the rail or sitting on the porch chairs at Jack's while Jack and Preacher sat on the steps, watching. Jack's hand was plunged into a bowl full of ice when the sheriff's deputy pulled into town. He had to carefully drive around the man in the street and parked at the bar, right in front of Jack.

It was the same deputy who had attended the shooting Jack had been involved in over a month ago when a drug addict, looking for narcotics from Doc's drug cabinet, had held a knife on Mel. The deputy, Henry Depardeau, got out of the car and hitched up his gun belt. "Sheridan," he said. "I'm seeing a lot more of you these days than I like."

"Ditto," Jack said. He lifted his swollen hand. "I'd shake, but…"

Henry threw a look over his shoulder. "You do that?"

"I did. The man threw my pregnant wife to the ground so he could kick the shit out of his own pregnant wife."

"Whew." Henry shook his head and looked down. "He punch you?" Henry asked, pointing to his own cheek, indicating the bruise Jack still wore.

"Nah. I wasn't going to let him hit me. This is old," he explained. "I walked into a door. A big, stupid door."

"Then you beat him. That's two batteries, Jack. His and yours. Might have to hook you both up."

"Whatever you have to do, Henry. He did try to kick me in the head, though. That count for anything?"

"Maybe. At least you didn't kill him."

"Saved his life," Preacher said. "I *was* going to kill him."

"How'd you get that blood on you there, big fella?" Henry asked Preacher.

"Carrying Paige to Doc's. Paige being his wife," Preacher said, looking down at the wide smear of blood on his shirt. To Jack he said, "Shew—I better change this shirt before Chris wakes up from his nap. The things you don't think about with kids." And he got up quickly, going inside.

"So," Henry said to Jack. "You did that all by yourself."

"All by myself."

"And the woman?"

"She's been taken to a specialist—an OB. She might be losing that baby. He knew she was pregnant, by the way," Jack added, throwing a glance in Lassiter's direction. "Last I heard, besides being thrown to the ground by her hair and kicked in the stomach, she's bleeding real bad."

"Witnesses to this beating?"

"Plenty. There's me, Preacher, Rick here, my wife, who took the woman to the doctor in Grace Valley. You can catch up with her later. It was an emergency."

"Hey!" Lassiter yelled. "I'm over *here!*"

Henry glanced lazily over his shoulder and said, "Yeah? Then shut up." Back to Jack, he said, "I suppose I can trust you to stay right here?"

"Where am I gonna go, Henry? I want to be sure Mel's okay."

"Tell you what we're going to do. I'm going to book him. And if the sheriff wants you to come in, you drive on over. Okay?"

"Sure thing, Henry."

He shook his head again. "I just can't figure out why anyone in his right head would bother these Virgin River women."

"Yeah. Makes no sense," Jack said.

The baby spontaneously aborted—miscarried—before Doc and Mel could even get Paige to Grace Valley. John Stone and June Hudson loaded her in their ambulance and took her to Valley Hospital where, thankfully, a D and C caused the bleeding to slow and no further surgery was required.

When Paige woke from her procedure, she was told that fortunately it appeared there had been no further damage to her reproductive organs. She would only stay through the night for observation and could be released in the morning, but Dr. Stone wanted her to stay off her feet for at least a couple of days.

The next face she saw was Preacher's. "Hi," he said softly.

She reached for his hand. "Where's Christopher?" she asked sleepily.

"He's with Mel and Jack. They're staying at the bar till I get back. I'll keep him in my room through the night and bring him with me to pick you up in the morning."

"Hmm," she said.

"Paige, are you awake enough for me to tell you some things? I want to tell you without the boy."

"Hmm," she said. "I think so."

"Here's how it is. Wes was arrested. Paige, they found drugs on him. They wouldn't tell me what, just that he's going to be arraigned for a couple of felonies—battery, possession, defying an order of protection. He might make bail but he's going to have to go to trial. Judge Forrest promises he'll at least get a fast trial—and believe me, if I have to stand over you twenty-four hours a day until he's in prison, I'm willing to do that. I'm so sorry I let this happen to you."

"You did all you could, John," she said sleepily.

"He's not getting off this time. You did it, Paige. Okay? You with me, Paige?"

"Yeah. Yeah, I'm with you."

"Then…" He stumbled. "Then, when he's convicted and locked up, you can go home if you want to. Get your custody and divorce. He can't get custody if he's in prison. No ifs. Felons can't get custody. He can't keep you from getting a divorce."

"Home?" she asked.

"You can do whatever you want."

"How long will he be in jail?" she asked.

"No idea," he said. "Your lawyer is trying to get them to add attempted murder to his charges, given the baby, but that's a real stretch. Paige, I'm awful sorry about the baby."

"That baby," she said weakly. "I tried, but it just didn't have a chance."

He put his big hand softly against her tummy, the most personal he'd ever been with her. "I know you did. It wasn't your fault. It was more my fault than yours."

"John, stop saying that. Of all people, it was least of all your fault."

"You're as good as free."

"Free. I won't know how to act."

"Think you'll want to go back to L.A.?" he asked.

"I don't know. So many bad memories."

"If you want a place to sit for a while, while you think things over, you can have that room that smells like bacon in the morning for as long as you want." Then very quietly, almost to himself, he said, "For life, if you want."

"I could help out," she said. Eyes closed, she smiled sleepily. "I could do dishes." Her eyelids fluttered a little, but she couldn't keep them open.

He brushed her hair back. "Jack wants to build a house," he said. "It's going to take him away from the business. I could always use the help. You and Christopher…"

"Hmm," she said.

"Okay," he said. "You're done. You have to sleep."

"Hmm."

He leaned over and gently touched his lips to her forehead. "I'll be back for you in the morning."

"Okay."

He started to leave and she said, "John?"

He turned back to her bed.

"Could I? Stay there until I feel better?"

His chest felt suddenly full, as if it might burst. He tried to tamp down hope, but it was impossible. "Of course. I love having you there. Everyone loves having you there."

"It's nice there," she said, and her eyes closed.

# Seven

Paige was once again burrowed into the room over the kitchen, but this time her injuries were not terrible. She had to recover from her D and C by staying off her feet for a couple of days, and although she'd received a bloody nose, it was not broken. While she rested, Preacher watched Christopher. Via long distance, Brie helped line up a lawyer in L.A. to appeal to the court to reverse the order to return Christopher to his father, given his pending trial. Wes Lassiter made bail after three days and went back to Los Angeles, returning to his job before his employer could sniff out the arrest. Preacher was not content to take Lassiter's lawyer's word for that—he called Mike Valenzuela, who was happy to check, twice a day if necessary, to be sure that Lassiter was back at his job, hundreds of miles away from Virgin River.

It seemed as though things might calm down, at least until the trial, but then Mel was surprised by a patient she wasn't expecting. A patient and condition she would never have anticipated.

Doc was off fishing when Mel's friend Connie came to the clinic. Connie was in her early fifties, a good-natured little redhead who was still recovering from cardiac bypass surgery that she'd had last May. She was almost back to her old self. With her was her niece, Liz. Upon seeing Liz's face, Mel's first reaction was to smile brightly, but then, noting that Liz's eyes were downcast, her smile froze. Mel's gaze drifted lower to the very slight rounding of her tummy, and she felt her heart plummet. Oh-oh. Then she stole a glance at Connie's face and saw her friend grimace, then shrug, helpless.

Connie's sister had sent Liz to her from Eureka last spring, right around the same time Mel had come to Virgin River. March. The reason was that Liz was a handful, too much for Connie's sister to handle. She'd been reportedly running wild in Eureka. Both Connie and her sister thought Virgin River might calm the girl down, or at least prove to have fewer opportunities for getting in trouble than were available in the much larger town of Eureka. But when Connie had a heart attack in May, Liz was sent home to her mother.

"Hey there," Mel said cheerfully. This was Mel's work—she knew how to get beyond the shock, the panic. "Welcome back. How are you?"

"Not totally great," Liz said.

"Well, it's good to see you, anyway," Mel said, reaching out and taking her hand. "I bet you're here for an exam. Why don't you come with me."

Liz let herself be led to the exam room. The girl looked quite a bit different than she had last spring. She came into town looking like a hussie; she wore skirts no bigger than napkins, high-heeled boots, abbreviated tops, belly button ring, glossy lips and thick black mascara on her sexy long lashes—like an ad for *Playboy.* And at the time she was all of fourteen, a very beautiful, provocative fourteen who looked more like eighteen. No wonder her mother had been terrified. Now she was clad in jeans and a bulky sweatshirt that was pulled down to cover her tummy, but it was still evident she was pregnant. Her makeup was much more natural looking and conservative than it had been, but she really didn't need it at all. She was lovely. And she actually looked younger today than she had last spring. Younger and more vulnerable.

Rick had taken one look at Liz last spring and went bonkers. Jack and Preacher had been looking out for Rick for years, kind of surrogate big brothers or dads. According to Jack, he'd had a serious talk with Rick about the dangers of intimacy, especially with such a young girl. After Liz went home to her mom, Rick had told Jack that they were no longer seeing each other. Knowing Rick, the kind of young man he was, Mel couldn't imagine that he would get her pregnant and abandon her. He just didn't seem like that kind of boy. Mel thought perhaps Liz had wasted no time in finding herself a fella back in Eureka.

"So," Mel said to Liz. "Want to tell me why you're here?"

"I'm pregnant. Obviously."

"Have you been examined by a doctor yet?"

"No. I wasn't sure I was until… I thought I was just getting fat."

"Liz, how many periods have you missed?"

She shrugged. "Who knows? I hardly ever got any, anyway. I never knew when I was supposed to."

"Do you have any idea how far along you might be?"

"I have a perfect idea. Since there's only been one person. One guy. One time." She lifted her clear blue eyes and looked directly into Mel's.

Mel had a brief and delusional hope that Rick had escaped this mess. She asked, "If that's the case, if you can remember the approximate time of conception, it will help us set a due date."

"May 7th," she said, and her eyes grew moist.

Rick, she thought. Damn. Two days before the heart attack that sent Liz home to her mom. And it made her even further along in her pregnancy than Mel was. "Well, first things first. Let's examine you and see how you're doing. Can you put on his gown for me? Everything off, bra, panties, the whole bit."

"I've never… I haven't ever had one of these…."

"It's okay, Liz. It's not terrible. I'll give you a few minutes to undress and when I come back, I'll explain everything as I go. I promise you'll be fine. Once you're sexually active, it's very important to have regular exams, pregnant or not."

Even if Liz hadn't delivered that date of conception, any of Mel's curiosities would have been quickly answered when she found Connie in the waiting room. "My sister," Connie said with an ounce of disgust. "She said, she got knocked up in Virgin River, she can go back there and have the baby. You'd think I did it."

Mel shook her head. "It happens, Connie. Too often."

"I don't know which one of them I want to kill most."

"No killing," Mel said, reaching out and giving her hand a pat. "Let's just get them through it and see if they can have their young lives back."

"Stupid idiots," Connie said. "What were they thinking?"

Mel sat down beside Connie for a second. "What gives you the impression they were thinking? If they were, they were thinking below the waist. How are you feeling? We don't want your blood pressure up."

"Ach, I'm fine. This just took me by surprise."

"I have a feeling it's going to take everyone by surprise."

"How the hell could she not know?"

"Oh, Connie, you'd be amazed at how tight denial can keep those fourteen-year-old tummy muscles."

"She's fifteen now. Not that it matters too much."

Mel heard herself laugh, though humorlessly. "It's slightly less stunning. Let me take care of my patient while you practice deep breathing. Hmm?"

Liz was already more than five months pregnant. Almost six. She might've felt the baby move already, but she wasn't sure. She thought it was just gas. She thought her breasts were sore because her period was coming. This was so typical of a young girl, especially a young girl who wasn't getting regular periods. She was oblivious to the changes in her body, combined with an overwhelming desire for it not to be so.

"You're staying here now?" Mel asked. "With your aunt Connie?"

She shrugged. "I guess so. If she doesn't just throw me out."

"You know she wouldn't do that. Does this mean you've decided to have the baby?"

"Yes. What else can I do?"

"At this stage, your options are definitely limited."

"I'm having it. I can't do anything else now." She took in a ragged breath. "This is going to be really bad."

"How can I help you, Liz?" Mel asked.

She just shook her head miserably. "I don't think anyone can help me now."

"Honey, you're not the first teenager to get pregnant. I won't kid you—there will be some tough times, getting through this. But you will get through it."

"I'm just hoping to get through today."

"What's so important about today?" Mel asked.

"I guess I better tell him. Huh?"

"He doesn't know," Mel said, and it was not a question.

"No." She lifted her eyes and they welled with tears. "He's going to be so mad."

"Sweetheart, you didn't get this way alone. You remember that. I'll give you a few days to settle in, then we'll drive down to Grace Valley and get an ultrasound. You'll be able to see your baby. I think you'll be able to determine the sex, if you want to know."

"Okay," she said. "Yes, I want to know."

"You can think about who you would like to deliver your baby. You'll meet the OB in Grace Valley when you have the ultrasound, and given this is a first pregnancy, there's plenty of time for you to get to Valley Hospital. Or, you can have the baby here, but I don't administer anesthesia, something you might want to keep in mind."

"Okay. I don't know what to do yet," she said.

"You take your time. Some advice?"

"Sure," she said. "Join the club."

"Don't wait. Tell him right away. Get that part behind you."

Liz shuddered. "Yeah," she said. "I know."

Rick parked his little truck right next to Jack's behind the bar and, whistling, he bounded up the back steps and into the kitchen. Preacher was rolling out dough for pies, and right beside him, sitting up on the counter crosslegged and pounding at his own little wad of dough, was Christopher. Preacher's shadow. Rick tousled the boy's hair. "How you doing, buddy? Makin' pies?"

"I'm making my own," he said, concentrating.

"Good for you," Rick said.

Preacher said, "Rick, there's someone out in the bar here to see you."

"Oh, yeah?" he said, grinning.

"Listen, Rick," Preacher said. "Nice and easy, Rick. Take it nice and easy. Use your head. Think before you talk, okay?"

"Yeah?" he said again, in question.

Rick went into the next room and saw that Jack was behind the bar serving beer to a couple of men. He met Rick's eyes and his expression was real serious. Then he inclined his head slightly, into the room. Rick glanced across the room to a corner table, and when he saw her there, his eyes lit up and he grinned. Liz, he thought. Oh, God—*Liz!* His heart actually started to hammer—he hadn't seen her since last May and he had missed her like mad! He couldn't imagine the number of times he thought about her. He'd *dreamed* about her.

As he walked quickly around the bar toward her, she stood. And as she stood, her hands automatically went to her middle, as if holding up her round tummy, and the bottom suddenly dropped out of Rick's world. He stopped dead in his tracks, stunned. Paralyzed. His mouth hung open and his eyes went from her face to her belly to her face. He wanted to run for his life. He wanted to die.

From across the room he could see that tears instantly gathered in her eyes. She was scared, he could see that. He heard Preacher's voice in his head—nice and easy; think before you talk. He managed to close his mouth, swallow and take slow steps toward her. As he neared, she lifted her chin bravely, even though a big, fat tear spilled over.

His head was spinning. How could this be? It couldn't be his—she said she was okay—no baby. Next thought— I'm a senior in high school and the only girl I ever did anything with is pregnant, standing here right in front of me, scared to death of me. While I'm scared to death of *her*... Please, God, let this not happen to me.

Then, helplessly, What does she think—I'm going to blame *her?*

And then he concentrated real hard, as if grabbing hold of his brain—get a grip. A pregnant girl you did it with is standing in front of you, scared to death of you. He heard Jack in his head—it's not enough to feel like a man, Rick—you have to think like a man. Do the right thing.

He had limited options. He could run, he could deny, he could pass out, and when they brought him around, she and her belly would be gone.

Another tear spilled down her cheek while he was in

shock. He tried to imagine what Jack would do, because he admired and respected Jack. What would Preacher do? And he got a picture in his mind of Preacher watching over Paige and Chris. He decided that no matter what he was feeling, he'd just act like them. He'd deal with the real issues later. For now, he was at least going to look like a man.

He stood in front of her, looked into her eyes, her terrified eyes, and managed a soft smile. He put an arm around her waist and drew her close enough to put a kiss on her forehead. His life was unraveling, but what he noticed was that she smelled so good—like he remembered. "Lizzie," he whispered. She let her head drop against his shoulder and he could feel the trembling, feel her shoulders quaking. He pulled her against him and held her. "Don't cry," he whispered. "Come on, Lizzie. Don't cry."

He looked over his shoulder at Jack and Jack solemnly inclined his head toward the door. He turned back to Liz. "Come on. We have to go somewhere and talk. Come on," he said, his arm around her waist, leading her out of the bar as she leaned against him in tears.

He led her out behind the bar where there were no people, where they were alone, and stood with her under a tree. "Here now," he said. "How we gonna talk if you cry?"

"Rick," she said, leaning her head against his shoulder. "I'm sorry, Rick."

He lifted her chin with a finger and took in her red eyes, her chapped cheeks. He tried to keep his voice soft. Tender. "What happened, Lizzie? You said it was all right."

She shrugged. "I thought it was. It seemed like that's what you wanted me to say."

"Only if it was true," he said.

"I didn't know, that's all. I just didn't know."

"I thought you got your period. Didn't you tell me that?" he asked her.

She shrugged again. "I never got 'em very much. I only had, like, four last year, all year. You asked me every day, so I said it was okay, so you'd stop asking me. And you broke up with me. Right then. That minute. On the phone. Pretty soon, that was all I thought about…not anything else. Just that you broke it off. That you didn't want me. Like I did something wrong, something bad. I felt like such a—"

"Stop. You didn't do anything wrong," he said, ashamed of how he'd made her feel.

"That's how it felt," she said in a whimper.

It took him less than half a minute to remember those details, and to feel like total crap at the accuracy. Just a couple of days after the little mishap that caused this pregnancy, Liz went home to her mom in Eureka. He called her all the time, kept asking her if she was okay, if she'd gotten her period so they could relax that they hadn't been caught. Finally she said yes, they were okay. And in that very same conversation he told her they should cool it, not see each other anymore. He told her he cared about her, but holy God—they obviously couldn't control themselves. And they were both too young to get caught with a baby.

Except, no, they weren't.

He pulled her into his arms. "Oh, Liz, baby," he said. "I broke it off to keep you safe!" *To keep* me *safe!* "I didn't want to lose control again and get you in trouble." *Get* me *in trouble!* "You're so young! Too young!" I'm *too young!* "Oh, God, Lizzie. You should have told me the truth."

"I didn't know," she said again, crumbling into sobs against him.

"Okay, baby, don't cry. It's not your fault. It's my fault. Come on, don't cry."

But she was going to cry for a long time, it seemed.

First, because she'd been so scared of what he would say, and second, because she was so relieved. He held her for what seemed like forever, but it at least gave him time to think of what he might say next. When finally the tears abated, he said, "Can we go for a ride? Is that okay?"

She nodded.

He wiped the tears from her cheeks with the backs of his fingers. "Should you tell your aunt Connie?"

"It's okay," she said. "She knows I came to talk to you. To tell you."

"Okay, then. We'll go for a ride, settle down a little bit, and then we'll face the music with Connie. Hmm?"

"Should you ask Jack?"

He put an arm around her shoulders and led her to his little truck. Jack had seen her belly, had seen Rick take her out of the bar. "Jack knows exactly what I'm doing right now." The only thing I can do, he thought. What I should have done before this happened. Try to act like the grown-up. A little too late…

"Where are we going?"

"Let's go out to the river. We'll sit on a rock and talk about what's coming. How about that?"

"You're sticking by me?" she asked.

"Sure I am, Liz."

"Do you love me, Rick?" she asked him.

He looked down at her round belly; he'd put that there. Holy shit, he thought. Love? That was a stretch. He wanted no part of this. So he forced himself to think about Preach and Jack, how they were around women. And he put a soft kiss on her temple. "Of course I do. I want you to stop being afraid now. Everything is going to be okay. Maybe not so easy, but okay."

Ordinarily Jack would have left the bar as soon as possible after the dinner hour had passed. Preacher was occupied with little Christopher and Paige, and he had a sense that Rick might come back. Rick would feel that he had to explain things. There wasn't too much to explain—it had been pretty obvious by Lizzie's presence. But still, Rick looked to Jack as if he were a father, and Jack had never been unhappy about that. Not even now.

Jack had talked to Mel briefly, before she went home for the night. "We have a situation, and I think you know all about it."

"I can't talk about it, darling," she said. "I'm sorry."

"I just want to help," he said.

"I know, Jack. I still can't talk about a patient."

"Can't you give me any advice?" he asked.

She leaned toward him, kissed him and said, "You don't need any advice. You'll know exactly what to do." She looked down at his swollen hand, up at his black eye. "You're a mess. Try not to get into a fight tonight." She smiled her sweetest smile. "Follow your instincts with Rick. It's not as though you haven't been there yourself."

There was that, he thought. He was certain their baby had been conceived the first time they'd been together. The only time he'd had unprotected sex in more years than he could remember.

It was about eight-thirty and he was close to giving up. Preacher had bathed Christopher and put him in the bed beside his mother and was back downstairs, pouring a short whiskey with Jack, when Rick came in. He was tall, already six feet. Hard work around the bar had honed his arms and shoulders, made him strong. He was seventeen now, and this was his last year of high school. With his high cheekbones, square jaw and thick, expressive brows, he was a handsome youth. But as he walked into the bar, head down and hands in his jacket pockets, he seemed to have new lines on his face. He might have aged about ten years in the past few hours.

The bar was empty but for Jack and Preacher, so Rick jumped up on a bar stool and faced them. He ran a hand through his hair and looked at the two men who, if they hadn't just about raised him since he was thirteen, sure had mentored him. "So, by now you've figured most of this out. Right?"

"Liz seems to be pregnant," Jack said.

"Yeah. That little slip last spring—it hit solid ground. The baby is due in February, as near as she can figure out. As near as Mel can figure out. She's *very* pregnant."

"Jesus, Rick," Preacher said, almost weak. "Aw, man…"

Rick shook his head. "Well, it's mine. I did it."

"It wasn't just you, buddy," Preacher said, remembering too well the little sexpot act Liz was putting on back then.

"She's carrying the baby," Rick said. "The least I can do is take the blame. Besides, she didn't hold me down." He took a breath. "Guys. I'm sorry. I let you down. I fucked up. Big."

Jack felt a proud smile threaten his lips. Any other seventeen-year-old boy would be on his way out of town, but not Rick. He was stepping up the best he could, like a man. Accountable. Facing Jack and Preacher had to be as hard for him as facing this disaster. "You manage to work anything out?"

"No, not really. You can't really do too much the second you find out. You know? But I told her I'm in this with her. And I want her to not be afraid anymore. Then I told Connie that I'll pay for everything, no matter what I have to do."

"How'd Connie and Ron hold up?" Preacher asked him.

"Oh, I think they pretty much want to kill me right now," Rick said. "I did an awful lot of groveling. Apologizing. Begging. Promising to work till I drop dead seemed to ease the pain a little bit."

"You probably won't have to do that," Jack said. "We

can always help you with extra hours. School's important, Rick. No matter what else comes."

"Thanks. The most important thing right now is that she not be scared. She's so frickin' scared, it kills me. I not only knocked her up, I terrified the shit outta her! Holy Jesus! Aw, guys. I know you expected better out of me than this."

"Rick, you didn't let anyone down," Jack said. "Shit happens. You handled yourself real well. Better than most guys in your position would."

"You see how scared she was? You know why? She told me everything was okay because I kept asking and asking, like that was all I cared about. And the second she let me off the hook, I dumped her!" He scrubbed a hand along the back of his sweaty neck. "I knew I screwed that up, I just didn't know how bad. I thought I was keeping us out of trouble—instead I was keeping her from telling me sooner. If I'd known sooner, maybe we could've done something about—that baby," he said softly, almost reverently. "That baby's moving inside her. I felt it *move*. Holy God."

Jack felt something in his chest stir. He was over forty and more than ready for a family, true, but he could relate to Rick's shock and awe just the same.

As for Preacher, no one in the world knew how much he'd give for a mess like this one. Not even Jack.

"She's just a kid," Rick said. "I don't know how I'm going to make this up to her."

"For starters, you're in this with her," Preacher said. "You treat her good, sweet as you can, with respect. You treat her like the mother of your baby, no matter what's coming for that baby."

"Yeah," Rick said. "She asked me if I loved her," he said uncomfortably.

Silence hung in the air for a second. Then Jack got down a third glass and tipped the whiskey bottle over it, a short shot. He pushed it toward Rick. He probably needed it right about now.

"What'd you say?" Preacher asked.

"She's got my baby in her, Preach. She didn't ask for it. What the hell was I gonna say, huh? Maybe I should've said, I sure thought I did last spring when we were doing it—that'd be a real stand-up guy." He looked down into that short shot and shook his head. "I said, 'Of course I do.'"

"Aw, Rick, that was the right thing," Preacher said. "What else could you do?"

Jack clinked Rick's glass; he was damn proud of the boy. No feeling sorry for himself, no whining about how he got screwed. No blaming. It took a lot to straighten your back like that, hold your head up, be the strength and not the victim. Took a lot to do that at any age—and at seventeen, it was admirable. "You're going to be okay, buddy," he said, hoping it was true.

"I feel like I have to do something, and I have no idea what," Rick said.

"Right now, you do nothing," Jack said. "You take some time to think. Don't get crazy on me and run off and get married or something. You're seventeen, she's fifteen, and the only thing for sure is a baby's coming. You just hang close to her, treat her right, and we'll figure it all out."

"Jack, Preach," he said, his eyes getting a little wet. "Guys, I'm sorry. You tried to warn me about this and I—"

"Rick," Jack said, stopping him. "You're not the first guy to walk down this road, okay? Take it slow." Jack lifted his glass and had a little sip. "We're gonna get through this. Might be tough, but thank God—we're tough."

# *Eight*

All of Judge Forrest's determination to get Wes Lassiter to trial quickly hit a predictable snag—Forrest was in Mendocino County and Lassiter was arrested in Humboldt County. His case would go before a different judge.

Lassiter had been found to be in possession of methamphetamine at the time he assaulted his wife, a condition that his lawyer argued contributed to his crazed behavior and lack of judgment. The prison sentence could be impressive, if he was convicted. But his lawyer pleaded for drug treatment and the judge allowed bail on the condition that Lassiter would stand trial for one misdemeanor and two felony counts after drug rehab, and that successful completion of treatment could be held in sentencing consideration. There were other conditions— if he checked himself out of treatment early, his bail would be revoked and he could sit in jail, awaiting trial. And while ordinarily treatment centers operated under a code of strict anonymity, in Lassiter's case, the prosecutor's office would be able to check in, make sure he was still under wraps and not a threat to his family.

Brie called Paige. "Don't take this decision as bad news," she said. "It's entirely possible that sobriety will make a huge difference in his perspective. My recommendation is that you proceed with the dissolution of the marriage and custody arrangements. He can stall you while he's in treatment—but given the facts of the decision, my bet is that he'll prove cooperative to keep his sorry ass out of prison."

"How long will he be in treatment?" Paige asked.

"It's hard to say. A month is a minimum, but meth is a pretty tough drug and I've heard of people staying as long as several months. In order for this agreement to work in his best interest, he can't just quit. He has to be released by a supervisor."

"I have no idea how bad his drug problem is," Paige said. "I suspected drugs. I found something that looked like drugs once, but I was afraid to ask him about it. If it's a matter of convincing a supervisor he's cured—he's very manipulative."

"Yeah, they all are. Believe me, if there's one place in the world the pros are on to the cons, it's drug treatment."

"I'll be looking over my shoulder for months…."

"Paige, with what you've been through, as long as he's *alive* you'll be looking over your shoulder. Ask Preacher to teach you how to shoot."

It took her a couple of days of thought before she broached the idea to John.

"That's worth thinking about," he said. "We could do that. In the meantime, I called my buddy Mike to be sure scum-bucket was where he belonged in L.A., but now that he's gone to that treatment center in Minnesota, you should call the prosecutor's office and check on him."

"Oh," she said, kind of squeamish. "Maybe I could have my lawyer do that?"

"Think about it, Paige," Preacher said. "Take control. You know I'm glad to look out for you, but it's important you get your confidence back. That confidence I know you had before…all this."

Yes, she thought. I did have confidence once. Not as much as some young women, maybe—but enough to carve a little space out of the world for herself. And although it seemed barely noticeable to her, it was coming back, piece by tiny piece. She was going to have to reclaim her former self-assurance, self-trust—she was going to be a single parent to Christopher.

She hadn't thought she could ask for that restraining order or custody; fear had had her in its grip. But with John at her side, encouraging her, she had. It was ugly and terrifying, but she'd gotten through it and Wes had been taken away in handcuffs. He might be in a cushy treatment program right now, but it wasn't over. He had a lot to atone for, and his atonement might come behind bars, freeing her and her son for years. Now that she was on this track—getting free, getting her life back—she was determined to stare it in the face. No matter how scared she was.

She paced back and forth in front of the kitchen phone, then picked it up and called. The next day she paced less, and when she got the A.D.A.'s secretary on the phone, she was told they hadn't checked that day and might not have time—perhaps she could call back the next day. Suddenly, she was furious. "No!" she said. "Do you understand my life and my child's life are in constant danger from this man? That he's threatened to kill me, and if you take a look at my medical records, it's obvious he *tried?* No. I'm not waiting until tomorrow. I'll call back in an hour!" She hung up the phone, heart hammering, and stole a look at Preacher. She could feel the heat on her cheeks.

He lifted one eyebrow and smiled slightly. "There you go," he said.

Her call was returned twenty minutes later by the assistant district attorney himself. He reassured her, then gave her the number of the treatment center and the name of a counselor with whom he'd been in contact, inviting her to call directly, as many times a day as it took.

Again she paced in front of the phone. "What's wrong?" Preacher asked her.

"I don't know. It's like I'm afraid he'll answer or something."

"And what if he did?"

"I'd die!"

"No," he said calmly. "You'd hang up, because you don't have to talk to him ever again. Right?"

"I don't," she said, a little bit surprised by that reality. Her mind started spinning—what if he denied ever having touched her? What if he convinced them he was sorry? She picked up the phone immediately, punching in the numbers, though her brain twisted with possibilities. What if he wanted a message delivered to her? What if he asked to call her, to talk to Christopher? He never talked to Christopher, but she wouldn't put it past him to act as though he cared about his son.

The phone was answered, the counselor she asked for was put on and she said, "This is Paige Lassiter. I'm just calling to be sure Wes Lassiter is still there."

"All tucked in, ma'am," he said, his voice calm and friendly. "Rest easy."

"Thank you," she said weakly.

"You try to have a nice day."

She hung up the phone, trembling for a moment. Then she looked at John and found him smiling. "I know it's hard," he said, his voice soft. "But every day you take your life back a little more. That's how it's done, Paige."

There was a road into Fallujah, Iraq, that held a strong reputation for mortal danger. American troops had fallen there before. When Sergeant Major Jack Sheridan led his platoon in, one of his squads, led by Gunnery Sergeant Miguel—Mike to his friends—Valenzuela, was separated from the platoon by a suicide truck bomb. They were holed up in an abandoned building with injuries, pinned down by sniper fire. Joe Benson and Paul Haggerty were bleeding dangerously, along with others wounded by sniper fire. Gunny held off snipers with an M16 he fired repeatedly for hours until the rest of the platoon—Preacher among them—could subdue the insurgents and effect a rescue. When it was over, Mike could barely move his arm and his shoulder was frozen. He was decorated for his heroic performance.

Mike, an L.A. police sergeant, had been activated for an eighteen-month tour in Iraq. He was never injured. He had saved lives.

And now he lay in an L.A. hospital bed, comatose, with three bullet holes in him. The shots were fired by a fourteen-year-old gangbanger. The one place the kid hadn't hit was square in Mike's bulletproof vest. Another officer got off a fatal shot to the kid. Investigation suggested it might have been an initiation right of passage to get jumped into the gang—and bringing down the sergeant under which the gang unit served was a major feat.

Preacher had called on Mike about Paige, and Mike had done everything he could to help. Now Preacher had received the call.

It was early—the coffee barely brewed, Chris not yet racing downstairs in his pajamas, the loud crack of the ax in the backyard just begun. The shooting had occurred the night before and it took Ramon Valenzuela, Mike's oldest brother, a few hours to get to someone in the old Marine squad. In the meantime, Mike had undergone emergency surgery and lay comatose in an intensive care unit.

Preacher went to the back door of the bar. "Jack!" he called. "Come in!"

Jack had an anxious look on his face when he came through the back kitchen door.

"Valenzuela was shot on the job," Preacher said without preamble. "He's critical. L.A. trauma center. I'll call Zeke, have him pass the word, and close up the bar."

"Jesus," Jack said, rubbing his chin. "What chance they give him?"

"His brother Ramon said he thinks he'll make it—but he's in a coma. He said something about him never being the same." He shook his head. "See if you can catch a flight. I'll make the drive."

Paige appeared at the bottom of the stairs and knew something serious was happening. She stood, waiting.

"What about Paige? Christopher?" Jack asked.

Preacher shrugged. "I'll have to take them. I'm sure as hell not leaving them here without me."

"Take me where?" she asked.

Both men turned to look at her. "L.A.," Preacher said. "One of our boys was shot in the line of duty. He's in intensive care and I have to go."

"L.A.? John, I can't go to L.A."

"Yeah, you can. You have to. My friend Mike, the one who helped you so much, he's in the hospital. Jack?" he said, looking at his best friend. "Go ahead. I'll call Rick's grandma and have her tell him to check on the bar every day."

"Right," Jack said, taking off at once.

Preacher turned back to Paige. "It'll be all right. You'll be safe. You can call that treatment center every day. If you want to, you can go get a few of your things while he's in there. Maybe there's someone you want to visit— you could do that safely. But I have to go." She stared at him, unmoving. "I have to go right away, Paige. I need you to do this with me, so I can go to my friend and be sure you and Chris are safe. Please."

She shook herself. "I'll get us ready," she said, running back up the stairs.

She didn't hear Preacher let out his breath in a long, relieved sigh.

Jack stood on Doc's front porch with Mel, his packed duffel on the bed of his truck. "Reconsider," Jack said. "Come with me. I don't want to leave you here alone."

She put a hand on his chest, looked up at him and said, "I won't be alone. I have a whole town. Nothing is going to happen to me."

"But Preacher won't be here. He's taking Paige and Christopher because he can't leave them. I think he's scared to death to leave them."

"Of course. Jack, Doc needs me. I have things I have to do. And I'll be fine. No one's going to bother me. Here's the name of a doctor to speak to," she told him, tucking a piece of paper into his shirt pocket. "Just tell him you married his old nurse. He'll give you any information he can about Mike."

"You worked with him? When?"

"It's been a while, but he won't have forgotten me. He's a trauma surgeon—he may have operated on Mike. Be sure to tell him the news—that we're having a baby. That'll make him so happy."

"I'll find him." He lowered his lips to hers and kissed her deeply, one hand at the small of her back while the other ran over her expanding middle. "Leaving you is the hardest thing I've done in some time," he said.

"You'd better go. You want to get there as quickly as you can."

Jack drove like mad to Eureka, charging Mel's old cell phone in the truck so that he could use it to call her from the L.A. hospital. He picked up a flight that made only one stop in Redding, getting him to L.A. in less than three hours. Preacher, however, was making the whole drive, which would take eight, maybe closer to ten, hours.

When Jack got to L.A., he didn't even stop at a hotel. Mike was still on the respirator with visitors limited to immediate family for just a few minutes every hour, but the crowd at the hospital was very much what Jack expected—impressive in numbers. Cops were known to gather for one of their fallen and there were dozens, in and around the hospital. They had parked an RV in the parking lot where Mike's family could take occasional breaks from the stress of the hospital and they stood virtual guard around it. Mike had been married twice, but was at present single. There was no shortage of family— a big family of parents, brothers, sisters, nieces, nephews. There was probably an ex-wife around somewhere, and an inevitable girlfriend or two. A couple of their boys from the squad were there, the ones who could get away on short notice—Zeke, a firefighter from Fresno, and Paul Haggerty, a builder from Grants Pass. Others might make an appearance if they could. "Where's Preacher?" they asked.

"He should be here soon. He made the drive. How's Mike doing?"

"We don't know too much. Three hits—one each in the head, shoulder and groin. He lost a lot of blood and hasn't regained consciousness. There was a long surgery."

Jack pulled the piece of paper out of his pocket. "Anyone know the surgeon's name?" he asked.

They looked at one another, shaking their heads.

"Okay, let me look for this guy," Jack said. "An old friend of Mel's. He's a doctor here—might be able to tell us something. I'll be back."

Jack spent the better part of an hour going from nurses'

station to nurses' station, looking for Dr. Sean Wilke, leaving messages for him to no avail. It wasn't until two hours later that a man about forty years old wearing a white coat over scrubs was heading for the ICU and the name embroidered on his coat in blue thread read "Wilke."

"Dr. Wilke," Jack said, stepping forward and stopping him. Jack put out a hand. "Jack Sheridan, Doctor. I'm here for Mike Valenzuela." The doctor seemed cool and distracted, accepting the handshake absently. After all, there were a ton of people here for Mike—the doctor couldn't speak to all of them. "I'm married to Mel Monroe," he blurted.

The man's expression changed instantly and dramatically. "My God," he said, grasping Jack's hand enthusiastically in both of his. "Mel? How is she?"

"Great. She gave me your name. Said you might be able to get me some information about my friend."

"Let me see my patient, then I'll tell you whatever I can. That work for you?"

"You bet," Jack said. "Thanks."

About fifteen minutes later Jack realized he had hit the jackpot when he saw Wilke pausing outside the ICU to have a brief conversation with Mike's mother, father and brother. So—he was the surgeon. After leaving the family so they could go back into ICU, Wilke walked toward Jack. "Come on," he said to Jack. "I've got a little time."

"He's gonna make it, isn't he?"

"I'd give him a ninety-eight percent chance of making it—but we don't know the extent of his potential disabilities." Dr. Wilke took Jack to the employee lounge in the back of a busy emergency room. Wilke poured himself and Jack coffee. Jack took a sip and almost gagged. It was horrible. He wondered if it was possible they got the tap water mixed up with the mop-pail water. "Yeah," Wilke said. "I know. Pretty bad."

"I own a bar and restaurant up north. Our coffee is fantastic, better than Starbucks. I think I hooked Mel with the coffee first—she's a caffeine junky. Tell me about Mike, Dr. Wilke."

"Please, call me Sean. Here's the situation so far. He remains unconscious because of the head wound, although it was really the least traumatic. The bullet, miraculously, doesn't seem to have damaged the brain, but we had to do a craniotomy to remove it, and that has caused swelling, for which a shunt and drain has had to be inserted, and I believe that explains his coma. The bullet to the groin was his worst injury—the most complicated repair. We repaired bowel and bladder and he lost a lot of blood."

"Jesus. He made it through eighteen months in Iraq without a scratch…."

"The shoulder is bad. We're looking at a permanent disability there, I'm almost certain."

"Damn," Jack said, shaking his head. "What about his job?"

Sean shook his head. "I don't see it. His injuries are critical. We're looking at long-term rehab. The shoulder's stitched up real nice, but it's going to be weak. He'd be compromised in defensive tactics."

"But he's tough," Jack said.

"Yeah," he said. "It's keeping him alive."

"Thank you," Jack said. "For everything you've done. For taking the time to tell me—"

"You're welcome." He leaned forward. "I know he's your first concern right now, but I'd love to know how Mel's doing. I haven't heard from her in a long time."

Jack smiled, happy to catch him up on Mel's trek to the mountains, her first inclination to bolt, get the hell out of there. And how all that turned into not only her decision to stay, but remarriage and a baby on the way.

The shock on Wilke's face was evident.

"Yeah, plenty of surprise to go around there. I know she didn't think that was possible. Here she was, a woman who didn't think she could ever be happy again, a midwife who would never have a baby. And I'm almost forty-one, a retired marine who never married. Hell, I was never attached, never intended to be. The day I met her was the best day of my life. A new life for both of us, I guess. She's everything to me."

There was a tablet on the table and Jack pulled it toward him. He reached toward Sean, holding out a hand for his pen, which the doctor took out of his coat pocket.

"You should call her. Don't take my word for it—ask her how she's doing. She'd love to hear from you. She gave me your name—told me to look you up." He scribbled the number on the yellow pad and turned it toward Sean.

After a moment's hesitation, Sean tore the page off, folded it and put it in his pocket.

"Really, give her a call. She'd like that. And one more thing. Any chance you can sneak me into ICU? Mike—he was one of my best guys. He was a fine marine. He saved lives. He was a hero. I love the guy. I do. Lotta people do."

"You bet," Sean said.

Jack sat at Mike's side through the night so that the family could sleep. Mike's head was shaved on one side, tubes and drains everywhere, but probably the hardest thing to see was the respirator breathing for him. Nurses and therapists moved his extremities, but Mike didn't move them himself.

After briefly talking with Mike's family, Preacher took Paige and Jack's duffel and secured a couple of hotel rooms nearby and came back in the morning to give Jack a key. Jack went there to take a nap, but was back by afternoon, and again, spent the whole night at Mike's bedside. Every hour at least he would stand up, lean over the bed and talk to him. "Everyone is here, buddy. Your family, your cops, some of your squad. Everyone's waiting for you to get up. Wake up, buddy."

On the third day, the respirator was removed and Mike opened his eyes, but looked at Jack and his parents blankly. The nurses tried to stimulate him, but he was groggy and listless.

While Jack took his place at his friend's bedside to wait out another long night, Mike's mother put a hand on his shoulder. It was the middle of the night when he turned to look up into her dark eyes. Mrs. Valenzuela was a handsome and strong woman in her sixties; she had raised eight kids and had a passel of grandchildren. When she wasn't in the ICU she was in the chapel worrying the beads; by now the rosary that dangled from her hands should have caused blisters. She hardly slept. "You're a very patient man, aren't you, Jack?"

"Not in this, I'm not," he admitted.

"I know about you. Miguel is not the first young man you've kept vigil for. He said you'd never leave your man— no matter how dangerous staying with him could be."

"He exaggerates," Jack said.

"I don't think so. I'm going to get some rest so I can be alert in the early morning. Thank you for doing this."

"I wouldn't leave this one, Mrs. Valenzuela. He's a good troop."

In the middle of the sixth night, Mike opened his eyes, turned his head and said, "Sarge?"

Jack was on his feet instantly, leaning over the bed. He saw clarity in Mike's eyes. "Yeah, Gunny. Right here. Lotta people here for you, buddy. You have to stay with us now—the hospital staff is ready to throw us all out."

A nurse was instantly at the bedside. "Mike?" she asked. "You know where you are?"

"I just hope I'm not in Iraq," he said weakly.

"You're in the hospital. In intensive care."

"Good. No snipers here."

"Mike, I'm going to call your mother," Jack said. "I'll be nearby."

Jack walked out of the ICU and down to the lounge where family and friends could wait, make phone calls, rest. The Valenzuelas were in the trailer provided by the police department, but there were easily a dozen men passing the night in the lounge, just to be close by. "He's awake. He's recognizing people."

A collective sigh of relief came out of the room. Jack called the trailer to bring Mrs. Valenzuela to her son's bedside, then went back to ICU. By the time he got there, two doctors were examining his friend. One of them was Sean, the other a neurologist.

Sean came around the bed and, his hand on Jack's arm, led him away from Mike. "I haven't called Mel yet, but I'm going to. I just wanted to say something—you've been here every night, through the night, for almost a week. I'm damn glad you decided not to let her be lonely. You're a good man, Jack. A good friend."

"I told you—he's a good guy. He'd do the same for me." He smiled. "As for Mel, when she took me on, she made my life."

While Jack was away Mel had one important errand to occupy her. She picked up Liz at the corner store to make the trip to Grace Valley to see Dr. Stone, the OB. Liz was waiting outside for her. "Are you sure you don't want to invite your aunt Connie along?"

"No, really," she said. "I want to go with just you."

"That's fine. You look very pretty today," she said.

Liz smiled. "Thanks," she said.

It pleased Mel that Liz had gone to some trouble to

look nice today, since she'd be meeting Dr. Stone for the first time. Her hair was shiny clean and curled, her makeup tasteful. She had on those tight jeans with a long sweater pulled down over the belly that wouldn't allow them to close anymore.

"Are you looking forward to this?"

"I think so," she said. "I'm nervous."

"Nothing to worry about—it's completely painless."

When they got to the Grace Valley clinic, Mel realized that the appointment was probably not the only reason behind Liz's primping, and there was definitely another reason Liz didn't invite Aunt Connie. As they pulled up to park, a very familiar little white pickup was waiting across the street. Rick got out of the truck and began to walk toward them. When Liz saw him, she beamed with happiness and ran to him, meeting him halfway. Now, Mel had seen them together since Liz returned to Virgin River—at the bar and around town. They were pretty cautious, especially around Connie and Ron, and Connie and Ron seemed to always be around. Rick would hold her hand, drop an arm over her shoulders, maybe put a mature little kiss on her temple.

But this was different. She ran into his arms. He held her closely, lovingly. She saw Rick in a different light, his arms full of a pregnant girl. Tall, broad, strong, handsome, yet a boy—full of all that seventeen-year-old testosterone.

They embraced and kissed in the middle of the street, kissed like grown-ups. Liz's hands were on his cheeks, pulling him hard against her mouth. Hungry, eating each other's mouths—there was enough passion in their kiss that steam was rising. He held her tight against him, his hands running up and down her back. He slid a hand over her tummy while he talked and smiled against her parted lips. This was no boy, but a man. Man and woman, yet children.

Mel cleared her throat.

They reluctantly parted and walked toward Mel. "Hey, Rick. I didn't know you were coming."

"I had to cut school. I don't think an ultrasound appointment for the father is the usual excused absence. But Liz wanted me here."

"I can understand that." So old. So young. They were kids; it was disconcerting. In fact, their apparent love for each other was somehow more unsettling than getting a poor young girl through something like this alone. These two seemed to want to have this baby together, and what could be more impossible for kids so young?

"Well, let's go in and meet the doctor."

Mel had talked to John Stone, told him about her patient. The exam got under way. Rick took his place beside Liz, holding her hand, like any young husband might. She looked up at him adoringly while his eyes were more fixed on the monitor. John moved the wand over her belly, and on the screen the baby fluttered and kicked. "Oh, man," Rick said. "Man, look at that."

"Can you make it out? Arms here, legs, head, butt. Penis," John said.

Mel hadn't been prepared for this—she watched a slow transformation come over Rick. His eyes grew wide; they began to mist. He gripped Liz's hands tighter and his mouth fixed in a firm line as he struggled for control. It's one thing to see a round tummy and know it's yours, to feel movement there and understand it had life. But it was a whole lot more to see that baby, and know it's your *son.*

"Oh, God," Rick said. Then he lowered his head and his lips touched Liz's brow while she held on to his hands. Then she started to cry and Rick began to whisper to her, "It's okay, Liz. It's okay. It's going to be okay." He kissed her tears away and Mel thought she might cry with them.

Mel had known this boy for quite a while, since her

first night in Virgin River. She was at once amazed by him and felt that she didn't know him at all. When had he crossed over into this other life? What was he doing here, looking at his son on a monitor when he should be in his calculus class?

John finished with the ultrasound, printed them a picture to take with them, then, pulling Mel's hand, led her out of the room, leaving the kids alone for a few moments.

"Whew," Mel said. "I didn't know he was going to be here. I know that boy pretty well, but I never knew him like that. A father. Growing up way too fast."

"Young and dumb, and so in love they make me ache. You think it's too soon for me to get Sydney into the convent?" John asked.

"At eight? Maybe just slightly."

"She's almost six months along. Fifteen years old. Holy shit, huh?"

"Shh, don't let them hear you."

"Mel, they're not going to hear me. In fact, we'd better knock on the door or they'll be doing it again. Right in the exam room."

"They're not doing it, John. Their hearts are breaking. How can there possibly be a happy ending here?"

On the drive home, Mel asked Liz, "Why didn't you tell me Rick was going to meet us there?"

Liz shrugged. "Connie wouldn't like it."

"Why not? He's the father."

"Aunt Connie's pretty mad about this. Mad at me and Rick. And my mom—jeez. She's on the moon, she's so pissed. She doesn't want me to see Rick at all…."

"She sent you back to Virgin River, but doesn't want you to see Rick?" Mel asked, wondering, How does this make any sense?

"I know," Liz said. "Stupid, huh?" She rubbed her hands over her belly. "A boy," she said quietly. Sadly.

Mel stole a glance and saw a tear running down the girl's cheek.

If a woman is old enough to have a baby, Mel found herself thinking, then she's old enough to love what's inside her. Old enough to love the man who put it there.

# *Nine*

While in Los Angeles, Preacher was able to leave Paige and Chris at the hotel for short periods of time while he went to the hospital. He was confident there was no danger to her. Although she still made phone calls to that treatment center regularly, even if Wes somehow slipped away, he had no way of knowing where they were. But whenever he returned, she would sigh audibly, her relief obvious, when he was back, shoring her up. He wasn't quite sure if it was that terror from her marriage or something deeper. There were still some very large holes in his understanding of her. The largest of which was her family.

On the long drive to the city from Virgin River, hours and hours in the truck together while Chris slept on and off in the backseat, there had been lots of time to talk. Paige shared happy and animated stories about the soap-operaish beauty shop in which she had worked, good times in the old half a house she'd shared with her best friends, and she even talked about old boyfriends. She had opened up more about life with Wes, in hushed, careful tones so that Chris wouldn't hear and possibly become upset. But when it came to her widowed mother and older, married brother, she seemed to clam up, grow tense and gloomy. There was deep ambivalence, but she didn't explain. "I haven't had much of a relationship with my family since I married," she said. "And Bud and I were never close, not even as kids."

"Maybe that will change now," he replied. "Listen, you don't want to miss an opportunity. I'd give anything for an hour with my mother. I joined the Marines to get brothers."

"I know," she said. "I know."

"Hey, don't let me talk you into anything. But if you're right here…"

"You might not like my family, John," she said.

"Hey, Paige, I don't have to like 'em. They don't have to like me. I'm just saying, you have a chance to visit now, if you want to."

It was four days before she called her mother, another two before a meeting was arranged. She invited John to take her to her brother's house for dinner with the family; her mother would be there.

Preacher suspected within three minutes what the problem was, but it took him about an hour to put it all together. Fifty-eight minutes too long. He wasn't slow; he hadn't been around too many people like this. A big, silent, loner type of guy like Preacher, when he got a whiff of something *off,* he gave it a wide berth.

Bud, Paige's older brother, met them at the door of a small tract home in a dusty little suburb where there were only about four different styles of homes, very few trees, and where people worked on their cars in driveways. Bud's house had an above-average front lawn, trim and green, right next door to a house with a cyclone fence around a grassless yard. Bud was wearing a T-shirt with his khaki pants, holding a beer. "Hey, hey, hey," he said, coming out onto the stoop and down the sidewalk toward them. "There's my girl. How you been, baby?"

"All right, Bud," she answered, letting him embrace her.

Her arms, Preacher noticed, didn't quite get into the game. Preacher hung back, holding Christopher's hand, watching.

Bud released her and approached Preacher big grin, hand extended. "This the new boyfriend? How you doin'? How about a beer? You look like a beer man to me."

Preacher took the hand; he concentrated on not squeezing too hard. In fact, he wasn't much of a beer man. Nor was he much of a boyfriend. "Thanks," he said. "I'm not the new—"

"Come in. Welcome to the *humble* home."

Preacher caught the inflection. "Nice place," he said, stepping into the living room. He didn't know anything about decor, but it looked comfortable. Spotlessly clean, with a couch and La-Z-Boy recliner and a real big TV. "Nice yard. Bet you work hard on that."

"Nah," he said. "Gin does most of that. She says she likes it, but I think she's competing for first prize in the neighborhood." He didn't greet Christopher. Bud put a hand at the back of Christopher's head and seemed to try to physically direct him through the living room and away. "Kids are in the playroom, Chris. Go play with the kids."

Chris pulled back, clinging to Preacher's leg.

Leaning down, Preacher said, "You can stay here if you want."

Chris said nothing but clung harder.

"Whatever," Bud said. "Come on back. We got snacks, we got steaks. This is nice, sis. Glad you could stop by. Now, what did you say brought you out of hiding?"

Preacher saw her flinch slightly. "John's friend… He's in the hospital. He's a police officer…."

As they moved into the kitchen, an older woman separated herself from the salad she was making and came around the counter. "Paige," she said in a breath. "Oh, Paige…" She was smaller than Paige and very thin. She wore slacks and a blouse, long-sleeved and buttoned high, so conservative that for a split second Preacher was reminded of his own mother.

They embraced, both of them seeming to get a little misty. And Paige responded, "Mom. Mom." This time her arms cooperated in the embrace. The younger woman followed, having waited for her turn. Again, the embraces were mutual. "I'm so glad to see you," she said.

"Dolores, Gin, meet John, the new boyfriend," Bud said.

"I'm not the new—"

"Bud Lite okay by you, pal? I figure a guy named Bud drinks Bud Lite. So what about this friend of yours? In the hospital?"

Preacher accepted the beer and said, "He's a cop around here. He was shot in the line of duty. He was hurt pretty bad—so I came down."

"Hey, did I hear about that on the news, maybe?" Bud asked, giving the neck of Preacher's bottle a tap with his own. An odd time for a toast, Preacher thought.

"Maybe. Probably."

"Yeah, I heard about that, I think. You have a lot of cop friends?" Bud asked, moving to the table. "Chris, go play with the kids. They're in the playroom. So, you have a lot of cop friends?"

"Just the one," Preacher said, a steady hand on Chris's shoulder. It was already beginning to reach him—Paige's brother was a bully. A bossy, immature, irreverent bully. He watched Bud go to the kitchen table, take his seat at the head. In the middle was a bowl of chips and one of salsa. Out the back patio doors he could see a manicured backyard surrounded by a high wall. There was an above-ground hot tub covered with a green leather tarp. A grill, a birdbath, some patio furniture, but no toys. Hadn't Paige said three kids?

Bud indicated a chair with his hand and Preacher took the seat next to him. Bud wasn't a small guy—probably six feet with some good arms on him. His hair was cut really short, the sleeves of his T-shirt rolled up a couple of notches to bring his biceps into focus. His smile was constant, which was a signal—you only smile when something makes you smile. If you smile all the time, you're hiding something. He told Chris once more to go play. Preacher pulled Chris onto his lap.

The women followed like lemmings, sitting at the table with the men. Bud started on the chips and salsa with his beer and said to Paige, "Tell me about this place you're staying."

"Virgin River," she said. "It's in the mountains, way north. It's very pretty—lots of big trees."

"And how'd you end up there?" he asked.

"We were on our way to visit a friend and got lost," she said, her voice just a little quieter than Preacher had grown used to. "Chris had a fever, there was a doctor there, and we stayed over."

Preacher tried not to frown as he listened to Paige give an almost fictional account of what had happened. This story was accurate enough for her new friends in Virgin River, but there was something so wrong about telling it this way to her family, people who knew her intimately. She had to stay a while because of Chris, she said. She fell in love with the place, the people were so nice, they needed some help in the bar and grill, and she thought maybe it was just the change she needed. She decided to see if it worked for her. Bud asked what Wes thought about that and Paige said, "Well, Bud, he wasn't real happy about it— but I had made up my mind." Not real happy? Preacher thought. She and her brother were nibbling around the edges of the real drama. Preacher found himself wondering, Don't they know anything about her life? About the sad and dangerous state of her marriage? About her flight to save her life? To save her children?

One of the kids ran through—a little girl about seven or eight. She had a wild look in her eyes. She grabbed a fistful of chips, her father barked at her to go play and she was gone.

Paige talked a little more about the area, about the redwoods, the people, the simple lifestyle. Bud got up and got two more beers, and when he put one in front of Preacher, Preacher said, "I'm good." But Bud left the beer in front of him.

Chris reached for a chip, tentatively, and Bud said, "Those are for the grown-ups, son." And Chris yanked his hand back as though he'd touched fire. Preacher tried not to glare at Bud, but pulled the bowl closer to himself and Chris and said, "He might be hungry." He took a chip out of the bowl and handed it to Chris and noticed out of the corner of his eye that Paige watched this action with the slightest smile on her face. He also noticed that Dolores and Gin weren't talking much and partaking of the hors d'oeuvres, such as they were, sparingly. Cautiously.

Another kid ran through—another girl—scruffy, her hair wild, her shoes untied. Whatever was going on in the playroom got the kids as gamey as an afternoon outdoors on the playground. She grabbed at the chips, got yelled at to go play and disappeared. Now Preacher might manage a bar and hang out with men primarily, but he was unaccustomed to fathers who pushed their children out of sight. Rudely, at that. In his crowd, families were appreciated. Most of his friends were married with children, and the children were a part of everything. The women were nearly worshiped.

He was starting to know things were not kind and respectful here. He was already unhappy with the way Bud regarded Paige. Preacher was real close to saying, "This meeting is over." Then a child started to cry, from the playroom, presumably, and Bud's wife, Gin, jumped up and ran. A few minutes later she carried a child of about two into the kitchen. This beautiful child had short blond curls and streaks of tears on her chafed cheeks.

Bud turned to Preacher and asked him what he did.

"Me? I'm a cook. My buddy bought a bar. I went up there for some fishing, and stayed."

They talked a little about the bar and Preacher was trying. This guy wasn't his cup of tea, but he didn't have to love everyone. He thought it was a good idea to get along if he could, for Paige's sake. This was family; sometimes you're stuck with family. He was sure good old Bud had his fine points. He wasn't sure he'd come in touch with them tonight, however. But they landed on a conversation about how much fishing and hunting there was to do up there, and Bud loved that. He might just come up, check it out. Bud would do a lot more of that, if he didn't have to work so goddamn hard all the time, but with three kids… Three kids almost never seen, Preacher thought. But, Preacher talked more than he usually did, because he wanted Paige to know he was giving it his best shot. He could be cordial. Friendly.

During this time, Gin, holding her youngest daughter on her lap, cajoled Chris over to her and acquainted them. Chris was not intimidated by a child younger than he and they began to get friendly. The child came off Gin's lap and with a little push of her hands, she sent both children off to the playroom.

"So, what did you do before being a cook?" Bud asked.

"I was in the Marines about twelve years."

"Marines!" Bud said. "Should've known. Ever been to war?"

Preacher gave a solemn nod. "Couple of times," he said. "No fun."

"So, you're the cook," he said, laughing. "Looks more like you should be a bouncer."

"We don't usually need a bouncer."

"Speaking of cooking, how's that salad coming?"

Paige's mother and sister-in-law got up from the table and instantly went to the kitchen. Paige rose, too, asking if she could help, but Bud directed her back to her chair, saying, "They'll do it." And she *sat*.

Plates were brought out—five of them. Preacher counted twice. "What about the kids?" he asked.

"Gin'll give 'em something in the playroom. She's got some dogs, some beans. They love it. Kids. I like to have some grown-up time, sometimes."

The salads appeared, as well as another beer each. "You're slowing down there, my friend," Bud said. "You're going to have to catch up!"

Preacher had his ear tuned in to the "playroom." Just as he was sharpening his listening and they were starting on their salads, Bud looked at Paige and said, "What's going to happen to Wes?"

She lifted her eyes steadily to her brother's, but she didn't answer at once. "I don't know. He's admitted himself into a drug treatment program."

"Why?" Bud asked.

Again she paused. "For drug treatment. It's not unusual for some of those traders to get hooked on… You know… Uppers?" It was stated as a question. And Preacher thought, it was meth. It wasn't a little bitty innocent drug.

"And you couldn't do anything about that?"

"Like what, Bud?" she returned.

"I don't know. Like help him with that. I mean, what did you have to *do?*"

Paige put down her fork and glared into her brother's eyes. "No, Bud. I couldn't help with that. It was completely beyond my control."

Bud tilted his eyes toward his lettuce, stabbed a piece

with his fork and muttered, "Maybe you could've kept your stupid mouth shut."

Preacher's fork went down sharply. And Preacher, who rarely used profanity and only in the most heated moments, said, "You're fucking kidding me, right?"

Bud's eyes snapped up to Preacher's face. His jaw ground and he scowled. "She tell you she had six thousand square feet and a pool?"

Preacher glanced at Paige, Paige glanced at Preacher and then swiveled her eyes slowly to Bud. She spoke to Preacher while she looked at Bud and said, "My brother doesn't understand. The size of the house you live in has nothing to do with anything."

"The hell," Bud said. "I'm just saying, there are times to keep your mouth shut, that's all I'm saying. You had it fucking *made*."

It took every red blood cell in Preacher's body to stay in his chair. He wanted to shout, *He beat her up in the street in front of me! He killed their baby with his foot!* He was squeezing and releasing his fork with such tension, he was unaware he was bending it. It wasn't his right to speak out; he was a guest. He didn't see himself as Bud's guest, he was Paige's guest. He got a sick feeling in his stomach at the thought he could've dropped her here for a visit, alone. He felt his blood pressure going up; his temples were pulsing.

"Bud, he was abusive."

"Jesus Christ, you had a few problems. The guy was *loaded,* for Christ's sake!"

Preacher thought he might explode, his heated blood was expanding so fast. He could hear his own heartbeat. And he felt a small, light hand on top of his coiled fist. He raised his eyes and met the dull, nervous stare of Paige's mother, pleadingly looking at him from across the table.

"Bud doesn't mean exactly that," she said. "It's just that we've never had a divorce in the family. I raised the kids to understand, you have to try to get beyond the problems."

"Everyone has problems," Gin said, nodding. Those same eyes. Begging.

Preacher didn't think he could do it. Sit through it. He was pretty sure he'd never get to the steak without shoving Bud up against the wall and challenging him to keep his mouth shut through something like his fists. The struggle was, that was like Wes. Get mad, take it to the mat. Beat the living shit out of someone. Someone you could beat into submission real easy.

"They weren't *problems*," Paige said insistently. "He was *violent*."

"Aw, Jesus Christ," Bud said, lifting his beer.

A piercing cry came from the playroom. Preacher was on his feet at the same moment Chris came flying into the kitchen, holding his forearm with his other hand. He ran to his mother, with a look of pain and fear, his mouth open in a wail, tears on his face. Paige instantly drew him in, asking, "What's wrong? What's wrong?"

Preacher leaned over, pulled Chris's hand away, saw the perfect outline of a juvenile mouth, and with an expression of sheer horror and disbelief, leveled his gaze at Bud. "Someone *bit* him!"

"Aw, kids. They'll work it out," Bud said, waving his hand, as though leaving them completely unsupervised had nothing to do with him.

Gin said, "I'll get something for that," and jumped up.

Dolores left the table saying, "Ice. I'll get ice."

Preacher gently drew Chris away from Paige and lifted him up against his broad chest. Chris put his head on Preacher's shoulder and cried. He met Paige's eyes and he was sure that despite his greatest effort to remain calm, his were ablaze.

Paige stood, regally, Preacher thought with a touch of pride, and said, "We'll be going now."

"Sit down," Bud said sharply, and Preacher was as close as he'd ever been to coming completely unhinged.

He passed Chris back to his mother as calmly as he could, then leaned both hands on the table, pressed his face close enough to Bud's so that Bud actually leaned back a little bit. Out of the corner of his eye, he saw that Paige had her bag over one shoulder and Chris lying against the other, headed for the front door. "We're going to miss those steaks," he said in a very menacing whisper. Then he picked up the fork he'd been squeezing and saw that it was a little bent. He bent it the rest of the way, folding it in half with one meaty hand. He dropped it on top of Bud's salad. "Don't get up."

By the time Preacher caught up with Paige, she was halfway down the walk toward the truck and already the women were fluttering out the door, calling after her. With no experience at this at all, having never before been in this position, Preacher knew what was going down. They were going to make excuses for Bud, maybe apologize for him, probably beg Paige to come back. He put a soft hand on her shoulder and she stopped, turning toward him. He reached for Chris. "Here," he said, taking the boy tenderly. "Say goodbye. We'll get settled."

He got Chris in the car seat while Paige and the other women were still on the walk. Each one of them took one of Paige's hands, but she pulled out of their clutch.

"Lemme see that arm, buddy," Preacher said to Chris. "Aw, that's going to be all right. Hey, how about pancakes? Breakfast for supper, huh?"

He nodded and sniffed back tears. Preacher wiped a big thumb under each eye. "Yeah, pancakes. And chocolate milk." Chris nodded again, a slight smile on his lips.

Preacher got into the front cab and waited, watching

as Paige finally embraced both the women, then walked quickly to the truck. She got in and he pulled away from the curb before she could even get her belt fastened.

They drove a little then Preacher said, "Chris and me, we're thinking pancakes. And chocolate milk."

She sighed deeply. "I really thought about trying to explain them," she said. "And why I really didn't want to—"

He reached across the console and picked up her hand, holding it, giving it a squeeze. He smiled and shook his head at her. It's okay, he mouthed silently. He didn't let go of her hand. "After pancakes, I'd like to take a swing by the hospital, see if there's any change on Mike."

"Of course," she said.

Another moment of silence, then, "You know, my mother—she was a little like your mother. Skinny, but stronger than she looked. I was six feet by the time I was twelve. I might've been taller than my mother in the fifth grade. But my mother, Church Lady, she had this move— she could reach up and grab the top of my ear and give it a twist. If I swore or spit or showed disrespect, so fast you never saw it coming, she'd wrench that ear and bring me to my knees. She was still taking me down like that the week before she died. I think she learned it from nuns— some of 'em were mean as junkyard dogs. But she made her point." He squeezed her hand. "I don't think your mom ever perfected that move."

Paige laughed lightly.

"Paige, the way you just stood up and left like that, I was awful proud of you. Really, you're stronger than you let on."

She sighed. "I should've stood up and left sooner. I was real close."

"Me, too," he said. "I think maybe we tried too hard with Bud. Both of us. He always act like that?"

"When he's not real quiet and sulky."

"He get along with Wes okay?" Preacher asked.

"Bud thinks Wes is awesome. Because he thinks Wes is rich. Wes thinks Bud's an idiot."

"Hmm." Preacher contemplated. He didn't let go of her hand. "You think Bud really believes it would be all right to get your head bashed in a few times a year for six thousand square feet and a pool?"

"I believe he does," she said. "I really believe he does."

"Hmm. Think he'd like to move into *my* big house—test that theory?"

She laughed. "Do you have a big house somewhere, John?"

"Not at the moment." He shrugged. "But for Bud, I'd be willing to look around."

It had been flowing over Preacher like a steady wave since the very first night she came to Virgin River, and it grew. Being around her gentled him, steadied him. Made him want to be a better man. It also had another, more disquieting effect; when she brushed up against him, when he caught a whiff of her sweet, natural scent, he could almost become aroused.

The three of them had been in each other's constant company for weeks, and his attachment to Chris was strengthening, his affection for Paige deepening by the day. By the hour. When he took her small hand in his, she never pulled it away and he loved that. Sometimes he'd drape an arm over her shoulders, just to let her know he was right there, watching, caring, and she would lean into him a little.

He wanted this to never end.

They shared a hotel room while in Los Angeles—two queens. Preacher in one bed, Paige and her son in the other. Lying in the same room with her was both blissful and painful. He would hear every soft noise, every little snuffle in the bed, and wonder what it might be like to lie beside her, bring her against him. When he would shower after her in the morning, he'd get heady from the smells of her soap, shampoo and lotion.

Mike Valenzuela was sitting up and taking nourishment, though still in pain and a little goofy in the head. There was very little hope of him returning to the police force and his recovery and physical therapy was going to be intense. But with the crisis past, the number of cops sitting constant vigil at the hospital was thinning. Zeke and Paul had gone home; Jack and Preacher were talking about getting back to Virgin River.

At Preacher's urging, and the last step before leaving Los Angeles, was a trip to Paige's house. Right after loading a few things into the truck, they would head north. Christopher was dozing in the backseat of the truck in his car seat, for which Preacher was grateful. He had the passing worry that the boy would want to stay home, not understanding the dangers his father posed.

"I don't think you're prepared for this, John," she said. "It's a lot of house."

"Yeah, so Bud said. It bother you at all, leaving a big fancy house?"

She shook her head. "I'll be quick. There's really not much I want."

They drove through a security gate into an upscale, exclusive neighborhood and Preacher had to keep himself from reacting to the ostentatious setting, but he gulped. The houses within seemed monstrous to him, sitting back on manicured lawns, landscapers at work, cleaning ladies approaching front doors. Paige's house was a big brick two-story with a wide, curving drive and wrought-iron gates. Like a country estate. They must have rattled around in there like marbles in a tin can. It was enormous.

Preacher backed into the drive so that the truck bed was handy for her things. "God, that's amazing," he muttered. "There has to be a part of you that felt, for maybe five minutes, what a big deal that was."

She put a hand on his knee, looked up at him and said, "Not for five minutes. I begged him not to buy that house. He was constantly angry about the cost, the bills, but he had to have it. Do you want to come in? Look around?"

He didn't. He was putting her up in a room above a country bar—a bedroom with no amenities. In a little town with no school. "Nah, I don't need to see any more. I'll wait out here and keep Christopher with me."

When she opened the door with her key and went inside, Preacher leaned against the truck and thought, what must it be like for someone like Wes to lose all this—the woman, the kid, the big, fancy house? Would it ever cross his mind that if he'd treated this with care, it might still be his?

Paige filled four small, soft canvas bags with clothing for herself and Christopher. She packed up some toys and books. As an afterthought, she threw his Big Wheel tricycle in the back of the truck and Preacher drove them out of town. They were a couple of hours out of L.A. when she reached over to Preacher and put her hand over his. "God, that's a relief. I hope I never have to walk in that front door again."

"It's too bad, to have all that and lose it. That's like the American dream. What every man thinks is the perfect life. A family, success, stuff."

"Is that your idea of the big dream, John?"

He laughed. "My idea is a lot smaller."

She stared at his profile for a long moment. Then very quietly she said, "I bet it's not really smaller. But maybe a lot less complicated."

And he thought, not anymore. His idea of the perfect

life, the best he could have in the universe, was sitting right next to him. So close, yet so far out of his reach.

Rick had lived in Virgin River his whole life, had gone to school with the same kids for years, and he enjoyed popularity among his peers. He was a senior, on the home stretch, when his high school experience made a drastic detour. Now, every morning, he was picking up a pregnant girl and taking her to school with him.

Liz was barely recognizable as the girl who had spent a couple of months in Virgin River the year before. In fact, the pregnant sophomore looked younger than the freshman girl in the short skirts and high-heeled boots of the year before. Lizzie had seemed much more worldly then. She was no longer strutting her stuff; she was shy, self-conscious and vulnerable. She was just a little pregnant girl, and totally dependent on Rick.

Rick stayed as close as he could, trying to get her to classes. He couldn't leave her to fend for herself, alone, making her way through the snickering girls, half of whom would've done anything for a date with Rick. Sometimes he was late for class because he'd been getting Liz to hers. His teachers weren't real sympathetic. He didn't pretend this was some fling or second cousin—he straightened his spine and claimed her. His girl and his baby. He wished he didn't have to, but he had to. She had no one else.

It didn't take too long for him to get into a fight. A loudmouthed, dimwitted junior by the name of Jordan Whitley made a crack about Rick "gettin' him some every night" and it just tipped him over the edge. Rick shoved Whitley up against the lockers and slugged him. Whitley got one off on Rick before teachers pulled them apart, so when Rick went to work that afternoon at the bar, he brought a shiner with him.

"What the hell happened to you?" Preacher asked.

"Nothing," he said. "Some asshole had an opinion about my love life."

"That right? And you felt you had to get your face bashed in?" Preacher said.

"No, Preach. I decked him. He never should've gotten up. I guess I didn't hit him hard enough."

"Man. Feeling a little out of control?"

Rick shrugged. Truthfully, he hated that little punk and had secretly wanted to hit him for at least a year. "He has a real mouth on him. Maybe he'll keep it shut now."

As far as his love life went, it was pretty bleak. Oh, it was true, he was having sex.

He couldn't deny that it scratched a certain itch, but it was beyond strange. Liz needed to be touched, to be loved, but the girl who so softly curved to him now was worlds away from the hot little number that squirmed wildly on his lap last year. And not only did these brief sessions often end with her in tears, he could sometimes feel his baby move while he held her, loved her. When she cried, he'd just collect her against him and soothe her, tell her it would be all right, that they'd figure it out. He said that, doubting it constantly.

And here they were, having a baby and expected to act like grown-ups, with Aunt Connie watching them like a hawk, making sure they weren't doing anything adult. The only time he could get with her was by taking a detour on the drive home from school to park for a little while, an action that got him all worked up even as he felt guilty about it. Even with everything that had happened between them, they weren't allowed to lie down on a bed together. God forbid! What if Liz got pregnant or something?

She wanted to run away and get married. Fifteen and seventeen, holy Jesus. And when they'd made this little error in judgment, they'd been only fourteen and sixteen.

It was a real wake-up call. He was holding her back, holding her off, telling her he'd never abandon her, but he didn't think they should do anything as drastic as marriage—it was too soon to make that leap. The leap they'd made was terrifying enough. Most days he thought he had her convinced they should wait at least until they decided what to do about the baby.

Doing the right thing, knowing what the right thing was, just seemed to get more confusing all the time. Around Liz, he tried not to let that show. She was having a hard enough time without Rick letting on that he didn't know what he felt, didn't know what to do.

It was eating him up.

# Ten

On the drive back to Virgin River, Preacher asked Paige a lot of questions about the missing girlfriends, Jeannie and Pat. He asked, "You think they did all right when they got married?"

"They picked up on Wes so easily, I assume they had much more on the ball than I did. I met their families— parents, brothers and sisters. They seemed okay."

When they got back, Preacher got on the Internet. It was quick, but it took him a few days to work up the courage to present his findings. When she came into the kitchen right after putting Chris in bed for a nap, he put down his chopping knife and said, "I… ah… I hope this wasn't out of line. I found them. Your friends." He pulled a slip of paper out of his jeans pocket—their married names, addresses and phone numbers.

Her mouth actually gaped open as she stared at him, her hand hesitatingly reaching for the paper. She stared at it for a moment, then her eyes went from the page to his face to the page, back and forth. He shrugged and said, "I was getting in your personal business again, but I just thought—"

She shrieked his name, threw her arms around his neck

and hugged him so fiercely he took a step back and started to laugh. He put his arms around her and held her off the floor in her excitement. She kissed him on both cheeks, several times, making loud smacking noises. He laughed at her, hanging on, hating the thought of letting her go. He had to put her down too soon. Large, liquid green eyes stared up at him, overcome, and on her lips a phenomenal smile. "How did you do this?" she asked in a breath.

"It was easy," he said. "I need to show you how to work that computer. I can't believe you didn't use a computer before."

She just shook her head and stared at the paper. Wes wouldn't allow her use of his computer; it would have put her in touch with the outside world too much.

"Go on," he said. "Call 'em. Use the phone in my place instead of in here. Have a little time alone with the girlfriends."

She got up on her toes and kissed his cheek again, laying her small hand against the other cheek. She looked at him with such gratitude, it melted his heart. Then she whirled and ran to his apartment, gripping that paper like a lifeline.

"Yeah," he said to himself, under his breath, nodding. "Bet there's lots of little things I can look up for her. Yeah." And he went back to chopping.

Jack came into the kitchen, looked at Preacher and frowned. "What are you grinning about?" he asked.

"I'm not grinning," Preacher said.

"Preacher, I didn't know you had that many teeth."

"Aw, Paige. I looked up something for her, got her all excited. That's all."

"Kind of looks like it got you a little excited, too. I think you're flushed. And Jesus, you sure have a mouthful. You never showed *me* a grin like that."

Yeah, he thought—big mystery. You put your arms

around me and kiss all over me like that, I'll show you a mouthful—of *fist*. But he couldn't stop grinning. He could feel it and couldn't stop it. Jack just shook his head and left the kitchen.

There was another by-product, as if all that affection wasn't enough. Paige had so much to tell him. Pat was still in L.A., working part-time now in a new salon, a real upscale salon, and she had a baby daughter. She even had some celebrities as clients—little celebrities, but her reputation was growing. Jeannie was in Oregon, of all places! And she had her own shop! She'd married a guy twelve years older who'd never been married before. He flew cargo, so he went out on ten-day trips, then was home for at least two weeks. They bought her shop a few years ago and here they were, thirty and forty-two, thinking about a family if she could just get the management of the shop under control.

"She offered me a job, can you believe it?" Paige said excitedly. "She said she'd love to have me there, and would train me as assistant manager."

"Wow," Preacher said. "That must have made you feel pretty good. Think you could do that?"

She laughed and put her hand on his arm. "I have one or two things to get settled before I even think about anything like that," she said.

There were all kinds of details about her old girlfriends' lives, and she didn't seem to leave out even the smallest one. They sat in front of the fire until very late. She said, "I don't know how to thank you. It was so wonderful to talk to them."

"You should talk to them as much as you can. Catch up on things."

"It's long distance, John."

"Aw, that's not a big deal. Call every day if you want. Think you'll get to see them soon?" he asked her.

"Well, Pat's in L.A., and I'm not going back there. The very thought gives me shivers. But maybe when things are resolved a little, I'll check out Jeannie's new husband, new shop."

Paige's attorney had filed divorce papers while Wes was still in treatment, warning her that they might not be able to serve him.

He was as protected as he wanted to be while there. But within a couple of days her lawyer called her to report that the papers had been served, accepted, and the message from Wes was that he had a great deal of remorse and wanted to be cooperative. The only exception to her terms: he wanted at least supervised visits with his son. He hoped to finally be released from treatment with a good report by Thanksgiving.

Paige asked John to use his apartment to place a long-distance call, but this one was not to one of the girl-friends. She told Brie what she'd learned.

"I don't trust this for a second," Paige said.

"You shouldn't. Here are some facts—we have no idea how he's doing in treatment. There's no way to find out if he's committed to recovery or one of their problem children. Also, if I were his lawyer, I'd advise him to be repentant, cooperative, ashamed and docile. I'd tell him if he could cry at his trial and blame the drugs for every-thing, it would go down a lot better than getting his back up about how bad he's getting screwed by the woman he knocked into the middle of next week."

"Lovely," Paige said.

"Lawyers aren't all bad. Advice like that often puts the defendant in that mind-set—he has to change his awful ways, be sorry, be nice. It doesn't always work that way, but often. He can't get what he wants if he has an attitude with the court. And we might not know what's happen-ing with him in treatment, but him not getting released with a good report after thirty days is an indication he hasn't exactly given himself over to the gospel. Two months isn't bad. He hasn't screwed himself up yet."

"But it's his third battery offense," Paige said. "It's automatic prison. Right?"

"Aah," Brie began. "Sentencing requirements vary. He can be charged, tried and convicted, and his sentence can still be less than you're hoping for. He's got a good lawyer. It could be light—short time, lots of probation. It's still a sentence, still a conviction. The judge has the power of discretion as long as he's within the law. My advice? Deny the visitation and go after this divorce like a bulldog. If he really does clean up, he can revisit the custody issue when he's proved himself. That'll take years.

"Meanwhile," Brie said, "watch your back. Stay alert. Remember who this guy is. You know him better than anyone."

"Oh, Jesus, is he going to get out of treatment and show up here again?" Paige said in near panic.

"He could. But my guess is, he's going to honor the conditions of his bail to stay out of jail, go with this trial and try to get out of the felony convictions. Or at least plead them down. Freedom, Paige—that's the big carrot right now. And the trial can come soon, maybe early in the new year."

"I'll be completely gray by then," she answered.

Paige brooded a little bit, hoping it didn't show too much. Strangely, it wasn't Wes or the divorce that occupied her thoughts, but John. November came in rainy and cold and she'd been in Virgin River more than two months. There were times she could become lost in the present moment—oddly satisfied with the day-to-day simplicity of her life, content to work alongside him in the kitchen. They were in sync, and it wasn't rehearsed;

he would chop the scallions, she would scrape them into the bowl. He would shred the cheese, she would clean the grater. She'd beat the eggs, he'd make the omelet. He'd mix the dough, she'd roll the piecrust. She loved watching John—his movements so slow and steady, confident. And to talk with him in the evening after closing, even for a while, was like a reward. The sound of his voice as he read to her son, kind of raspy and soft, comforted her as much as it did Chris.

She found herself wondering what it would feel like to be enfolded in those big arms, to feel his lips on her neck. She couldn't remember last feeling desire. She would have thought that being in his company for so many continuous hours each day, at least some minor faults would be revealed, but she couldn't find one. He could be so sweet and tender with her, but then at other times—like when they were with her family in L.A.—he was every bit her champion. Now and then she'd ask herself, was she turning a blind eye to his true character? Was he somehow fooling her, reeling her in? But no— there wasn't an unchivalrous bone in his body. And it wasn't just her opinion—his closest friends and the entire town trusted him implicitly.

She was falling in love with him. She couldn't remember being in love. The delusion of love she'd experienced in the early days with Wes didn't even come to mind.

Sometimes she asked herself if she should brave rejection and tell him. *I want to stay right here with you forever.* But she was terrified that he'd get a stricken look on his face and explain, in his patient and direct way, that he thought of her as a good friend, that he was just doing the right thing.

After Chris's bath in the evening, she went down to the kitchen and said, "John, did you want to read tonight, or should I go ahead?"

"I'll do it," he said. "I look forward to it. Is he ready?"

"Squeaky-clean," she said.

When John went upstairs, she went into the bar to find Jack wiping down the bar, putting up his glasses for the next day. As she entered, the last two customers went out, giving Jack a wave and thank-you as they left.

"Preacher reading?" Jack asked.

"Yup. If you want to take off, I'll keep an eye on things. He'll be down in a few minutes."

"Thanks. You feel okay with that? Down here by yourself?"

She smiled at him. "I'll lock the door. How long do you think it would take John to get downstairs if I yelled?"

"I guess you're in good hands. It's wet out there tonight. I sent Rick home a half hour ago."

"Go visit with your wife," she invited.

She stayed in the bar and it wasn't long before John joined her there. "He was asleep before we finished. I guess he was just knocked out." He took down a glass. "Feel like something tonight?"

"No, thanks."

"You're a little quiet. Have been the last couple of days," he said.

She leaned her elbow on the bar, her chin in her hand. "I've been thinking a lot. I'm going to be divorced soon. That's eerie. Though I have no idea what's coming next."

He poured himself his nighttime drink. "I have something that might perk you up," he said. "Sit tight." He went back to his apartment and was quickly back with a long white envelope. He handed it to her. "I took a chance on this. If it doesn't work out for you, no big deal."

She opened it up and found two round-trip plane tickets to Portland. "What's this?"

"You've got a lot on your mind," he said. "I figured you

were probably worrying about what's ahead for you. Might be a good time to visit that old girlfriend—check on that beauty shop of hers. Just in case…"

"In case?"

"In case you decide to get back to that kind of work.…"

She put the envelope on the bar. When she said she didn't know what was coming next, she had meant from Wes. Not what she would do, where she would go. She was right where she wanted to be. "John, tell me the truth—are you about ready for me and Chris to move on? The truth, John."

His expression was stunned. "No!" he said emphatically. "I didn't get you the tickets because I want you to leave. Hey, they're round trip! I just thought—I know you miss her. And I know that eventually…" His voice trailed off, incomplete.

She bit her lower lip and looked up at his face. "I should know what you're thinking. What does *eventually* mean to you?"

"Paige, I don't kid myself. I know you can't be happy here for long. I mean, once you get your life back, get on your feet…"

*Tell him,* she challenged herself. *Tell him the only thing in the world that would make you happy is to be here forever!* "Right now I can't think of anything I'd rather do."

"That's why I got you the tickets, for you and Chris. For a visit. You should have options. I didn't call her and ask, by the way. And it's over the Thanksgiving holiday, so I got them refundable. If you have to change dates…"

She thought for a second. "Maybe I will have something to drink. How about a little red wine? You have something open back there?"

He looked under the bar and pulled out a bottle of cabernet, showing it to her. She nodded and he poured.

After a sip, she picked up the envelope again. "This was very nice of you. Very expensive of you."

"Think of it as a Christmas present, if you want. Has Chris ever been on an airplane?"

She shook her head. "What if I go to Portland and love everything? How would you feel about that?"

He smiled sweetly, then leaned across the bar and pressed his lips against her forehead. "Nobody I know deserves to be happy more than you," he said, his voice soft.

Preacher wanted her to be free to choose, that's why he'd done it. He wasn't stupid, he could tell she enjoyed herself in his kitchen, in this little town. It made her feel safe and protected, her son was happy. But she should know if there was something better for her. He didn't want her to stay because it was the path of least resistance—it had to be her ultimate desire.

If she left, he was going to lose his mind. If she stayed, he was going to lose his mind.

She hemmed and hawed about the trip, but in the end she went. She drove herself over to Eureka, left her car at the airport and flew with Chris to her friend. She called when she got there, called a couple of days later to say the city was lovely and Jeannie's shop was great. They had a dog, a big, friendly Lab, and Chris was in love.

Preacher concentrated on planning Thanksgiving dinner, a custom at the bar. He was grateful to have a big cooking job ahead to take his mind off things. He was making his lists, getting out his recipes. And he stopped shaving his head the day she left. Within four days a cap of short black hair covered his dome.

"What's going on with this?" Mel laughed, reaching up and rubbing a hand over his bristly, dark head.

"Head's cold," he said.

"I like it. Do you grow it in every winter?"

"Head hasn't been this cold on other winters," he said.

And he hadn't been infatuated with a woman who had cut hair for a living other winters, either.

"Have you told Paige you have hair on your head?"

"Why would I do that?" he asked her.

She shrugged. "I guess things that pass as news to women are not quite as interesting to men," she said. "Have you heard from her this week?" she asked.

"She called. She says they're having a nice visit. Her friend has a dog and Chris is crazy about the dog." He wiped down the counter. "You think a dog would get in the way around here?"

She laughed at him. "Preacher, what's that matter? You just miss them so much?"

"Nah, it's all good," he said. "Paige hasn't seen her friend in years."

"He's killing me," Mel told Jack. "Look at him—he's miserable. He's so in love with her he can't think. But will he say anything? To anyone? And seeing him without that little blond angel riding his shoulders is kind of like seeing him with an amputation. He needs to call her—tell her he misses her."

Jack lifted an eyebrow and peered at his wife. "You don't want to get into that," he said. "He might try to break your jaw."

At night, after Jack had gone home and the last customer of the night had left, Preacher went up to Paige's bedroom above the bar and went inside. That she had left so many of her things behind, including Christopher's toys, did not encourage him. He couldn't believe she'd come back here. To him. If she returned at all, it would probably only be for her things. He didn't think he had anything to offer her beyond a safe harbor. Probably Jeannie and her husband could give her that, and more.

Her nightie was tossed on her bed and he lifted it to his nose. He inhaled the fresh scent of her. It brought tears to his eyes.

*  *  *

A major cooking event always helped Preacher take his mind off things. It would be just a small Virgin River crowd—but not a small meal. Besides Jack, Mel and Doc, there would be Hope McCrea, Connie and Ron and Liz, Rick and his grandmother, Lydie, Joy and Bruce.

On Thanksgiving Day Mel and Jack were at the bar by noon to help with the cooking. Mel rolled dough for Preacher's pies and peeled potatoes while Jack cleaned up cooking pots. They talked about Christmas with his family in Sacramento, about next Christmas with a baby. Preacher was silent, doing his work. He had his recipe books propped up, stuffed a twenty-five-pound bird, whipped cream, filled pie shells and put them in the oven, all the while glum. When he went into the bar to put out plates and utensils, Jack said, "What's up with Preacher? He coming down with something?"

"Yeah, he's coming down with something!" Mel whispered back. "Paige and Chris, that's what. It's like he thinks she's never coming back."

"She's due back Monday, right?"

"Of course! He bought her the tickets, told her to go, and it's killing him. He looks so handsome with hair, I wish she could see him. He did it for her, I'm sure of it. Who knew there was more to his face than that big, bald head and bushy brows?"

Since Preacher was never a force of personality, his dour mood was only noticed by his best friends. When people started to arrive for dinner, the tables were pushed together into a long one, places set, and Jack started setting up drinks and glasses of wine. Preacher brought out a couple of trays of hors d'oeuvres, put the bread in the warmer and had the turkey out of the oven to sit a minute before carving. Great smells filled the bar and the fire in the hearth was bright and cozy.

Preacher found himself wishing this were over with so he could be alone. He looked forward to everyone leaving; he'd take his time with the cleanup, have a shot of whiskey and go to bed. Hopefully he would sleep.

It was minutes before five, about time to carve, when the door to the bar opened, and there, in the frame, stood Paige. She held Christopher's hand and looked into the room, scanning the faces until she found Preacher. When she spotted him behind the bar, her eyes lit up so much, they glittered. As for that big man, shock settled over his features; his mouth actually gaped, obviously shocked.

There might as well have been no one else in the room. As she walked toward the bar, he came around it. "I'm sorry I didn't get here in time to help," she said.

Preacher stooped to pick up Christopher, who put his arms around his neck first, then rubbed his head. "You din't shabe it," he said.

Preacher kissed the little boy on the cheek. "My head was cold," he said.

Paige wrapped her arms around his waist and, looking up at him, said, "I hope you have room for two more."

"What are you doing here?" he asked softly.

She shrugged. "I changed the tickets. I wanted to be here. With you. I hope you missed me a little bit."

"A little bit," he said. And then he smiled and put an arm around her shoulders and pulled her close.


The Thanksgiving party broke up a little earlier than planned, everyone in the room being aware of the hot gazes that Paige was sending Preacher and Preacher was clearly receiving even if he didn't seem to be successfully interpreting them. The women all helped with the dishes, quickly, so that the couple could finally be alone.

"Maybe they had some kind of fight before she left,"

Mel suggested to Jack. "Do you have any idea what's going on with them?"

"Before or now?"

"Before," she said.

"None whatsoever."

"And now?"

"Right now I bet that old bar is shaking so hard it's about to come off its moorings."

When the last of the dishes were put up, the floor swept, the Open sign turned off and the door latched, Preacher trudged slowly up the stairs to his old room. When he got there he found Christopher was jumping on the bed while beside it Paige stood holding his pajama top, trying to get him to settle down after his bath. She threw a look over her shoulder with a wan smile that said she was coming to the end of her rope. After all, she'd been trapped in the plane and car with him much of the day.

"Okay, cowboy," Preacher said, coming forward. He took the top out of Paige's hands and held it for the boy. Christopher slipped his arms in and turned around so that Preacher could snap it up the back. "That a boy," he said.

Paige put a hand on Preacher's forearm and said, "Please tuck in the cowboy and I'll meet you downstairs."

Christopher lunged at Preacher, jumping on him, arms around his neck and legs around his waist, hugging him tight. "Wanna kiss Mommy good-night?" Preacher asked.

Christopher leaned around Preacher a little, puckering, but didn't let go. He got his kiss and Paige left them alone. "In you go," Preacher said.

"Read," he said.

"Aw, c'mon. It's been a long day."

"Read," he said. "One page."

"Okay, one page." Preacher sat on the bed beside him

and accepted the book. He read three pages. "Now you have to settle down."

He started whining and wiggling around.

"Did someone give you sugar?" Preacher asked him. "Get into bed. Enough of this." He tucked the covers around him and kissed his head. "See you happy in the morning."

"G'night," Christopher said, snuggling down in the bed.

When Preacher got downstairs he found Paige in the bar, at the table by the fire, and she had poured him a shot and herself a glass of wine. A new log had been added, an unspoken signal they would sit there together for a while. Her silky, light-brown hair caught a shine off the flame; her cheeks were pink and her curved lips soft and inviting. An ache of longing he couldn't suppress spread through him.

"I poured your shot. And helped myself."

"Thanks," he said. "He's a little wound up tonight. I asked him if anyone gave him sugar and then realized, it was me. Pie and ice cream, two helpings. And I think he had a cola, too."

"Well, he's exhausted, so as soon as he detoxes, he should be out like a light. It was a wonderful dinner, John. I think you outdid yourself."

"I wasn't expecting you to come back early." He pulled out the chair and sat down with her. "Did something happen?"

She shook her head. "It was a fantastic visit. Jeannie's husband is a great guy, great with Chris. She's working like a dog in that shop of hers, but it's going to be successful and she's so proud of herself. Thank you again for doing that."

"You missed her," he said.

"And guess what?" she said, smiling. "After a few days, I missed you. I missed Mel and Jack, some of the others." She laughed. "I missed the kitchen."

"Did she offer you that job?" he asked tentatively.

"She did. I told her I'd keep it in mind, but I didn't think I'd end up doing that."

He was pretty sure he hadn't heard right. "You have a better idea?" he asked.

She lifted one eyebrow. "You think a string of shops would make it in Virgin River?" she asked him. "Right now, I'm fine. Chris is fine. I've asked you before and I'm trusting you, John, to tell me the truth—you say it's okay I'm here. And when it's not really what's good for you, for the bar, I hope you'll tell me."

"Paige, I wouldn't lie to you. Have I ever lied to you?"

She laughed. "No, not really. But you have been known to delay the information."

"Aw, not so much," he said. "Paige, does he—does Christopher ask about him? His dad?"

She shook her head. "He asked about his Big Wheel." She looked down. "I'm really worried about something, John. Between my brother, who is a copy of my scrappy dad, and Wes, I'm afraid Chris could get cursed with some nasty DNA thing that causes him to be angry, to hit, to hurt people. I'm really scared about it. Maybe you could look it up?"

"I could," he said. "But I think you can see, he's sweet and happy every day. It's probably a good idea to keep an eye on that, though. I would." He took a small sip of his drink. "Wes," he said. "Does he have people somewhere? Family?"

"No one," she said. "He grew up real rough. Foster homes, group homes. A lot of bouncing around." She laughed ruefully. "I thought it was pretty admirable that someone who came up hard made something of himself. I was looking at the outside, ignoring the inside. He didn't come through it—he brought it with him."

He was silent, thinking. "I served with a guy who grew

up in foster homes," he finally said. "Had a really hard time as a kid. Sweetest guy you ever met. His childhood made him want a nicer life. You can never tell about that. Which way it's gonna go. You just have to try your hardest to raise him right." He grinned at her suddenly. "I can show you that ear-twist of my mom's…."

Paige smiled at him, sipped her wine. She'd had a lot of late-night talks with Jeannie about John, about Virgin River. Jeannie put in real long days at her shop and Paige had tried to help out by cleaning up the house and starting dinner. But her old best friend, though she may have been tired, sat up and listened to the saga of meeting John, of John's confrontation with Wes, of visiting her family in L.A. and John holding up to them—holding her up. John and Chris. Jeannie saw the bear with the blue-and-gray flannel leg. She had stroked it and said, "Oh, God. I've never known a guy who does something like this. This is amazing."

"It's one of the first things that convinced me to stay. The way he is with Chris."

"That's really awesome," Jeannie said. "But you can't stay there forever because of how he is with your child, you know."

"That isn't all there is," she said softly. "It's how he is with me. But he's so quiet. So…reluctant. I don't know if he's just shy or if he's a big Boy Scout, doing the right thing and counting the days till I leave and he's free of this obligation…."

Jeannie had laughed and said, "Make him tell you."

"Huh?"

"You've completely forgotten how to flirt. No surprise. Let him know you want to be there. You love it there, and he's the biggest draw. Let him know he makes you feel wonderful. Be coy but get him the message—you're a girl ready for a guy like him. If you flirt with him a little and he's not interested, he's going to set you straight eventually.

If he's really shy, you don't want to confront him and scare him off. So, what have you got to do in the meantime?"

Paige said to John, "You're sure it's okay that we're still here? I mean, with the holidays coming…"

"I don't know what I'd do without you here," he said.

"That's good," she said. She took a final sip of her wine, stood and kissed his forehead. She let her lips linger there. "This is the only place I want to be. By the way, the hair is sexy. Very sexy."

With that, she went through the kitchen and up the back stairs to her room. And he thought, I'm going to pass out.

Late in the year the salmon and sturgeon fishing on the Virgin was at a peak, and fishermen came in droves to the river, which meant the bar had plenty of visitors. Many of those who traveled to this part of the world had been here before and had at least a passing acquaintance with Jack and Preacher. But they met with delight the new face on the scene.

Paige was alive with happiness. She delivered drinks and meals, bussed tables, laughed with the patrons and, it did not go at all unnoticed, threw adoring looks at Preacher when they were both in the same room at the same time.

The conversation in the bar always seemed to center around the size of the catch, the conditions on the river, the weather. But something that also came up was Preacher's apparent catch.

A couple of fishermen were seated at the bar where Jack served when Paige took a tray of dirty dishes back to the kitchen. "This place gets better-looking all the time," one of them commented to Jack. "Business is bound to pick up on account of the new help. Where'd Preacher find this young beauty?"

"I think she found him," Jack said, lifting his coffee cup.

"Shouldn't he be smiling a lot more?"

"You know Preach—he doesn't like to show too much emotion."

As for Paige, she thought John was responding to her, in small ways. He certainly wasn't pushing her away, and she took that as encouragement. Lips touched cheeks and brows more often; there was the occasional embrace. The best part of her day, her life, was that time after the last patron left the bar and John flipped off the Open sign. Christopher was bathed, dishes were done, bedtime story was read, then she and John would spend their private time together. Talking in soft tones in front of a late-night fire. He had begun giving her a very brief kiss on the lips as she headed toward the stairs and he to his room in the back of the grill.

He was the best thing that had ever happened to her. Soon, she hoped, he would realize that what she felt for him was not just gratitude.

Jack had been watching Rick closely. He hadn't expected him to be carefree, but the boy's troubled frown seemed to grow deeper and Jack was determined he wasn't going to let Rick be swallowed up by this, his one mistake.

"You look like a man who needs to go fishing," Jack said.

"I need to work," Rick returned.

"I'm a really good boss," Jack said, grinning. "I'm willing to keep you on the clock if you're willing to talk about it."

"You'll be sorry," he said. "I'm such a mess, a world-class psychiatrist couldn't straighten me out."

"Good thing you have me, then," Jack said. "Get your gear."

It was their way that they didn't broach the subject right off. They drove out to the river, got into their waders and began casting. There were a lot of fishermen this time of year, but that wasn't a problem; they simply staked out their own little piece of river where they could quietly talk without being overheard above the rushing water. After a little while, a little casting, Jack said, "Lay it on me, pal. What's eating you?"

"I don't think I can do it, Jack. I can't give up my son."

"Whoa," Jack said. He hadn't prepared himself for that, but probably he should have. Where was Mel when he needed her? "What are you going to do?"

"I don't have a freaking clue," Rick said. "I saw him on the ultrasound, kicking around in there. I saw his *penis*. My *son*. I can't have someone else raising him. Not when I made him. I'd worry all the time. You know?"

It was not as though Jack had a hard time understanding those feelings. "I've heard of adoptions where you can stay in touch, stay involved."

"I don't know if that'll do it for me," Rick said. "I know this is crazy…"

"What does Liz say?"

He laughed, but it was a hollow sound. "She wants to quit school right now. Run away and get married. You have any idea how awful school is for her?"

Jack suddenly felt pretty stupid—of all the things he could focus on, be aware of, it had never occurred to him how terrible it might be for a fifteen-year-old pregnant girl to attend school every day. And since she'd only been in that school a couple of months the spring before, it was practically a new school for her at that. She might as well have a tattoo on her forehead. "Aw, Rick," he said. "I'm so sorry to hear that."

"I try to be there for her after every class, get her to the next class. I'm late a lot. I'm getting in trouble a lot. It sucks so much." He sighed deeply. "Lizzie is so young. She didn't seem that young before. Before we got into this mess. She was… I couldn't keep my freaking hands off her, she was so hot. She was that way with me, too. She seemed so…experienced. But she wasn't, you know? There wasn't anyone before me and there hasn't been anyone after. And now she's just this scared little girl who would give anything not to have these problems." He took a breath. "She needs me so much."

"Jeez," Jack said. "I'm sorry, Rick. My mind has been on so many other things, I never thought—"

"Hey, it's not your problem, okay? It's my problem. If I'd listened to you in the first place…"

"Don't kick yourself. You're not the first guy to have one occasion of unprotected sex. But guaranteed you're among a very select number to get a girl pregnant on that first and only shot. We're a small fraternity, for sure."

"This happened to you?" Rick said, amazed.

"Yeah. Sure did."

"How old were you?"

Jack turned and met Rick's eyes. "Forty."

"Mel?" he said, astonished.

"Between you and me, right?" Jack said. "I don't know how Mel feels about me talking about it. But yeah, near as we can figure out—first strike. Difference is, I'm an old man, and not sorry. I wouldn't have it any other way. In my case, I really did get lucky."

"Shew. I guess if a midwife can screw up, I shouldn't be so embarrassed."

"My screwup, bud. All my adult life, that condom's been automatic," Jack said. "Not just because of the pregnancy issue, but because you don't want to expose a woman to anything. If a woman's willing to share her body with you, you don't want to take a chance of giving her some STD you don't even know you have. And you don't want to be exposed. I lost my head. I didn't protect her. If I weren't so grateful for the baby, I'd feel bad about that. But hell, that stuff happens to people, pal. At least we're old enough to take it on—

and want to take it on. But you? Damn, buddy—you kids sure got hit hard. I can't imagine how rough this is for you. Both of you."

"My life is so weird right now," Rick said. "I'm in high school, and I'm sneaking around to be alone with the girl who's got my baby in her. And it's not like it's a punishment, being alone with her, you know? But I'm not even doing it for me—she's the one who needs attention. I can't refuse to touch her when she needs to be touched, not when she's going through this. Can I?"

"She'd think you didn't care about her," Jack said.

Rick's voice grew quiet. "Sometimes she just cries. We do it…I want it to be nice for her, hold her, keep her safe, and when it's over, she cries and cries. And I don't know what more to do."

I think I might cry, Jack thought. "I think it has to be up to her," he said. "Not what you want—what she wants."

"That's what I think, too. Maybe I should just do it. Talk to my grandma about letting Liz move in with us, into my bedroom. Marry her or something."

"I think you need somebody's permission for that."

He shook his head, laughing. "We're having a freaking baby! In less than three months!"

"Well…"

"They want her to give him up. No discussion. It's best for him, everyone is saying. Even if they can convince her, I don't think they can convince me. Do you have any idea how hard it is to keep my mouth shut right now?"

"Oh, man…" Jack was wishing about twenty things at that moment. Top on his list—he wished Rick was his son, so he could step in and help handle things. He understood they were too young to have a baby together, but it was going to happen anyway, and Rick shouldn't be marrying anyone at seventeen. Still, that baby shouldn't go away from its mother and father. And how could they do otherwise, at their tender ages? "You're the father. Aren't there papers you have to sign to let him go?"

"I don't know. What the hell do I know?"

"You should talk to Mel," he said. "Seriously—this discussion is for you and Mel. She does babies, I do other things."

"Jack," he said, "there's a part of me that is so sorry I crossed that line like I did and set this up for us, for me and Liz. What a disaster. But there's another part that saw that little guy on the ultrasound and just wants to hold him. Show him how to catch a ball…" Then he shook his head. "No matter how much talking people do, there's no way anyone can get you ready for what happens to your life when you don't get that condom out of your pocket."

"Yeah," Jack said.

"Jack, I'm sorry. I let you down."

"Nah. I don't feel let down. I feel really bad for you, but not disappointed in you. You've done pretty good with this, all things considered. Now we have to figure out a way for you to get your life back, both of you, before it gets even worse."

"No matter what you come up with, Jack, I'm never getting that life back. And neither is Liz."

As Jack came out of the kitchen into the bar, there was a man seated at the end. He wore a western hat, a shady brady, and as Jack entered the bar he lifted his dark eyes. It took Jack less than five seconds to recognize him as a man who'd been in his bar a few months ago and tried to pay for his boiler-maker with a hundred-dollar bill peeled off a thick wad of bills, all of which carried the skunklike odor of green marijuana. Jack wouldn't take his money.

If that alone wasn't enough to give Jack a bad feeling about the man, he was also the one who had lain in wait for Mel at her cabin to take her out to some hidden grow back in the hills where a woman was giving birth. For that, Jack felt an urge to go a few rounds with him to be sure he knew better than to ever try that again. Instead, he wiped down the bar in front of him. "Heineken and Beam, isn't it?"

"Good memory," the man said.

"I remember important things. I don't want to get in the habit of comping you drinks."

The man reached into his back pocket and pulled out a thin leather wallet and withdrew a twenty, laying it on the bar. "Freshly laundered for my fussy friend," he said.

Jack set him up his drinks. "How you getting around these days?" he asked. The man's eyes lifted swiftly to Jack's face. "I came across your Range Rover," Jack said. "Off the road, down the side of the hill. Totaled. I told the deputy where."

The man threw back his shot. "Yeah," he said. "My bad. I didn't make that turn. Must have been going too fast. Got a good deal on a used truck." He lifted his beer, took a long pull. "That everything?" he asked, indicating he'd rather not have a conversation.

"Not quite," Jack said. "There was a birth back in a trailer somewhere…."

The man put down his beer rather sharply, glaring at Jack. "So much for medical confidentiality."

"The midwife is *my* wife. That can't happen. We straight on that?"

The man's eyes widened in surprise, his hand tightening around his cold beer.

"That's right, cowboy. She's my wife. So. Are we clear? I don't want her taking those kinds of chances."

He made a lopsided smile. He lifted his beer and took another pull. "I doubt I'll ever find myself in that spot again." Jack stared, hard, into the man's eyes. "She wasn't at risk, but you're right. She probably shouldn't do that."

After a moment of quiet, Jack said, "Clear River might be a better place for a drink."

The man pushed the shot glass across the bar. "Quieter, anyway."

Jack served him up again, then took the twenty to change it, indicating the man was done here. Then Jack went to his own end of the bar and busied himself wiping it down, straightening glassware and bottles. He lifted his head as he heard the stool scrape back. The man stood, turned and walked slowly out of the bar without looking at Jack. A glance showed Jack he hadn't left any money behind and, in spite of himself, he chuckled under his breath.

Then he went to the window to see what kind of truck it was. So—he'd lowered his standards a little. A dark Ford, jacked up, lights up top, tinted windows. He memorized the license plate, but knew that wouldn't matter.

It was only a minute before the door opened again and in came Mel. Her jacket stood open and her belly protruded slightly. She wore an odd expression.

"You see that guy, Mel?" Jack asked her. She nodded. "Did he say anything to you?"

She got up on a stool. "Uh-huh. He gave me a long up and down look and said congratulations."

"You didn't talk to him, I hope."

"I asked him how that baby was. And he said, they have everything they need."

"Aw, Mel…"

"That man never scared me, Jack. There might be lots of scary people out there, in those hidden grows, but something tells me he's not one of them."

# *Eleven*

After two weeks in the hospital, two weeks in a rehab facility and two weeks with his mother, Mike Valenzuela was stir-crazy. He was still crippled in one arm and totally out of his mind with cabin fever. Not to mention shook up by how long it had taken for his mind to come back. Nothing scared him quite as much as memory loss and not being able to find the right word, or looking at the right word and thinking it was wrong.

Physically, he was getting by, but there was pain. Most of it was in his shoulder, arm, neck and scapula, and at night it could get so fierce he couldn't sleep, couldn't move. At those times, he could barely get out of bed, and the only thing that worked was a big ice pack and a pain-killer. The other pain was still stiffness and weakness in the groin area, and that kept getting better, but he was using a cane for left-sided weakness when he walked.

When he looked in the mirror he saw a thin and wasted body where a toned and muscled one had been. A man stooped slightly because straightening hurt his groin, his abdomen. His right arm was bent at the elbow and held protectively against his midsection, the hand curled inward and too stiff and weak to open all the way. A head of thick black Mexican-American hair that had been shaved on one side of his head to remove a bullet was barely growing back. A man who, at thirty-six years of age, was retired from the police department with a one-hundred-percent disability. A man staying in his mother's house because he'd given houses to two ex-wives and given up his rented apartment when he was shot.

There was another little matter. Something that didn't show—it was still hard to pee and he hadn't seen an erection in a long time. And what came to mind was, I pissed away my life and here I am, hardly able to piss.

Mike had been into living hard, living on the edge. The fighting Marines, the police department. Women. Lots of guy stuff—lifting, sports, poker, hunting, fishing. More women. Life in the moment. Fun, fun, fun. Ah. Instant gratification. He'd married twice because he was in the mood, married women he wasn't really committed to, obviously. And he had pursued too many others. That was certainly not going to be an issue now. Maybe you get only so many erections, and I had all of mine, he thought.

Driving a long distance wasn't advisable, but he managed. The right leg was good, the left arm worked fine. The doctors disapproved; they had ideas about further rehab and treatment, but he was a stubborn man and desperate to get away from it all. He threw the stuff he needed in the back of his Jeep SUV and headed north. "Stay as long as you want," Jack had said. "You'll have to stay with us, though. Preacher's filled up the spare room in the bar. You might remember the woman—the one that Preacher called you about—she showed up in the bar, beat up, running from an abusive husband."

Mike remembered, but vaguely.

What Mike wanted was a place to go where his family wouldn't be in his business, hovering, breathing down his neck. Where his buddies from the department wouldn't keep calling to see how he was doing, because he wasn't doing that great. The doctor said that he might eventually get back close to a hundred percent of his arm, but it would take a long time and hard work. The other things, the peeing, the erection, that stuff would either return spontaneously or not—nothing they could do about it right now.

Virgin River had always been a place of good memories for him. Of sanctuary and challenge at once. He and the boys from his squad went a couple of times a year, camped, stayed a week or so, fished every day, did a little hunting, played poker and drank all night, laughed themselves stupid, had a good time. And what Mike had to do was work on the arm, the groin. Get his body back. Then he could think about the future. At the moment, it seemed like the things he wanted were out of his reach.

The last time he'd been to Virgin River had only been a few months ago—August—not their usual fishing/hunting/poker trip. Jack had called saying he'd had to kill a man—a lunatic from out in the woods had held a knife on Jack's woman, demanding drugs. Jack got together a couple of guys to go clean out the woods, so Mike had rounded up the boys and, of course, they all took emergency time off from their jobs and were there by the next morning. When one of them called, they rallied. They hadn't found anything dangerous in the woods except a big, mean, smelly, pissed-off bear.

And they'd found Jack, their leader, for the first time in his life, hooked into a woman. Mel, a petite, stunning, delicious woman. Jack, who'd always played the ladies with little care and a lot of useless charm, getting ready to commit to a woman. Now Mel was Jack's wife and carried their child. Mike was amazed this had happened. He assumed Jack had finally stumbled on a woman who could trip him up, catch him. And make him think he was happy to be caught.

That, and the three bullets, had set up a real strong sense of regret in Mike. And a longing for a different kind of life. He felt like he'd missed out on something.

So, he went to Virgin River with his clothes, his guns, his weights, a rod and reel he wasn't sure he'd get to use again. He was going to keep rehabing his arm, get some rest and gain some weight back eating Preacher's food.

When he got to the bar he honked the horn and Jack came out on the porch. Mike got out of the SUV using his cane for balance. Jack was tough—he didn't look at Mike as if he was pathetic, thin, limping slightly, his arm crimped and still useless. Instead, he embraced him like a brother would, but more carefully than in the past. And said, "Damn, I'm glad you're here."

"Yeah," Mike said. "Me, too. I have so much work to do to get strong. Again."

"You'll get there."

Mel came outside. She was showing now, and it made her more beautiful than ever—she was glowing with Jack's life in her. She wore a smile that was sincerely welcoming and opened her arms to him, as well. "I'm glad you're here, too, Mike," she said. "I can help you with that arm. We'll get it back."

He hugged her with the good arm. "Yeah," he said. "Thanks."

"Come inside," Mel said. "There's someone you haven't met, even though you helped her."

Jack let Mike navigate the stairs up onto the porch himself, obviously resisting the urge to help him. When they were inside, Jack yelled for Preacher and the big man came out, wearing his apron. He cracked a rare grin when he saw Mike and he came around the bar, arms open.

"Oh, man," Preacher said, embracing him. He gave him several pats on the back, causing Mike to wince painfully. Then he held him away and looked at him. "Damn, it's good to see you!"

"Okay, great. Now, never do that again."

"Oh, man, I'm sorry. You still in pain?"

"Some, yeah. What's with this? Hair on my Preacher-man?"

"Head got cold," he said, ducking shyly. "You okay? I didn't hurt you, did I?"

"Maybe you could set me up a beer. That'd help."

"You bet, buddy. Coming up. And maybe something to eat, huh?"

"Beer first, okay?"

Preacher went around the bar and fixed him a draft. Mel and Jack each sat on one side. Mel leaned in. "How bad is the pain?" she asked.

He shrugged. "It's all soft tissue," he said. "But it can get real…real."

"What are you taking?"

"I'm trying to hang in there with the anti-inflammatory, maybe a beer, but every once in a while I have to cave in to the Percodan. I hate doing that. Makes me weird."

"You're already weird," Jack said. "Preacher, let me have a beer with my man here." When his glass was poured, Jack lifted it toward Mike. "Here's to your recovery, bud. It's going to be quick and powerful."

"Hope God heard that," Mike said, and took a long, refreshing pull. "The doc said I'd need three months to start feeling better and I've only given it six weeks, but…"

And then she came out from the kitchen. Mike almost choked on his words. She smiled at him and said, "Hello. You must be Mike." She went to stand next to Preacher, and he, with his eyes focused on the shine in Mike's, dropped an arm around her shoulders, claiming her. God, Mike thought. Preacher has a woman. And what a woman.

"Yeah," Mike said slowly. She was gorgeous. Soft,

light brown hair fell in silky curves to her shoulders. She had skin like creamy satin and peach-colored lips, a little line, a scar in her lower lip. He knew what that was about, he remembered better now. And warm, sexy green eyes surrounded by a lot of dark lashes and perfectly arched brows. With Preacher's arm around her, she leaned against him.

"I just don't get it," Mike said with a laugh. "You two somehow found the most beautiful, sexiest women in the state right here in the backwoods. Shouldn't there be at least one of you in Los Angeles?"

"Actually, we were both from Los Angeles," Mel said. "And fortunately, both found our way to the backwoods."

No way Preacher knows what he's holding, Mike thought. And Preacher, knowing Mike's careless ways with women, just about anyone's woman, might feel a little threatened at the moment, even given the crippled hand and cane. Little did he know…

"Well, damn," Mike said, lifting his glass. "To your good fortune. All of you." Then he looked at Jack and said, "I'm sorry, Sarge, but I've had it. That drive—it was way more than I thought it would be. Do you mind if I…?"

"Come on," Jack said. "You can follow me out to the cabin and I'll help you unload your gear. Take a nap. Maybe you'll feel like coming back for some of Preacher's dinner later. If not, I'll bring you home something."

"Thanks, pal," he said. He stretched his good hand toward Preacher for a shake.

Preacher's expression lightened up. "Good you're here, Mike. We'll beef you up in no time."

In the mornings, Mike drank the protein shakes that Mel gave him, though they were god-awful. Then he'd lift piddling weights and stretch. By 10:00 a.m., drenched in sweat, he'd need a shower and nap. Lying down always produced the same effect—soreness and pain when he got up. He'd roust himself up, try to ice it out, and if he could, get himself to the bar by three so he could have a beer to tamp it down a little before meeting Mel at Doc's. Once there, she'd work on him, as vicious as any physical therapist. She would start with a deep massage of his shoulder and biceps and then the exercises would start. It was enough to make him cry like a baby.

He was lifting a one-pound weight laterally with the right arm and could not yet raise it to shoulder level, yet she praised him for it, but it was agony. Mike still couldn't lift three plates out of a cupboard. He'd broken a couple, trying, and forced himself to drive all the way to Fortuna to replace them.

Every once in a while he'd try to lift his 9 mm right-handed and hold it out in front of him, looking over the barrel. No way.

"I really think we should set you up with an orthopedist. I can find you one on the coast," Mel said.

"No. No more surgery," he said.

"This could take a lot longer."

But he was worried about trade damage, where they go in to fix one thing and muck up something else. "Where am I going? Save the orthopedist. I'll work it out."

"Any other issues?" she asked. "The head and groin?"

"Fine," he said, but he didn't connect with her eyes.

Almost two weeks in Virgin River, eight weeks post op, and he still couldn't do a sit-up. But he had gained some weight and walking straight was easier, so things were looking up somewhat. And his friends, Jack, Mel, Preacher, Paige—they were hanging in there with him, encouraging his every movement.

Some days, if the sun was out, he could drive out to the Virgin and watch some angling. He particularly loved watching Jack and Preacher casting; he loved it even better when they had the boy Rick with them. They'd trained the kid and he was a master angler. The three of them, side by side, their lines soaring through the air in perfect S-shapes, flies touching down in the river with such grace and finesse, pulling in their catch. It was like ballet.

Mike had been a damn fine angler himself in days gone by. He'd been pretty good at a lot of things.

It was in that kind of a mood that Mike found himself a little later than usual at Jack's. There were only a few fishermen at a table by the fire with a late meal. Mike was up at the bar when Preacher came back downstairs from story time. Jack exited, leaving Preacher to lock up, and Mike asked for another drink. Then he started to grumble. He was frustrated with the arm, the pain, the clumsiness. A few other things.

Preacher poured himself his closing shot and stood behind the bar, listening to Mike complain, nodding every so often, saying, "Yeah, buddy. Yeah."

"Can't lift the gun, can't lift a lot of things. Know the true meaning of 'weak dick,'" he said morosely. Preacher's eyebrows lifted and Mike looked up at his face, glassy-eyed. "That's right, the old boy's dead and gone. May as well have shot it off...."

Preacher lifted his drink. "You're the only guy I know who'd complain about not getting laid in a few weeks because he's been in a coma," Preacher said. "I guess you thought you could get lucky even while you were unconscious...."

"That's what you know," he slurred. "Do I look like I'm unconscious now?"

"Hey, man, there aren't all that many women around here. You just might have to do without for a bit...."

"What do you see when you wake up in the morning, Preacher? A nice tent, huh? I see the...the... the great plains."

Preacher frowned. "You have a pain pill tonight, Mike?" He didn't answer. "Mike? You have a pain pill tonight?"

"I dunno."

"Hmm. Sit tight. Don't move. I'll be right back."

Sit still? Mike thought vaguely. Like moving was an option…

Mike might not have even known he was gone when Preacher was back; he was still peering into his drink, babbling to himself, slumped over the bar. It didn't seem like any time at all had passed when Jack was helping him to his feet.

"Come on, Mike. There you go. Forget the cane, just lean on me."

"Wha—"

"Yeah, you're going to sleep good tonight, that's for sure," Jack said.

Preacher got the door and as Jack was helping him through, said, "He might've had more than one pill, Jack. I asked him if he took a pain pill and he didn't know."

"You know how many drinks?"

"Not his usual limit, that's for sure," Preacher said. "A couple, maybe three."

"I gave him a couple," Jack said, Mike kind of lolling against him.

"I gave him one," Preacher said. "Tell Mel. She'll know if it's anything to worry about."

"Yeah, okay. Thanks for calling. I got it now."

Mike didn't get to breakfast at the bar the next morning, but by afternoon, right before his appointment with Mel, he was looking pretty decent. He called Preacher and asked for a lift into town where his SUV waited.

"How'd you sleep?" Preacher asked when Mike got himself carefully into the truck.

"Probably good," Mike said. "Couldn't tell you."

"You gotta watch those pain pills and drinks. I think

maybe you had a couple pills, a couple of drinks, and went straight to la-la land."

"Yeah, could'a been. Sometimes it gets terrible…"

"Then there's depression," Preacher said. "Depression after major surgery is real common, you know that? Especially if it's heart surgery or something violent. I think you qualify for violent. Three bullets."

"Could qualify," Mike said evasively.

Preacher reached in the pocket of his denim shirt and pulled out a folded piece of typing paper. "And then there's the morning tent…" he said. "I looked all this stuff up last night. Erectile dysfunction—common after major surgery, after violent crimes, while taking narcotic drugs, et cetera. There was a list of things. Besides waiting until you get better, which you will, you should get checked for chronic bladder infection, which happens after being in the hospital, having those catheter things. You can tell Mel about it, no problem. Mel doesn't even tell Jack stuff. I printed it out for you."

Mike took the paper gingerly, unfolded it. "Aw, Jesus, I couldn't have told you about this…."

"It'll come back, I think. If it doesn't, you can always get a rod put in it. But I don't know, Mike… I don't think I'd get a rod put in my dick. I think I'd try prayer first…."

"Aw, fuck…" Mike said.

"But one thing you oughta really think about—something for that depression. Mel can hook you up. And maybe count the pain pills. Man, you were a goner."

"Preacher, I swear to God, if you ever—"

"Why would I say anything? Gimme a break, huh?"

Mike looked at the printed page. "Where'd you get this stuff?"

"On the computer. You just tell Mel. Or Doc. But I'd tell Mel, even though she's a girl. She's a lot more up on some stuff than Doc. I don't know that Doc sees a lot of this with the sheep ranchers. You know?"

"I hate you so much right now," Mike said.

"Yeah? You'll get over it. Probably real soon—when you next want food."

It took him a few days of pouting, but then Mike brought up his issues with Mel during one of their rehab sessions. He got a round of antibiotics for a chronic bladder infection and an antidepressant that he'd probably only have to take for a few months. But he'd be damned if he'd thank Preacher. Guys just don't talk about those things. At least sober.

But he secretly found this rather amazing, coming from Preacher.

He walked into the bar early one afternoon, between lunch and dinner, and found Preacher seated on a stool with a towel around his shoulders. Paige had scissors in her hand and was trimming him up. He cocked his head and looked at this activity.

"I was a beautician," she said, smiling. "And if John is going to have hair, he's going to have to keep it decent. I see to that," she said, smiling. Then, taking a comb to his bushy eyebrows, said, "Not to mention these evil things. I've never seen a man with so much hair here."

"He is looking better these days, I've noticed," Mike said. "I figured it was you."

Preacher glowered.

Laughing, Mike ran a hand over his own bizarre head of hair. It was longer on one side than the other, still a little sparse over that temporal scar.

"Want me to try to straighten that up for you? While I've got my stuff out?"

"Hey, that would be great. You don't mind?"

"I'd be glad to. John's done here," she said, whipping off the towel.

"Okay if I let your girl touch me with her scissors, Preacher?"

Preacher merely scowled and stood up from the stool. But he turned toward Paige and placed a small fatherly kiss on her forehead. Just in case there were any questions.

Then she put a hand on his forearm and looked up at him with adoring eyes. But Preacher seemed not to see it. Mike wondered if Preacher had any idea what was going on here.

"I'll go see if Christopher is waking up," Preacher said.

"Thanks. Then I'll be in the kitchen to help." And to Mike she said, "Next?"

He sat on the stool and she draped him with the towel.

"Ah, yes," she said, "I can work with this. Does this still hurt?" she asked, gently touching the scar.

"No, it's fine. But it seems to be having trouble growing hair."

"I'll fix you up. Let me take it a lot shorter, give you a chance to catch up over here. I promise, it won't be awful. You'd look good with shorter hair."

"Yeah, that's what the Marine Corps thought. They thought I was cute as a button as a jarhead. Anything you do is fine. I appreciate it."

"You must have been terrified, when it happened," she said.

"I don't remember anything. Instant lights out."

"That's good, I guess." She snipped a bit, black hair falling to his shoulders and onto the floor. "I should thank you, I think. I know that John called you about my…situation. My ex-husband."

"Ex now?" he asked.

"Yes, very recently. I don't even carry the name anymore."

"And I guess, if you're still here—"

"I love it here. I don't know when I've felt more...I don't know, normal. And Christopher is so happy—he loves John so much."

"It's pretty clear how Preach—how John feels."

"Is it?" she asked.

Mike laughed. "Okay, he's not the most demonstrative, but you can bet I've never seen him act like this before. It's pretty obvious."

She picked up the mirror off the bar and handed it to him. "What do you think?" she asked.

"You're gifted," he said. "Anyone who can get a silk purse out of that mess should have her own chain of shops."

"Not in Virgin River, I don't think," she laughed. "Besides, I love working with John."

Unable to sleep one morning, Mike hoisted himself out of bed, iced down his shoulder and went outside with his 9 mm. He stood on the porch and lifted it with his left arm, peering over the barrel.

Jack came out onto the porch, dressed to go into town. "Is the wildlife in danger?" he asked.

Mike turned. "I think I should start perfecting the left hand. In case... You know. In case I don't get it back."

Jack shrugged. "Never hurts to know what you can do. But I wouldn't give up on the right arm. Not yet. It hasn't been that long, Mike."

"It's frustrating as hell. That's all." He holstered the gun. "There a place around here I can shoot?"

"There's a range about thirty minutes from here just outside of Clear River. I'll write down some directions for you."

"You on your way into town?" Mike asked.

"Headed that way pretty soon," he said. "I'm going to get Mel out of bed."

"I'll see you there," he said, carefully maneuvering the steps and climbing into his SUV.

Jack stood there until Mike had driven out of the clearing. Then he pulled off his boots and left them on the porch. In his bedroom, he got down to his boxers and slipped into bed beside his wife, pulling her into his arms. "Hmm," she said, snuggling close. She sniffed. "You've had coffee already."

"Mel," he whispered. "We're alone."

Her eyes popped open and she turned toward him only to find her mouth instantly covered in a blistering kiss. It took her a second to realize what he'd said, and when she did, she returned the kiss. "You're sure?" she asked.

"I watched him leave," Jack said, smiling down at her. "You can make as much noise as you want."

"I don't make that much noise," she said. She tugged his boxers down. "Oh-oh. I might make a little noise."

"You go right ahead, baby. I might, too."

Mike pulled up in front of the bar and parked, but he stayed in his car. There, slumped in one of the porch chairs, was a woman. She was a big woman wearing long men's trousers, boots that hung open unlaced, a plaid shirt and quilted down vest. Her head lolled to one side, her arms dangled over the arms of the chair, and on the floorboards of the porch, an empty bottle.

He tucked the 9 mm under the seat and left his cane in the car. He had to use the porch rail to assist in getting up the steps. He went to the woman and pressed two fingers to her carotid artery—at least she was alive.

Mike tried the front door to the bar and found it was still locked. No need to wake anyone. He went back to the SUV and pulled a blanket out of the back. He covered the woman and used a book of matches to light one of the gas space heaters Jack kept on the porch in winter. Then he took a chair on the other side of the porch. Waiting.

After about fifteen minutes, he got a clue. Jesus, he was stupid sometimes. Suddenly, he began putting the pieces together. Great detective work, Valenzuela, he found himself thinking. At night, when everyone turned in, he could hear them softly talking. He couldn't hear what they were saying, but their muffled voices in late-night conversation drifted to his room. And in mornings after he'd had trouble sleeping, Mel would usually say something like, "It was a bad night, wasn't it? You okay?" Every groan, every flush—it was one big room. They might as well be camping together.

Just because he wasn't getting it up didn't mean no one was. Jack and Mel needed some time alone. My God, they were newlyweds, and Mel's pregnancy wasn't too advanced for her to enjoy a healthy, satisfying sex life. He made a mental note to pay attention to that—to find things to do that would free up the cabin. To be sure, they knew he wouldn't be back for quite a while so they could have a private life.

He could look around for another place to stay and get out of their hair. But Jack was pleased that Mike had come to him. Mel was happy to be helping with his rehab. It would be better if he could just delicately find ways to give them the place to themselves for a few hours here and there.

He looked over at the woman, wondering who she was and what she was doing here. That bottle could be bar stock. Did Preacher give her the whole bottle and send her on her way so he could lock up? But if she'd been passed out here since last night, she might be frozen by now. The temperatures at night were pretty low; it was getting damned cold. Cold enough to give her some serious hypothermia.

It was thirty minutes before Jack's truck pulled in next to his SUV. When he got out of the truck, his brow was furrowed. "What's this?" he asked.

"I was hoping you could tell me," Mike said.

"Preacher's not up yet?"

"I don't know. He might be back in the kitchen, but the door is still locked and I didn't want to take a chance on waking up the house. You know?"

"Hey, buddy, I'm sorry. I—"

"Jack. You don't have to explain. I should be the one trying to explain. Sometimes I just don't think."

"Jeez, Mike…"

Mike tilted his head and laughed suddenly. "Holy shit, are you blushing?" he asked, astonished. "The woman's your wife, for God's sake. I've been whoring with you and you never—"

A strong hand was clamped on his good shoulder. "That's where we're going to stop talking about it," Jack said.

"Except to say, luckily for you, I am now sensitized. You and the *comadrona* deserve the life of man and wife."

"*Comadrona?*"

Mike laughed. "The midwife. I'll be a better house-guest from now on."

"Don't worry about it. Getting strong is your first priority. *Our* first priority."

Mike laughed. "This is when you really know who your friends are," he said. "Now, who's this?"

"Her name is Cheryl Chreighton. I'm afraid she's an alcoholic."

"She wind up here a lot?"

"No. This is a first."

"She get that bottle out of your bar?"

"No. We don't serve her," he said. "I can't say where she got the bottle. She used to stick to that nasty Everclear, kind of hard to find around here. We're the only place in town with a bar." He rubbed a hand along the back of his neck. "We should probably get her out of here."

"Where you going to take her?"

"Home," he said.

The lock on the door moved and it opened. Preacher stood in the doorway, looked out, assessed and said, "Oh, crap."

"Preacher, you have coffee yet?" Jack asked.

"Yeah."

"Let's have a cup of coffee while we think about what to do with her. She'll keep." Jack bent down and picked up the empty bottle to throw away.

Twenty minutes later Mel came into the bar, her jacket collar pulled up around her neck, hands in her pockets, all that blond hair scrunched up at her shoulders. Mike looked at her appreciatively; her cheeks were rosy with love, her eyes bright, lips bruised pink. "Jack, Cheryl Chreigton is kind of weaving down the street with a blanket around her shoulders. You know anything about that?"

"Yeah," he said. "That means I don't have to take her home. She was passed out on the porch when we opened up this morning."

"Oh, Jack, there must be a way to get that woman some help. My God, she's only thirty years old!"

"If you think of something, I'll be glad to pitch in," he said. "But, Mel, her parents have been trying for years."

"They're obviously not trying the right things," she said. She shook her head sadly and left the bar.

Jack had barely finished splitting logs when Connie was in the bar, visibly upset. "Well, they did it," she said. "They ran off."

"Aw, Jesus," Jack said. "When?"

"Who knows?" She shrugged. "Could've been the middle of the night—I didn't hear anything. Ron's out driving around now. I can't stand the thought of calling my sister."

"Well, don't," Jack said. "Give me a minute. Help

yourself to coffee." He went into the kitchen, pulled out the business card that was stuck between the phone and wall, dialed up the sheriff's department and asked if they'd dispatch Henry Depardeau, the deputy assigned to their area. He called the California Highway Patrol. Both times he gave a description of Rick's truck and said that family in Virgin River needed to get in touch with the young couple. Then he went back to Connie. He refilled his mug with coffee. "I've tried to stay out of this, Connie. But maybe I shouldn't have."

"Why do you say that?"

"Well, Rick's just got Lydie, and she's old and not too well most of the time. If Rick has anyone coaching him into manhood, trying to teach him, it would be me and Preacher. Probably not the best father figures in the world, but that's all he's got. We should do better by these kids right now."

"Look, Jack, I'm doing the best I can."

"I know that. Do you know why they ran off? Because I have some ideas. One is—they don't want to give that baby away. Holding that hard line with them, even if it seems to make the most sense, might drive them to do more drastic things."

"What are they going to do with a baby, Jack?"

"When Rick found out there was a baby, he said he was going to make sure Lizzie wasn't afraid. He's going to protect her, whatever it takes. He must have felt like he was facing a firing squad—you know any seventeen-year-old boy looking to be a father? Huh? But he said he was going to stick close to Liz. Me and Preach, we were damn proud of him for that. He's trying to be a man here, take care of the mother of his child. He shouldn't be protecting her from us."

"I agree, he's a good boy, but still, Jack…"

He shrugged. "Rick's going to be eighteen in a few

months. Young, but not the youngest father on record. But he's living with his grandma, Liz is living with you, and they can't even be alone together."

"Jack, they shouldn't get any more involved! They're children!"

"They made a baby together, Connie. Do you think you can un-shoot that gun? Every day is a hard day for Liz— and sometimes she needs the only person she thinks is on her side to put his arms around her. It isn't a good time for her to think she doesn't have love in her life, when it's growing in her every day. She needs him, Connie."

"But, Jack, Lizzie is fifteen…."

He gave a nod. "I know this, too. Now, Connie, I hope I never say anything about a woman that isn't gentlemanly, but I'd like you to do a quick memory check. When Rick and Liz got involved, she was only fourteen— fourteen going on twenty-one. Two kids with grown-up bodies and adolescent minds. I don't know about you, but I think it's better if they don't get married just yet. And being in somewhat the same position as Rick, nobody would get my baby away from me. Not at knifepoint."

She looked down and shook her head. "I didn't have my own kids," she said. "My sister shouldn't have stuck me with this. She told me to watch that they don't get any more serious, make sure that baby gets adopted by someone who can give it a good home."

"You're right there—she shouldn't have done that to you. But I'm glad she did. Doesn't sound like your sister has the wisdom or patience for it, and I've known you for some time now. I know you're up to it. It might be better if you start playing by your own rules, not someone else's. After all, Liz is living under your roof."

"I don't know what's the right thing, the wrong thing…."

"Sure you do. They're a couple, Liz and Rick. Unfortunately for them, they got into this so young, we don't know if they can make it stick, but they're a couple right now. They should be getting ready for the baby, because I can tell you, that baby's coming no matter what they decide to do. Even if Liz can be forced to give him up, Rick can't. Maybe we should put our heads together and see if we can help them be parents and finish school, because the only thing for sure right now is, they're going to be parents. No matter what we do. We might as well offer up some support."

"I'm not taking on a baby full-time," she said. "I don't think my health is up to it."

"Lotta help around here, Connie. Preacher and I— we'd do anything for Rick. I think Mel and Paige fall into that category, as well. Instead of telling them what they have to do, we better start asking them what they need." He shrugged. "Connie, if those kids need each other right now, it's time to back off. She's not going to get more pregnant. It might keep them from getting married before they're old enough to vote." He took a drink of coffee. "Unless we're already too late."

The phone rang and Jack went to the kitchen. He was back in seconds. "We got 'em. Henry Depardeau is holding them out on 99, changing a tire. I'll go get them if you'll keep an eye on the bar until Preacher gets out here. Okay?"

Jack drove down the highway for only about fifteen minutes before he saw the sheriff's car, and right in front of that the little white truck. He pulled up in front and got out. Rick already had the old tire off and the new one on. The minute Liz saw Jack, she put her hands over her face and began to cry.

Rick put his arm around her shoulders and she leaned her face into his chest. Jack came up behind her and with strong hands on her upper arms, pulled her back from Rick and into his embrace. "Liz, honey, I want you to stop crying. Everything is going to be all right. Go sit in my truck and let us get this tire changed. Go on, it's all right."

Rick held the lug wrench in one hand. He looked at Jack. "You pissed?" he asked.

"Nah. What happened?"

Rick applied the wrench to one of the lugs and gave it a sharp, angry twist. Jack noticed, not for the first time, how strong the kid was. "Lizzie hit a wall—total panic. Hysteria. She's afraid of losing the baby. Losing me."

"Shew," Jack said. "You must have felt like you had to do something about that."

"Yeah, I was trying." He tightened another nut. "I thought if I took her somewhere…Oregon. Married her. She'd settle down. She's getting kind of close, Jack. I can't have her all messed up like that. It worries me." He applied the wrench again. "I should be with her as much as I can. Try to keep her calm."

"You're right. But you can't run off. Take her home, sit down with Connie. Tell Connie you need to be in the driver's seat now. You have to take care of your girl, your baby. I think maybe she'll listen to you. I had a talk with her."

"Yeah?"

Jack hung his thumbs on his belt and looked down. "Rick, I know you're trying to keep everything from spinning out of control. You gotta keep your head, buddy. Before you do something as crazy as running away to marry a fifteen-year-old girl, talk to me. Will you, please? Between us, we can keep things sane."

"Sometimes that seems impossible," he said, tightening the final lug nut.

"I know, Rick. But—"

"I want that baby," he said flatly.

"I would, too," Jack admitted. "Let's focus on getting this to come out the best we can. I'm on your team, Rick."

"I really don't know how you could be," he said. "After all, I didn't exactly listen to you in the first place."

"I never saw it like that. We've been over this. You're not the Lone Ranger on this fuckup. Okay?"

"All I ever wanted was to make you guys proud of me," Rick said.

Jack grabbed the kid's upper arm and gave him a little shake. "Don't you ever think otherwise. The only thing that could make me more proud is if you were my son."

# Twelve

There were only four anglers in the river, die-hards. The weather was cold and rainy, the salmon had almost finished running for the season, snow was falling in the higher elevations and Christmas was just around the corner.

Preacher pulled in his third catch of the day, a good-size fish, and started out of the river, his head down. This was getting ridiculous. It wasn't as though Jack and Preacher had a lot of long talks, but the glum, preoccupied silence had been stretching out. Something had Preacher on the ropes.

Jack, shaking his head, went after him. "Hey, Preacher," he called. "Hold up." Jack caught up with him. "We have enough fish to clean for tonight?"

Preacher nodded and turned away, moving toward the truck. Jack grabbed the sleeve of his slicker. "Preacher. I gotta ask you something. What the hell's eating you?"

"What do you mean?" he replied, frowning.

Jack shook his head in frustration. "You have this beautiful little family under your roof. You watch over them like a papa bear. That kid adores you, you have a sweet, cuddly young beauty to knock boots with every night, and you're *depressed*. I mean, you are obviously depressed!"

"I'm not depressed," he said somewhat meanly. "And I haven't knocked boots with anybody."

"What?" Jack said, confused. "What?"

"You heard me. I haven't touched her."

"She have issues?" Jack asked. "Like the abusive ex or something?"

"No," Preacher said. "I have issues."

He laughed. "Yeah? You don't want her? Because she—"

"I don't know what to do," Preacher said suddenly. Then he averted his eyes.

"Sure you do, Preacher. You take off your clothes, she takes off her clothes…"

Preacher snapped his head back. "I know where all the parts go. I'm not so sure she's ready for that…."

"Preacher, my man, do you have eyes? She looks at you like she wants to—"

"Jesus, she scares me to *death!* I'm afraid I'll hurt her," he said, then shook his head miserably. What the hell, he thought. Jack's my best friend. If I can't tell Jack, I can't tell anyone. But he said, "You say anything about this and I swear to God, I'll kill you."

Jack just laughed at him. "Why would I tell anyone? Preacher, you're not going to hurt her."

"What if I do? She's been through so much. She's so soft. Small. And I'm—hell, I'm just a big, clumsy lug."

"No, you're not," Jack said, laughing again. "Preacher, you don't even break the yolks. You're—well, you're big, that's for sure." He chuckled. "You're probably big all over," he said, shaking his head. "Believe me, women don't mind that."

Preacher's chin went up and he frowned, not sure whether he'd just been complimented or insulted.

"Listen, buddy, you don't have the problems you think you have. You have to trust yourself."

"That's just it—I don't. I'm afraid I'll go out of my mind. Do something that—I'm afraid I'll break her in half." He looked down at his hand, fingers splayed. "What if I leave a bruise on her? I'd wanna die."

"Okay, you listen to me. Here's what you're gonna do. You're gonna tell Paige what's been bothering you. Okay? That you haven't touched her because you're afraid you might not know your own strength and be too rough with her, and you don't want to be. She'll help you, Preacher. She'll get you through this. Goddamn, man— the girl wants you so bad it's distracting." He shook his head. "Man, the way she looks at you, I figured you haven't let her sleep in two weeks!"

"I don't think either one of us is sleeping…."

"Well, hell—how could you? You gotta get this monkey off your back!" And Jack immediately thought, I can relate. I've had a houseguest in the cabin with paper walls for weeks now. It was catch as catch can at his house, and while he was a man who could appreciate a quickie now and then, a steady diet of that wasn't getting it. He'd give anything to be alone with Mel for a long, slow night. He was just about out of his mind himself. The house he was going to build would be soundproofed.

"There haven't been… I haven't been with a lot of women," Preacher said. "Sure not a tenth as many as you."

"That's good. That's a good thing. You're a serious guy—you get points for that! You just have to be willing to— Jesus, I can't believe I'm doing this." Preacher frowned blackly. For a second Jack thought, if he hits me, I'm not letting him get away with it again. "Okay, listen. You just have to be willing to pay attention to details. The details, Preacher. The sounds she makes when, you know, you touch her. Tell her to show you what… Argghh," he growled in frustration. He forced himself to go on. "Okay, you ask her to show you what she likes. Ask, is this okay?

Listen to her. You can tell by the sounds she makes if you're on the right spot. Ask her to put your hand where she wants it. To tell you where she'd like you to touch her. *How* she'd like the touch. It's pretty simple. You just want to make her feel good."

"Aaww, man," he said, helpless.

"Well, hell, I guess someone has to tell you. You need me to dig you out a movie or something?"

"No! Jesus!"

"Just as well. They don't do it so well in those movies, anyway. You'll be better off if you just admit you're not sure and you want it to be good. You guide each other, Preach. That's the best way."

"I never had—you know."

"Someone you loved," he said. It wasn't a question.

"Yeah," he said, hanging his head. "God. It never mattered so much before. I guess I should feel like crap about that, too.… But…"

"Get a grip, Preacher. You're not rough. You're gentle, but you're strong. It's a great combination, believe me. All you really have to remember is, she goes first." Preacher frowned. "Come on, man, you know what I mean. You hang in there until you're sure she's been satisfied. Then you're free and clear. That's the best advice I can give you. That, and you better not wait any longer. I have a feeling you've put this off too long already."

"You tell anyone about this and I swear to God—"

"I know. You're gonna kill me. Shit, Preacher. You better do something about this right away. I mean, Jesus, man, are you at all confused about why she's still hanging around here? That girl's been waiting for you and you have to get the job done. Now, come on, let's go clean fish." Jack threw his pole and catch in the back of Preacher's truck. Damn, Jack thought. The poor guy. The poor *girl!*

* * *

When Mike walked into the bar, no one was there. Well, the place tended to stay pretty empty on rainy afternoons. That was just as well—he only wanted a beer to take the edge off the pain in his shoulder and neck. It was amazing how bad it could get sometimes, and the rain and cold always made it feel worse.

The fire had begun to die down, so he went to the hearth, leaned his cane against the wall and opened the grate. With his left hand he lifted the poker and stirred the logs a little, sending up a flame. Then, holding his right arm protectively against his middle, he reached for a log to put on the fire. Then another.

He looked at his watch. Three o'clock. He could pour himself a beer. Jack and Preacher wouldn't mind. But he walked back into the kitchen. Paige was in there, kneading a big wad of dough, her back to him. "Hey," he said.

She turned around and, as quickly, turned back. There had been tears on her face. He frowned. What was this? Trouble in paradise? "Hey," he said, walking up behind her, squeezing her upper arm with his left hand. "What's going on?" he asked her.

"Nothing," she said with a sniff.

He turned her around to face him. He looked down at her pretty face and for the hundredth time thought, that damn Preacher. I bet he doesn't know what he has here. "This isn't nothing," he said, wiping a tear from her cheek.

"I can't talk about it," she said.

"Sure you can. Seems like maybe you'd better. You're all upset."

"I'll work it out."

"Preacher do something to hurt you?"

She immediately started to cry and leaned forward, her head falling on his chest. He put his good arm around her and said, "Hey, hey, hey. It's okay."

"It's not okay," she cried. "I don't know what I'm doing wrong."

"Maybe if you talk to me, I can help. I'm so good with free advice, you'll be impressed."

"It's just that…I care about him. But he just doesn't find me…"

Mike lifted her chin. "What, Paige?"

"He doesn't find me attractive."

"Bull."

"Desirable."

"Paige, that's nonsense. The way he looks at you, he eats you with his eyes. He's wacko for you."

"He won't touch me," she said, a large tear spilling over.

That almost knocked Mike down. "No way."

She nodded pathetically.

"Oh, man," Mike said. He'd thought, everyone thought, they were doing it all night long. The way they looked at each other, like they couldn't wait for everyone to leave so they could be alone, get it on. Those sweet little kisses on the cheek, the forehead. The way they touched—careful, so no one would see the sparks fly, but the sparks were flying all over this bar! The sexual tension was electric. "Oh, man," he said again. He put his arm around her. "Paige, he wants you. Wants you so bad it's showing all over him."

"Then why?"

"I don't know, honey. Preacher's strange. He's never been good with women, you know? When we served together, we all managed to find us a woman somewhere. I killed two marriages that way. But not Preacher. It was very rare for him to—" He stopped himself. He was trying to remember—were there women at all? He wasn't sure; he knew Preacher never had a steady girl. He thought he remembered a woman here, there. It's not as though he was focused on Preacher's love life; he was too busy taking care of his own. He probably lacks sexual confidence, Mike thought. It would be hard for him to put the moves on anyone he felt he had to win over.

"I bet he's scared," Mike heard himself say.

"How can he be? I've practically thrown myself at him! He knows he isn't going to face rejection!" She dropped her gaze, lowered her voice to a whisper. "He has to know how much I—"

"Oh, brother," Mike said. "I bet he's not worried about rejection. Aw, Paige, Preacher's so shy, sometimes it's just plain ridiculous. But I promise you, Paige, I've known the man a long time—"

"He said he'd trust you with his life. That he has…"

"Yeah, we have that, it's true. It's funny with men—you can trust each other with your lives and never talk about anything personal, you know? Sometimes Preacher seems a little naive in the ways of the world." Then remembering their talk not long ago about depression et cetera, he said, "And at other times, he makes the Grand Canyon look shallow." He shook his head. "He can be a mystery. There's more to Preacher than… You really care about him?"

"I do."

"Then you be patient. He'll come around. Paige, it's obvious—he cares about you, too. You and Christopher. I've never seen him like this with anybody."

"Maybe he wants to be sure I'm not just—"

Mike was shaking his head. "He wants to be sure of himself, Paige. Preacher's real cautious. I think the man could be terrified of disappointing you. That's my bet."

"He couldn't possibly," she said, and a tear fell again.

Mike wiped it away. "You just have to trust me on this—he's a bundle of nerves. He's really good in a fight, really good in a war, and who'da guessed how good a cook he turned out to be, huh? But with women? Paige— he's never been a hustler. I don't know of any women.

He's never been that kind of guy. Just not a tomcat like some of the rest of us."

"That's one of the things I love most," she whispered.

Mike smiled. "You give him some time, huh?"

She nodded. She smiled weakly.

Mike dropped a brotherly kiss on her forehead. "It's going to be all right."

"You think so?"

"Oh, yeah. Just hang in there. Don't give up on him." Mike thought, that lucky son of a bitch. This woman adored him. Wanted nothing so much as to make him happy all night long. "Go wash your face. I'm gonna get myself a beer." He gave her shoulders a final squeeze, and as she turned away from him, Preacher was standing in the back door with his catch.

Paige skittered past Preacher, keeping her head down so that he wouldn't see her tears. Preacher scowled at Mike. "Need something?" he asked.

"I need a beer before I walk over to Doc's and let Mel torture me. Want me to get it myself?"

"Help yourself," he said, throwing his fish in the big sink.

Jack came in right behind him. "Hey, Mike. How you feeling today?" He threw his catch on top of Preacher's.

Mike rubbed his right upper arm with his left hand. "A little better every day. Need a hand? I have exactly one."

"Nah, but if you want to drink your beer back here while we clean fish, you're welcome."

Preacher had a stuffed trout that was nothing short of amazing. It was a lot of trouble—fileting the fish, stuffing it with a delectable corn dressing, slipping it back into the trout skin and under the broiler. It was one of Paige's favorites. He served it with spinach soufflé, warm pasta in a white garlic sauce and bread. It was good to make a meal that was labor intensive; it took his mind off things.

He'd seen her leaning against Mike; seen Mike kiss her forehead, smile and whisper to her. Well, he wouldn't be surprised if she fell for Mike. Mike was the sexy one, the romantic one, even when he was a little scraped up. Always successfully wooing women. He'd had more women than he deserved. So, if that was how it went, that wouldn't surprise Preacher. He'd thought from the beginning that Paige just saw in him a true friend, a man who could protect her against the world. All that business with the sweet smiles, the embraces—she was probably just ready, period. Not necessarily for Preacher.

Now it embarrassed the hell out of him what he'd said to Jack.

She made the bread. "You did good here, Paige," he told her.

"I did exactly what you said would work," she said. "You okay?"

"I think I got stuffed up from the rain," he lied. "It was so cold out there today."

"Did you take anything?"

"No, it's okay."

"Why don't I go get you something. Aspirin or something."

"Naw, forget it. I'll be fine."

There were only a few for dinner, typical for a rainy night. Jack sat at a table with Mel, Doc Mullins and Mike while Paige and Christopher sat at the bar with Preacher standing on the other side, coaching Christopher to eat a little more. Everyone was done before seven and Jack was picking up the plates. Mel went back to the kitchen with him where they started washing up.

"Hey, man," Preacher said. "I got that."

"We're almost done here. Then we'll get out of your hair."

"No hurry, man. I have sweeping up to do."

"I could get that, too," Jack offered.

"Don't worry about it."

In ten minutes, Jack was holding Mel's coat for her. Mullins was edging out the door and Paige was taking Christopher upstairs for his bath.

"You coming, Mike?" Jack asked.

"Yeah, I'll be along in a minute."

"Don't overstay your welcome," Jack advised.

"I'll be right behind you."

When everyone had gone, Mike moved to the bar. Preacher started putting chairs up on the tables so he could sweep. But Mike said, "Hey, Preacher, come here a minute, would you, buddy?"

Reluctantly, Preacher went around the bar. Don't tell me now, he was mentally pleading. Don't tell me about you and Paige. I don't want to hear it. Just let it happen and I'll live with it. I'll find a way to live with it. Never really thought I had a chance, anyway.

"Have a drink with me. A short one. No pain pills today, I swear."

Preacher got down two glasses and poured them each a shot.

"I'm gonna tell you something, and you're going to act like you never heard it. You get me?"

"Sure," Preacher said, throwing back the shot for courage.

"I caught your girl crying today."

Shock settled over Preacher's face.

"That's right, old man. She can't figure you out. I think she loves you, Preacher. She's waiting. She needs some attention. You with me?"

Preacher nodded solemnly. He wasn't going to go there with Mike.

"She thinks you don't find her attractive. Desirable."

"Aw, that's crap," Preacher said. He poured himself another shot.

"I'm telling you. You don't have any excuses here, pal. If you don't step up, she's going to think you don't want her. Don't care about her. I'd hate it if she thought that because I'm looking at the two of you, the three of you, and I think it'd be a damn stupid shame if you three lost one another because you're an idiot. Now, I'm not going to try to guess why it's not happening for you two. Preacher, buddy, it's time to make it happen."

Preacher threw back that second shot while Mike merely lifted his, not drinking.

"I thought you were messing with my girl," Preacher confessed.

"No, I was telling her to try to be patient with you because of your, you know, extra-low IQ." Then he grinned at Preacher's scowl.

"You always used to mess with anybody's girl," he said.

"Not just anybody's girl, Preach. I'd never touch a brother's woman, you should know that. Even I don't cross that line. Even if you haven't made it clear to Paige, you've made it clear to everyone else—she's your girl. Besides, I'm no threat to you. It's you she wants. Bad enough to make her cry about it." Mike took in about half his drink and stood up. "Do yourself a favor, Preacher. Your girl needs you and you don't want to let her down now. Don't waste another minute." He left the rest of his drink. He stared into Preacher's eyes. "You better take care of business. You copy?"

Copy, Preacher thought. Cop talk. "Yeah. I copy."

Preacher went upstairs to put Christopher to bed. Christopher was running around the room bare-assed, dodging his jammies; the kid loved being naked. Preacher grabbed him up, swung him around as he giggled and stood him on the bed. "Enough," he said. "You're going to bed."

"Read to me," Christopher said, bouncing.

"Your mommy is going to read tonight. Ten minutes. And then lights out."

Preacher got him in the pajamas and gave Paige a little slap on the rump. "I'll see you downstairs in ten."

"Okay," she said, a little surprised by his apparent playful mood.

Preacher, his insides tight, went to his quarters. He shaved and showered quickly. He put on a pair of sweatpants and a T-shirt. He looked at his bed and drew the quilt down, folding it. And he thought, I'm going to think of this as something I have to do for a friend. Not for me—for her. That's what it'll be.

She hadn't come downstairs yet, so he stirred up the fire a little bit and sat on the chair, his feet up in front of the fireplace. When she came into the room he said, "Come here, Paige." He held out a hand to her and brought her onto his lap. He ran his big hands down her sides to her waist and leaned toward her. She met his lips for a short kiss, but when he didn't pull back, she went there again, making it long, slow and lovely. His lips opened slightly, and with the back of his hand, his knuckles, he brushed against her breast and felt her sigh against his open mouth. He put his big hand over her breast.

She rubbed a hand along his cheek. "You shaved," she said.

"Uh-huh. I wouldn't want to go hard on your skin with whiskers. Mmm. Paige, you have any idea how I feel about you?" She just looked at him. "How much I feel for you?"

"You haven't really said…."

"I should've said. But I—" He stopped and took a breath. "It's hard for me to put into words, but what it is… This thing I feel for you—it gets stronger every day." She smiled into his dark eyes. "You're so soft. So small compared to me. I want you, Paige. My God. But haven't been sure if you're ready…"

"I'm ready," she said in a whisper.

"I've been worrying. I don't want to do anything to hurt you. Especially after everything… Everything that came before me. Before us."

She was stunned for a moment. Seeing the precious look in his eyes, she pressed her lips against his and kissed him again, lightly. Against his mouth she said, "You're the gentlest man I've ever known. You're not going to hurt me."

"I'm not experienced with women," he said. "I'm never sure of the right things to do. And I never wanted to do the right things more than with you."

"Good." She smiled. "We'll make up our own right things to do. It'll be fresh. New."

"My buddies, they know a lot about women. I never paid much attention. Until now. Until you."

"I know," she said. "I love that about you."

"You do?"

"It makes me feel really special," she said.

"Even if I don't know everything I should know about women…?"

"I'll tell you what you need to know," she whispered.

He groaned and pulled her harder against his mouth, kissing her deeply, feeling her small tongue enter even as her arms tightened around him. "You think he's asleep?" Preacher asked, a little breathless. "Because we're going to have to close the door."

"He was almost asleep before I left him. He's not going to get out of bed, John."

He kissed her again. And again. And then with his arms beneath her, stood up, lifting her. As he carried her toward his room, he felt her mouth against his neck, pressing soft kisses there, sucking gently at his earlobe, making small, beautiful noises.

He put her on his bed and she came up on her knees, facing him. His lips against hers, he began to work the buttons of her shirt. She slipped her hands under his T-shirt and ran them over his smooth chest, teasing his nipples. He spread her shirt open and over her shoulders, letting it drop. He looked down at her; bruises healed, her skin was flawless. She reached her hands behind her and unhooked the bra, flinging it away. For a moment he just stared, filling his eyes with her lush, ivory skin, her full breasts. When he met her eyes, she was smiling up at him, pleased to have his eyes on her.

Preacher ripped his shirt over his head and pulled her against him. He was already making a nice big tent in his sweats. "Paige," he said, holding her close. "Oh, this could be over way too fast…."

She laughed softly, kissing his neck, his cheeks, his lips. "Lucky for us, we don't get just this one chance."

The thought had never even crossed his mind. In his panic about doing the right things, making her happy and pleasing her, it hadn't even occurred to him that this was the beginning, not the final exam. He could mess it up, like he half expected to, and he could still get a second chance. His hands went to the snap on her jeans and popped it. "I have condoms, Paige."

"Have you been screened…since the last time…? Because I was checked after the D and C and I'm on the pill."

"I haven't…." He kissed her again, drowning in her mouth. His hands on her hips, he slowly slipped the jeans down. "There hasn't been anyone. There's no chance. Oh, I can't believe how good you feel. I can't believe I get to touch you like this…."

She closed her eyes, feeling his hands run up and

down her sides, over her bottom, along her hips and up again. His hands were so big and powerful, but as she expected, his touch was careful and tempting. Slow and delicious, driving her crazy with longing. She put her hands on his hips; the sweats came down easily, despite the obstruction of an amazing, beautiful erection. "Look at you," she said in a breath, smiling, taking in his broad, hairless chest, narrow hips. She finally saw the rest of that tattoo on his left upper arm that peeked out from under the snug sleeve of a T-shirt—an American eagle.

"Tell me what you like," he whispered against her mouth.

Still kneeling, she directed his lips lower, to her breast. With a soft, easy tongue he circled her nipple and she dropped her head back, sighing. That nipple came to life under his tongue and he pulled her harder against his mouth and gently suckled, drawing a deep moan from both of them. He felt her pull his hand from around her until it was in front of her. With her hand over his, she slid it down, over her belly, past her soft mound and deeper. Her fingers on top of his, she pressed them into her and moved them. "There," she whispered. "There," she said again. He memorized the place, the sound. The details.

He would have no way of knowing that his skill as a lover was not an issue with her, but the fact that he wanted only to please her, to make her happy, that was huge. It took only a second of showing him where and how to touch and he was on his own, driving her absolutely mad with desire. Maybe it didn't occur to him that he wasn't the only one who'd been a long time without this pleasure in his life. For Paige, it had been a lifetime. And she was so ready to feel both love and pleasure.

John pinched his eyes closed and prayed for control. He hoped he would be able to tell when she was satisfied— he wasn't completely sure how that worked. He'd never paid attention before. A lot of panting and squirming, he assumed. Maybe he'd get lucky and she'd just tell him.

The sensation of her breast against his mouth, his fingers in her soft, slick folds made him light-headed. Then her hand went to his erection and he groaned miserably. He lifted his head. "You better not do that yet," he told her. "I'm sorry. I wanted you so bad, it's lucky we made it to the bedroom…."

She let herself slowly drop back onto the bed, pulling him down with her. "Not a problem, John," she whispered. "I wanted you just as bad." He held himself over her and she put his finger back on that spot, reminded him how to move it and said, "Oohh," just before she kissed him again, her tongue sweet and strong in his mouth. He worked it a little bit and her moans came stronger, her hips pushing against his hand.

"Tell me what to do. Tell me what you want. I'll do anything you want," he said. "I want this to be right for you."

She touched him boldly again and said, "John, let's take care of this, right now. Right away. We can experiment later…."

"I wanted to do it for you first," he said. "I want to make you feel really good."

She laughed softly against his lips. "I do feel really good," she said.

She opened her legs for him and he lowered himself over her. As she guided him with her hand, he pressed himself slowly and deeply within her. He was amazed by her strength, amazed that she seemed not at all overpowered by him, but rather a formidable partner as she rose to meet him, pulled him in. "Ah," she said. "That is so perfect." He heard her hum deeply, felt her move her hips beneath him, and he began to pump his hips to her rhythm. He figured he'd be good for seconds, not minutes, and hoped it would be enough. But he remembered then, remembered what brought that deep moan from her and slid his hand between their bodies and down, inching his finger toward that spot that she loved. And he heard it again. "Oh, John…." She moved harder, throwing a leg over him and pulling him deeper and deeper. He rubbed that hard little knot while he thrust his hips, and beneath him, she was pounding against him, meeting him with each movement.

Something happened immediately. Her body tightened around him and he felt a clenching, a squeezing, a pulsing. It startled him, it felt so good. It was so amazing, he was able to hold himself back because he was in a trance. This was a first for him; he'd never noticed this before. Never felt it. He froze as her breath caught and she strained against him, hot spasms closing around him, drenching him in liquid heat. "Paige," he whispered, overcome. "Oh, Paige." She cried out softly, again and again, grasping him powerfully, lost in her own orgasm, and then her mouth was on his again, devouring him, sucking at his lips and tongue. He rocked with her as she climaxed, while she pulsed with such power, until it felt like there was nothing left in her; then she slowly began to relax beneath him, weak in his arms. Weak and limp and satisfied, all the strength he'd felt a moment ago turned to nothing but softness in his arms. He was in awe of her response. Looking down at her, brushing her hair away from her face, he asked in a hoarse whisper, "Was that it?"

She smiled dreamily. "That was it."

"That's *incredible*," he said.

She laughed softly. "Yes," she said. "But, John," she said, moving her hips beneath him. "We're not done."

"No," he said, smiling. "I guess we're not."

She wrapped her legs around his waist, and with his hands on her bottom, he drove himself into her until he let it go, and it was more powerful than anything he'd ever known in his life. It shook him to know he could do this for her, feel this with her. Every muscle in his body flexed, then trembled, and then slowly began to relax. It took him a long time to stop panting; took him quite a while to breathe evenly. He rose above her. "Paige," he said weakly. "I never felt anything like that in my life."

She touched his face. "You're just too good to be true, you know that?" she whispered. And kissed him. She knew it would be like that—his every touch was powerful yet sweet, so like him in every way. "John, promise me something."

"Anything."

"You can tell me anything, John. Never be shy with me again."

"Never," he said, and slowly lowered his mouth to her breast, drawing gently on a nipple. And she said, "Oooh, John." He memorized the place, the sound.

So this was what it felt like when you loved someone, when you wanted to please someone rather than just be pleased. When you paid attention to what made her purr and sigh. He hadn't known about it. As he held her close, he couldn't stop kissing her, couldn't stop touching her, tasting her and exploring her body with gentle fingers. With kisses. With his mouth, his tongue. "I don't think I can get enough of you," he whispered to her.

"Good. I'm not tired at all. And your hands on me… Your hands are like velvet. You're so careful, but you don't miss anything. It's how I knew it would be, John. You're so perfect."

"Paige, is this how it is? Do other men know all about this?"

She laughed softly. "I don't know what other men know. I'm not very experienced, either."

"I've never… I swear, I've never felt like that."

"Neither have I. You're a wonderful lover. Wonderful."

"I didn't think you could want someone like me," he told her.

"You don't see yourself at all—I suspected that. John, you're so beautiful, so smart and kind and strong. You don't even realize how handsome you are. And you have the most incredible body—so big and hard and fit. Not an ounce of fat or flab." She ran a small hand over his shoulder, down his biceps. "Your hands are so perfect—powerful and soft—all that kitchen work, I bet. Your hands on me… It's everything I dreamed it would be. You just don't see yourself."

"I couldn't believe it was really me you wanted. I thought maybe—"

"Shh," she said. "Don't you think after the kind of life I've had, I know a good man when I find one? How could you doubt me?"

"I'm sorry about how I made you feel before," he said. "Like I didn't want you. When, God, you were all I've wanted since… Since almost the first day."

"Somebody said something," she said, but she didn't say it angrily.

"Mike told me I'd better step up, take care of my girl, or I might lose you."

"I think you're stuck with me. But just the same, I'm glad you didn't wait any longer."

"You make it so easy," he said. "All I wanted was to make you feel good. I didn't know it was going to be that wonderful for me, too. And when I felt it—your pleasure— I thought I was going to pass out, it felt so good."

She put her hand on him. He was already rising again.

"I want to make you feel like that every night for the rest of my life," he said.

"I kind of like that idea," she said. "John. I don't want to scare you away, but I'm in love with you."

He buried his face in her neck, in her soft hair. "Baby, I love you so much, I think I'm going to die of it."

"Do you see, John? This is all I want. You. You loving me. Me loving you."

"Now what?" he asked her, her hand on him, his hands on her.

"Now we do it again. Slower."

# Thirteen

The sun came out, and though the December air was cold, the day was bright and sunny. When Mel got to town, she checked in with Doc to see if anything was going on. Then she went over to the bar to have a cup of coffee with her husband.

Jack was a definite morning person; it was his best time. He got his exercise splitting logs if the weather was decent, and he did this year round, even in summer when there was no need to lay a fire. He'd leave Mel sleeping and sneak away quietly. He liked to be around the bar first thing in the morning, check on what Preacher planned for food, inventory his supplies, make a list of chores to finish, be sure everything was set for the day.

She found him behind the bar with his coffee mug, Christopher sitting up on a stool, a bowl of cereal and glass of orange juice pushed slightly to one side as he colored on a page of his coloring book. His box of crayons was flipped open, at the ready.

Mel jumped up on a stool beside him and said, "Morning, buddy. How are you?"

"Mmm, good," Christopher said, paying attention only to the page.

Jack poured her a mug of coffee. "Christopher, tell Mel what you told me this morning."

"What?"

"You know. About how big you're getting."

"Yeah," he said. "I'm getting big."

"You are," Mel agreed.

"And…?" Jack prompted.

"And John says I should have my own bed. My own room. Because I'm getting so big."

"Well," Mel said. "I suppose you should."

Paige popped into the bar from the kitchen. "Hi, Mel," she said brightly. Her cheeks were chafed pink, her eyes twinkling behind sleepy lids, and her smile was a tish secretive. Her lips were ruby, maybe a little swollen from kissing all night long. She seemed to flow into the room, serene. Mel thought, How amazing that you can always tell when someone's had sex. Lotsa sex. "How are you doing on that cereal, kiddo?" Paige asked Christopher.

"Hmm," he answered, coloring.

"I think he's done," Jack said. "He hasn't touched it since the last time you checked on him."

"Okay," she said, picking up the bowl. "But please drink your juice," Paige said, taking the bowl back to the kitchen.

Mel looked up at her husband. Jack lifted one eyebrow and gave her a half smile. Mel leaned across the bar and grabbed a fistful of Jack's shirt, drawing him to her. She whispered, "What's going on here?"

"That should be pretty obvious."

"I want you to take me home this minute and…"

"I can't," Jack whispered back.

"Why not?"

"Because we have company. And you're a screamer."

"God, this is ridiculous. I'm so jealous I could spit."

"It isn't fun, that's for sure. Well," he said, throwing a

look over his shoulder in the direction of the kitchen. "Some of us are having fun. Finally."

Within a few minutes, Mike made his entrance. He said good morning to everyone, ruffled Christopher's head of floppy hair and accepted a mug of steaming coffee from Jack. "How's everyone doing this morning?" he asked.

"Beautiful morning," Jack said, sipping from his cup.

"Sure is. I had a pretty decent night last night." He leaned his cane up against the bar and went to the kitchen. He poked his head in and found Paige and Preacher in a serious lip-lock. Feeling somewhat the author of this hot embrace, he watched for a minute. Paige had her arms around Preacher's neck while he had both his big hands on her bottom, holding her close against him. They were completely oblivious to being watched and he couldn't resist. He cleared his throat.

Paige jumped and withdrew her arms, but Preacher refused to release Paige, not moving his hands. He looked over the top of her head with narrowed eyes.

"Beautiful morning," Mike said. "Whenever you get a second, could I have breakfast? I'm starving." He grinned and left them.

When he got back to the bar, he hoisted himself carefully up onto the stool and picked up his mug. "Things are working out pretty well around here," he said. "I don't think I'm the only one who had a good night last night."

"That a fact?" Jack asked.

"I just hope I get breakfast before noon."

Preacher had taken apart his weight bench and put it in the storage shed behind the bar, keeping back barbells and a couple of weights. There was a small tree there instead, as well as one in the bar. He had taken Christopher out into the woods to chop them down and they decorated them together. Beneath the one in the apartment, ready for Christmas morning, were gifts thoughtfully chosen by Preacher and Paige, some bought together, some individually.

Mel and Jack left for Sacramento for a big Sheridan family gathering a few days before Christmas and Mike could not be convinced to join them. Neither was he interested in going home to L.A.—not yet. He'd only been in Virgin River a few weeks and promised he would be fine at the cabin, so Mike would be with Preacher and his new family for Christmas Eve and Christmas Day.

Preacher was still in a state of shock and euphoria at the turn his life had taken. It had been more than three months since Paige had happened into his life and a matter of days that they'd been intimate. Nothing could have prepared him for the joy he felt. Working by her side through the day, he found in her a partner in full. They shared everything from the managing of the bar and cooking to the parenting of Christopher with complete compatibility. She was ever at his hand, looking for ways to help him just as he was always near, taking care of her every need.

And at night, when the little one was asleep, Preacher found he had become a master lover, something that had never in his wildest dreams seemed possible. He had never even considered it. And especially not with a woman like this—a young woman of what he considered stunning beauty with the disposition of an angel.

In no time at all he had learned every way to draw a sigh from her, to make her cry out. Preacher, so easily embarrassed and quiet, had become bold and daring with Paige. Experimental. He had begun to trust his hands, his instincts, much to her satisfaction. And this idea of paying attention to details, memorizing touches and sounds, asking her what she wanted, what she liked—well, this was pure genius. If he didn't find this amazing thing he had with Paige to be so private, he might even thank Jack for the advice.

As he held her against him, flesh on flesh, he asked her, "Will you tell me if it's too much? If I'm too demanding?"

"Yes, John," she said, breathless. "Will you tell me?" she asked.

He answered with a lusty laugh. "Yeah. Sure. But you'll have to dig me up to ask me."

"Then do that thing you do… Again," she said.

"And again and again and again?" he asked, teasing her.

"Ooh, John…"

This business of the female orgasm Preacher found to be the best discovery of his lifetime. It had to be better than a man's; better for a man than his own. The one thing he didn't even know he was capable of, he'd quickly become an expert at. He was quite sure it wasn't even as much fun for her as it was for him. He had a dozen methods, but one of his favorites was to torture her delightfully by kissing her whole body, from her eyelids to her toes, spending a little extra time right in the center of her body. He liked to start with soft kisses, end with a strong tongue, and when he sensed, *knew* that she was ready to explode yet again, he'd get right inside her so that he could enjoy it. There was nothing in this world like it— that hot, gripping spasm that sometimes caused her to cry out his name and grab hold of him as if she was afraid he might float away. When he rocked with her through that miraculous release, more than once he said, "I think I could do this forever. I could do this for a living…."

He liked to catch her as she fell back to earth, gasping, breathless, weak from an electrifying orgasm. It was so pleasurable for him that he'd hold himself back, delay his own release so that he could bring it to her again. He'd let her have a moment to recover and then begin on her once more, slowly at first, sweetly, gently. Her responses would let him know that it was time for him to be more aggressive, put a little more muscle into it. It was she who determined the pressure and pace—and it made him laugh to think he was so worried that he might break her. She was like finely tempered steel—and she surprised him with her strength. Her power.

It wasn't unusual for her to wrap her legs around his waist and refuse to let him go, or push him onto his back and climb on him, treating him to a bit of his own medicine, taking the choice to wait any longer away from him. Giving back what she'd gotten.

He had no idea his life could be so satisfying. So utterly fulfilling. Nor had he ever considered that it could be so much fun. Their sex was hot, then afterward they could laugh, banter a little, bring the lightness to their life that balanced everything.

"How can I love you this much?" he asked her.

"Or this often?" she countered, laughing.

"Paige, I want you to know something. I know it's too soon for you to think about a whole lifetime, but I'm not fooling around here. I don't have any expectations, I swear. I just want you to know that. I'm in all the way. Committed. I don't want you to ever worry that I'm just passing the time."

She ran her fingertips through the short hair at his temple. "Aren't you a little afraid you could get tired of me, John?"

He shook his head. "I'm not that kind of guy. I take it slow—too slow, sometimes. I give things a lot of time—being sure is a good thing. But I don't change my mind. I know in some things that can be bad. I like things to stay the same."

"I won't hold you to anything," she said. "I'm just so happy to be here, like this, right now…."

"There's something else I want to say about that, about us. I'm not the kind of guy who doesn't want you to talk back or have your opinions or expects you to never have a bad day when you're all cranky and annoyed. I want all of that—I want you to speak up, make demands, insist on the most exceptional treatment and get pissed off if you don't get it. I want you to feel safe to yell at me just because you're in a mood. If I'm not what you want for the long haul, I can live with that. What I could never live with is you being afraid of how I'll act when you're just being yourself."

It was impossible to keep tears from gathering in her eyes. "John... No one's ever loved me like that...."

"Well, baby, I do. In fact, that's the only way I love you. Every part of you—strong and bossy, scared and needy—it doesn't matter. If I'm gonna have you, it has to be all of you, not some little part that feels safe."

She kissed him, quick, on the lips. He brushed a tear off her cheek.

"I know that baby you lost wasn't planned, and it still hurt you pretty bad that it didn't make it. Maybe someday, when you're ready, you'll talk to me about adding to our family. Giving Chris a little brother or sister."

"You'd like children?" she asked.

"I never thought I would. But with you, it comes to mind." He laughed. "It comes to mind pretty hard. It'll keep, Paige. It's just an idea...."

She gently touched his face. "You do understand that if there's a baby between us, you might have to cut back a little?"

"How much?" he asked, that frown that she had come to adore drawing his brows together. And she laughed at him.

"You're teasing me," he said. "Okay, you asked for it," he said, starting on her eyelids.

She grabbed his face in her hands and stopped him.

"John," she said. "I want it, too. Everything. All of you. I've never been this happy."

He smiled. "More where that came from," he said. "Forever, if you want."

Mel was so excited about Christmas in Sacramento, she could barely contain herself. All of Jack's sisters and their families would be around both Christmas Eve and Christmas Day, but the bonus was that Mel's sister, Joey, husband Bill and the three kids were flying in. There was plenty of room at Sam Sheridan's house for them—Jack's sisters all having their own homes in town. Mel and Joey, being the only family they had, had been generously and affectionately drawn into the Sheridan clan. This was only Mel's third visit to Jack's family, and she already felt as though she was going home.

She had left the Hummer for Doc's use, in the event he had to get someone to a hospital. The back of Jack's truck was loaded with gifts, many of which they bought when they stopped over in Redding to spend the night and finish shopping. And to enjoy the comforts of a hotel room, which did not have paper-thin walls or one of the Marines across the hall.

Though they didn't consider the money wasted by any means, it was not a night of wild passion as it might have been a few months earlier. Mel was now seven months pregnant, a little baby girl literally romping inside of her. Sex was lovely, but way more tame than it had been at the time they conceived this little genius. Instead of crying out Jack's name with passion in the aftermath of her orgasm she said, "Ugh."

"You know, if I weren't an incredibly secure man, that might really bother me," Jack said.

"I'm sorry, darling. My back hurts, my boobs hurt, and I think I'm carrying a marching band, not your baby girl."

"I guess that kind of eliminates the potential for lots more sex tonight."

"It's starting to eliminate the potential for lots more sex before spring," she informed him.

She lay on her back, her belly sticking up like a mountain on top of her little frame, and Jack couldn't keep his hands off of it. While there was a time he couldn't keep his hands off the rest of her—and she had no doubt they would be there again before long—right now it was the antics of his baby within her that occupied him thoroughly. He would let go a loud bellow when her entire abdomen shifted, caving in on one side and protruding enormously on the other. And he especially liked when it appeared a foot was sliding in a large lump up one side. She could actually doze while he occupied himself with her pregnancy. It brought to her mind what he was going to look like rolling a ball on the floor with their baby girl, bouncing her on his knee, twirling her around over his head.

"We should think about naming your new playmate," she said.

"I have a suggestion," he said. "Emma."

"I like Emma," she said. "Old girlfriend?"

"Mother. My mother," he said.

"Aw, that's sweet. I think your mother would be happy you're finally serious."

"Mel? Are you nervous about—you know—giving birth?"

"Not at all. You know why, big fella? Because I'm meeting John Stone at Valley Hospital, and if everything goes to hell, I'm having a big fat epidural. Afterward, I'm having a rare steak and a tall beer."

"Mel," he said, running a hand down her hair onto her shoulder. "I want you to have the epidural."

"Jack—are *you* nervous?"

"Oh, baby, *nervous* doesn't touch it. You're my whole

world. I don't think watching you hurt is something I can do. But I gotta be there, you know?"

She smiled and shook her head. "You know how you always said I should trust you? Well, now it's time for you to trust me. I know what I'm doing, Jack."

"Yeah. Well, that makes one of us."

When they were getting ready to leave the next morning to complete the trip to Sacramento, Mel was drying her hair in the hotel bathroom, which was large and had plenty of mirrors. In their little cabin in the woods there was just that one mirror at eye level. Jack was mesmerized by the sight of her, naked in front of those mirrors. He hadn't really seen her like that. He'd seen her naked, of course, but lying down or standing almost a foot shorter than he as they showered. Now he bent, looked at her profile and said, "My God, Melinda. You're huge."

She threw him a look that suggested a different choice of words.

"I mean, you look awesome, Mel. Look at that!"

"Shut up, Jack," she said.

When they got to Sam Sheridan's house, Mel preceded Jack up the walk toward the front door while Jack began toting luggage and gifts. "Mel," he called, causing her to turn around to see him smiling brightly. "You're starting to *waddle,*" he said proudly.

"Uh!" she exclaimed, tossing her hair as she turned abruptly away from him.

Although Christmas Eve wasn't until the following day, all of Jack's sisters and at most of the husbands if not all the kids were there to meet them. Mel's sister and family had arrived ahead of them, so it was, as usual, a teeming throng. When they got inside, the women rushed to her, embracing, examining her growth, exclaiming, "Oh, my God, you're *huge!*" To which Mel giggled happily, proudly letting everyone rub their hands over her belly. Joey screeched, "You're waddling like a duck!" and they all crumbled into hysterical laughter, including Mel.

Jack was frowning darkly. A couple of the brothers-in-law, Dan and Ryan, came forward and said, "Need a hand unloading, Jack?"

"Yeah," he said, his brows drawn together.

"What's the problem?" Ryan asked.

"I said exactly those two words to her—*huge* and *waddle*—and she was very pissed about it."

The men laughed. Bob clamped a hand on his shoulder. "Come, my brother. Let's get you unloaded, get you a beer and teach you the facts of life. Out back, where men will be men and the women won't hear us."

Outside on the patio, now too cold for picnicking, there were a couple of large space heaters thoughtfully provided by Sam, who knew the men of the family would want their beer and cigars without interference. And where Sam also wanted to be, while his daughters overran his house and bossed people around. With Mel and Joey, there were six, not to mention granddaughters—a formidable and intimidating group of women.

It was there that Jack learned from the experience of four brothers-in-law and the occasional comment from Sam, that if having children was a partners' project, pregnancy was definitely a team sport. The women were the ones who knew the rules. What a man said and what girlfriends or sisters said were viewed from entirely different perspectives. If your sister said you were huge, it was a badge of honor. If your husband said that, he thought you were fat. If your best friend said you waddled, it was adorable. If your husband said that, he thought you walked funny and he no longer found you attractive.

"And look out," said Joey's husband, Bill, father of three, "if you try to make love to her, she thinks you're a pervert, and if you don't, she'll accuse you of no longer finding her desirable as she sacrifices herself to bear your child."

"The last time we had sex, instead of crying out 'Oh, God, Oh, God,' she said 'Ugh.'"

Ryan spewed out a mouthful of beer and fell into a fit laughter. "Been there, brother," he finally choked out.

"You wanna know what's coming, or you wanna be surprised?" Bob asked.

"Oh, please, I can't take any more surprises," Jack said.

"Okay, you're coming up on where you love the baby more than her. Everything is about the baby—you consider her your brood mare."

"What do you do about that?"

"Well, for starters, never talk about breeding."

"Grovel," said someone else. "Beg for forgiveness."

"But don't trip yourself up and claim she's *way* more important than the baby, which brings you a whole new set of problems."

"Aw, Jesus."

"And since you don't have the big belly and the backache, it would be advisable not to mention that this is all completely natural. She might deck you."

"You'd think a frickin' midwife could rise above these ridiculous notions."

"Oh, it's not her fault. There was an estrogen explosion in there—it's beyond her control."

"You want to be especially careful about admiring her breasts," Jeannie's husband, Dan, said. He took a pull on his cigar. "Especially since they're, you know, only temporary."

"God, that's gonna be so hard. Because—"

"I know." Someone else laughed. "Aren't they *great?*"

"Pretty soon there's going to be labor and delivery," Bill said. "And the love of your life, whose back you're trying to rub and whom you're doing everything in your power to encourage, to keep comfortable, is going to tell you to shut up and get your fucking hands off her."

Everyone laughed so hard at that, even Sam, that it appeared to be a universal fact.

"Dad," Jack said, stunned. "Did Mom ever say *fuck?*"

Sam drew leisurely on his cigar. "I think about five times," he replied, throwing the men into a new fit of laughter.

"Why doesn't anyone tell you these things before?" Jack asked.

"What difference would it have made, Jack? You didn't know you were about to score a pregnancy, anyway. I know, I know—you thought you knew everything there was to know about women. Turns out you're just as stupid as the rest of us."

A few more jokes made the rounds before Jack said, "Someone's missing."

Everyone, even Joey's husband, Bill, seemed to look down. Brie's husband, almost an ex, was the only spouse not in attendance. Brie was the only sister no longer tethered; the only one without children. And she had so wanted a baby.

"Anyone seen him?" Jack asked.

"Nope," someone said, the group shaking heads as one.

"How's she doing?" he asked.

"She says she's fine, but she is not so fine."

"According to her sisters."

"And he's at the new house with the new woman, who was the old woman in Brie's life. Having a family Christmas with her and her kids."

"While my sister, who wanted a baby, is here with us," Jack said.

"Yeah, the son of a bitch."

"Can't we have a few more and go over there?" Jack asked. "Just beat him up a little or something?"

"I wish. They'd all secretly love that, and we'd be grounded for life."

"Can't any of us stand up to those women?"

"Nope," said at least three men in unison.

"I just don't get it," Jack said, for the millionth time.

"Jack, have you asked yourself, what if you'd been married to someone else when Mel came along? What would you do?"

"We've all asked ourselves that," Ryan said dismally.

Jack *had* asked himself, though it was an unfathomable idea. There had been lots of women, yet no one before Mel. He'd been really fond of a few, yet somehow managed to not marry anyone. "I'd like to think I'd do the right thing and just kill myself." He looked at the boys. "She getting out of this okay? Like with the house and stuff?"

"Shit. Don't ask that," Dan said.

"Oh, don't tell me…"

"She's getting the house," Bob said. "She's buying him out. And paying him alimony."

"No way!"

"You were told not to ask."

"How does that happen?"

"She's an attorney, he's a cop. She's making the most money."

"See—we need to go over there, beat him up."

Christmas Eve they had ham and potatoes au gratin while Christmas Day it would be stuffed turkey. The clan started to gather at about four and the house throbbed with noise and laughter. They ate, drank, gathered in the family room, *stuffed* themselves into the family room, and sang carols. The men sang too loudly and off key and the women, to the last one, had to drive home. Mel and Joey steered their husbands to their beds, where they flopped down and would surely live to regret having beer, drinks and then brandies and cigars. The only thing that annoyed Mel more than Jack drinking too much on Christmas Eve was that he couldn't stand up long enough to shower off the smell of illegal Cubans.

The kids were tucked in and the men were asleep, to put it politely. Joey was in her pajamas and Mel was in a soft and roomy sweat suit. They met in the family room. Mel brought the quilt and pillows out from her bedroom and they huddled on the couch together, eating ice cream and talking.

"You're feeling well, except for the heartburn?"

"I'm feeling pretty wonderful," Mel said. "For someone who has an entire gymboree inside of her."

"And things in Virgin River are great?"

"Oh, Joey, you should see Preacher and Paige—I've never seen a transformation like that in my life. They are so in love, there's practically a halo around them both. When they look at each other, there's steam."

There was a sound that caused both women to lean forward on the couch and look toward the front door as it opened. Brie came in. She was wearing her coat, her purse slung over her shoulder, tear stains on her cheeks. She stood in front of them and said, "I don't want to go home. Alone. On Christmas Eve."

"Oh, baby," Mel said, opening her arms.

Mel and Joey instinctively slid apart so that Brie could sit between them. Brie dropped her purse, shed her coat, kicked off her shoes and climbed onto the couch in that little space they provided. And cried.

"It's not like I haven't gotten people through divorces," she said. "But you can't imagine what it's like when the man you love, a man who's leaving you, asks you to be his friend."

"God, what nerve!" Mel said.

"You know what's worse? I hate him for what he's done—and I still can't stop wanting him back."

"Oh, Brie…"

"If he came to me tonight and said, 'I've made a terrible mistake,' I think I'd forgive him. Do you know he's asked me for alimony? That he's going to spend on her and her kids? She's getting alimony and child support from her husband, and I'm paying them, too, and they both have good jobs. They're going to make money on the deal."

"The bastard…"

"And I can't wait to start hating him for that. But I'm so afraid I'll start hating him, which closes the door on letting him back. I want him back," she wept. "I think I still love the son of a bitch."

Mel and Joey put arms around her and held her as she cried.

"I'm so sorry," Brie said. "It's Christmas. And I bet this is the first really good Christmas you've had in a while, Mel."

"We're family," she said. "We rejoice together. We share our pain. You're staying right here with us. We're sleeping on the couch tonight, anyway. I bet it pulls out."

"Why are you sleeping on the couch?"

"Our drunk husbands stink," Joey said.

# Fourteen

Jack rolled over early Christmas morning with a loud moan and a splitting head, and some memory of learning the facts of pregnant women over far too much alcohol. Or was that the previous night? He wasn't sure. There might have been inappropriate joking in the presence of the women, but he hoped they'd all been too drunk for that. His mouth tasted vaguely like a kitty litter box. He opened one bloodshot eye and saw that the bed beside him was empty. "Oh-oh," he said. The sudden knowledge that the only man in the Sheridan family not in trouble would be Sam did not comfort him much.

He dragged himself out of bed and looked at the clock—6:00 a.m. There was time to mend his fences before the masses descended on them again, but he would first have to find his wife. He hoped she was still in Sacramento.

He rinsed his mouth and ran a brush over hair that was spiking every which way. The only thought he had was that he really hoped his lousy brothers-in-law were all in worse trouble than he undoubtedly was. Because surely they had done this to him. Bad influences, to the last.

He still had on last night's trousers. Not a good sign. However, she had not killed him in his sleep—and that *was* a good sign. She was probably saving his execution for later, when he could feel it. He stood up straight in front of the mirror. He stuck out his hairy chest. He flexed, popping out tattooed biceps. I am a marine, he said to himself. She is five foot three. He sagged visibly. Who am I kidding? was his next thought.

He crept out of the bedroom into a silent house. Ah, there they were. Mel, Brie and Joey, on the sofa bed. Brie? Well, he'd find out about that later. He knelt on Mel's side and gently moved her hair away from her eyes. One eye opened and there was not a smile in it. "Baby, are you pissed?" he asked gently.

"Yes."

"I'm sorry. I might've had one too many."

"I know. I hope you're in agony."

"What are you doing out here?"

"Trying not to sleep in an ashtray."

"What's Brie doing here?"

"We'll talk about that later."

"Am I going to be punished?" he asked.

"Yes," she said. And she closed her eye.

It turned out that the great lover, Jack Sheridan, didn't know his way around women nearly so well as he thought. He decided to shower and dress, in an attempt to get some points for effort. That accomplished, he crept quietly to the kitchen to make coffee and take aspirin. He was in no condition to fight; he had a hangover. And within a few hours there would be that huge gang of people back at the house, tearing into presents, yelling, laughing, making his head want to explode.

Sam met him there. "Gonna be fun today," he said. "You boys, you sure know how get the women all spooled up."

"Save it. Want me to help you get the bird ready?"

"Yeah, we should do that. Then we make brunch."

"I'm good with brunch," he said. "Did you notice Brie is here?"

"I noticed that," Sam said. "And I noticed that so far, two of the five married women in this family did not spend the night in bed with their husbands."

"Okay, *save* it. Since I'm going to get it later, I don't need your two cents."

"Whatever you say, son," he said. "If you get in really deep, maybe you can take her back to my office and show her all your medals, tell her how you've barely escaped death a dozen times and she just doesn't scare you."

Jack glared at his father. Sam laughed, having far too much fun with this. Then Jack got busy cooking. He sautéed onion and celery in butter, washed the turkey, mixed the stuffing, peeled the potatoes. He had noticed that when Mel saw him doing domestic things, it softened her.

Brie was the next one in the kitchen, cozy in one of Mel's long flannel nightgowns—the kind she used when she'd be around other people in her nightwear because at home, with Jack, his body heat was so intense, she could hardly bear to wear anything at all. Brie put her arms around Sam and said, "Morning, Daddy. I just couldn't go home last night."

It tore at Jack's heart and he wanted to kill Brad. Wanted to put his arms around Brie.

"I'm glad you were here, honey," Sam said. "You know this is always your house. Stay tonight, too."

"Maybe," she said, burying her face in his chest as he held her.

Next came Mel. She was still in last night's sweat suit. But when she walked sleepily into the kitchen, she walked right into Jack's arms and he must have breathed an audible sigh of relief because she whispered, "You're still going to be punished. But not on Christmas."

He smiled and kissed the top of her head because here

was something he thought he knew about women for sure—if there was any kind of delay in the execution, they tended to lose interest. If she wasn't mad enough to go after him right now, she wasn't mad enough.

Christmas in Virgin River was a much quieter affair. For the first time since opening, the bar was closed for the day. Christopher had his gifts in the morning, which left him with plenty to occupy him throughout the day. Preacher turned out a delicious roast duck and all the trimmings while Paige worked on pies. Mike showed up at five with gifts—books for Christopher, a green cashmere sweater for Paige the color of her eyes, and for Preacher, specialty items for the kitchen purchased at Williams-Sonoma. "This is *great!*" Preacher said with enthusiasm.

"I don't even know what some of that stuff is," Mike said. "But it's guaranteed for someone who loves to cook."

"Let's see, we have a mandoline, a thermostatic tray—Jesus, this stuff is incredible. A gravy separator, which I don't really need 'cause my gravy is *perfect.* A grip-and-flip spatula, scoop-and-strain ladle, micro grater. Good work, Mike," he said, grinning.

As they were sitting down to dinner, Paige came into the bar wearing her new sweater and, Mike noticed, dangling in the V of the neck, a very beautiful diamond pendant necklace. "Well," he said, "someone had a very nice Christmas."

She touched the necklace, a huge and lovely surprise from her man. Who knew Preacher could buy jewelry? Who knew Preacher knew what jewelry *was!* "I feel badly, Mike. We had nothing for you."

"Being here with you three is Christmas enough for me," he said, meaning it.

"Did you talk to your family today?" she asked him.

"Oh, yeah—about a hundred of them. All at Mom and Dad's."

Preacher set about carving the duck. "You don't miss being there, with them?"

"Not yet," he said. "Not until I get a little something back, you know? I need the space. They're Latino and Latina—very demonstrative. Close. Intense, you know? Anxious and annoyingly well meaning. I want to at least be able to cut my meat with my right hand before I visit."

"I get that," Preacher said. "You watch. You'll have it in no time."

After dinner Paige left the men to a game of cribbage in front of the fire while she cleaned up. A little while later Christopher was downstairs, all scrubbed with one of his old books in his hand. He crawled up into Preacher's lap as if he'd been doing it since he started walking. And Preacher drew him up like a father would. "This the one you want?" he asked Christopher.

"Horton," he said.

"You don't want to try a new one? We read Horton every night."

"Mazy the lazy bird…" Christopher pointed out.

Mike turned his chair toward the hearth and put his feet up, enjoying the sound of Preacher's voice telling the story by heart, Christopher adding lines that Preacher deliberately left out just for fun. My man Preacher, he was thinking—all soft and sweet, his voice rough and gravelly as sandpaper, holding a kid on his lap like he'd been doing it all his life. This was a guy who you didn't want to see coming at you with a scowl on his face and his fists up. A picture of him in fatigues, toting an M16, a snarl on his face… The guy could take down a whole army. Mike looked at him now with new eyes. Transformed into a big, cuddly bear. Committed. Devoted. All in.

It wasn't long before he stopped reading, dropped a

kiss on the head of his sleeping boy and said to Mike, "Pour us a little something. I'll be right back."

Mike picked out the whiskey Preacher seemed to favor—a nice mild Canadian—and brought the bottle and two glasses to the table. When Christopher was tucked in and Preacher back, Mike lifted his glass to Preacher. "To you, old man. I think maybe you have it all."

"I have to drink to that," he said, sitting down. "Thing is—I really am going to have it all. When all that crap with Lassiter is settled and behind her some more, we're going to talk about making a lifetime commitment. And children. More children, you know, because we already have a perfect family." He took a breath. "Man, I never thought this would happen to me."

Mike was shocked at first, but recovered quickly. "Well, hey," he said. "Congratulations. I guess everything worked out like it was supposed to."

"Whew," Preacher said before he could stop himself.

Mike chuckled. Good for him, he thought. It's not as though Preacher hadn't waited long enough to find this kind of happiness. "She's a great girl, Preacher."

"Have you seen how good that kid is?" Preacher asked. "Because she is just an awesome mother, that's why."

"And she'll be an awesome wife, too," Mike said.

"We have a few issues to work out. That business with her ex—it's still pretty ripe," Preacher said.

Mike sat forward. "How so?"

"Well, he's called here. He's not supposed to, but he's called."

"You tell anyone about that?" Mike asked, sitting up straighter.

"Yeah, we got in touch with her lawyer, who will get in touch with the judge. She didn't talk to him, but I had to tell her. I'm not going to be keeping things back from Paige. He called a few times, thinking she'd talk to him.

He wants to know if anything can be worked out, if he can at least have Chris for weekends or something. Jesus, man—I'd be scared to death of that. I can't imagine that."

"Paige doing okay?" Mike asked.

He shrugged. "Stirred her up pretty good, but she never caved. The woman is brave. I see it grow, more every day. She refused to get sucked in, even if it did make her shake a little bit. But I gotta tell you—I'd be tempted to take Paige and Chris and run for it if there was any chance the court would turn him over to that brutal lunatic." He took a sip of his drink and said, "I couldn't let that happen. I have to do better by Paige and Chris than that."

"Yeah," Mike said. "I sure understand."

"Yeah? You do?"

"Of course I do. You have to take care of your woman. Your family. Whatever that takes."

"Right after Christmas gets handled, we're going to call Brie. She knows everything about this kind of monster. And, she knows everyone in California. She'll have advice."

"Good idea," Mike agreed.

"Yeah," Preacher said. "You know, I never figured myself for a family man. I thought I'd be fishing and cooking it up for the other fishermen in this little bar for the rest of my life. There aren't any women around here, not to speak of. What are the chances some woman wanders in here and needs me."

"She more than needs you," Mike said.

"Yeah," he agreed. "She does."

"You and Jack," Mike said with a bit of a laugh. The two most unlikely candidates for domestic bliss Mike could think of. Jack, because he'd always had a woman somewhere, but never one that held his interest long enough for any kind of commitment. Jack used to say, "Me? Marriage? I highly doubt it's possible." And then Preacher, who seemed not to notice women existed.

"Jack," Preacher said, shaking his head. "You shoulda been here for that," he said, laughing. "Our Jack—Jesus, I hate to think the number of women he ran through, never lost a minute of sleep." Preacher looked over at Mike, grinning. "Took Mel about thirty seconds to turn him into a big pile of quivering mush."

"Yeah?" Mike said, smiling.

"Then it got fun," he said. "She wasn't having any of him."

"Wait a minute—I was up here last year to fish with the boys. Looked to me like he had a lock on her. Next thing I hear, she's pregnant and he's going to marry her. I figured he finally ran into one that could trip him up."

Preacher whistled. "Nah, it didn't go down like that. Jack went after her like a bobcat goes after a hen, and she just kept dodging him. He rebuilt her whole cabin for her without being asked, and I think *maybe* it got him kissed. Sometimes she'd come in the bar for a beer and he'd light up like a frickin' Christmas tree. And she'd leave and he'd head for the shower. Poor bastard. He was after her for months. I guess no one ever said no before."

They used to all say yes to me, too, Mike thought.

"Now when you look at 'em, it looks like they've been together since they were kids," Preacher said. Then more softly, "And that's how I feel with Paige. Like she's been in my life forever."

Mike thought about that for a moment and then said, "Good for you, man." Mike finished his drink and stood up. "I'm going to let you get back to your girl. I'll make it an early night."

"You sure, man? Because I think Paige is busy putting away Christopher's gifts."

"Yeah, I'm going to head back out to the cabin. Hey, dinner was fantastic. One of your best ever." He carefully stretched out his back, then his arm. "I'll see you sometime tomorrow, I guess. Thanks for Christmas."

Funny the way things work out, Mike thought. Jack and Preacher, two men who thought they'd never hook up, totally down for the count. Their women had them both in the palms of their pretty little hands.

Now Mike, he thought he'd hook up. Actually, he thought it would be automatic, which probably led him into marriage without him giving it enough serious thought. All his brothers had fat, happy wives and lots of kids. His sisters had made good marriages for themselves, added to the grandchildren. But he'd screwed up his marriages, thanks to that good old Latino prowess, that itch that has to be scratched real quick, without thinking about the consequences. Well, that was no longer an issue.

But he watched Jack and Preacher and had to wonder about how good it would feel to have someone in his life he'd die for. Damn, what a buzz that would be. He'd never felt that way about a woman.

He was glad, in a way, that it hadn't found him. He'd hate to have a beautiful, sexy, devoted wife in his bed and leave her wanting. So—the bullets had decided. He'd be on his own from now on. One thing he had discovered, it was a little easier to be alone here than a lot of other places. There were loyal friends and the air was real good. If he kept at it, kept working and practicing, he'd be able to fish and shoot just fine with the left arm and hand.

When Jack was driving back to Virgin River, he got off the road right before they got to town. "Aren't we going home?" Mel asked.

"One quick stop," he said. Then he pulled onto that bumpy, narrow road that went up and up until it opened into a clearing with a view that went for miles.

"Why are we here?" shé asked.

He reached in front of her and opened the glove box, pulling out a thick document. He handed it to her. "Merry Christmas, Mel. It's ours. I'm going to build you a house right here."

"Oh," she said, a little breathless. "Oh, God," she cried, tears coming to her eyes. "How'd you convince them?"

"It was easy. I told them it was for you. Do you have any idea how much this town loves you?"

This was what she'd dreamed of when she decided to come here—good country people who would appreciate her help. "They all mean an awful lot to me, too. Then there's you…"

They sat in the truck for a long time, just looking out over the land, talking about the house. "A great room with a fireplace, a kitchen so big that your entire family can gather in it," she said.

"A soundproof master bedroom," he said.

"And master bath with two closets and two sinks," she supplied.

"Three bedrooms in addition to ours, and maybe a guest house—a one-room guest house with a refrigerator in it, and a roomy bath. In case my father, you know—"

"In case your father what?" she asked.

"Ever needs a place with us. In his old age."

"Wouldn't he want to be with one of your sisters?"

"Actually, I think he's been trying to get away from them for years now." Jack laughed. "Haven't you noticed how bossy they are? No, you wouldn't notice because—" He stopped suddenly and she threw him a look. He thought, What am I? Suicidal? "Because you all get along so well."

"Nice save," she said. "What do you need all those bedrooms for?"

"You never know." He shrugged. "Emma might be having company."

"As in siblings? Jack, we weren't supposed to get this one!"

"I know. And yet—"

"That'll never happen again," she said. But she shivered.

"What was that?" he asked.

"I can't help it. Sometimes when I think about that night… That first night… You know, I think she was conceived the second you touched me."

He was sure that was accurate. "Thus, the bedrooms," he said.

"And Jack?"

"Hmm?"

"There will be no dead animals on the walls of my house."

"Awww."

"None!"

Jack and Mel immediately labored over a floor plan and rendering that they could send to Joe Benson, the Marine architect in Grants Pass, Oregon. After Joe's first tour in the Corps, he went into the reserves, got his degree and started his business, but then was called up for Iraq, where he served with the others under Jack. He was thrilled to be asked to draw up their plans. In January, the initial plans were complete and Joe brought them down to Virgin River. When he walked into the bar, Mel was there with Jack. Joe had the plans rolled up under one arm and Mel jumped up with an excited gasp.

Joe stood right inside the door, a smile growing on his lips and a wonderful warmth lighting his eyes as he looked her up and down. "Oh, honey," he said in a breath. "Look at you. You're gorgeous."

Mel laughed. These guys, she thought. To the last one, they loved pregnant women. It was very amazing, very sexy. No one could better appreciate that kind of man than a midwife.

He dropped the plans on a table and moved toward her with his hands stretched out, tentative.

"Go ahead," she said.

His hands were on her belly in no time. "Ah, Mel." Then he pulled her into his arms to give her a hug. "Ripe and ready," he said. "You're so beautiful."

"I'm right back here," Jack said from behind the bar.

Joe laughed. "Be right with you, buddy. I have my hands full of woman right now."

"Yeah," Jack said. "My woman."

"You need your own woman," Mel said. Another one who was, like her husband, a big, handsome man, an angel of a man, and though he was surely over thirty-five, completely unattached.

"I do," he said. He touched her nose. "Why don't you find me one?"

"I'll get right on it," she said, pulling out of his arms and grabbing the rolled-up plans from the table.

They looked them over together, then Jack and Joe went out to the property to walk it. Before pounding in stakes or painting an outline on the ground, Mel and Jack would take at least a couple of weeks to consider changes. Joe stayed over one night, Grants Pass being a four- to six-hour drive, and had a nice evening with Preacher, Paige and Mike.

The plans tended to stay at the bar. Every time someone who was interested in their house came in, they asked to see the plans. Doc Mullins said, "Lot of wasted space in that kitchen."

"I like a big kitchen," Mel said. Though for what, she was uncertain, since Jack seemed to do most of the cooking when they were at home and they took the majority of their meals at the bar. "Jack likes a big kitchen," she amended.

"That Jack," Connie said. "You sure have him trained."

"I found him trained," Mel said.

"Love this bathroom," Connie said. "What I'd give for a bathroom like that."

"All I need in a bathroom is a hole in the floor," Ron said.

Jack and Mel spent a lot of their time together looking at the plans, people looking over their shoulders. One morning Mel came into the bar to have coffee with Jack, who was out splitting logs. Preacher and Harv were found poring over the drawings by themselves.

Mel backed out of the bar and went around back to find Jack. He stopped what he was doing as she approached.

"Do you know what's going on in there? Preacher and Harv have our plans spread out and are going over them. Our house has become a community project."

"I know. Don't let it worry you. We're going to do what we want."

"But does it bother you that everyone has an opinion? That usually disagrees with our ideas?"

He grinned proudly. "I hired excavation," he said. "They start the first week in February. They'll clear and level the land, widen the road. I'm having them clean and stack the trees for firewood."

"It's happening," she said. "It's really happening."

"Yep. It's happening."

"Jack? Not even fish. No dead animals."

Rick was cleaning out the ice machine under the bar, whistling. "Looks like you're doing better these days," Preacher observed.

Rick stood up. "Yeah, things are a little better. Probably thanks to Jack having a sit-down with Connie."

"Yeah? What's going on?"

"We have a couple of things ironed out," he said. "Lizzie's staying with me. I gotta have her close, Preach. Keep her reassured, you know."

"'Course. You gotta keep an eye on that."

"We're spending nights with my grandma—I think it makes her feel good to have people there. And my grandma has always said that house will be mine someday, anyway. Not a lot of room there," he said with a shrug, "but enough for now. We have a little crib in the room and a couple of things for the baby. Lizzie is helping out at the store during the day. She's taking a leave from school for a little while. She didn't go back after Christmas break and she's a lot happier. Lots calmer. The baby will be here in a couple of months, then she'll need some time with him. She'll get a little behind, but I'll graduate on time. Then we'll work on her diploma."

"Planning to keep that baby?" Preacher asked.

"Can't do anything else, man. It's not going to be easy. I'll take care of the baby while she's at school, and when she gets home in the afternoon, I can come in to work till eight, nine, whatever. We're not going to try to get married till we have a year or two together. And get a little bit older."

"You thought about college?"

Rick laughed. "Not for a few months now."

"One thing at a time, bud. You have a family to think about. Then, there's always community college when Liz is in high school. All I'm saying is, these things don't have to come in a hurry. No point in taking on things that will only tip you over the edge. You're only seventeen—there's time."

"That's kind of what Jack said…."

Preacher grinned. "Did he, now." He and Jack had talked about this. A lot.

"God," Rick said, shaking his head. "You guys. You're the best friends I've ever had."

"So are you, pal. You just have to never panic. Things can fall into place."

"Maybe that's right," Rick said.

"Sure that's right. You're doing fine, kid. Give yourself a little credit. You make us old boys real proud."

Mel went to the bar in the afternoon, looking for Jack. Preacher told her he was out at their property, shooting with Mike. "Where's Paige?" Mel asked, looking around.

"Lying down with Chris, I think. She took him up for a nap and said she might."

Mel looked at her watch. She had twenty-five minutes to kill before her next appointment and had been looking for an opportunity just like this. She jumped up on a stool facing Preacher. "Paige seems very happy," she said.

The look that came over Preacher's face was wistful. Angelic. "She does," he said. "It blows my mind."

Mel couldn't help but chuckle. "Could I have a ginger ale?" she asked. "I've been meaning to talk to you about something…."

He poured her a drink, put it on a napkin in front of her. "Yeah?"

"You remember that time several months ago, after the boys were up to fish and play poker, Jack had that meltdown. Got tanked, passed out, had to be carried to bed. You said sometimes the past snuck up like that and it would take him a while to get his stability back." Preacher gave a single nod, frowning slightly. "So—you know what that was, right? I'm sure if you served in combat, the Marine Corps talked about it some." He just looked at her. "Post-traumatic stress disorder. PTSD."

"Has he been having trouble with that?" Preacher asked.

"No, he's been good. I watch, though. I want to tell you a story. A short one. I had a friend back in L.A., in the hospital where I worked. She was an administrator, older than me. A brilliant woman. When I knew her she'd been in her second marriage for twenty years. One night over a glass of wine she told me that her first marriage, a brief marriage, had been extremely abusive. She got beat to a pulp regularly. And while her second marriage was totally kind and loving, sometimes she'd see an expression on her husband's face or he'd have a tone of voice—completely innocent for him—yet it would conjure something from her previous life with her ex-husband and there'd be a rush of emotions—fear, anger. Terror. It would put her in a funk, depress her, really challenge her ability to cope. She said it was as if her nervous system was programmed to react a certain way, which had helped her to survive the first marriage. But she felt bad about the way her reaction would make her second husband feel. Like he'd done something wrong, when really, the wrongdoing was ages ago."

Preacher looked down. "You mean I could remind her of that shitbag somehow?" he asked.

"Not really, no," Mel said. "It's way more subtle than that. Something harmless and innocent 'suggests' that earlier time…because…" Mel's explanation trailed off.

After a moment of silence, "I can get that," he said. "Like a war veteran hearing fireworks and suddenly feeling like he's back in a firefight."

"Exactly," she said. "And then there's the thing about shame. My friend, she told me that sometimes she would be chased by it. It's hard to understand why a woman who has done nothing wrong and has been abused would ever feel shame—it's the shame of letting herself get into that situation, at not getting out faster, shame at having let it happen. It's not a right or wrong thing, it just is. We can't judge feelings. John, I wanted you to know about this. In case you run into it."

He was quiet for a minute. Finally he said, "Is there something special I should do?"

"Nah," she said, shaking her head. "If you sense a

chronic problem, behavior you can't understand or explain, think about support counseling. Maybe none of this will happen with Paige. I'm only telling you because it can. It might. You should be in the know. I think you do the things that come naturally—be loving. Forgiving. Patient. Understanding. That night with Jack? I held him in my arms and told him it was all right."

Again he was quiet for a minute. "That woman, your friend. Those times her husband did something… Did she stop loving him? Even for a little while?"

"No. Never had anything to do with love. Plus, he saved her life, loving her in a pure way like that. It had to do with being hurt real bad once. A little time, a reality check on her part, a solid partner… She could always manage to get back on track. Kind of like Jack. Lucky to have good people around. Lucky to be safe."

He smiled a small smile.

"If you ever sense something is wrong, don't be too private about it. Let me help you with it. I know a couple of things about this." She glanced at her watch. "I have a patient due. I have to go. I just wanted to talk to you about that. You take it easy," she said. She jumped off the stool.

# *Fifteen*

Wes Lassiter didn't have to go to court. A plea agreement was reached by the prosecutor and the attorney for the defense, and it did not give Paige any peace of mind. The judge was disappointed in Lassiter for breaching the conditions of his bail by phoning Paige and trying to leverage her, but in the end he sentenced the man to forty-five days in jail, five years of probation, and two thousand hours of community service. Also required, a meeting at Addicts Anonymous every day, the order of protection was enforced and the custody agreement upheld. And he immediately went to jail.

"I know it doesn't feel like it, but you're winning," Brie told Paige over the phone. "He's been compromised—he's not getting away with anything. Even though the jail sentence is short, it might be enough to modify his behavior. Jail is ugly. Mean and dangerous. And the scuttlebutt is that he has to liquidate to pay his lawyer, which means you'll be getting your divorce settlement."

"I don't care about that. I don't care about money. I just want to be safe from him."

"I know," Brie said. "But in the grand scheme of things, forty-five days with the threat of the judge going bonkers and sentencing him to ten years if he screws up is better than three to five. Really."

"Why doesn't it feel that way?" Paige asked.

"Because you're scared," Brie said. "I would be, too. But this is good. No one's letting him off. And the chance of him calling or approaching you in that five years of probation and getting hammered for it—that's a strong deterrent. During that five years, he could actually move on. I don't hold much hope of him becoming a different kind of human being, but, God help me, he might find a new target. Oh, God really help me."

"I don't know if that's encouraging, or the worst thing I've ever heard."

"I know," Brie said. "So it goes in our business."

Paige was notified that the house was listed for sale, and that her signature was required. Her lawyer sent her papers regarding the liquidation of 401Ks and retirement accounts. The closed checking and money-market accounts were accounted for, as well as the charge accounts and mortgage balances.

In a quiet moment, Preacher asked her, "Are you worried about money?"

"No, I'm worried about never being free of him. I don't want to be afraid anymore."

"I don't know what I can do about that, besides promising to do everything I can to keep you safe. But, it looks like you're going to get a few bucks here—maybe something you can put away for emergencies. The being afraid part, we'll have to take it as we go. I'll do whatever I can to help."

"I know you will, John. I'm sorry you're stuck with this basket case who's afraid of her own shadow."

"I'm not stuck," he said, smiling. "I've never felt stuck. I live a real simple life, Paige. I've never really worried too much about money. Maybe we should talk about that a little bit. Money."

"Could we not?" she asked. "Money and things—it was so important to Wes. It drove him mad, trying to be rich, to have a lot, to look like he was successful. It leaves such a bad taste in my mouth that if a check comes in the mail, I might not even be able to cash it!"

"Understandable," he said. "But I don't want you to think that if you and Chris are my family, you'd have to worry about your future. His future."

"When I look at the difference between my life then and now, I feel richer now. I have everything I need. Chris and I—we're so much better off."

Preacher decided to let the matter rest, at least for the time being. He'd never talked to anyone about money. He and his mom had been pretty much lower middle class, maybe poor. They lived in a two-bedroom cinder-block house with a cyclone fence around the yard and roof that wasn't dependable. There weren't any side-walks or streetlights on their block. She kept it real nice, but he couldn't remember a stick of new furniture in his lifetime. When she died, there was a policy paying off the little house plus a life insurance benefit and a small pension through the church. It was a small piece of suburban Cincinnati real estate in a declining neighborhood plus a modest amount of cash. He was only seventeen and didn't care about what a sale might bring—he wanted his mom, their home together.

When he went into the Marines, he had to let it go, had to realize he'd never have that life back. It was a hundred and forty thousand dollars in total, a fortune for an eighteen-year-old kid with no family but the band of brothers he signed on with. He'd felt a little like Paige—like he couldn't even cash the check. So he did the next best thing. He put it in a safe place—a CD. A few years later he put it somewhere else—a mutual fund. Since he had no attachment to it and it meant so little to him, it caused him no stress at all to move it around a little, here and there. He had his first computer by then—and he was looking things up, his favorite pastime next to fishing, shooting, reading military history. He learned a little about investing on the computer, then began doing some online. In fourteen years his investments had grown considerably—they approached nine hundred thousand dollars.

The only pleasure Preacher had ever gotten from his nest egg was watching the balance grow—he had no use for it. But now he had a boy who'd be going to college in fifteen or so years. With any luck there'd be more kids needing college. He could keep going—investing and re-investing—but it occurred to him to stuff a couple hundred thousand in bonds, which were safe, so that by the time it was needed, it would be handy.

Later, when the time was right, he'd tell Paige that if she couldn't cash that check from her divorce settlement, it couldn't matter less. She really did have everything she needed. She just didn't know it yet.

Mel's mind might have been wandering a little—pregnant women were known for that sort of thing. She was in Clear River where she'd been gassing up the Hummer, and while stopped at the only light in town, it turned green and she didn't move. By the time she looked up to see that it had changed, there was a loud bang and a jolt; the Hummer was pushed into the intersection. When she got out of the vehicle, a hand pressed to her back and her stomach protruding like Mount Kilimanjaro, the man in the pickup truck who'd rear-ended her went completely pale. She recognized that man—he wore the shady brady on his head, and he had all but kidnapped her to deliver a baby in an illegal grow in a trailer a few months ago.

Mel looked at the bumper of the Hummer. One side was smashed in pretty good.

"Shit," she said.

"You okay?" he asked, a panicked look skittering across his face.

"Yeah, I think so."

"Oh, Jesus, I really don't want to have to deal with your husband on this," he said.

"Me, neither."

"I have insurance. I have a license. I have whatever you need. Just say you're all right."

"Sit tight," she said. "Try not to go nuts on me. Don't flee the scene or anything really stupid."

"Yeah," he said nervously. "Right."

There were no local police in Clear River, so Mel walked back to the gas station and called the California Highway Patrol. She called Jack, assured him she was just fine, knowing that wouldn't cut any grass with him and he'd be flying across the mountain.

About thirty minutes later CHP responded, pulling into the intersection, the car lit up to keep the traffic away from the accident. When the patrolman stepped out of his car, he found Mel sitting in the passenger seat of the Hummer, door open and feet in the street, listening to her belly with a fetoscope. He frowned down on Mel's big belly. "Oh, boy," he said. "You okay?" he asked.

"Yeah," she said, rubbing a hand over her belly. "I'm fine."

"Um. You're awful pregnant," he said.

"Tell me about it."

"You a doctor?"

"Midwife."

"Then I guess you know what you need," he said.

Right at that moment, Jack's truck came screeching into the intersection and he was out and striding toward them. Mel looked up at the officer. "Well, that's probably going to be irrelevant."

Jack took one look at his old friend in the shady brady and got himself all stirred up. The jaw pulse ticked, his complexion went dark and angry. She put a hand on his arm. "I know it's technically his fault, but the light had changed and I didn't go. So try to leave your personal feelings out of this and let the cop do his job."

He glanced over at the cop collecting the man's data and said, "It might be real hard for me to not get personal here."

"Okay, then," Mel said. "Let's shoot for rational."

Forty minutes later, she was lying on the exam table in Grace Valley, the ultrasound bleeping beside her. Jack was nearly distraught, but no one else was particularly worried. John said it wouldn't hurt to check, make sure everything was all right. Clearly the baby was not traumatized; she was bouncing around like a gymnast. June Hudson and Susan Stone were peering over Mel's big belly, looking at the baby on the monitor while John moved the wand around. Then John said, "Well, shit."

"Oh, brother," John's wife said.

"That doesn't happen very often," June said.

"What?" Jack said. "What?"

"But I have all these pink things! From Christmas!" Mel shrieked.

"What?" Jack said. "What the hell is it? Is the baby all right?"

"Baby's fine," John said. "It isn't Emma, that's for sure. Look—femur, femur, penis. I blew it. And I'm so damn good, I can't imagine how that happened."

"It was probably just on the early side," June said. "We should've done another one at twenty weeks to be sure."

"Yeah, but I'm so damn *good,*" John insisted.

"Penis?" Jack asked.

Mel looked up into his eyes and said, "We're going to have to come up with another name."

Jack had a dumb look on his face. Mel didn't recall

having seen that look before. "Man," he said in a breath. "I might not know what to do with a boy."

"Well, we got that news just in time," June said, leaving the exam room.

"Yeah, right before the shower," Susan added, following her.

"I really thought I had it nailed," John said. "I feel betrayed, in a way."

Mel looked up into her husband's eyes and watched as a slow, powerful grin appeared. "What are you thinking, Jack?" she asked him.

"That I can't wait to call my brothers-in-law, the slackers."

Mel was ready to leave Doc's for the day, to walk across the street and have dinner with her husband, when Connie came in assisting Liz to the front door. Connie had a hand under Liz's elbow while Liz was gripping her belly. A dark fluid stain ran down her jeans from between her legs and she was crying. "It hurts," she wailed. "It *hurts!*"

"Okay, honey," Mel said, coming forward and taking the other hand. "Let's see what's going on. When did you see Dr. Stone last?"

"A couple of weeks ago. Oohh."

"Is she in labor?" Connie asked.

"Maybe. We'll know in a minute. Come into the exam room and let me check you. Then we'll see if you should go to the hospital."

Mel and Connie helped Liz undress, peeling off the wet jeans and helping her into a gown she could get onto the exam table. "I'll take it from here," Mel told Connie. "I want to see where we are."

"Call Rick," Liz cried. "Please, Aunt Connie! Please! I need him!"

"Sure, honey." Connie left the room, pulling the door

closed behind her. Mel applied her fetoscope to Liz's belly, though Liz writhed. She waited for the contraction to pass, but it was a long, hard one. Finally her uterus relaxed, not that it gave Liz much relief.

Liz's cries became quieter and Mel worked hard at listening, moving the fetoscope all around. Then she hung it around her neck and pulled out the Doptone, a fetal heartbeat monitor. She moved it over Liz's belly as calmly as possible, despite Liz's squirming and groaning.

"Is the heartbeat okay?" Liz asked.

"It's hard to hear with the contractions right now. I'll listen again after I check your cervix." Next, she put on gloves. "All right, Liz, let me examine you. Feet in the stirrups, slide down for me. I'll be as gentle as possible. There you go. Take some slow, deep breaths." She carefully slipped her hand into the birth canal. Six centimeters. No, seven. Bloody fluid.

"Liz," she said, "it's time. You're going to deliver soon." Mel tried with the Doptone again, her heart plummeting. Liz was a little early; she hadn't even started the weekly visits she would pay to John Stone during her last month. She probably hadn't had an internal exam since the one Mel gave her when she returned to Virgin River.

She got a blood pressure and listened to her heart. Normal, under the circumstances. She applied the Doptone again. "Have you been having contractions long?" she asked Liz.

"I don't know. All day, I guess. But I didn't know what it was. It just kept getting worse and worse. It wasn't like those Braxton things. It was like a *knife!*"

"Okay, honey. It's okay. Have you been feeling the baby move a lot?"

"No. Just my back hurting and lots of… And a stomachache on and off. Gas, I think. Was it gas?"

"I don't know, honey. When did you last feel the baby move?" she asked.

"I'm not sure," Liz cried. "Is he all right?"

"Try breathing like this," she said, demonstrating a deep inhale, slow exhale. But Liz was too far into this. Mel showed her panting, short puffs of air, which seemed to work a little better. "There you go. I'm going to go make sure your aunt Connie called Rick. Okay?"

"Okay. But don't leave me."

"I'll only be a minute. Try the breathing."

Mel left the room, pulling the door closed. "Connie, did you find Rick?"

"Jack sent him over to Garberville to pick up some beef for the bar. He should be back pretty soon."

"How soon?" Mel asked. It was her gut instinct to tell Liz immediately—there was no heartbeat, no movement. But she was so young, vulnerable, so dependent on Rick.

"Minutes, Jack said," Connie answered.

"Okay, good. Liz is in labor and she's dilated. Will you please go stay with her for a couple of minutes? I should call Dr. Stone. It won't take me long."

Doc Mullins caught her in the hallway. "What's going on?" he asked.

Mel leaned close and whispered. "I have no fetal heartbeat, no movement, seven centimeters and she can't remember when she last felt the baby move."

His white brows drew together more and more as Mel spoke. When she was done he said, "God*damn* it!"

"Will you go in there and try? Please?"

"Your ears are a lot better than mine."

"Use the Doptone and try anyway. Please," she asked. "I'm going to call John. He's been seeing her."

He put his old hand on her shoulder. "You couldn't have done anything."

"I know, but please try, Doc," she asked. But she knew he wasn't going to find anything. The fetus had expired in utero. They could try to transport her to Valley Hospital, but as advanced as her labor was, it wouldn't do any good—wouldn't help the baby—and she would be too far advanced in her labor by the time they got there for an epidural, so they couldn't relieve her from the pain. What Mel was focused on was getting Liz through the labor, get the baby out as quickly as possible. But first she had to call John. Thankfully, he answered the call immediately, and she explained the situation.

"I saw her about two weeks ago," John said. "We were fine then. Is she preeclamptic?"

"No. Her blood pressure is okay, and it won't do any good to check her urine with blood present and I don't want to use a catheter now, with so much going on. But I'm saying no—I don't see any edema. She's had a bellyache, can't remember the last fetal movement and her contractions are coming on like gangbusters—her uterus is working hard. She was seven a few minutes ago."

"All you can do is get the baby out," John said. "Want me to come up?"

"What can you do?" Mel asked.

"I can deliver for you, Mel. I hate for you to go through this, being pregnant yourself. It's traumatic."

"I can get her through it," she said. "But damn!"

"Yeah, damn," John said quietly.

"At least this seems to be moving very quickly," she said before she hung up. Then she immediately called Jack. "I need some help over here," she said. "Liz is in advanced labor and I can't get her upstairs."

"On my way," he said.

Doc came out of the exam room just as Mel was headed there. He was shaking his head sadly. All Mel could think was, Oh, God, could things get any harder for these kids? If having a baby too young wasn't difficult enough, having a baby that wasn't alive was horrific.

Hold it together, she told herself. There's going to be a lot of crying—hold it together. Someone has to be strong. Someone has to get them through this.

"Jack's on his way over," she said to Doc. "He can carry her upstairs for us. Send him right in, okay?" Then she went back into the exam room. "Liz, I have to be straight with you—this is going really fast. There isn't going to be time to get you to the hospital. We're going to take you upstairs to the bed. I'll get you through this."

"What about that pain shot?" she asked, already sweating profusely.

"I don't want to slow you down or zone you out, honey. I can give you something when we get situated upstairs… But let's get on with it. I'll help you with the breathing. And Rick will be here soon."

Jack stepped into the room. He was too perceptive for his own good. His expression said he knew that things were not okay, even if he didn't know precisely what was wrong. Mel stepped away from the exam table and Jack leaned over Liz. "Come on, sweetheart," he said tenderly. "I'm going to take you upstairs." As he lifted her up into his arms, the sheet that covered her slipped away, her bare bottom hanging out, but that was the least of Jack's worries. "Here we go. Nice and easy."

He carried her up the stairs to the room in which Mel had attended her very first birth in this town. Liz was writhing and crying as he gently placed her on the clean white sheets. As he pulled his arms out from under her, one of his sleeves was wet with bloody fluid. "Rick?" she asked.

"On his way, Liz. He'll be here any second."

"I need him with me," she cried.

"On his way, honey," Jack said.

Mel was applying the Doptone again, praying for a

miracle as she did so, but there was nothing. Nothing but fierce contractions and no life inside.

"Doc, stay with Liz for a minute, will you?"

"Sure thing," Doc said. He went to her and lifted her hand into his and started to coach her. "Let's try some of those panting breaths, Lizzie," he said.

Mel stepped into the hallway with Jack and Connie. Jack was rolling up his soiled sleeve as the front door to Doc's opened and Rick yelled. "Liz? Mel?"

Mel put a hand on Jack's arm, gesturing for him to stay. "Up here, Rick," she called. He came bounding up the stairs, anxious lines etched into his young face. He was all wound up and obviously scared.

"Is it too soon?" he asked.

Mel took one of Connie's hands, one of Rick's and said, "Rick, I have something to tell you, and I need you to be stronger than you've ever been. For Liz. You're going to help us get through this." Jack stepped up behind Rick and put strong hands on his shoulders. "The baby, Rick. There's no heartbeat." She didn't bother with medical terminology. To this seventeen-year-old boy she said, "He died, Rick."

"What?" he asked, confusion wrinkling his brow. "What did you say?"

"There's no heartbeat. No movement. Liz is laboring and she's going to deliver him soon, and he's not going to be alive."

Connie caught it the first time and began to softly weep, her head down, her shoulders shaking. It took Rick a minute. He shook his head, trying to make it not be so. "Why?" he asked. "How?"

"We don't know, Rick. I talked to Dr. Stone just a few minutes ago—everything was fine when he saw her last. Liz doesn't seem to have any complications. It's been a while since she felt movement. It could have been a few hours, a few days.... These things are rare, but it happens. And we're going to have to tell her."

"I thought he was just quiet last night. Was he...?" Rick asked. "Last night, when I held her, I didn't... No," he said, shaking his head. His eyes watered, though he stood straight. "No," he said again. Mel took him into her arms, this big, solid boy, a father too young, a grieving father too soon. He leaned against her, shaking his head, saying no, no, no, no, over and over. She thought it might be best if he vented a little first, before going to Liz, but then a cry came from the labor room and he raised his head sharply, as though he heard a gunshot. She could see his brave struggle to try to control his own tears.

"She's going to need you so much. It doesn't get any harder than this."

"Maybe we shouldn't. Tell her."

"We have to tell her. It's her baby. Can you do this with me? Because I really need your help."

"Yeah," he said, sucking back the tears and wiping a sleeve across his nose. "Yeah, I think I can. Oh, God," he said, briefly losing it. "I did this to her!"

"No, Rick—this just happened. It's cruel and it's horrible, but it isn't anyone's fault. We have to somehow get through this."

"What if we hurry up and take her to the hospital?" he asked.

"I'm sorry. It wouldn't help anything. Come on, let's—"

"But maybe you're *wrong*."

"You'll never know how much I wish I was wrong. Come with me. She's getting closer and she has to know." She took his hand. "You're going to have to be there for her." She pulled him into the room and, as they entered, Doc left, leaving Mel to do her job.

"Rick," Liz cried, reaching for him. She was bathed in sweat, her hair damp and her features twisted.

Rick rushed to her and took her into his arms, holding her against him, silent tears running down his cheeks. Liz was gripped by too much pain to wonder what was wrong with him. When the contraction passed, Mel took her hand and said, "Liz, Rick and I have to tell you something…." Rick lifted his head from her shoulder and looked at her, his expression strong though his cheeks were wet.

"What?" she asked weakly. "What's the matter?"

Rick brushed the hair back from her brow and barely whispered, "The baby, Liz. He's not okay."

"What?" she asked again.

Rick looked at Mel imploringly. "The baby is no longer alive, Liz," Mel said, struggling against her own tears.

"How do you know?" she asked hotly, scooting up in the bed, suddenly alert and frightened. "How do you know that?"

"There's no heartbeat, sweetheart. There hasn't been."

And then she was gripped by another hard contraction.

"Can't you give her something?" Rick asked.

Mel put on a pair of gloves so she could check Liz. "I'll give her something to take the edge off without slowing her down or blacking her out. But we need to keep this moving," she told them both. "Let me have a look, honey. Knees up. That's my girl. There you go. Good—we're getting close. It won't take too much longer."

"Why?" she asked through sobs. "Why? What happened?"

"No one knows, baby," Rick was saying. "A freak of nature—no one knows."

"Oh, God, Rick!"

"I'm here, baby. I won't leave you. I love you, Liz. I love you so much. We'll get through this."

"Can't anybody do anything?" she shrieked.

"If they could, they would. I'm here, baby. I won't let you go."

As they cried together, held each other through one painful contraction after another, Mel couldn't help but feel tragic pride in these two kids, helping each other through what had to be the most terrible experience anyone can possibly endure, at any age.

"I'm going to want you to push in a minute, Liz." She went to the door and opened it, finding Doc there, waiting. "It's almost time," she said. "She's real close to ten centimeters."

Back in the room, she coached Liz and Rick through pushing, an arduous process. Liz was heroic, and between every hard contraction, she sobbed uncontrollably. Then John Stone stepped into the room. "I thought you could use some help," he said. "I'm right here if you need me."

Mel mouthed a thank-you, then looked back to the field of birth. John donned gloves, set up clamps and scissors.

Liz pushed a couple of times and clung to Rick between contractions. Mel met Rick's eyes a few times and saw that, remarkably, he was holding it together. She briefly thought how like Jack the boy was—his eyes were clear, but his cheeks damp, and he clenched his jaw. But as he lowered his lips to Liz's brow his expression softened and he murmured sweetly to her, telling her he was there, he loved her.

Mel saw the labia separate and the baby's head crown. He was going to come out quick; he was premature and smaller than average.

The baby's head emerged. Right away she could see the arrested development, the slightly blue tinge, but his skin was intact—this baby had expired perhaps a day ago. "Once more, Liz, then it's over." She edged a shoulder out.

Mel left the limp, lifeless baby boy on the bed between

Liz's legs while John clamped and cut. Then Mel wrapped the baby in its blanket, lovingly and gently as if he were alive, his face showing. His eyes were shut, his arms and legs floppy.

"Give him to us," Liz said. "Give him to us!"

Mel passed the baby into Liz's arms. Rick and Liz held him, wept over him, their heads together. While Rick's shoulders silently shook, Liz's cries were wrenching. Then Mel watched as they slowly unwrapped him, touched him, examined every inch of him as though she'd presented them with a living baby. Mel's vision blurred with her tears; she felt them on her cheeks. Inside, her own baby kicked.

Mel gently massaged Liz's uterus for a few minutes, then the placenta came. As she examined it for completeness, it came to mind that this was where the baby had lived, and died. There was no sense to this. When she looked at Liz and Rick she saw that despite the fact tears ran down their cheeks, they were studying the naked baby, touching him with soft, loving strokes, holding his tiny fingers in their hands. Mel looked down, overcome.

John's hand was on her shoulder. He whispered in her ear. "How about I finish up for you here?"

She nodded and moved away. Ordinarily, she'd have insisted on completing the cleanup, but the combination of this sudden, intense loss and her own pregnancy put her in a whole different place. She watched as John examined Liz to see if she needed stitches and covered her up. He checked Liz and Rick to make sure they were okay, though neither of them seemed aware of him. Then he dropped an arm around Mel's shoulders and said, "Let's give them a few moments. Come on."

He pulled Mel out of the room, and once she was outside, she leaned against him and sobbed. John held her while she cried hard tears. While he held her close, he felt her baby move inside her and in spite of his desire to be the strong one, his eyes became wet. At long last she drew a jagged breath and looked up at him. She smiled and wiped some wetness from his cheek. "Thank you for coming."

"I couldn't let you go through that alone," John said.

"I wasn't alone," she said softly. "I was with two of the strongest, bravest kids I've ever known."

Doc transported the baby to Valley Hospital, where an autopsy would be performed, but it wasn't unusual in such situations to find no distinct cause of death. Liz had come through the delivery well, despite the devastating outcome. It took Mel a couple of hours, with John's help, to get everything situated and cleaned up. John gave Liz a sedative and soon after, she slept. By that time, Doc was back and Rick was stretched out on the narrow bed beside Liz, holding her in his strong arms. Mel offered Rick a sedative, as well. "No," he said stoically. "I'm going to stay awake for Liz. She might need me."

It was ten when John left and Mel walked across the street to the bar, each foot dragging in depressed misery. When she walked in, she found that not only had Jack stayed, but Paige, Preacher and Mike were still up, waiting this out for her. Jack stood up from the table.

She walked in, looked at them, and shook her head. "Those poor kids," she said.

Jack enfolded her in his arms, and for a moment she laid her head against his chest. Then she said, "I'm so cold inside—I need the fire. And a brandy. Just a swallow of brandy, please."

He led her over to the fire and when she sat there, Paige reached for her hand. "Bad?"

"The baby was gone before she delivered." To anyone else she might have reported it as very sad. To her intimates, she said, "My heart is in a million pieces, it hurts so bad for them."

Jack brought Mel a small snifter of Remy. She lifted it to her lips with a shaky hand and took a sip, then put it back on the table. She pulled her coat tighter around her, her back to the fire. "You never know where you're going to find courage," she said. "My God, those two kids. They clung to each other and got through the worst day of their lives."

"At least they're young," Paige said.

"Yeah, at least that."

Then the room was silent while Mel absorbed the heat of the fire, quietly partaking of half her brandy. Then she said, "Jack, I want you to go home and get some rest. I'm going to stay with the kids tonight, in case they need me."

His back straightened immediately. "Mel, Doc can do that. Or you could've asked John to stay—Liz is his patient, after all. You're—"

"I'm going to stay at Doc's. And I'd like you to go home and try to sleep. Rick's going to need you tomorrow."

"I'll wait here in case—"

"Please," she said. "Let's not argue about this. You must know I won't leave them now."

"Mel…"

"I've made up my mind, Jack. I'll see you in the morning."

Although Preacher offered Jack his bed or at least the couch in his apartment, Jack did as he was told and went to the cabin. Of course he didn't sleep. On a night like this, he really needed his wife's belly pressed up against him, feeling his son move around in there, alive. But he understood; Mel was as stubborn as she was strong and had she gone home with him, she'd have worried about Liz and Rick all night.

At four in the morning, he'd had all he could take. He got out of bed and dressed. He put on his heavy suede jacket and leather gloves and drove back into town. He parked his truck outside of Doc's, right next to Rick's, got out and leaned against the door. He could have let himself into the bar and started coffee, but there was no point in waking the house; Preacher and Paige should be allowed whatever sleep they could manage. This would have deeply affected them, as well.

Jack stood there, unmindful of the cold, his breath swirling in a steamy cloud above him, until the very first rays of winter sun began to creep over the mountain, more than two hours later. He was going to be right there when Mel came out, when she gave up her vigil, and he would get her breakfast and take her home to make sure she got some rest. He spent a lot of time just looking at the ground, wondering how such an unkind thing could happen.

When the door to Doc's opened, he lifted his head. It was not Mel but Rick who stepped out onto the porch. All Jack could think was, what a damned awful way to become a man. Rick just stood there for a moment, then he slowly stepped down from the porch into the street. He met Jack's eyes and there was such pain, such loss.

Jack stepped toward him and put a hand behind the boy's neck, pulling him onto his shoulder. He heard Rick let go a deep, painful sigh. Jack put his other arm around him and Rick let it go. He fell against Jack and the tears began. "Yeah, buddy. Get it out. I got you."

"Why couldn't I do anything?" Rick asked softly.

"None of us could, son. It's damned awful. I'm so sorry."

Rick cried softly and mournfully, his shoulders shaking while Jack held him. Through all the challenges of this pregnancy, all the sadness surrounding Liz and Rick's situation and their struggles to get through it like grown-ups, with a little dignity, nothing could have prepared any of them to face this. The boy who had become a man, who stepped up and took responsibility, leaned against Jack, shattered, quietly weeping in the anguish of grief. His heart was shredded, and Jack's was aching as he held him.

A single tear traced a path down Jack's stubbled cheek.

# Sixteen

Liz stayed two nights in Doc's hospital room, Rick with her the entire time. They did a lot of weeping and holding on to each other. Mel spent a good deal of time there, trying to comfort. She told them that it was important to remember two things: that it was nothing they or anyone else did, and there was no reason to believe that it would ever happen again. It was extremely rare for an intrauterine death not precipitated by eclampsia or another complication of pregnancy, but sadly, it happened from time to time.

Jack and Mel made the arrangements for the burial of Rick and Liz's baby. Liz wanted to take him home to Eureka, where she'd grown up and her grandparents were buried. And then Liz wanted to stay with her mother, who had become much more sensitive to the young couple, given their tragedy. She extended to Rick the invitation that he was welcome as much and as often as he wanted to be there, for his support was desperately needed to get Liz through these dark days.

Mel grieved. It was certainly not the first fatality for her, but medicine and midwifery in a small town made your patients your friends, and these young people were very special to her. Jack, not really knowing what to do for his wife, took her to June Hudson's house in Grace Valley where John and Susan were present with June and Jim and old Doc Hudson. They had a solemn dinner together, talking about their worst moments, their tragic losses. It was far from cheery, but it got Mel through it—remembering that this was the downside of medicine and that she was not alone.

During that dinner, Jack had the passing thought that the need for these clinicians to share their war stories was not unlike what soldiers did, what his Marines had done. It was a leveler; it reminded you that everyone had a role in holding one another up, in sharing the victories and the tragedies.

Rick took his strength from Jack and Preacher, who watched over him closely, spending long hours at the end of the day talking and giving him the sturdiness of their shoulders, the camaraderie of their shared experiences. These men who had been to war had buried those they loved, young lives cut tragically short. Loss was no stranger to them. And Rick had joined their ranks too soon.

The whole town seemed to suffer for Rick and Liz, but it was clear to Paige that Mel's pain was unique. As she grew round with her own baby's birth imminent, a time that should bring her great joy, she was too quiet. Paige was familiar with the story of how Mel came to Virgin River, and just as she was about to flee, an abandoned newborn was found on Doc's porch and Mel put her own needs aside to stay, to take care of that baby until a home could be found for her. For many weeks and months after Lilly Anderson had fostered the baby, Mel had gone to the Anderson ranch to hold her. Their bond was a strong one.

So Paige went to the clinic one afternoon and asked Mel to go for a ride with her—she had an errand and didn't want to go alone, she said. She drove up to the Anderson ranch and Mel said, "What are we doing here?"

"Good medicine," Paige said. "Come on."

Paige put her arm around Mel's shoulders and led her up the porch. When Lilly came to the door, Paige said, "Someone needs to hold a living baby."

Mel shot her a look, began to shake her head, but Lilly reached for her hand and said, "Of course you do," and drew her inside.

Little Chloe was sleeping, but that didn't matter to Lilly. If there was something Mel needed, there wasn't a person in Virgin River who wouldn't move heaven and earth to help her. Chloe was almost a year old now. Lilly lifted her daughter out of the crib and handed her to Mel. Mel held that little life against her, drawing strength from the baby's cuddle, from her sleepy sighs. It wasn't quite the same as holding a newborn, a healthy baby pulled from its mother's womb, but it served its purpose. Lilly left Mel alone in the baby's room and Mel rocked Chloe for a long time while Paige and Lilly had tea in the kitchen. The warmth of life against Mel's chest seemed to give some healing. Inside her, her own baby kicked and squirmed, letting himself be known. For each movement, even the ones that were uncomfortable, she gave grateful thanks.

On the way back to town, Mel said, "How did you know to do that?"

Paige shrugged. "It hasn't been that long, Mel. It wasn't a full-term baby, but—"

For a moment Mel was shocked speechless. Then she reached across the front seat and grabbed Paige's hand as she drove. "Oh, Paige, I'm so sorry."

"Thanks, Mel. But—"

"No, I'm *sorry!* We were all so focused on how dangerous your husband was, the fact of losing his baby just didn't seem… Oh, God, me of all people! That was *your* baby! Paige, please forgive me. I should have helped with your grief. And instead, you're helping with mine."

Paige cast her a sweet smile. "I'm so glad I could help.

As for me, I'm going to get another chance. And the next time, it will be safer and easier. Sweeter."

Mel squeezed her hand. "Have I told you how glad I am you came to town?"

The first week of February arrived, bringing with it the excavation crew. The second week in February brought two baby showers, one in Virgin River at the home of Lilly Anderson and the second one in Grace Valley, hosted by June Hudson and Susan Stone.

As February aged and Mel's own time drew near, her step might have become slower, but her eyes were brighter and she glowed. Joe Benson brought the final plans to Virgin River and Mel sat beside her husband in his truck and watched as the foundations for their house and the one-room guest house were laid out so they could be poured.

As she grew heavier by the day, it became obvious she wasn't going to be answering many more, if any, emergency calls with Doc. Mel had no babies due, and while she was in town every day, she came later in the mornings. And her husband was never very far from her side.

When Mel and Jack left the bar together at the end of the day, Paige leaned against Preacher and whispered, "I can't wait until we're like that."

"Fat?" he asked, chuckling.

"Fat, full, ready to pop with a new baby. I'm thinking of going off those birth control pills," she said.

"Anytime you're ready," he said, putting his arms around her. "I told you, I'm in all the way."

"Hmm, that's so nice. I'm going to give Christopher his bath while you finish up and close the bar."

"I'll be up in a minute," he said, giving her a loving pat on the rump.

It was this time of day that Preacher had come to regard as the magic that made his life work. Every little piece of it. He liked the act of cleaning his kitchen and never failed to feel grateful for all that was his. Had he not been here, working the place for his best friend, he would not have found Paige, and Christopher, who had become his son.

He locked the door and went upstairs to Christopher's bedroom and, finding him already in the bed, waiting with his book, Preacher sat on the bed beside him. Chris crept closer, climbing up on his lap and touching the pictures in the book while Preacher softly read. Before long, the little guy slept and Preacher was able to kiss him, tuck him in and turn off the lights.

In his own room, he found Paige in front of the bathroom mirror brushing out her hair. She wore her pajama top, which came to her thighs. He came up behind her and moved her hair over one shoulder to kiss her neck, running his big hand up her thigh to her hip, finding, much to his liking, that she was naked under there. It wasn't as though she had to be psychic to anticipate him—he wanted her all the time. She wanted him to want her, and she let him know.

His hands crept higher under the shirt until he held one breast in each hand. She leaned her head back against him and hummed in pleasure. He pulled his hands out and slowly began unbuttoning her top, watching himself and her in the mirror. Her right arm came up, reaching behind herself to his shoulder, and curled her hand behind his neck. Her top unbuttoned and hanging open, he slipped one hand inside to cup her breast while his other fell over her soft pubic mound. And he looked at their reflection. Her head turned, she rested against his chest with her eyes closed, one arm lifted high above her head to embrace him, the other resting lightly atop the arm that had captured her breast. He never dared hope for this—that he would be half of a couple, a handsome, erotic, loving and perfect couple. And something surprised him—he didn't look scary at all. He looked like a man in love, a man holding his woman with sure, strong and gentle hands. And his woman leaning into his embrace, filled with desire for him, her lips parted slightly in a soft sigh. Sighs that would soon become powerful as she gave herself over to him completely. Within her adoring, he had flourished.

Preacher had no idea he could be like this—so sexual, so confident, so deeply in love. He leaned down and kissed the top of her head. "Baby, I'm going to make you feel so good."

"I know, John," she whispered. "I know."

The night that Mike Valenzuela lay in bed and listened to Jack toss and turn after the loss of Liz and Rick's baby, he knew it was time. And yet—time for what? He had no interest in going back to L.A., though his family was due a visit. There was nowhere else in Virgin River to stay. But three months in the same small space with Mel and Jack was already too much—though you'd never know they felt a strain.

That night he knew. They had to have their home back. That had provoked thought, which stimulated ideas.

He'd come so far—his right arm was stronger, his shoulder pained him less. His hand had a decent grip. He couldn't cast with the right arm yet, but he saw hope for that because he could now shoot a pistol with his right hand as long as he gave it an assist with his left. Added to that, he had perfected his left-arm aim with both the rifle and the pistol. He could easily keep up with Jack, who was a decorated sharpshooter.

This was the place for him, he realized without much surprise. He didn't know what he'd do here, but it didn't really matter, because he could retire if he wanted to. He had his disability, his pension. And it cost nothing to live here. Until something changed in his head, he wanted this easy life in a small, uncomplicated town. By the time Jack was ready to frame his house in early summer, his right arm and shoulder would be strong enough to help. He'd add to the menu at Jack's with his own fish; he'd help around town where needed. He'd live as Jack and Preacher had lived, at the center of a town that appreciated their good works and loyal friendship.

Now when he stood in front of the mirror, stripped to the waist, he saw a muscled chest, shoulders, arms. His right side was still smaller than his left around the shoulder and biceps, but it had come a long way and was barely noticeable. Sit-ups were easy; he had his six-pack back.

It was easier to pee, thanks to a round of antibiotics prescribed by Mel. But that other thing—it might be gone for good. He'd had two false alarms, waking up with a good pee hard. He'd gripped it like a drowning man, filled with hope. But, nothing. It just went back down, like the docile memory it had become. He was afraid to hope, but being a man, he held out for a miracle.

So, Mike drove to Eureka, where he bought an RV—his new home. It was his goal to be free and clear of the cabin before the baby came so that Jack and Mel could have their life back. He could park it anywhere he was needed—behind the bar, out at Mel's cabin, even on the property on which Jack was going to build. When he drove it into town, towing his SUV behind, he pulled it right up to the front of the bar. It was the end of the workday—dinnertime. Preacher and Paige would be cooking, Rick would be working, Jack and Mel would be having that after-work drink with Doc. Friends and neighbors would be gathering soon.

He extended the bedroom and living room walls with the pop-outs and pressed the switch for the awnings, for the full effect. Once these walls were pushed out, the bedroom and living room became comfortably large. Then he honked the horn, bringing everyone out on the porch.

He jumped out—sans cane for weeks now—and stood in front of the RV, leaning against it. Mel was the first one out, Jack close on her heels.

"My new apartment," Mike said.

"When…? What…?" Mel stammered.

He reached out his left hand to help her descend the porch steps. When she was down, he dropped an arm around her shoulders. "I wanted to get out of the cabin before the baby—it's time to put that nursery together and I'll help do that."

"But where are you going?" she asked, looking up at him with eyes that had suddenly grown moist.

"I'm not going anywhere, sweetheart. I love it here. But I need my own house. More important, you need your own house."

And when he said that, she fell against him and wept.

"Aw," he said, putting his good arm around her. "I hope those are glad tears."

She lifted her head and looked up at him. "I didn't want us to lose you," she whispered. She wiped impatiently at her eyes. "God, I'm sorry. You have no idea what it's like to be this pregnant. My emotions are like a landslide."

"Naw, I'm honored, Mel. You guys—you've been everything to me these last few months. I started thinking I'm well enough to go home—then realized that this feels like home."

She hugged him tightly around the waist. "I'm so happy to hear you say that."

"Want a tour?"

"Of course. Jack," she said, "get Preacher, Paige and Rick."

When Rick came out on the porch, his face split in a

huge grin and it filled Mike up inside. Rick had been coming along real well since his loss, but the goofy kid the Marines had all come to think of as a little brother had been replaced by a somber and quiet young man. "What the heck?" Rick asked.

"My new digs. What do you think?"

"I think that's awesome," he said, jumping off the porch to join the tour.

They combed through the RV, admiring the accoutrements. Full kitchen with a nearly full-size refrigerator, freezer, washer and dryer, roomy bedroom with a queen-size bed, large closet that occupied a whole wall, large bathroom with a two-person shower, TVs in both the bedroom and living room with roving satellite reception. Plenty of cupboard and closet space for a bachelor and storage compartments underneath.

Before long, there were a number of people trailing dirt through the new RV—Connie and Ron, Doc, Hope McCrea, the Bristols and Carpenters. Christopher loved the big bed, tucked back in the end of the RV.

"Where you going to park this thing?" Preacher asked.

"I don't know. Probably out at Jack and Mel's, till I get a better idea. I could always park out there behind the bar, near the tree line, where the boys all sit when they come to town to fish. Or, I might even look around for land. But not yet. For right now, I'm just going to hang out. Near my friends."

Over dinner they talked about the baby's room, the spackle, paint and papering Mel wanted done. Mike told them he planned to clear out of his room in the morning and then wanted to help get that room set up for the baby. He'd take Mel to Ukiah where there was a Home Depot to pick out what she wanted. And, he told them, after that room was set, he was going to drive down to L.A. to see his folks, brothers and sisters, so he could be back when

Mel delivered. "I figure to be one of the many uncles, so this is where I should be when it's time."

"This is where you should be," she said, covering his hand with both of hers.

Four days later, Mel stood in the doorway of the second bedroom of that little cabin and looked at a room painted yellow, trimmed in blue, papered with tiny hand and foot imprints. A white crib and bureau changing table stood ready to catch the next Sheridan and all the little blankets, onesies, outfits, socks and miscellany had been laundered and lovingly folded away. While she was admiring the room, Jack came into the cabin carrying the most beautiful rocking chair—it seemed to match the cradle given to her by Sam.

She ran a hand along the edges and arms. She couldn't wait to rock their baby in this chair.


The first week in March, Paige received a check for one hundred twenty-some thousand dollars—the balance left after the sale of a three-million-dollar home, the liquidation of 401(k)s and modest liquid cash, minus debts and fees. "I almost can't touch it," she told Preacher.

Preacher stared at the number and thought how pathetic that a man who managed to earn enough to live in a small mansion, put pretax dollars toward retirement and smoke or shoot a lot of white powder could have a net worth so low. Probably the white powder. "Put it aside for a while, but don't lose track of it," he said. "After the shock settles, I can help you find some kind of trust for Chris. You really don't need it."

"I hate even having it. All I wanted from that marriage since the honeymoon was *out*."

"I understand that. But someday you'll be practical and see how you can make something good out of it. Use it to help your kids or something."

She handed it to him. "You keep track of it, then. If I ever get over this, we can make a decision."

It wasn't long after that conversation that it happened— what they'd been trying to prepare themselves for, but which was inevitable. Wes Lassiter was released from his jail sentence. The district attorney called and reported that he'd returned to Los Angeles to begin his required Addicts Anonymous meetings, probation reports and community service. But the community service hadn't been selected and approved by the court, the probation meetings hadn't begun and AA wasn't likely to cooperate with anyone inquiring about whether he was turning up for meetings.

"We'll watch closely," Preacher said. "It'll be neighborhood watch around here, don't you worry. This is one nosy town."

But Paige got tears in her eyes, ran to their bedroom and cried.

When Rick came in for work, Preacher was leaning on his work counter, staring down at nothing. "Hey," Rick said. "Where's the little guy?"

"Nap," Preacher said shortly.

Rick's head lifted, listening. Paige's sobbing could be heard, though muffled. "Everything okay?" Rick asked.

"It'll be fine," Preacher said.

When Rick got into the bar he found Jack behind the counter with his clipboard, marking things off, and Mike up at the bar, giving him some grief about his unwillingness to let Preacher put inventories and receipts on the computer. He walked up next to Jack. "Something's wrong in the kitchen," he said. "Preacher's pissed off and Paige is crying. You can hear her. Like maybe they had a big fight or something."

Jack and Mike exchanged glances briefly, then got up and went to the kitchen. They'd also been counting the days. Rick followed.

"What's up, man?" Jack asked Preacher.

Preacher kept his voice low. "He's out. They say he went back to L.A., but there's no way to check. Paige's scared. Upset. I'm not sure what to do."

"Get ready for anything," Jack said. "Isn't that what we were trained to do?"

"Yeah, but, there's Chris. We gotta be so careful how we do that. I don't want him scared, you know. And I don't want him thinking it's about his dad."

"We can work with that," Jack said. "We won't keep a loaded gun under the bar or anything. If there was a robbery the next town over, we could carry sidearms for a while, till it looked like things are cool. Sidearms around here—not even interesting. Chris, he should stick real close—because there was a robbery the next town over, huh?"

Preacher was shaking his head. "I don't want him scared."

"I know," Mike said. "But a little nervous is better than a little abducted. We need to play it smart, Preach."

"I think Paige is going crazy right now," Preacher said.

"You should go in there," Jack said, giving his chin a jut in the direction of Preacher's quarters. "Tell her we're going to keep a gun or two, but there won't ever be one set down where a kid could touch it. We'll do that till it feels better around here, right?"

"How long's that, you think?"

"I don't know," Jack said. "I could do it a year without feeling the strain. Can you cook with a sidearm? Just because there was some trouble the next town over?"

He was shaking his head again, but not in denial so much as frustration.

"I was gonna go to L.A. for a week to see the family, but I can stay," Mike said. "I can see them later."

"No, go," Preacher said quickly. "Maybe you have a

contact or two that can tell us if he's there, doing what he was ordered to do. That might help."

"I can check that out," Mike said. "I'll make it a quick trip, see if I can find out anything. How's that?"

"Good," Preacher said. "Thanks."

"I'll wear a gun around the bar," Rick said. When all three men swiveled their heads toward him, frowning, he said, "What? I'm licensed to carry! Why wouldn't I get in this?"

"No," Jack said.

"You'll be sorry when I'm caught without a gun."

"Nothing like that's going to happen," Mike said calmly. "He's not going to storm the bar and get himself shot. If he does anything, he's probably going to call Paige, try to convince her he's a changed man, see if he can work a deal with her to get that order of protection lifted, maybe take a new look at custody. His type is manipulative."

"He attacked her once," Preacher said. "Right here, in the street."

"So, defense makes sense. And watching him makes sense. But remember, that was before he was risking a long-term prison sentence. He's a badass, but he's a smart, manipulative badass. Let's see if he went home…."

"The house is gone," Preacher said. "Sold."

"Well, Jesus, finding him could be a challenge. But anybody can be found."

"Preach," Jack said. "Go to Paige. Tell her we're on board. We'll do everything we can to keep her and Chris safe. Best-case scenario, we get the message he's doing his chores in L.A., trying to get his life back, and we can move on. But we don't quit early, huh? Tell her that. We don't quit early."

"Yeah," Preacher said. "Yeah."

Getting used to seeing Jack wearing a gun behind the bar was not easy for Mel. She had adjusted to the fact that everyone in Virgin River owned guns, out of necessity. They had livestock issues, wildlife concerns. Those guns in the racks of pickup trucks were loaded; children were educated in gun safety early. But where she'd come from in L.A., people with guns were either law enforcement or dangerous.

Paige was understandably upset when she'd learned her ex-husband was released from jail, but a week later and a phone call from Mike in L.A. saying Wes seemed to be making his probation and community service arrangements put her more at ease. It gave her hope that maybe all this precaution could be just an exercise.

In the meantime, Mel's baby was lowering and her back was aching. She was a small woman for such a load, and the pressure could be intense. The back pain came and went for a few days. Sometimes if she took a break and lay down for a while, it would go away. She knew she was getting close.

"You're starting to look like you should stop working," Doc said.

"I'm starting to look like I'm going to give birth to a whole football team," she returned. "What am I going to do with myself if I don't come into work? Sit out at the cabin all day and watch fuzzy TV?"

"Rest up," he said. "You're going to wish you had."

"You know, I'm only wishing for one thing right now. My mouth waters at the thought of that stupid epidural…."

"How about a little gin? After you wax me, you can go home and take a nap."

"Sounds good to me." She got out the cards, but before they could deal, a patient came in. Doc stood up to see who had come in the front door, Mel behind him.

Carrie Bristol had her hand under the elbow of her thirteen-year-old daughter, Jodie, while Jodie was gripping her tummy. "Bad tummyache," Carrie said.

"Let's have a look," Doc invited, preceding them down the hall and standing aside so they could enter the exam room ahead of him. A few minutes later, he called Mel to the exam room. "I have a possible positive appy," he said, meaning inflamed appendix.

"Ew," Mel said. She went into the room and looked down at Jodie's squinting eyes. "Bad, huh?"

"Fever, vomiting, pain," Doc said.

"You tap the soles of her feet?" Mel asked. If that technique jarred the appendix painfully, it was a sign.

"Of course. Start an IV for me, will you? I think we'll take her."

"Do you have to operate?" Carrie asked. "How can you be sure?"

"You know what, we often aren't," Mel said. "In fact, surgeons remove a fair number of healthy appendixes simply because to err on the side of surgery is safer than to err on the side of a rupture. If there's time at the hospital and her appendix isn't too hot, they'll do a few blood tests to see if her white count is elevated—that's a sign it needs to come out. But Jodie's symptoms are strong—it's better to just hurry and go. Let the surgeon decide."

Mel got out her IV setup and started a line. Before long they were ready to put her on the gurney.

"Want me to go?"

"Hell, no," Doc said. "Carrie can ride in the back with her. I don't need a delivery along the way."

"We'd be going in the right direction," Mel put in.

"Just close up the office, go home and take a nap."

"Well, at least you're not going in the back of a pickup. Take the Hummer," she told him.

"Right. Let's go. Carrie, you help me with the gurney. Melinda is ready to whelp."

Mel walked outside with them and gave Jodie's hand a pat. "You're going to be fine."

She stood on Doc's porch for a few minutes after they were gone. She noticed Cheryl Chreighton weaving around the side of the boarded-up church, an unmistakable bottle in her hand. Mel ran a hand over her belly and silently vowed that after the baby came, she'd find a way to get that woman some help. That she wasn't a patient was irrelevant. She was a human being in need. When Mel saw a need, she went to work on it.

The breeze picked up and became a brisk wind and the sky was darkening. A few heavy drops fell on the street in front of her and she thought about how much she'd enjoy a heavy rain on a lazy afternoon. It took Mel only a couple of minutes to decide Doc was probably right—she should take the rest of the day off. Her back was killing her. A hot shower and nap sounded fine.

She went over to the bar and hopped up on a stool. "Hello, gorgeous," Jack said, leaning across the bar to put a brief kiss on her lips. "How are you feeling?"

"Huge," she answered. "How are things around here?"

"Calm. Quiet. Nice."

"Can I have a ginger ale, please?"

"Coming up. What's going on with you?"

"Doc took a patient to Valley Hospital in the Hummer—possible appendicitis. So I'm going to take the afternoon off. Can I borrow your truck? Can you get Rick or Preacher to run you home later?"

"I think that can be arranged. Want me to take a break and drive you home?" he asked.

"That's sweet, but I like having the truck. I hate being stuck out there without wheels. If you need it, I can scrounge around for Doc's keys…."

"Nah, take it. I'd rather have you in my truck."

She took a sip of her ginger ale and lifted her eyes toward the ceiling as there was a loud crack of thunder.

"I think I'm going to have a hot shower, put on my flannel nightie and let the rain on the roof rock me to sleep."

"I can come wake you up a little later," he said. "I'll rub your back."

"It's driving me crazy," she said, pressing a hand against the small of her back. "This kid must be sitting on my spine. When he's not dancing on my kidneys."

Jack held both her hands across the bar. "I know this has been rough lately, Mel. Pretty soon he'll be here and you can start to feel better."

She smiled prettily into his eyes. "You know I wouldn't trade this for anything."

"It's the greatest thing anyone has ever done for me," he said. "I love you so much." He came around the bar, fishing his keys out of his pocket. He walked her out onto the porch. She took a deep breath. "Smell that air? Don't you love the smell of rain? It's going to bring us flowers."

He kissed the top of her head. "I'll see you in a few hours. See if you can get some sleep. I know you don't sleep through the night."

She gave him a pat on the butt and went down the porch stairs to his truck. She waved as she cut a wide U-turn and drove out of town. Her back started to really throb as the wind along the road picked up steam and was blowing hard, whipping the branches wildly against the truck. Then there were several bright flashes of lightning and the rain pelted the windshield with gale force. She was within a quarter mile of the cabin when a sharp pain ripped across the front of her abdomen, and when she pressed her hand there she felt the rock-hard tightening of her uterus and she thought, shit! You dummy! Who let you be a midwife? You're in labor! Back labor! All day long! And some of yesterday, too!

Right in front of her in the road lay a pine, obviously cut down by a lightning strike, and she was too late to stop. Swerving, she at least didn't hit it head-on, but she ran the left front bumper into it and caused the right front wheel of the truck to veer off the shoulder.

Distracted by the contraction, she'd almost had an accident. Make that, worse accident. At least the air bag hadn't deployed—that could've been bad, given her advanced pregnancy. She'd go back to Jack; go to the hospital.

She put the truck in Reverse and the tires spun. She tried again and again, rocking the truck. And now, she thought, I have made a real mess of things. Why didn't I stay at the bar ten more minutes? Time enough for this first really good contraction to kick in!

She had no option but to walk the rest of the way to the cabin and call Jack. It wasn't far; she wasn't going to drop this little acrobat on the ground. But, she thought, I am going to be very, very wet. And I'm having a baby a little sooner than I thought.

# Seventeen

Mel had to climb over the thick trunk of the tree, heavy with branches, which was a challenge, belly and all. She had her medical bag, the collar of her coat pulled up high. It was necessary to lean into the wind, bending a bit as she pushed forward. She hadn't gone far when another contraction seized her. Whoa, she thought—the last one wasn't long ago. But—first baby—there was lots of time. She was no doubt going to labor for hours, then have to push for more than an hour. Don't panic—there's plenty of time. But she hated the thought of trying to get back to a vehicle over that tree trunk. Well, she thought, he'll just have to carry me. Good that I picked me a big, strong man!

On the porch of her cabin, it happened again. Another contraction. She counted—it was nice and long. Little doubt—this was it.

When she got inside, she went immediately to the phone before taking off her boots or coat. She lifted the cordless and punched some numbers, then listened. No ring went through. She disconnected and listened. No dial tone. Oh, crap, she thought.

Now it would be okay to cry, she told herself. She started to snivel a little bit, trying to calculate in her mind where

she might be in her labor in a few hours, when it finally
occurred to Jack to hitch a ride home. She flicked the light
switch. Nothing. Okay, it was definitely okay to cry, she
thought. No electricity, no phone, no doctor, only one idiot
midwife on the premises. And baby coming. Coming.

Mel sat down at her kitchen table, her hand on her
abdomen, and tried to collect herself. She took several
deep, calming breaths. There was nothing to do but get
ready, in case the baby came at home. She was dripping
wet from the rain. She'd attempt to check her dilation,
which could be a challenge, given the big bulge in the
way. But first, she'd find a way to protect her mattress,
gather some towels and blankets, basin or pan, medical
bag by the bed. She'd take a quick shower—if she could
get her boots off. That always proved harder than she
thought, and before she had the second one off, the next
contraction came.

She found a couple of plastic trash bags. She stripped
off the bottom sheet on the bed and spread them across the
mattress. Over the plastic, she smoothed out a couple of
towels, then replaced the fitted sheet. A couple more towels
on top of the sheet. She pulled extra pillows out of the
closet to prop herself up. She gathered up the candles from
the kitchen, living room, bedroom and set them up on her
dresser and bedside table. Oh, she hoped she didn't have
to deliver herself by candlelight. In the middle of all this,
she was hit again—big one. She had to sit on the edge of
the bed for a few moments to get through it. Then she got
the baby blankets and more towels and put them by the bed.

Finally set up, she headed for the shower. She started
the water so it would get hot, stripped off her wet clothes,
kicking them aside, washed her hands thoroughly and
waited rather impatiently for another contraction to come
and go. When it had, she squatted, legs apart. She held
on to the bathroom sink with one hand to keep balance.

Slipping one hand under her belly, she slid her fingers into her birth canal, reaching. This was the best she could do. She pushed gently, reaching. This was a damn difficult maneuver. One, two, three fingers and some room—God. Already seven-plus—she was cooked. She knew at that moment, she wasn't going anywhere.

She pulled out her hand and with it came a gush of amniotic fluid, spilling between her legs onto the floor.

Okay. No shower.

She tossed some towels onto the floor to sop up the spill, then tried to dry herself off. If she were attending someone else in birth, she'd have the mother walking, squatting, rocking her hips side to side, using gravity to assist that baby downward and out—but this was a different ball game. She wanted some company—at least Jack, and preferably John Stone or Doc.

Her flannel granny gown would be a poor choice for a labor garment, so she chose one of Jack's oversize T-shirts. She pulled the shirt up around her breasts, got into bed atop a couple of thick, soft terry towels, covered her belly with the sheet and hoped to keep back the labor for a while. Long enough for someone to see that truck up against the tree; long enough for someone to try phoning her and discover the lines were down.

She pulled the fetoscope out of her bag and listened, very gratefully, to the baby's strong and regular heartbeat.

Thank God Jack was a worry wart. It might come in handy for once. She felt another contraction and looked at her watch. Two minutes long. She waited—less than three minutes later, another, and with every one, more amniotic fluid was being pushed out. Another couple of minutes—oh, Jesus, this boy was going to come barreling out of her.

Jack tried to call Mel, just to be sure she made it back to the cabin without incident, because the storm had really picked up right after she left. But there was no answer. Maybe it took her a little longer—given the rain. He tried again ten minutes later, but there was still no answer.

"She pick up yet?" Rick asked.

"Not yet. She said she wanted to go home and take a shower, get into bed. She's probably in the shower."

It was nearing the dinner hour and there were a couple of people in the bar. Jack brought them drinks, then went back to the phone. No answer.

"Could she have turned the phone off?" Preacher asked him.

"Probably. To keep me from calling her every ten minutes to ask her how she's doing."

Paige was getting rolls ready to put in the oven. She laughed at him. "Jack, she'd call you if she needed you."

"I know," he said. But he dialed. Nothing.

A little while later he was pacing. "You think she could be sleeping through the phone ringing?" Preacher asked.

"I'd be surprised if she actually slept," Jack said. "Her back is killing her."

"I hope she isn't having back labor," Paige said rather absently. "I had a lot of that with Christopher. It's awful."

"She'd know if she was in labor," Jack said.

"Yeah, I suppose. But I didn't," Paige said. "Not until it moved around to the front, and by then I was pretty far dilated."

Jack threw a look at Preacher, at Rick—a stricken look. How long ago had she left? A half hour? Hour?

"Okay, we're outta here," Jack said. "Come on, Rick, let's do it."

"It'll be okay, Jack," Paige said.

"I know," he said, but as he said it, he was rushing for his coat and flying out the back door, Rick on his heels. Jack went to the driver's side of Rick's little truck, because he couldn't ride. He was too wound up, too worried. Rick went along with this, knowing better than to argue with the guy now. He tossed him the keys and Jack started the truck, threw it into gear and tore out of town before Rick's door was closed.

It was a long ten minutes to the cabin, and through it all Rick kept trying to talk him down. "She knows what she's doing," he said. "You don't have to worry about Mel—she'd call." Jack said nothing. He flew down the road, taking those sharp turns real tight and fast. Rick felt his own panic rising, after what he'd just been through. He tried not to let it show. "You know everything is going to be—"

Rick was cut off midsentence as Jack screeched to a stop behind his own truck, the left front of which was rammed into a fallen tree. "God," he said, jumping out of Rick's little truck and running to his own. "Mel!" he yelled, opening the driver's door. Finding the cab empty, he looked for blood, for her bag. Neither was evident, so he took off at a dead run, bounding over the huge tree and racing toward the cabin.

He blew into the house and slipped on the wood floor, nearly falling on his ass, his boots and clothes dripping wet from the rain and muck. "Mel!" he called.

"Jack," she called back, her voice small and strained.

He saw a soft glow coming from the bedroom and went toward it. She was propped against the pillows in the bed, sheet drawn over her.

"It's happening," she said.

He rushed to her side and knelt. "I'll take you now. Take you to the hospital."

"Too late," she said. "I can't take the ride now—I'm too far into this. But you can get John, see if he can come…." She grunted against a contraction, grabbing Jack's hand. "Phone's out," she said. "Go back to town, call John, tell him my water broke and I'm at eight. Can you remember that?"

"Got it." He ran back to Rick and repeated the message, and then the boy was gone. Jack ran back to Mel and took her hand. "Tell me what to do," he said.

The contraction passed and she let out her breath. "Okay. Okay, listen to me. Mop up your mess before you kill yourself slipping in a puddle, get some dry clothes on, see if you can get a little more light in here and then we'll see where we are. It's going to be a while. Maybe John will make it. Whew," she said, leaning back. "I don't know when I've ever been happier to see you."

Her face took on a look of pain and she began to breathe, short and shallow, panting, while he stood looking down at her, helpless. When she recovered, she said, "Jack, do what I told you to do."

"Yeah," he said. "Right."

He started by going for a towel in the bathroom to wipe up the puddles he'd dragged in and there he found her clothes, hastily discarded, panties a little bloody, and wet towels left in a pile on the floor. He kicked everything aside, clearing a path in the bathroom. He opted for the kitchen mop, cleaning up the trail of water that went from the front door to the bedroom. He left his boots by the front door. Hurrying, he pulled off his jeans and shirt, adding them to the pile of wet towels and clothes, put on fresh, dry clothes and socks, and went again to her bedside.

"Do we have any more candles?" she asked him.

"Not that I know about."

"How about flashlights?"

"Yeah, I have a couple of those."

"Get the strongest one. If he starts to come before John gets here, I might be able to hold the light for you."

"For… Me?"

"Jack, there are only two of us here. One of us is going to push him out, one of us is going to catch him. Which job do you want?"

"Oh," he said, going for the flashlight. He took it back to her and demonstrated its strength by shining it right in her eyes. She winced and he turned it off.

She rubbed her eyes. "Oh, brother. Maybe you should push him out. I'm calmer. Yeah, I vote for you," she said.

He knelt with one knee on the floor beside her bed. "Melinda, how can you be sarcastic right now?"

"You know, you own a bar and you don't keep alcohol at home," she said, breathless. "I could have had a shot— it sometimes slows labor."

"We'll have some on hand for the next one."

"You keep talking like that's gonna happen," she said. "How ridiculous."

"I think my record speaks for itself. But, Mel, I just want to make them, not deliver them."

"I hear ya, buddy," she said, and then was gripped by another contraction. She tried to pant through it, but they were getting tougher—longer and closer together. She looked at her watch. "Oh, man," she said, breathless. "This is going to turn me into a much more sympathetic midwife. Yii."

"What should I do?" he asked.

"Pull up a chair... Or something. All we do now is labor."

Jack went to the nursery and got the rocker, bringing it to her bedside and sitting up on the edge, leaning toward her. "Did you hit the tree?" he asked her, picking up a towel from the bed and wiping it gently across her sweating brow.

"A little bit. I had a contraction, the first really good one, and it distracted me, and there it was, right in the road."

"So that didn't make you go into labor?"

"No. I suspect I've been in labor all day and didn't realize—it was all in my back. Killing me!"

"That's why I'm here. That's what Paige said happened to her."

"God bless her, huh? Uh," she said, grabbing her middle and going with another one. It seemed to go on forever. Finally, she relaxed against the pillows again, closed her eyes and caught her breath. "Oh, man, this is harder than it looks. At least he's off my back."

"God, I wish I could do this for you."

"That makes two of us." She closed her eyes for a moment. Two minutes later she was seized by another one. She panted through it. Jack went to the bathroom and wet a washcloth, going back to her to wipe her brow and neck. "That's nice," she said.

"You have to wait for John," he said.

"I'm doing the best I can, Jack."

He held her hand and wiped her brow through several more contractions, murmuring, "It's okay, baby. It's okay…."

And then she snapped, "I know it's okay! Stop saying that!"

Oh, he had heard about this—when you're doing whatever you can, but she hates you, anyway.

"Sorry," she said. "That's transition talking."

"Transition?" he repeated.

"It's getting closer." When the next one passed she said, "Okay, something is a little different. I think he's moving down. I feel like in a minute—" Before she could finish her sentence, she was nearly lifted off the bed by the urge to bear down. She seemed to catch herself, stop herself by panting. Two minutes is a long, long time when you're going through that. When you're watching someone go through that. When it passed, she collapsed back on the pillows and had trouble catching her breath.

"Jack," she said breathlessly. "You're going to have to take a look. Get the flashlight and shine it right on my pelvic floor. See if the birth canal is opening. Tell me if you see him coming."

"How will I know what to look for?" he asked.

She narrowed her eyes at him. "It has hair," she said in a very snotty tone.

"Okay, don't get pissy, I don't do this for a living."

She lifted her knees and spread them while Jack held the flashlight on her. "Whoa," he said. He looked over her knees at her face. He looked a little bit pale.

"Show me how much, like this," she said, showing him a circle with her thumb and forefinger. He responded by showing her a circle, larger than hers. "Ho, boy," she said.

He turned off the flashlight. "Melinda, I want you to wait for John…."

"I am sick to *death* of being told to wait for John!" she said meanly. "Jack, listen to me. I'm having this baby. Period. And you're going to pay attention and help. Got that?"

"Aw, Melinda…"

She grabbed his wrist and dug her nails into him. "Do you think this is my *first* choice?"

He thought briefly about suggesting, again, that she try to hold off. But he knew he was not in the driver's seat here, plus he was resisting the urge to look at his wrist to see if she'd drawn blood. It was going to be impossible to get her to listen to reason. He'd always been good at following orders—he'd do that again. "Gotcha," he said.

"Okay, here's what we're going to do. Spread out a blanket at the foot of the bed, down there. A small blanket for the baby. Okay?"

"Okay."

"Okay, in my bag here, get out two clamps and a pair of scissors. The suction bulb. We're going to need a basin for the placenta—a large bowl or saucepan will do. Then go into the bathroom, roll up your sleeves and scrub your hands up to the elbows with soap, lots of soap and the hottest water you can stand. Dry with a clean towel. When you get back, done with that, there's going to be a bigger circle. Okay?"

"Okay." He opened the bag. He had to hold up a couple of things before she confirmed he had a clamp. The suction bulb was a complete mystery. As this process was going on, she reared up again and with a loud and very primal grunt, was bearing down. She held on to her thighs and pushed until her face was red. He took the flashlight on instinct, shining it on her pelvic floor. Oh, Christ, he thought. That circle of hair that was his son's head was indeed getting larger. He supposed there was no point in telling her to stop that. "How much time do we have?" he asked.

"Go. Wash. Don't screw around."

"Done," he said. But it was awful, standing at the sink sudsing himself while she was in the bedroom, groaning and grunting and pushing his baby out of her. He wanted to yell at her to stop that, but he knew it would only piss her off. When he got back to the bed, he reached for the flashlight and she yelled, "No! Don't touch that! Pick it up with a clean towel! Hand it to me!"

He looked around and upon locating the towels up by her pillow, he took one and passed the flashlight to her. She struggled to sit up a bit and held the flashlight, pointing it down. "Holy shit, Mel," he said.

She thought she knew what that meant. She collapsed back on the pillows and looked at her watch. It had been almost an hour and a half since Rick lit out of here. Where the hell was John? "He's coming, Jack," she said weakly, collapsing against the pillows.

He took the flashlight from her with the towel and said, "Gimme that." He propped it on a rolled-up towel so that it shone on the field of birth and said, "Okay, now you can think about one thing."

"Giving birth?" she asked.

"Two things," he amended. "Giving birth and telling me what to do."

On the next contraction, she pulled herself up, grabbing her thighs, and the baby's head, crowning, grew larger. "Holy shit," Jack said again. Three more pushes and the baby's whole head emerged. "Oh, my God," he said.

"Jack, look for a cord around the baby's neck. It's purple and ropey. Ahhh," she said, struggling against another contraction. "Use your index finger to see if you can feel anything around the baby's neck. Ahhh!"

Right at that moment, the front door slammed open with a bang.

"John!" Jack yelled. "John, come *on!*"

John, soaked and coming into the bedroom at a pace far too leisurely for Jack's tastes, appeared. Jack started to stand and John said, "Get back in there, man." He peered into the field. "Good. You feel for a cord?"

"Yeah, but what the hell do I know?"

John let his coat fall off his shoulders. He grabbed the flashlight and brought it in closer. "Nice," he said. "Jack, get your hands in there—she's going to bring him out. Be ready."

"Are you out of your fucking mind?" Jack asked, really at the end of his tether with this business.

"You're there, Jack. Now." He looked over Mel's raised knees. "Little push, Mel," John said.

Mel gave a grunt and a shove and the baby came sliding out, neat as pie.

"Hold him face down, your hand on his chest, and rub his back," John said. Before Jack had even accomplished that, the baby was crying. "Ah, good," John said. John spread a blanket on Mel's abdomen. "Good work. Put him down right here. Let's get him dried off and wrapped nice and warm."

Jack's hands were shaking as he did so, wiping the

muck of birth from his son's little body. Mel was strain-
ing up to see him, her fingers reaching toward him to
touch him. For a moment Jack was paralyzed. Trans-
fixed. Before he could close the blanket around him, he
stared at him in sheer wonder. His son. Brought right out
of his wife's body. Naked, covered with muck, squalling,
and the most beautiful thing he'd ever seen. His little
arms and legs were flailing, his mouth open in a wail. He
was so tiny, Jack was thinking, when John said, "Jesus,
Melinda, he's big. Where were you keeping him?"

"Oh," Mel said. "That feels *so* much better."

John was finally in the ball game, gently massaging
Mel's uterus. "What a woman," he said. "No stitches necessary." He applied the clamps to the cord, handed Jack
the scissors and told him where to cut. Jack, finally
numbed by an event in which he'd felt entirely helpless,
did as he was told, freeing the baby from his moorings.

"Good work," John said. "Let Mel have her baby, Jack.
I'll wash and help with the cleanup."

John disappeared into the bathroom while Jack
lovingly lifted the baby. Mel was tugging at her T-shirt
as Jack was handing her the baby. She held the baby's
cheek against her warm breast, running her fingers over
his perfect head. The baby stopped crying and appeared
to be looking around. Mel glanced up at Jack and gave
him a little smile.

"Come on, little guy," she cooed, serene, totally
focused on her son. "Do your job here. Stanch the
bleeding, bring out the placenta." She pinched her nipple
to fit the baby's mouth, trying to entice him with it. Jack
felt a river of emotion run through him. He didn't know
if he was about to burst into song or faint. He dropped to
his knees to be closer and watched Mel tickle the baby's
mouth and cheek with her nipple and then the baby turned
his head instinctively and clamped on, took hold, suckled.

And Mel said, "Oh, my! You're very good at this." Then she looked at Jack, who knelt by the bed, dazed. She smiled weakly and said, "Thank you, darling."

He leaned closer to her, his face next to his son's head. "My God, Melinda," he said in a breath. "What the hell did we just do?"

An hour later the lights came on and Preacher was on Jack's front porch, looking for information. John had helped clean Mel up and washed the baby, helped Jack get clean sheets on the bed and was ready to leave them. "There's no point in taking them out in this weather," John said. "They're in good shape. You need a sedative, man?" he asked Jack, laughing.

"I could use one, yeah. Got a good single malt in that bag there?"

"Wouldn't that be convenient?" He slapped a hand on Jack's back and said, "You did a good job, buddy. I'm proud of you."

"Yeah? What choice did I have? It was all her."

"Show Uncle Preach the baby. I'm going home. And I think you have like *tons* of laundry to do."

"Tons." Jack laughed.

Jack carried the baby to the living room and let Preacher have a peek. "You deliver him?" Preacher asked.

"It wasn't my idea," Jack said.

Preacher grinned hugely. "Looks like you did okay."

"I'm not looking to do it again, however," Jack said. But he smiled. Where's Paige? Chris?"

"Rick's standing guard," Preacher said. "Wearing my sidearm. He's a little too happy about it."

"Yeah? Well, you better get back there. Disarm him."

Jack put the baby back in the cradle next to Mel, whose face had resumed those soft, beautiful lines that had been there prior to her hard work. He went around the house collecting clothes, towels, sheets. He laundered, he cleaned, he set the house back in order. At nine o'clock there was a soft knock at the door and he opened it to find Preacher had returned. He lifted a bottle. "John said you might need a sedative," he said.

"Yeah. Come on in. Be real quiet."

Jack found a couple of glasses and Preacher tipped the bottle over them. Then he lifted his glass, Jack lifted his, and Preacher whispered, "Congratulations, Dad."

Jack threw back the shot and when he brought back his head, his eyes were misting over. "My wife," he said in a whisper. "You have no idea the strength that took. She was amazing. I watched her face—she went to a place of power I've never been. And then, when I handed her the baby, when she put my son against her breast…" He took another swallow. "When she nursed my son, she was in another place—there was such peace and love…. God," he said.

"Yeah," Preacher said. "That was God." Preacher opened his arms and gave the man a huge hug, patting his back.

"I've never seen anything like that in my life," Jack whispered.

Preacher clamped strong hands on Jack's upper arms, giving him a little shake. "I'm real happy for you, man." And then he left, Jack quietly closing the door behind him.

At midnight, Jack blew out most of the candles and sat in the rocker by her bed. By his bed. He lifted the baby to Mel at two in the morning and watched, mesmerized, as she nursed him for a few minutes on each side, burped him and handed him back to Jack with sleepy instructions to change him. Which he did.

At 5:00 a.m. he repeated the process of lifting his crying son to his mother's arms, again watching as she breast-fed him. Again, changing him and cleaning him up. He held him and rocked him for an hour before putting him back in his cradle. At eight in the morning, it happened again, a feeding and changing, and Jack had not taken so much as a nap. He had watched every rise and fall of his son's chest, each breath, frequently reaching out to gently touch his perfect little head.

At nine in the morning he heard the sound of saws and he went to the front porch. He couldn't see that far down the road because of the fallen tree, but he knew what was happening—Preacher was having the road cleared.

At noon, Mel got out of bed. He was astonished by the fact that she sat up, put her feet on the floor, stood up and stretched. "Ah," she said. "I think I'll have a shower."

"Are you all right?" he asked.

"I feel so much better." She put her hands in the small of her back. "My back doesn't hurt anymore." She walked into his arms, hugged him close and said, "Thank you, Jack. I couldn't have done it without you."

"Yeah, I think you could have." He looked down the length of her.

"What's the matter?"

"After seeing what you did last night, I can't believe you can stand."

She laughed softly. "Amazing, isn't it? The way a woman's body can open up and deliver a child that size? You don't realize it yet, but that was a very wonderful experience you had. Delivering your own child."

He kissed her brow. "What makes you think I don't realize it?"

She touched his face. "Have you slept?"

"I can't," he said, shaking his head. "I'm still too wired."

"Well, maybe you do realize it. I'm going to get cleaned up a little, then I have things for you to do."

"What things?" he asked. "I did my laundry."

She laughed at him. "Jack, we haven't eaten anything.

And you have phone calls to make. You have to go into town. I heard saws—you think your truck will be pulled out by now?"

"It's sitting in front of the cabin."

She shook her head. "This place. The way people just act on instinct, without being asked. Okay, I'm starving. I'm going to clean up."

When she got out of the shower, he had a bowl of hot soup waiting for her. "You sure you'll be all right here by yourself?" he asked her.

"I can take it from here, cowboy," she said, diving into her soup.

Jack hurried through his phone calls while Paige and Preacher packed up a nice takeout for him—a scrumptious stew, bread, some sandwiches, fruit and pie. He quickly foraged for some groceries from the kitchen— eggs, cheese, milk, juice. Jack couldn't be away from them for long—he hurried back to the cabin. He found Mel and the baby napping, so he stoked the fire and leaned back on the couch, his feet stretched out in front of him on the chest that served as a coffee table. A kind of mellowness had settled over him, almost like having had a tranquilizer. He thought he might be visiting heaven, it was so sweet.

A couple of hours later, he felt her fingers threading through his hair and he opened his eyes. She was sitting on the couch beside him, holding the baby. "Has he eaten?" Jack asked.

"And eaten and eaten and eaten."

"Give him to me," he said, reaching for his baby. He kissed his head. "God," he said. "I still can't believe it. You know how I feel? Like I've never been happy before in my life, because this is so... This is just so much bigger than the happiest I've ever been." He touched her cheek. "No one's ever done anything this great for me, Melinda."

"That's good to know, Jack," she said with a laugh.

"Kiss me," he said, leaning toward her. She obliged him, covering his lips in a deep and loving kiss.

"Did you make your phone calls?"

"Uh-huh. Joey's coming, but I hope you don't mind—I asked her to give us a few days. I want to be here with you, alone, for a little while."

"That's fine. Till you come down to earth. How about things at the bar? Aren't you needed there for Paige?"

"Ron and Bruce are taking turns, hanging around. Am I going to come down to earth? It doesn't feel like it's going to happen."

"It's going to happen," she said. "But I hope not right away. I really like you like this. All sweet and overwhelmed."

"I like me like this, too."

After school, Rick went to Mel's cabin instead of to work. He tapped softly at the door and it was opened by Mel. She smiled sweetly. "You okay?" he asked.

"I'm wonderful," she said in a whisper. She put a finger to her lips and reached for his hand, drawing him inside. "Be very quiet," she whispered. "Come here."

She led him into the living room. Jack was asleep on the couch, his feet up on the trunk. She gestured to the chair. "Give me your jacket and sit," she said. He shrugged out of it, handing it to her, and did as he was told while Mel left the room. She was back in seconds, carrying the little bundle. She took the baby to Rick and put him in his arms. Then she went down on one knee, very nimbly for a woman in her condition, and put her arm around Rick's shoulders, her face near his face.

Rick held the new life, Jack's son, and admired the

handsome round head, the little, pink, heart-shaped mouth. The baby squirmed a little in his arms, making precious little noises.

Jack opened his eyes but didn't move. He looked the short distance across the small room and saw Rick holding the baby and Mel holding Rick. There was a slight glistening on Rick's cheek.

"This is how it's supposed to be," Rick whispered.

"This is how it will be," Mel whispered back. She pressed a soft kiss to Rick's cheek. "All in good time."

Then she went to the couch and curled up next to Jack. His arm lifted automatically to bring her close against him, and they remained like that, the four of them, for almost an hour.

# *Eighteen*

Mike Valenzuela had a friend in Parole and Probation, a man he'd used as a source of information when he was in the gangs unit. It was an excellent way of keeping tabs on gang members who'd been released from prison and were back on the street, with parole obligations. Even though he was no longer on the job, it was still a simple matter to ask questions about someone meeting probation requirements. Mike had been a highly respected officer. He was trusted.

"He's making his weekly appointments, bringing in his chits for attending daily meetings at AA," Mike told Páige and Preacher. "He's working two nights a week in a soup kitchen and trying to get his old job back."

"Soup kitchen?" Paige asked. She shook her head. "Hard to imagine."

"This will be easier for you to imagine. He's already trying to get his community service commitment bumped down and his probation appointments dropped from weekly to monthly. And…he's living with a woman he met in treatment."

"Oh, God," Paige said. "Brie said something like that might happen…."

"It's predictable, in fact," Mike said. "They discourage

any kind of involvement during the first year of sobriety—involvement with anybody, but especially another addict. Yet it happens all the time. Paige, it's impossible to believe he's forgotten about you, but his focus seems to be on lightening his sentencing burden right now. And maybe, a new woman."

"He hasn't called or anything," she said. "You thought he might."

"I did," Mike said. "If his mission was still custody or having you reconsider the relationship, I would have expected a call before anything else, the reason being a phone call could really annoy the judge, but if he sets foot in Virgin River to harass or threaten you in any way, he'll serve time. It's a pretty good deterrent—especially to a man who's been in jail. It ain't pretty in there."

"You think we can relax?" she asked.

"Just a little, maybe. Try to be alert. I think he'll turn up again someday. Guys like him, they nurse grudges, rarely abandon obsessions, and I don't believe they change. But he's pretty busy right now. It could be ten years before you have to deal with him again."

Preacher put his arm around her, pulling her close against him. "Just the same, will you check sometimes?"

"Absolutely," Mike promised. "Every week."

Preacher would have expected Paige to be at least somewhat relieved; there was no question Mike had delivered good news. But he found her to be sullen. Maybe a little depressed. When the day was at a close, their special time together, and he pulled her against him, he lifted her chin and asked, "Why aren't you a little bit happy? Is it because you can't trust him? Wes?"

"Oh, I can't. We can't. But it's the idea that I might never be really free of him, and I brought this into your life. Insanity and trouble. Maybe even danger. Oh, John... What a bad deal you got with me."

He smiled at her, touched her lips with his. "You can't believe for one second that's how I feel. Paige, I don't care if you have an army of loaded Huns on your tail. The day you and Chris came into my life, that was the biggest miracle of my life. I wouldn't trade you for anything."

She tightened her arms around him. "Do you know you're the sweetest man who ever lived?"

He laughed at her. "See, that's the thing. Until you, I was just a fisherman and cook. Look at me now." He grinned at her. "Now I'm not only the sweetest man alive, I'm like the world's greatest lover."

That was the beauty of John. He could turn her mood that fast, by simply speaking his mind. If there was one thing she understood about him—he said what he felt. "You think so, huh?" she asked, smiling back at him.

"Well, let's see if I'm getting any better. How about that, huh?"

Joey had been the first to arrive when the baby, David, was only five days old. Then Grandpa Sam, who tried very hard not to impose but found that he couldn't stay away. Mike, still parked out by Mel and Jack's, took the sofa in the RV and gave Sam his bed. Then, one at a time, Jack's sisters and a few nieces. Day after day, nearly every resident of Virgin River paid a call, bringing a covered dish or cake or plate of cookies. Weeks of visiting and celebrating seemed to pass quickly. The only member of Jack's family who hadn't yet arrived was Brie, who was in the middle of one of the biggest trials of her young career—a rape trial that had become a media circus.

May brought a bright sun and flowers and deer in the yard. And a baby who was held so often, he barely needed the sheets changed in the cradle. Jack was starting to wonder if other women had had babies before Mel,

because he had never seen a transformation quite as star-
tling. Quite as distracting. She dropped a lot of that baby
fat quickly, thanks to the miracle diet of breast feeding.
The first thing to happen—her beautiful face returned to
its former oval shape with high cheekbones and she
glowed with happiness. Everything about her seemed
brighter. Although she complained that she had a long
way to go to regain her figure, from his perspective, she'd
never been sexier. He worshiped her body, especially
after helping her deliver their son. Her belly slowly flat-
tened out and her breasts were full and high; her laugh
was quick and contagious. And when she held and nursed
his son, she seemed to shine as though there was a light
within her. To Jack, she was a vision. He was dead in love.

Jack was dying. He was splitting a lot more logs and
trying to avoid seeing Mel in the shower. She was having
a terrible effect on him. Without that baby between them,
he found himself longing for the days when he would
swoop her off her feet, up into his arms, bear her quickly
to the bed and fall on her, hungry. Starving. And have her
meet that hunger with her own, which was impressive. He
found himself fantasizing about being a little wilder,
ready to revisit that heat and power they had in the beginning, before she began to swell with little David;
before he felt he had to protect her from the strength of
his desire.

When he kissed her these days, when she opened her
mouth under his and let his tongue inside, he would groan
with such depth that she knew. And she would whisper
against his lips, "Soon, Jack. Very soon."

Not nearly soon enough, was all he could think. It had
turned him selfish and impatient. Then Brie's trial ended
and she arrived. She needed a rest to recover from the trial
that had gone badly for her; she needed to bond with her
brother, sister-in-law and new nephew. While Jack was

always happy to see his sister, especially to see her recovering very well from a difficult and disappointing trial and regaining her own former confidence in life since her divorce, the one thought that came to his mind was, now it's going to be at least another week.

Brie found that life had changed in her brother's little cabin in many ways. Mel and Jack were keeping the baby next to their bed, and in the night and in the early mornings, she could hear him stir, fuss, and then the soft murmurings of her brother and sister-in-law. She should have known that Jack would be awake for every feeding, often getting up with David, changing him, taking him back to the bed to Mel.

Another new development was that RV in the clearing. In the predawn hours, she would stealthily sneak out of the cabin and sit in one of the Adirondack chairs on the porch and listen to the soft melody of the Spanish guitar that came from the open window across the yard. He didn't know she was there, that she listened, that the music stirred her. His right hand was still a little tentative as he pressed down against the strings, but with his left he plucked and strummed with skill. He stopped often to start over. She imagined that once his strength was completely restored, his guitar music must be nothing short of magnificent.

Sometimes she would lean back, close her eyes and imagine that he played for her. Mike. She'd first met him years before in Sacramento during Jack's last leave before he left for Iraq, Jack's final assignment. Brie was newly married then. She had seen him again at Mel and Jack's wedding—they almost qualified as old friends. His name was really Miguel—she knew that. Although born in the U.S., he had managed to stay close to his cultural roots, the romance of his country. You could hear it in the music. That sexy Spanish guitar.

It had been more than six months since Brad had walked out on her. Soon she would be ready for a little attention from a man. But she would be more careful this time. She wasn't going to get hooked up to another man who lacked the power of commitment. Brie knew all about Mike—he'd been around Jack a long time and he was a consummate flirt. He probably fancied himself the great Latin lover; she had heard he'd been though two wives and a hundred girlfriends. Small wonder. He was handsome and sexy. They probably fell at his feet. She would enjoy the music and the fantasy; the man was clearly poison.

Brie was having a wonderful visit. With baby in tow, she and Mel drove around the redwoods, went to Grace Valley to see their friends, shopped in the coastal towns, visited with the locals. Mel handled the baby with such ease, wearing him in a sling around her body. And when she felt like a break, she would lengthen the straps on that baby carrier so that they fit Jack just right and pass his son to him. People in Virgin River were getting accustomed to being served a drink by a man with a baby slung around him.

On a typical dinner hour at the bar, Mel left Brie and Mike at the table and handed off her son to her husband so she could visit the powder room. Every time she passed David to Jack, his eyes would grow soft and warm, filled with love and pride as he took the baby. And then as he watched his wife walk away from him, another expression would creep into his features. The angle of his gaze lowered to her butt, and there was tension in his jaw.

"My brother," Brie said to Mike one day as they sat companionably together in the bar. "I never thought I'd see him like this, with a wife and son. He seems beyond happy. Though every once in a while I think I see a worried look on his face. Maybe he's just overwhelmed by responsibility."

"I'm not sure that's what you're seeing," Mike said, having just watched Jack's face. "I have four married brothers. Men talk."

"What do they talk about?" she asked.

Instead of answering, he asked, "How old is David now?"

"Almost six weeks. Why?"

He smiled and covered Brie's hand. "Why don't you come fishing with me tomorrow? You can borrow Mel's gear and her waders. We could stay out on the river for hours."

She pulled her hand out from under his. "Oh, thanks, but Mel and I were going to—"

"You could tell Mel and Jack that you're going to be out on the river for hours," he said. *"Hours."*

"But—"

He rolled his eyes. "Brie, you'd have a good time. I guarantee it."

She leaned closer. "Listen, Mike—understand something. I'm here to see Mel and Jack and the baby, not to—"

He glanced at the bar and saw that Mel was back, retrieving the baby. "We should get away from them for a few hours. Believe me, I wasn't thinking about us. I was thinking about *them.*"

She glanced over her shoulder at her brother and sister-in-law. They kissed just briefly over the baby's head. She glanced back at Mike. "You think?"

"I've seen that look before. If you go fishing with me tomorrow, you're not going to see that look on your brother's face after you get back. Most of those tense lines will be gone. I'm pretty sure of this."

"What if I don't much like fishing?" she said.

"Just say you're going fishing. We'll think of something else to do. Something that takes *hours.*"

She leaned close to him. "Will you bring the guitar?" she whispered. She was answered by a look of shocked surprise.

When Mel came back to the table, Brie said, "Mel, would you be terribly disappointed if I went fishing with Mike tomorrow? If I borrowed your gear?"

"No," she said, shaking her head. "That's okay. Gee, I didn't know you liked to fish."

"Well, I'm going to get a free lesson," she said. "If you don't mind, we'll be gone most of the day."

"That's okay," she said. "You about ready to head home?"

"Sure," Brie said. "What time, Mike?"

"How about ten? I'll get Preacher to pack us a lunch."

When the women left, Mike wandered up to the bar. "How about a coffee?" he asked Jack.

"You got it," he said, pouring a mug.

Preacher brought a crate of glasses out of the kitchen and slipped them under the bar. "Hey, Preach, can I get a favor?" Mike asked.

"What do you need, buddy?"

"I'm going to take Brie out to the river tomorrow. A little fishing. Can I get you to pack us a lunch? Something nice—so she thinks I'm debonaire? Maybe put a bottle of good wine in the basket?"

"Sure," Preacher said, grinning.

Jack picked up a glass and used a dish towel to wipe out any water spots. "You thinking of messing with my little sister?" he asked. "Because she's been through a tough time and doesn't need—"

"No, Jack." He laughed. "I'm not messing with anyone, trust me. But I figured if I kept her busy for a few hours, maybe you could mess with the baby's mother."

Jack's eyes narrowed.

Mike sipped from his mug. "I'll keep her out there through nap time," he said. "Maybe a couple of nap times."

Jack leaned closer to Mike. "You'd better not screw around with my little sister. Remember, I know you and your ways with women, and this is my sister we're talking about."

Mike laughed. "You think I'm looking to get shot again? Buddy, all that's in the past. I promise you, I'll treat Brie as a sister. You have nothing to worry about."

"In the past, huh? And what brought that on?"

"Three bullets." He drank a little of his coffee, left the mug on the bar and stuck his head in the kitchen. "Preach," he called. "I'll be by to get my lunch at about ten tomorrow. Okay?"

Jack found it strange that he felt even less confident about winning his wife's affection now than he had back when he'd been pursuing her. He greatly regretted that he hadn't said anything to her about the fact that they could have some time alone together—a major tactical miscalculation. He should have gotten an answer from her, because he dreaded going out to the cabin, lusty, all steamed up, only to have her tell him it was too soon, that she wasn't ready.

But he'd said nothing, opting for a more romantic approach, surprising her in the middle of the day, wooing her, seducing her. She had also known that Brie would be out with Mike for most of the day, and Mel was not shy. She could have suggested they take advantage of the opportunity. And she hadn't.

How does a guy know when his wife is ready for sex, right after having a baby? He knew the postpartum bleeding had long since stopped because he was the guy who threw the daily trash into the back of his truck to take into town to pitch in the Dumpster. Those little Peripads had dwindled and disappeared, replaced by more of the neat little disposable diaper bundles. And Mel's movements had gone from slow to spry; she had stopped complaining about soreness and there were no more bathtub soaks as of at least three weeks ago.

The closer he got to the cabin, the more thought he gave this adventure. She was having her appointment with John Stone in less than a week to be sure everything was all right after the birth—she was undoubtedly waiting for that. When he got there, he found her finishing up with David's bath in the kitchen. "Well, well," she said, smiling. "I don't often see you in the middle of the morning."

"It's real quiet at the bar," he said idly.

"When I'm finished here, I have to feed David and put him down," she said. And then she cooed and smiled and made faces at the baby, consumed by his needs. "Then I'll get to you," she said. Again, she had her face in David's, kissing him, making funny little noises at him.

Jack went out onto the porch. He sat on the steps and hung his head. He felt like a brute. Like a horny bull who was about to steal the milk out of his baby's mouth. This was no way to claim your conjugal rights—by jumping on the first opportunity you saw to take advantage of your own wife.

He took a deep breath and lectured himself. Have a cup of coffee with your woman, he said to himself. Spend a little time with her, talk to her, work into the conversation in a soft and gentlemanly manner that you can't wait for her to be ready to take you into her bed again, in that meaningful way. Ask her if she was waiting for an all-clear from her doctor, and for God's sake, take it slow. Give her all the time she needs—everything will be better that way. Being too hot to handle wasn't going to win any points now—she had a baby to think about.

"What are you doing out there?"

He turned to see her standing in the cabin door, wearing only his shirt. His heart was going to explode. He took in her full chest, her slim legs.

"You don't even have your boots off. I could have sworn you showed up to get reacquainted with your wife's body."

He swallowed. "Is that gonna happen?" he asked tentatively. Hopefully.

"Not a moment too soon," she said. And she turned and walked back into the house.

His boots were off on the porch, his shirt was off in the living room, his pants were down and kicked away in the bedroom doorway.

Mel lay back on the bed, barely covered by his shirt. She began to slowly unbutton it, starting at the top. Easy, boy, he told himself. You'd better find out what you're dealing with. She did just have a baby. He lay down beside her, brought her against him and, kissing her, holding her, he asked, "Are you okay with this? You're sure?"

"Jack, I'll never be exactly as I was before the baby. My body has changed."

"You're kidding me, right? Your body is amazing to me. After what you did—I'm almost envious, in a weird way. I worship this body."

She laughed at him. "You know the last two or three months?"

"Yeah?"

"All the things we would have done if we hadn't been so incredibly pregnant? If we hadn't just had a baby?"

"Yeah?"

"Can you please do all those things to me now? One at a time. Until you're almost dead from exhaustion. Please?"

"Oh, yeah!"

She opened the shirt to reveal her naked body, the sight of which he drank in greedily. She was fuller, rounder, so lush; there was a new richness to her shape that blew his mind. "Get started, big boy. I am insane, I want you so bad."

"Melinda," he said, filling his hands with her sweet body. "Have I told you how much I like being married to you?"

"Shh. Just show me."

Mike hadn't asked that the wine be packed in the picnic to get Brie relaxed or talking. He'd just thought it would be a nice touch, since he was pretty sure they wouldn't be fishing. And he was right about that. Instead, they drove through a redwood grove and down to the lower, more shallow, end of the river where the bank was wide and peppered with large rocks. He spread a blanket against a huge boulder near the river's edge, under the canopy of tall trees. And there wasn't much to do on a picnic besides talk, and at her insistence, attempt the guitar. His music was so rusty, he hated subjecting her to it, but she seemed not to notice his many mistakes. She leaned back against the boulder and closed her eyes, her lips curved in a half smile, listening to him play. In years gone by, Mike would've had her down on the blanket by now—but those were years gone by.

It was hard to imagine this tiny, young-looking woman as one of the toughest prosecutors in the Sacramento Valley. She was a little thing in slim jeans and moccasins, a light blue chambray shirt tied at the waist. Her hair was loose, a thick, light-brown mane that fell down her back almost to her waist. She had the most flawless ivory skin that would feel like silk under a man's hands. As he played, she let her warm brown eyes drift closed; her rosy lips tilted in appreciation.

Brie shivered in the breeze and Mike put aside the guitar. He went back to the car and got his jacket out of the backseat. He took it to her, spreading it over her shoulders, and watched, his eyes warming, as she pulled it tighter around her. Then he saw her sniff the collar and he grew weak. He did not think of her as a sister.

"Judging by your music, the arm is almost fully recovered," she said.

"Almost back," he said, sitting on the blanket again. "I think I'm going to recover one hundred percent, or damn close."

"And everything else is healed, right?"

"Not everything," he surprised himself by saying. "Every once in a while I have trouble getting the right word and I worry about my brain—but I notice that more than anyone else, so I could be overreacting. And I was shot in the groin. Bad spot."

"Oh," she said. He could tell she didn't want to ask.

"Nothing life-threatening," he said. Nothing for you to worry about, he wanted to add. You don't have to go to Jack and ask if they shot it off.

"And you're thinking of staying here?"

"Why not?" he said with a shrug. "My friends are here. It's quiet and peaceful. There's no pressure." He laughed a little. "I've had enough of that. I've lived in your world. When I was on the job, I worked with a lot of D.A.'s. You're what—thirty? Thirty-one? And locking people up for a living?"

"As many as possible. And I'm thirty. Thirty and already married and divorced."

"Hey, that's not exactly a scar on your face, Brie. The way Jack tells it, it didn't have anything to do with you."

"How does Jack tell it?" she asked him.

Mike looked down. Blunder number two, he thought. First, the shot to the groin, then the divorce tales. He raised his eyes. "Jack said that Brad wanted the divorce. That you were devastated."

"Brad cheated on me with my best friend," she said. "He left me and moved in with her and I pay him alimony. Her husband pays her alimony and child support. I gave him a big check for his half of the house and you know what he said? He said, 'Brie, I hope we can be friends.'" She gave a little laugh that carried all the weight of her anger.

"Ah, *Dios*," he said. "I'm so sorry that happened. *Tu no mereces esto*. You don't deserve that," he translated.

"What is it with some men?" she asked him angrily. "Why would a guy do something like that?"

He laughed ruefully. "At least I never did that," he said, mostly to himself. And then he wondered how he had managed to escape that indiscretion.

"I'm sure you have a multitude of things to be forgiven for," she said.

"You know what, Brie? I made so many mistakes, I can't even count 'em. And I know better than to think I'll ever be forgiven. If I made a million mistakes, I had at least that many excuses. Brad might end up like me— really sorry. And really too late."

"Cops," she said with some disgust. "You guys."

"Aw, come on—it's not just cops. Although, I'll grant you, a lot of guys with slick uniforms and a gun can make it with the girls pretty easy. But if that's the kind of guy he turned out to be, you're better off."

"Are your ex-wives better off without you?"

"You have no idea," he answered with an embarrassed shake of his head.

"Small comfort," she said.

"Brie, you're beautiful and brilliant and strong. A man who would cheat on someone like you, just flat-ass doesn't deserve you." He reached out and covered her hand with his. "You are too valuable, Brie, to be stuck with a man like that."

She pulled her hand out from under his. "And what did you do to screw up your marriages?"

"I was completely irresponsible," he said. "I knew how to be a lover, not how to love. Men take such a long time to become men, I think. Women have it easier—you at least grow up before you're old."

"You think you've finally grown up, huh?"

"Possibly," he said with a shrug. "Nearly getting killed tends to get your attention."

"What if you could start over? What would you change?"

He thought for a moment. "For starters, I wouldn't marry so fast. Not until I found the right woman, the kind of feeling that leaves no doubt. Jack did it right—he avoided commitment until the real thing came along. So did Preacher, although I'm not sure he did that on purpose. It's obvious they found that lifetime thing, that forever thing, though it didn't come to either of them early. Or easily. I didn't wait for that. I prowled and hunted, but I think the hunt was more important to me than what I would catch." He lifted his dark brows. "I admit I was stupid. Oh, *mija,* you don't know what I'd give to start over." He leaned toward her and said, "If I had a woman like you in my life, I think I would know what I had."

She laughed at him. "Good God, you're so obvious. You're coming on to me!"

Some habits die so hard, he thought. But he was close enough to smell her sweet perfume and it addled his brain a little bit. "*Dios,* no! I wouldn't dare! I'm admiring you, that's all."

"Well, you can stop admiring me—I'm never getting within a hundred miles of another one of you."

"Another one of—me?"

"You've been through two wives and a million other women. Not exactly a good résumé, Mike."

He leaned back on his hands and smiled at her. "For a little while, I thought you liked me."

She lifted her eyebrows. "I'm not about to be tricked by a flirtatious man."

He shrugged. "If you are, it will be kept in confidence, Brie," he said, smiling at her.

"This is a beautiful place," she said. "Why are there no fishermen?"

"It's too shallow here for the bigger fish. This is where the young people come to be alone," he said. "Down here where the grass is soft, the trees tall, and there are a few large boulders to hide behind. The river whispers past them while they whisper to each other. That old rock you're leaning against—it has seen some delicious things."

"The most delicious thing it's going to see today is Preacher's lunch," she said, but she smiled when she said it.

"Thank God," he said, teasing. "I admit, I was pretty worried. I wondered—if I gave you wine and music and you began to seduce me, how would I—"

"Get out of it?" she asked, amused.

"Not exactly, *mija*." He grinned. "How would I keep Jack from killing me."

"Don't take this the wrong way, Mike, it's not personal, but Jack isn't in charge of what I do. He thinks he is. But he's not."

"Big brothers," Mike said. "Very annoying people…" Then he sobered and said, "I am sorry about the divorce, Brie. And the trial. I don't know many of the details, but Jack said it was a terrible experience for you."

"Worse than terrible," she said. She pulled her hair out of the collar of his jacket and shook it down her back, looking upward. He found himself hoping a few strands would remain when he reclaimed it. "There are a lot of scary people out there to put away, some worse than others. It was a hard one to lose…one of the biggest trials of my career—a serial rapist—and I lost. He walked, and he's guilty as hell. That's not going to happen to me again."

"What went wrong?"

"My witnesses, my victims ran like rabbits. I can't prove it, but I suspect he threatened them. If I ever get another crack at him, I'm going to put him away for life. But that kind of criminal just pulls a territorial. He's going to get out of town—it's what they do."

"It took a lot of strength to take that on," he said in admiration. "You're amazing." He stood up and put out his hand to her. "You're welcome to come back in a little while and break my heart, *mija*," he said. "But right now, let's go back to town. Let's grab a cup of coffee and give the lovers another hour together."

"Breaking a few hearts interests me," she said, putting her hand in his to stand. But when they were both standing, she didn't pull her hand away.

He should have let go and stooped to gather up their blanket, but he didn't want to release her hand, small and soft but strong in his. He smiled at her. "I think the last time I had this feeling come over me when a girl held my hand, I was thirteen. You'll be good at it, I think. Breaking hearts." Still, she didn't pull away, didn't break the spell. It was he who finally let go, stooping to close up their basket, pick up the blanket. He handed her the folded blanket. "Thank you for today, Brie."

"It was a nice day," she said, her smile genuine. "You didn't seem to have any trouble finding the right word."

And, Mike thought, there are no words for what I'm starting to feel….

Paige walked out the bar's back door with a plastic garbage bag in her hand, tied off tightly so as to not let a whiff of garbage escape to tempt the wildlife. She went across the wide dirt yard where she, John, Jack and often Rick liked to park their vehicles. The Dumpster sat under a big old tree and was used by everyone on the street, not just the bar. She lifted the heavy lid, but before she could toss the bag in, her wrist was grabbed in a vicelike grip and she was pulled around to the side, out of sight of the bar or the street. The garbage bag dropped to the ground and she felt something hard and cold under chin. She gasped, staring into the lethal eyes of her ex-husband, the business end of a rifle lifting her chin.

"You made this easy," Wes Lassiter said, his voice low and dangerous. "I thought I'd have to go in after you. We have two choices. You can come with me right now, nice and quiet, or we can walk back in through that door, do a little shooting in the right places, and get my son."

"Wes," she whispered. "God. No."

"You did this to me, Paige. You could always find a way to provoke me, to make me crazy. You sent me to fucking *prison!*"

"Please," she begged softly. "Anything…"

"Go ahead, Paige. Try me. It's just you, right now. Or the three of us, and him out of the picture."

She blinked once, tears squeezing out of her eyes and running down her cheeks. Instead of praying John would hear and come, she prayed he wouldn't. If it was just her, Christopher would be all right. John would never let anything happen to him, would raise him right. She let herself be led to an old truck that sat behind the Dumpster. He pushed her in through the driver's door, slipping in next to her.

"Wes," she said, her voice shaking, tears running down her cheeks. "You're just going to make this so much worse. Not just for me, but for you."

He turned to look at her, his eyes narrowed, but even so she could see that his pupils were pinpoints. He was high. He laughed cruelly. "I don't think so, Paige," he said. "I'm finally going to get out of this mess." He started the truck, cut a U-turn behind the Dumpster and drove in the opposite direction of the bar rather than past it. Paige strained, but didn't see a single person on the street, no one on their porches. And no one saw her as far as she could tell.

She knew better than to try to reason with him. This surpassed any nightmare of her life. She knew that John wouldn't let very much time pass before looking out the kitchen's back door to see that bag of trash lying there, abandoned. She made up her mind—she would throw herself from the truck and if she survived it, she'd run. But not until they were farther away from town. Not until John had time to see something was terribly wrong and could protect himself and Christopher.

Wes didn't speak. The rifle lay across his lap and he sat forward in the truck, gripping the steering wheel. That tense jaw and the narrowed eyes that she remembered too well bore down on the road as they trundled along. The shocks on the truck were bad, the seat hard, bouncing her around. They were driving down the mountain, heading in the direction of Highway 101, which could take them to any of the local cities where they bought supplies— Garberville, Fortuna or Eureka. Or even as far south as L.A. if he kept going. They only passed a few vehicles, and none that she recognized.

After ten minutes of a silent drive, he exited at Alderpoint and went back up the mountain in the direction of Virgin River. This road could take them not through Virgin River, but around it. At least she knew roughly where she was. In a sudden and desperate move, she grabbed at the handle on the door and furiously tried to open it. She looked around for a lock, pushing on the door at the same time, but it wouldn't give. She popped the little button on the door next to the window—up and down, up and down, moving the handle, pushing. Nothing.

Her upper arm was gripped hard and she turned her watering, terrified eyes toward Wes. He scowled blackly, then his frown dissolved into mean grin. "Jammed, Paige. How stupid do you think I am?"

She swallowed hard and asked, "Do you plan to leave our son without a mother?"

"Absolutely," he said with terrifying calm. "But not until I'm sure I'm leaving him without a potential stepfather."

"God," she whispered weakly. "Why, Wes? John hasn't done anything to you!"

"No?" he asked. "Only took my family away from me. Got my family to turn against me."

"No," she said, shaking her head. "No, that's not what happened, Wes. I ran from you."

"Sure you did, Paige. And if it wasn't for that guy, you'd still be running. Running and running, and I would find you and find you. But what you did—ending it forever and sending me to fucking *prison,* that was *his* doing. We both know you don't have the guts for that." He turned his head toward her and grinned meanly. "He'll come after you, you know he will."

I'm bait, she thought. Nothing but bait.

"I wouldn't mind a piece of that other one, either," he said. "Sheridan."

Something came over Paige. It seemed to rise within her from her core. *You don't have the guts for that....* The thought that this dangerous lunatic would ruthlessly, without conscience, hurt John and his own son sizzled inside her like boiling oil. Her fear slowly gave way to rage. "You're going to burn in hell," she whispered. But he couldn't hear her above the noise of the old pickup.

When Brie and Mike walked into the bar it was deserted, but they could hear Preacher in the kitchen, and even muffled, his voice sounded riled up. Mike walked back to the kitchen to find him pacing with the phone in his hand, talking faster than Mike could ever remember; Preacher never said much, and when he did, it was measured and slow. Not so now. Before he could get a grasp of what Preacher was saying, he heard, "Mike's back. Come on, then. Right now."

Preacher hung up the phone and looked at Mike. "Something's wrong. Something happened. Paige. She took out some trash and she's gone. It's lying out there on the ground by the Dumpster and she didn't come back in. I've got Chris sleeping upstairs and can't leave. I called Jack—he's coming back to town."

"Did you call Connie's? Doc's?"

"Yeah, she's not there."

"How long ago?" Mike asked.

"Fifteen minutes or less. I would've looked outside sooner, but I was rolling dough and thought maybe she'd slipped by me and just went to our room. I gotta go down the street, see if she's around...."

"Yeah, okay. I'll go, too," Mike said. "Brie will stay here, stay with Chris."

"It's wrong," Preacher said, shaking his head. "This is all wrong. She doesn't do things like this. She always says where she's going. She's real, real careful."

Mike and Brie connected eyes. Brie frowned. "Go check with the neighbors." She slipped a hand inside her purse and pulled out a wallet. She opened it and withdrew a business card and lifted the phone off the hook. Preacher was out the back door, fast.

"What are you thinking?" Mike asked.

She leveled her steady gaze on him. "That it's wrong, like he said. Go on, and hurry back. Maybe you can get one of the neighbors to help you knock on doors. I'll make a couple of calls. See if I can learn anything."

Mike went the other direction, back to his SUV. He unlocked the glove box and pulled out his revolver, just to be ready. He hooked it on his belt and caught up with Preacher down the street. By the time they got down to Joy's house and the Carpenters', they had two women who were willing to do the door-knocking so they could go back to the bar. "Be sure to ask, everywhere you go, if any strange vehicles have been seen, if any unusual noises were heard," Mike instructed.

Just as they returned, Jack was getting out of his truck followed by Mel with the baby bundled against her. Rick pulled up behind the bar, reporting to work after school. They all walked in together to find Brie standing behind the bar, a very unhappy look on her face. "Okay," she said. "The A.D.A. is contacting the sheriff and local police in the larger towns. Someone is going to try to locate Lassiter in L.A., see if he can be found. I've reported Paige missing. Maybe this can be cleared up with a few phone calls. Meanwhile, let's see if we can find her around here."

Preacher's face fell. "Oh, Jesus," he said in a breath. "He did this. I know he did this…."

"We don't know that he came here, Preacher," Brie said.

"That's the only thing that could've happened. Paige wouldn't disappear like that. Her car's here, f'chrissakes. Her purse. Her *son!*"

"There's no evidence of a crime. Yet," Brie said. She reached into her purse again, this time pulling out a Glock 9 mm. She slid it out of its holster and checked it for a full magazine and one in the chamber, then returned it, tucking it into the holster and her purse. "You men should go look around town, call the outlying farms and ranches from Connie's and Doc's to keep this phone clear. Somebody look in that old church, very carefully," she said. "Mel and I will stay here with Chris, and if we have any trouble, I can take care of it. I'll answer the phone here."

"You're carrying?" Mike asked, stepping toward her.

"Hmm. It was necessary," she said. "And yes, I know how to use it. And no, I'm not afraid to do so."

Preacher was already out the door when Jack said, "Necessary?"

"It's not all that unusual to be threatened," she said. "Not for a person in my job. The people I prosecute are dangerous, often violent. And… I no longer have an armed husband in the house, you'll remember."

"Brie…"

"Not now, Jack."

"Yeah," he said unhappily. The idea of his baby sister being threatened just added to the tension he was suddenly feeling. He agreed with Preacher—something bad was going on. Paige had relaxed quite a bit, but she was still very skittish about being far from Preacher—it had only been about eight weeks since Lassiter got out of jail. He went to use Doc's phone to get Jim Post en route to Virgin River from Grace Valley, in case they had to extend their search. Jim had worked undercover for the DEA before retiring and marrying June Hudson and he knew a lot about hidden camps back in the mountains.

In an hour nothing turned up in town, nor had anyone on the ranches and farms they called seen or heard anything. But then the bad news came via phone. A couple of calls had revealed that Wes Lassiter had purchased airfare to Eureka from L.A. the day before. He couldn't possibly have carried a firearm with him unless it had been secretly and illegally packed in checked baggage, but he had rented a car. And there had been one truck theft in Fortuna in the early hours of the morning. A farmer's '83 Ford, tan, went missing. There had been a rifle in the rack.

"He's got her," Preacher said. "That's it, he's got her."

"If that's true, they're going to find that rented car not far from the farmer's property," Brie said. "Fortuna police are taking a look around immediately."

Preacher went straight to his quarters while everyone stood around, looking at one another. Within five minutes he was back, putting a couple of vests, rifles and sidearms on one of the tables. He also had jackets and flashlights, because night would come and it would get cold and dark. He was ready to move, whether or not he had more information.

Mike went to his vehicle and came back with his own rifle, bulletproof vest and down vest. There was no reason for him to carry a bulletproof vest in his vehicle, but when he worked gangs he always had it with him, in case anything that included gunfire was going down when he was in the area. Ever since Lassiter was released, he'd been at the ready.

Jack shook his head and left to fetch gear from the back of his own truck. When he'd been throwing stuff in the back of the truck, he'd been thinking—she'll turn up. It'll end up she was down the street, sitting on Lydie Sudder's porch, having tea, enjoying the afternoon sunshine. But Preacher didn't overreact, and on the off chance something sinister was going on, Jack wanted to be prepared. Mel had said, "Oh, for the love of God! Isn't this a little over the top?"

"I hope so," he had said. "I really hope so."

When he got back inside, Rick was putting on one of the bulletproof vests. "Uh, Rick. I'm thinking the women could use someone here in town…."

"Get Doc," Rick said, pulling on the vest, very big on him because it was one of Preacher's, and slapping the Velcro straps tight. "Doc can help over here. He's a fair shot."

Now, shrugging into his own flak jacket, Jack said to Preacher, "Tell me your plan."

"I'm sorry, Jack. My head is empty. I just know I have to try to find her."

"Right. Okay, here's the deal. The sheriff, Highway Patrol and Department of Forestry will be getting descriptions of vehicles and Paige. They'll have control of the roads, so we'll concentrate on going back in the woods. We'll look for old logging roads or broken-down brush indicating a vehicle passage. If he has that old truck, he won't be off road—he'll need a road to traverse. We'll wait for Jim Post. He knows the area pretty well—maybe better than we do. We'll concentrate on finding campsites, evidence of movement, maybe a hidden vehicle...."

"He could be far away by now," Rick interrupted.

"No, he's not going far," Preacher said. "He can't get away, not with Paige. Paige has changed since him—she doesn't go along quietly anymore. This show-off guy with the three-million-dollar house—he's not running back to L.A., to some cheap-ass hovel with the woman he thinks is his woman. If he's got her, he had to kidnap her. He's not running. He's hiding. He's gonna do something bad."

"Preacher could be right," Mike said. "Rick, we need maps of Trinity and Humboldt counties. Run over to Connie's and get some. We'll plot a course, select rendezvous points. That way we can get back here for new information. Jack, got a couple cases of bottled water?"

"Done."

"Preacher, are there pictures of Paige somewhere? Maybe in her wallet?"

"I'll see," he said, going immediately.

People started moving again, getting things handled. About forty minutes had passed as they gathered up weapons and studied maps when Jim Post walked in, already fully dressed out—the flak jacket under his shirt obvious, wearing sidearms. He took a glance at the search rings and rendezvous points when the phone rang in the kitchen. Brie went to answer it and came back into the bar, grim-faced. "It's not good news. Fortuna found the rented car. I'm afraid it's got to be him. In the truck."

Preacher went to Mel, who stood nervously jiggling the baby against her shoulder. "Mel, Chris is gonna be up from his nap pretty soon. You can keep him from getting worried, can't you?"

"Sure," she said. She put her small hand against his face and said, "It's going to be okay."

His eyes closed briefly. "It's already not okay, Mel."

"John?" came a small voice. There, standing in the doorway from the kitchen, was Chris with his favorite snugly toy, the one with the blue-and-gray plaid flannel leg. "What'cha doing, John?"

Preacher's face melted into a soft smile and he went to the boy. He lifted him into his arms. "Huntin'," he said. "Just a little huntin.'"

"Where's Mom?"

Preacher kissed his pink cheek. "She'll be back pretty soon. She's off on errands. And you're going to stay with Mel and Brie while we're huntin'."

While Wes drove, he talked. He didn't look at Paige—his eyes were roving a little wildly, as though looking for something he'd misplaced. She wondered if it was drugs or if he was lost back in these hills, for he often seemed to be driving in circles. He'd start up a road, then either turn around or back out. But while this was going on, she listened.

She learned how much he hated his life in L.A.; the woman was just a means to an end—she had a place he could stay. There was no way he was going to check in with some state flunky every week, go to those stupid meetings every day, but he knew how to play the game. And they had random drug tests, he said. "Did you know that? They want my pee on a regular basis." Then he laughed. "There're a lot of places to get good pee." And that's when she knew—he'd managed to stay one step ahead of them for at least two months. He was using something, and if he wasn't already just plain crazy, the drugs were helping it along.

Paige didn't respond. She listened and watched. Not only was it dark back here in the trees on these winding roads, but the sun was lowering. Although it was May, it was cold in the forest at night and she shivered. She had no idea where they were.

"You have any idea what it's like in jail?" He turned his face sharply toward her. "Ever see a prison movie, Paige? It's worse than the worst prison movie you ever saw."

She lifted her chin, thinking, Do they *beat* you, Wes? What's that like? Huh? But she said nothing.

"Still can't believe you did that to me. I just fucking can't believe it! Like you didn't know how much I loved you! Jesus, I gave you everything. Ever think you'd live in a house like the one I built you? Ever think so? I took you out of that dump you were in and put you in a decent place, a place with some class. What did you ever need that I didn't give you?" And on and on he ranted. While she listened, the first thought that came was that he was so delusional, it was as shocking as frightening. He really believed that a nice house, some material things, could make the abuse tolerable.

She thought about John—kind, loving John. She remembered what he'd said about being afraid. *They teach you to fake brave.* Every muscle in her body seemed to tremble with her rising anger. She would be damned if she'd let this delusional maniac take that sweet man away from her, away from Chris.

And the next thing that occurred to her—he never mentioned Christopher. Not since earlier, as he was abducting her—and that was only to leverage her, not because he wanted his son. He'd never wanted a son, never wanted children at all. He hadn't touched her sexually while she was expecting; it was as if a baby coming disrupted his focus. It was always supposed to be just the two of them.

She should have known those fierce beatings had been intended so that she'd lose the baby. It was a miracle she had Chris.

He drove up a spiraling road that ended at the top of a small rise with only a few trees. Looking down, she could see not only the road that wound its way upward, but the connecting road below. She noted a truck down there, whizzing past and disappearing around the mountain.

"This should be fine," he said, putting the truck in Park and killing the engine.

"Fine for what?" she asked.

He looked over at her, and while his expression was mean, he put his hand against her cheek. Gently. She shuddered at his touch. He hadn't hit her yet, and that's what he did best.

"Why didn't you just run?" she asked in a whisper. "If you didn't want to face court again, or the possibility of prison, why didn't you run? You have money, Wes. You might've gotten away."

He gave a huff of laughter. "You don't understand much about probation, do you, Paige? My passport was confiscated. Besides, the more I thought about it, about you and me, I decided it would go better like this. We'll just end it like this." He gave her a half smile, then reached under the seat and grabbed on to a roll of heavy duct tape. "Come on, Paige. We're getting out here."

Jack, Preacher, Jim Post, Mike and Rick lit out at about four, an hour after Paige went missing. They left a rough map behind showing the same rendezvous points as the ones on the map Jack carried. They'd cut widening circles around Virgin River. If they didn't find anything right away, they planned to swing back through town by eight, and again by midnight, to see if Paige had turned up or been recovered by police. But none of them planned to quit before she was found. They left in two trucks, drove first north of town into the hills. They parked along a wide curve in the road and, with flashlights, went into the trees on foot, looking for any kind of trail to track.

Whenever they came across a home or vehicle, they stopped and showed a picture of Paige and gave descriptions of the stolen truck and Wes Lassiter.

When they went back to Virgin River at eight, they found Buck Anderson and his three grown sons, Doug Carpenter and Fish Bristol, Ron and Bruce, and a few other men. Everyone took a glance at the map and this time they headed toward Highway 36, winding up into the mountains of Trinity County. Brie was able to tell them that the sheriff's department and CHP had nothing new to report.

While the majority of the trucks of men pressed on, Jack, Preacher and Jim stopped in Clear River. While Preacher and Jim talked to people on the street, Jack went into an old, familiar haunt of his—a little bar served by a waitress he'd been seeing before Mel came into his life. He viewed sentimentally the way her eyes lit up when she saw him enter. Charmaine was a handsome woman, older than Jack by about ten years, and one of the most kindhearted women he knew.

"Hiya, Bub. It's been a long time."

"Charmaine," he said with a nod. "I'm not here on a social call. Woman from our town has gone missing," he said, flashing a picture. "We suspect an abusive ex-husband, recently released from jail. The woman, her name is Paige, is my cook's girl."

"Aw Jesus, Jack, that's awful."

"Everyone's out looking. Can I get you to spread the word to anyone who happens in here for a drink?"

"You bet I will."

So Jack described the missing truck, the ex-husband,

and explained they weren't positive of the connection, but it was likely he had her—Paige was afraid of him and wouldn't have gone off. Her car and purse were left behind.

"I'll tell anyone who'll listen," she promised.

"Thanks." He turned to go and then turned back. "I'm married now."

She gave a nod. "I heard that. Congratulations."

"We have a new baby. A son. About six weeks ago."

She smiled. "It worked out, then."

He gave a nod.

"You wouldn't have been worth a damn if it hadn't."

"That's the God's truth. Anything you can do about this, Charmaine, I'd consider it a personal favor."

"I wouldn't be doing it for you, Jack. We all help one another out in times like this. Bet it's cold out there, even though it's almost summer. I hope she's okay."

"Yeah," he said. "Me, too."

When he left, a man in a denim jacket who wore a shady brady on his head slid down from the other end of the bar, sidling closer to Charmaine. "What was that?"

"You want to talk now?" she asked with a smile, giving the bar a wipe. "You probably heard—a woman from Virgin River's gone missing. They suspect her ex-husband, just out of jail, maybe driving a stolen '83 Ford truck. Tan."

"That a fact?" He finished his beer, put down a ten dollar bill, touched his hat and quit the bar.

Paige understood what was happening now. Wes sat her on the ground, her back up against a tree, and with duct tape, bound her hands in front of her, her ankles together, and put a strip across her lips. "That looks good on you, Paige," he said. "You can't talk back for once."

He positioned a couple of flashlights on her to bring her into sight in the dark. Then for the better part of an hour, sat on the ground not far from her and talked about the disappointments of his life, from the unhappy child-hood he'd suffered to the short jail term, which to hear him describe it could've been years. He had many com-plaints about their marriage—apparently in his mind, the strife had been entirely her fault. She drove him to abuse with her needling, her dissidence. But he spoke slowly. He had the calm and stoic composure of a suicidal man.

He had decided that Paige would draw John in search, and perhaps Jack, as well; they weren't far away from the town, which was why it had seemed he was driving in circles. Up here, he would see their vehicles approach. When Wes was done talking, he left the truck on the top of the hill in plain view, close to where she sat, flipped on the flashlights and went into the trees from where he could watch the approach of any rescuers. He planned to shoot John, then Paige and himself. "I'm done with this charade," he said. "You win." He smiled. "Sort of."

Though Paige, tape across her lips, couldn't respond, he couldn't stop her from thinking. And what she thought was, you have no idea about John. John and his friends. They're not only stronger than you, they're smarter. And then she closed her eyes and prayed, *Please let them be the most clever they've ever been.*

By the time the moon was rising, the search party was up to more than twenty men, some of whom were grum-bling about the wisdom of searching the dense wood for Paige at night when she could already be in San Francisco or even headed for Los Angeles. And if she were being held in the wood, it could be impossible—she might be lost in the vast acreage and never found.

"Are you worried about not finding her, Preach?" Rick asked him.

"I'm worried about finding her too late," he said.

They had traversed mountain roads, old logging roads, paths and trails, shone strong flashlights into ravines and gullies, but there was nothing. In the back of Jack's truck were harnesses and ropes in case they saw something down a hill and had to rapell down the steep glide to get close, but so far that had not been necessary. Most of them were fighting exhaustion, but Preacher was driven, and as long as he was driven his friends hung in there with him.

A man who had no name other than Dan had been having a drink at a bar in Clear River when he overheard the details of the search in the area and he thought he'd seen the truck earlier. There was probably more than one old tan Ford around these hills, but there had been a man and woman inside; the man was gripping the wheel pretty intensely, glaring through the windshield, driving nervously. Dan was a trained observer and he had taken note of that before even hearing of the suspected abduction.

Dan was a known illegal grower in the area. He'd gotten a little friendly with other growers over time; they were a real tight-knit group. Slow to trust. They could sniff one another out easily—they bought the stuff growers bought, they carried chicken manure to their grow sites in the back of trucks, pulled wads of stinky bills out of their pockets, but they *never* showed one another their sites or plants. After about three years, he'd gotten into their circle.

Most of them lived with their grow, but Dan preferred hired help. That gave him the freedom to move around at will, rather than being stuck in one place. It also allowed him to set up a lot of grow sites all around the three counties. And live somewhere else, away from all those folks he'd worked so hard to get tight with.

Dan didn't offer to join the search—they might have a problem with that. Nor did he mention he'd poke around on his own. But he'd been in that Virgin River bar a few times and had seen the woman, the cook's girl. The owner's wife, the local midwife, had done him a favor a while back; a woman who worked for him had surprised him with a baby coming and he thought he'd better get some help. Turned out to be a damned good thing he had. Without Mel Sheridan's help, that baby wouldn't have made it. That was not to mention that he'd rear-ended the midwife not so long ago and they'd been real civilized about it.

He'd spent a lot of time roaming back here in these mountains and knew his way around. He decided to have a look in places maybe no one else would think of. If anything turned up, maybe he could return a favor. Anonymously.

He knew exactly where to hide his truck off the roads, exactly where the abandoned logging roads and hidden trails were. He didn't always wear a sidearm, but on this mission he did. If the woman had indeed been taken by a dangerous ex, it could get ugly. The night was dark, but he knew where he was going and kept the flashlight on dim, pointed down. From time to time he'd see that search convoy whir by in a fleet of trucks, so he knew they weren't looking where he was looking and that alone kept him going.

That young woman, the cook's girl, she seemed a nice young woman, about the same age and size as Dan's own wife. Ex-wife now, but he really couldn't imagine what he'd have done if she'd been taken from him like that. He'd probably go crazy.

The moon was rising when he came upon the truck and the woman. One look told him something bad was going down. What was the point in leaving a woman tied up against a tree, flashlights illuminating her, the vehicle in sight, unless it was some kind of trap. He thought maybe she was dead and booby-trapped, but then he saw her move. She lifted her head, shivered and leaned her head back against the tree. Maybe she was alive and booby-trapped, and that made him sick to even think about it. As far as he could see, there was no one else there. He peered into the truck windows and bed—no one.

He tucked the flashlight into his belt and backed soundlessly down the dirt road. All the way down, until he could curve around to the left and start back up. The most obvious place to look would be right in front of her. Once he reached the bottom of the trail and prepared to start up, he was faced with two major challenges. One, he couldn't use a flashlight and it was darker than Hades. And two, he couldn't trip or slip in the dark and make a noise, in case he was right, and there was someone watching her.

He planned to cut a wide perimeter around the woman, and if he found nothing, no one, he'd move closer to her and assess. Look for some trap attached to her.

He'd barely begun the climb back up when the moon, high and full, cut a brightened path, for which he was incredibly grateful. Every time that nighttime breeze sifted through the branches of the tallest pines, creating a whispering and groaning effect, he'd cautiously place a foot. A couple of times he cracked a twig, and when that happened, he froze and listened. He was stone still; he didn't even breathe.

He wasn't very far up the hill when he could see there was someone at the top, hiding behind a tree. He heard the distant approach of vehicles and lifted his head. Under the cover of the engine noises, he rapidly made his descent back to the road. He chose his place under the cover of forest to stand in the road and, whirling his flashlight, flagged them down.

Jack lowered his window. "What the hell…?"

"This is it," Dan said quietly. "Pass this hill slowly so

it looks like you're moving on, and up there on the left, there's a wide space in the road. Take your trucks off road up there, come back on foot and I'll take you up. Kill the flashlights. They're up there," he said, giving his head a jerk toward the hill. "Let's do it."

Preacher leaned forward. "She okay?"

"I think so, so far. Come on, come on, let's not get his attention. *Pass* the hill."

Jack threw the truck into gear and drove on, the man by the road directing the second truck with his flashlight.

Dan waited a few moments and then he could hear them coming on foot. When there were five men gathered around him, he said, "He's got a plan. The woman is bound and in plain sight and I caught a glimpse of him in the trees, hiding. I couldn't see him, but I bet he's got a weapon on her, waiting. This old road goes to the top where he's parked the truck. Someone can follow me up the back side of the hill—but there's no path. Anyone here good at stepping light and soundless?"

"I am," Jim said.

"I'll keep your back—I'm pretty good," Mike said.

"All right, we'll circle up. You boys, take this road up nice and easy. Maybe one flashlight, dimmed, on the ground. Give us a head start—we don't have a road. With any luck, we'll meet up there."

Before he could lead Jim and Mike around to the backside of the hill, he found his jacket grabbed up in Jack's fist. "Why you doing this?"

"Hey, I was in the bar in Clear River when you came in," he said defensively. "I know the hills back here pretty good. You don't think I—"

Jim Post put a big arm between Jack and Dan and said, "Let's do this. C'mon. We'll sort it out later."

And with that the team separated—Jack, Preacher and Rick up the road, single file, Preacher in front, moving a little too fast, Mike, Jim and Dan rounding the foot of the hill to go at Lassiter's back. The climb was easy for Preacher's group, not so swift for Jim and Mike, being led up an overgrown hillside with no path.

Once Preacher reached the top of the hill, he spotted the old truck. He stopped in his tracks and crouched, sneaking up on it, Jack and Rick close behind him. And not far from it, he saw her sitting against a tree, her chin dipped down to her chest. She could be dead or asleep.

The second Preacher saw Paige up against that tree, her name came out of him in a stunned whisper. He started blindly toward her. Jack whispered to him not to go and grabbed for his shoulder, but missed. The second Preacher's footfalls began hammering toward her, she lifted her chin, her eyes wide with fear, and the next thing he knew there were a pair of arms around his ankles and he was on his way down. Midway there was a gunshot, a sharp, knifelike, stinging pain across his left biceps, and he hit the ground like a boulder, rolling with Jack.

There wasn't a second shot, but there was a disturbance in the trees. Rick stayed behind the truck, his weapon at the ready with nowhere to aim. The sounds heard in the trees suggested Lassiter could be on the run, hopefully only to be caught on his way down by Mike and Jim.

Preacher kicked out of Jack's tackle and belly-crawled toward Paige with incredible speed. He got behind the tree and reached long arms around, grabbing her arm harder than he ever had, and pulled her, still completely bound, to safety behind the tree with him. He put his fingers first on the tape that covered her mouth. "It's gonna hurt, baby," he whispered, then gave a sharp, quick yank.

She pinched her eyes closed tightly and held bravely silent. Then she said, "John, he's been waiting. He means to shoot you and me."

Preacher pulled his Swiss Army knife out of his pocket

and made fast work of the bindings around her wrists and ankles. "Crazy son of a bitch," he whispered, while slicing through the tape. He peered around the tree; someone was definitely on the run down that hill. Maybe even already caught and trying to fight his way out.

She touched his shoulder, the very top of his arm. Blood ran down his arm. "You're hurt," she whispered.

He put his finger to his lips and they froze, listening. The noise in the trees had weakened to a rustle; the night was otherwise silent.

A tense minute passed, then there was a shout. "Hey! Your bad guy's down! We're bringing him out!"

Paige whispered, "That's not Wes."

Preacher peered around the tree again. He saw Jack lying on his belly, his rifle up and trained in the direction of the trees. The man who'd led Jim and Mike up the hill had lost his shady brady, but he hauled Wes by the belt at his back, neatly folded in half, unconscious, through the trees. Wes dropped in a flop; the man wiped off his forehead with a hand. Then he shook his head. "Complicated," he said. Preacher helped Paige to her feet and, keeping her behind him, cautiously approached.

"What the hell did you do?" Jack asked, getting up on his knees, then his feet.

"Ah, shit. I should've known you couldn't hold off till we could get up on his back. Didn't I tell you to wait? Till we could get up that hill?" He crouched, pulled handcuffs off the back of his belt and, yanking Wes's hands behind his back, cuffed him. Jim was next out of the trees, holding two rifles, his and their guide's. Right behind him was Mike, both of them panting.

Jack looked down at him. "He dead?"

"Nah." He still gripped his flashlight. "But he's gonna have a headache. Pretty good thing he didn't see me—I can't be in this. For obvious reasons."

"You're going to be counting on a lot of people covering you. Someone might just accidentally tell the truth."

"Well, shit happens. Won't be the first time I've had to relocate. But I'm telling you—life's good right here, right now. I'd rather be left out of this."

Wes Lassiter lay facedown on the ground, unconscious. Mike Valenzuela stepped toward Dan, still trying to catch his breath.

"You whack him?"

"Well, your man there provided diversion, and I couldn't see good enough to shoot him…."

"You carry handcuffs?" Mike asked.

Dan grinned. "Yeah. You know. Kinky sex—you should try it."

"Think I will," Mike said.

Dan looked at Jack. "What if we made a trade here? Flashlights?" He pulled a rag out of his pocket and wiped his prints off his flashlight.

"Not this one," Jack said. "I used this one to deliver my son." He smiled. "I couldn't find a midwife."

Dan laughed. "I figured I owed you one. At least one. But seriously—I shouldn't be in this."

"Take mine," Jim Post said, and this made Jack just slightly more attentive. Jim tossed Dan the flashlight, received the replacement by a toss.

Dan touched his forehead. "Lost my damn hat," he said. "You'll be okay now. He's going away forever. No more trouble on that. I hear kidnapping's huge." He turned and moved down the hill, through the trees.

Silence reigned for a few moments while the sounds of his descent down the hill faded. The man on the ground began to squirm and moan. Preacher growled and pulled back a foot, but caught himself and didn't kick him with a boot behind which there was two hundred fifty pounds of pure rage.

Jim Post tilted his head toward the departure of the man who traded flashlights. "You know him?"

"No," Jack said. "He came into the bar for a drink with stinky Bens in a big wad. Then he took Mel out to a grow site to deliver a baby and I thought I'd lose my mind, it scared me so bad. Next time I saw him I told him that just can't happen." He shrugged. "He said she wasn't in danger, but it wouldn't happen again. Now this."

"This," Post said.

"The craziest part of our relationship so far," Jack said.

"Well, he was making that climb a little faster than we were," Jim said. "He must've heard you make the top of the hill, because he dropped his gun and took off up the hill at a run, through the growth. I heard the shot, then the struggle. He was taking a big chance there. If this guy was any better with a weapon, he could've turned on our man. Our friend."

"He's a good friend of mine," Preacher said. Paige came around him and Preacher lifted his good arm to drop it over her shoulders, the other dangling at his side, blood running down it.

Jim made eye contact with each of the men and Paige, one at a time. "I hit this guy in the back of the head, okay? We all good on that? Because your cowboy buddy there— I think he's not what he appears to be."

"Shouldn't the law decide that?" Jack asked.

Jim Post had been undercover in these mountains, in the cannabis trade, when he met and fell in love with June. "Leave that on me, okay? I still know a couple of people. Let it go. We owe him one."

"At least one," Paige said.

Wes Lassiter awoke from his head injury in the hospital, cuffed to the bed, with no idea who had struck him. He claimed no memory of abducting his wife and was, of course, a victim, not a perpetrator, in his eyes.

But there were many witnesses—from Paige to the search party to the man who found him pointing a gun at the location where Paige was bound and held, Jim Post. A witness testimony that would, strangely, never be required. The assistant district attorney promised they wouldn't accept any plea agreements—for numerous probation violations from possession, breaching an order of protection, kidnapping and attempted murder—but in the end he did. Twenty-five years without parole for kidnapping, the other felony charges to be sentenced later with possible parole on those—but he would be a very, very old man before it became even possible for parole. If he'd gone to trial, it was possible for him to get life without parole. Paige and the town of Virgin River were extremely grateful.

Often Paige would awaken in the night with a cry on her lips, shuddering, trembling, shivering in fear. John would pull her close and say, "I'm here, baby. I'm here. I'll always be right here."

She would calm. She was safe. "It's really over," she would whisper.

"And we have the rest of our lives," he always whispered back.

# Nineteen

Rick had taken an afternoon off from the bar after his high school graduation to go over to Eureka and visit Liz. He asked Jack and Preacher if they'd be around the bar till closing—he'd like to talk to them when he got back to town. It was almost nine by the time he walked in. "Thanks for hanging around, Jack," he said. "Preacher still in the kitchen?"

"Yeah. How's Liz doing?"

"She's getting by. She's back in her old high school—summer school to catch up—and she's getting some counseling there." He shrugged. "She has some real sad days, but she seems to be holding it together. Better than I thought she would."

"Glad to hear that," Jack said.

Rick got up on a stool. "I'm eighteen now," he said. "Not quite legal, but how about we have a drink together. You, me and Preach. Can we do that?"

"We celebrating something?" Jack asked, getting down three glasses.

"Yeah. We are. I signed up."

Jack's hand froze in midair. He had to force himself to complete the move, bring down the glasses. He banged on the wall that separated the kitchen from the bar to bring Preacher.

"We could've talked," Jack said.

"There wasn't anything to talk about," Rick answered.

"What the—" Preacher started, having come quickly from the kitchen with a pretty scattered look on his face.

"Rick signed up," Jack said.

His face fell from startled to stricken. "Aw, Rick, what the hell!"

"We're going to drink to it, if you can get under control," Rick said.

"It isn't gonna be easy for me to drink to that, man," Preacher said.

Jack tipped a nice whiskey over three glasses. "Want to tell us what was going through your mind?"

"Sure. I have to do something hard," he said. "I can't wake up every morning hoping that maybe today I'll be a little less sad. I need something tough. Something that will show me what I've got. Show me who I am again." He focused clear eyes on Jack's face, then Preacher's. "Because I don't know anymore."

"Rick, we could have found you something hard that wasn't quite as dangerous. This is a warring country. They're fighting Marines. They don't all come home."

"Sometimes they don't even make it out of their mother's womb," Rick said softly.

"Aw, Rick…" Preacher said, hanging his head. "It's been a real hard year."

"Yeah. I thought about a lot of things. School, bumming around the country for a year, logging, construction. I could beg Liz to marry me—but it turns out she's still only fifteen." He smiled lamely. "This is the only thing I can do, Jack. Preach. It's kind of what I was raised to do, if you think about it."

"So now it's not bad enough you're doing it, you're going to blame it on us?" Jack said.

Rick grinned. "If I do okay, you'll take all the credit."

They were quiet for a moment, then Jack said. "You giving notice?"

"Not really, Jack. I'm going right away. I was hoping you'd take me to the bus in Garberville."

"What's right away?"

"Tomorrow."

"You took the oath?" he asked, and Rick nodded. "We don't even have time to send you off?"

Rick shook his head. "All I wanted was to make sure Liz is okay. That I can go and she'll be okay."

"And…?"

"She's not thrilled, but she's gotten pretty tough. She says she'll write to me, but you know what? She's so young. When I'm out of the picture awhile, she'll have a chance to start over without this thing we went through together hanging all over her like a dark cloud. I'll almost be happier if she doesn't write to me. That would mean she's moving on."

"You want her to move on, man?" Preacher asked.

"That's one of the reasons I have to do something like this. I don't know that, either. Who knows what me and Lizzie had? Besides a baby that didn't live." He looked down. "I was working so hard at doing the best I could, I never had time to check, see what I'd be feeling if there wasn't any pressure. And neither did she. That's just not fair to her."

"What about college, Rick?" Preacher asked. "I thought between the three of us, one would go to college at least."

"There's time, if I want to do that. I didn't sign up for life. I signed up for four years."

"Just one thing," Jack said. "This isn't some idiotic idea you got in your head to make us proud, is it? Because you know we're proud. You know we couldn't be more proud. You get that, right?"

Rick smiled. "You guys being proud is what got me

through. Nah, it's not about that. I think if I grieve this anymore, I'll die inside. I have to go. Do something. Start something important. I have to push on something that'll push back."

"Semper, she'll push back, Rick," Preacher said. "She'll push back real hard, like you want."

Jack lifted a glass. "Do we drink to hardness?"

"That'll work," Rick said. "Say you support me. Say you respect my choice."

"You're a man, Rick. You thought it through, made a decision. Here's to you."

They drank. Preacher ducked his head away and gave a sniff. "You're killing me, man," he said.

Rick reached across the bar and grabbed the big man's good arm, giving it a shake. He swallowed hard. "Will you guys look after my grandma? Make sure she's all right?"

"What did she say about this, Rick?" Jack asked him.

He lifted his chin bravely. "She said she understands. She has a lot of pride, you know. She doesn't want me hanging out here, taking care of her. And she knows this has been really tough for me—that I have to get past it. Any way I can."

"There's a good woman," Preacher said. "We'll watch out for her."

"Thanks." Rick stood from the bar stool. "You guys gonna be okay?"

"Hey," Jack said. "We're tough. What time do we leave?"

"Seven in the morning. I'll be down."

The morning came way too soon for all of them. Rick showed up with his packed duffel, but couldn't escape the gathering at the bar. Mike was there to send him off. No way Mel was going to let him go without a tearful hug. Nor Paige nor Doc. Even Chris was up bright and early, and while still in his pajamas, he grabbed Rick's neck and had to be pried loose. Connie and Ron were there, emotional at the parting. Preacher almost killed him with his one-armed bear hug. "God," Preacher said, "you better be careful."

"Hey, it's just Basic. They can't do too much to me at Basic. But yeah, Preach. I'll be real careful, you don't have to worry about that."

It was pretty hard to talk on the way to Garberville. Jack was feeling a powerful ache in his chest. And a lump in his throat.

"I'm excited about this, Jack. It's the first time I've been excited in months. You remember how you felt when you first went in?"

"Scared shitless."

"Yeah." He laughed. "I've got some of that, too."

"Rick, they're going to try to pound the stuffing out of you. You're going to think it's personal. It's not."

"I know."

"You're going to want to quit, and you can't."

"I know."

"You don't have to fight, you know. There are two Corps—the fighting Marines and the support staff. You don't have to fight if you're not sure."

"Were you sure?" Rick asked.

"No, son." Jack looked at him. Rick sat tall. Strong. "No, Rick. I wasn't sure till I was trained, and then I still wasn't sure. It just felt like what I wanted to do at the time, and I went that way knowing I might be wrong. But I went that way."

"That's where I'm at. Just a feeling. But damn, it's good to have a feeling again. One that doesn't hurt."

"Yeah," Jack said in a breath. "I can imagine."

At the bus, there was one last hug. "I'll see you after Basic," Jack said. "You'll do good. I'm proud of you."

"Thanks," Rick said. And although Jack's eyes were

moist, Rick's were cool. Driven and confident, once again. Maybe a little bit like Jack had been a while back, when he was about that age.

Rick threw his duffel to the driver and climbed on. Jack stood on the sidewalk until the bus was gone. Then he walked down the street and found a pay phone. He plugged a pocketful of quarters into the phone and dialed. Sam answered.

"Yeah, Dad?" Braced against the phone box, he leaned his head on his arm. "Dad?"

"Jack. What's up?"

"Dad, I think I know how you must've felt. Back when I left for the Marine Corps. You must've wanted to die."

It was early June when the entire Sheridan family came to Virgin River en masse. They had rented RVs, brought fancy tents, campers and toy haulers. Also in evidence, the Marines—this time some of them brought their families. Zeke brought Christa and four kids, including a brand-new baby. Josh Phillips brought Patti and the babies. Corny brought Sue and the two little girls. Tom Stephens came from Reno but had to leave the family home. Joe and Paul were there from Grants Pass. Everyone was camping at the new Sheridan home site; quads and dirt bikes had come along for the entertainment of the pack. Flatbed trucks had brought picnic tables a few days before, plus a couple of huge barbecues and portable toilets. Jack had spent the past two months getting lumber ready for framing, and yesterday, amid much food, drink and celebrating, the men erected the frame of Mel and Jack's new home.

But that wasn't all that was taking place during this reunion. Since everyone was present, there was another special occasion. A wedding day.

Paige and Chris were at Mel's while Paige primped

and donned a sweet and simple floral sundress and high-heeled sandals. While she was getting dressed, the men and Sheridan women were sweeping out the foundation of the framed house and stringing garlands along the beams. Rented folding chairs were brought in and set up—one hundred of them—and that wouldn't be quite enough. Most of the town would turn out.

"I've never seen you look more beautiful," Mel whispered to Paige. "Nervous?"

Paige shook her head. "Not at all."

"When did you know?" Brie asked her. "When did you know for sure he was absolutely perfect for you?"

"Not right away," she admitted. "I wanted no part of a man who claimed he could take care of me, for obvious reasons. But John moves real slow." She laughed. "*Real* slow. It was all in the way his frown would slowly go away when he looked at me, the way his voice would get all tender and soft when he talked to me. His caution, his shyness. It takes a lot for a man like John to make a move. He has to be sure of everything. By the time he got around to telling me he loved me, I thought I'd die waiting for him. But he's a careful man—and he doesn't change his mind."

"How'd he do it?" Brie wanted to know. "Propose."

"Hmm." She thought. "Well, we've talked about this for a while—about making a commitment when things got under control. He told me at Christmastime he wanted to be with me forever, add to the family, and I wanted that, too. But when you come down to the exact, official proposal, he was peeling potatoes. He stopped what he was doing and looked across the kitchen at me. My hair was stringy, I was sweating from the heat of the stove and doing dishes, and he said, 'Whenever you're ready, I want to marry you. I'm *dying* to marry you,' he said."

"Well," Brie said, unimpressed. "That must have knocked you right off your feet."

"Yeah, it did," she said in a sigh. "John's the only person I've ever known who could look at me in my worst physical and emotional state and think I'm perfect."

Mel took her hand. "Come on. We're almost late. We have to go now."

The women loaded Chris and baby David in the Hummer and drove out to the home site. The widened road was lined with cars and trucks, and at the top of the hill, more vehicles, RVs and trailers. Mel drove all the way to the top and parked right near the structure that would one day be her house. Picnic tables were laden with food, the framed house was strung with flower garlands and the chairs on the foundation were full with people standing around behind them and out in the yard. Smoke rose from heated barbecues and children ran about. A ceremony, a picnic, a party, and some playtime. And for once, Preacher would do none of the cooking.

Paige, Mel and Brie got out of the Hummer. Someone immediately handed them simple bouquets and took David from Mel so she could attend the ceremony; a boutonniere was pinned onto Christopher's shirt and he clutched Bear under his arm.

There was no music, but this was not to be a traditional wedding, not meant to resemble other weddings, because John and Paige wanted this day to reflect who they were—simple, grateful people who loved each other more than the event. The bar was not big enough and the church had been boarded up for years. It was John who had said, "Once we get the frame of Jack's house up, not only will everyone we care about be there, there will be lots of room." Who gets married in a framed house? was Paige's first thought. Her next immediate thought was—people like John and me do.

But looking at it now, strung with flowers, it was so

beautiful that for a second she couldn't breathe. To the left was a view that went on forever, to the right, the majestic mountains. It had become an outdoor church, filled with friends.

Chris walked in front of her toward the plank that led up to the foundation, and Mel and Brie each held one of her hands. She smiled at the people—far more than she expected. They hadn't sent invitations—they posted a notice in the bar that anyone interested should attend, and they were here in droves. Of course it touched her to think how much respect they'd paid her, but even more deeply she felt the honor they paid to John, Preacher. He did right by everyone he met, not just her.

The foundation of the house being raised, she could only see the seated and standing wedding guests. Chris ran ahead, up the plank and down the aisle. She walked up the plank to the foundation carefully, her bridesmaids right behind her.

Then she saw him. Standing up front, at a place where a fireplace would eventually be erected. Chris stood in front of him; John's hands were on his shoulders. Jack and Mike stood beside him. Even from her distance she could see the light brighten his eyes. He was a pillar of a man, probably six-six in his boots. Today, for the first time ever, he wore a linen shirt with a button-down collar and she suspected his jeans were new, but she doubted he'd ever owned a tie. Before she could even make the walk to meet him at their makeshift altar he broke away from his groomsmen and strode toward her, reaching out a hand to take her the rest of the way. He didn't move slowly anymore, not where she was concerned. This man had saved her life, changed her life. To his very core, he was all goodness. He was so strong, so authentic.

He was so magnificent.

* * * * *